Before she started writing books, Helen J. Rolfe worked in I.T. until she came to her

journalism and writing. She
Health & Fitness magazines
content and media releases
organisation. In 2011 the fic
been writing fiction ever since.

Helen J. Rolfe writes uplifting, contemporary fiction with characters to relate to and fall in love with. The Summer of New Beginnings is her seventh novel.

Find out more at www.helenjrolfe.com, and follow her on Twitter @HJRolfe.

ALSO BY HELEN J ROLFE

The Friendship Tree

Handle Me with Care

What Rosie Found Next

The Chocolatier's Secret

In a Manhattan Minute

Christmas at The Little Knitting Box

The Summer of New Beginnings

Helen J. Rolfe

For Matthew & Oliver, the best brothers a girl could ask for…

Chapter One
Mia

Mia Marcello had spent her entire life proving her capabilities. As a little girl she'd helped fold laundry, prepare dinner and use the dustpan and brush to clean the floor when leaves from outside blew into the house. When her siblings were throwing toys in the cupboard at random, there she was sorting their possessions out into neat piles and restacking the shelves. When crockery was left in the sink she'd wash it up, when dirty socks were left on the floor she'd scoop them up and deposit them in the washing basket. And by the time her teenage years were upon her she'd never once neglected her sense of responsibility, especially if it meant she got to take charge rather than her brother, Will, who was given duties merely because he was the oldest.

As Mia transitioned from her teens to early adulthood she tackled any hurdles that came her way, knocking them down one by one so seamlessly they often went unnoticed. She spent her life worrying about not only herself but everyone else around her, and her doctor had told her more than once that she needed to realise she wouldn't be able to fix the world's problems on her own.

Still, sometimes it would be nice to solve at least one when it came to her family.

Echoes of Mia's childhood remained as she picked up the iPad ready to call her younger sister, Jasmine, in London. She'd already tried her brother, Will, in New York as she wanted to catch him before he left for work, but he wasn't picking up the landline or his mobile. She thought back to his teenage years when she'd spent many a time yelling at him to get out of the shower in the mornings. He was known to belt out a tune and take his own sweet time and she wondered whether this was what he was doing now. Wherever Will was, this wasn't the sort of announcement that could be left on a voicemail, especially when their relationship had been put through a lifetime of strain already.

Mia gave up on her brother for now. She'd have to call Jasmine first. She'd left her sister until last, because Jasmine worked late most nights and probably wouldn't appreciate the wake-up call, especially not from the sister she didn't particularly get on with for reasons Mia was too tired to think about. Mia, Jasmine and Will had somehow gone from children and teenagers with their petty squabbles over whose turn it was to empty the dishwasher, or who should really have sole possession over the remote control, to adult siblings scattered across three different continents. Thousands of miles separated each of them now and that was only the physical distance, never mind any other gap that existed between them. Sibling rivalry had become so much more as the years went on and Mia wasn't sure they could ever find their way back. But they had to now. Their family was falling apart and no matter what their differences were, no matter how far apart they lived from one another, family had always been everything to the Marcellos.

Mia sighed with exhaustion as she tapped on Jasmine's name in her iPad contacts, ready to tell her sister about everything that had been going on here in the Melbourne suburb of Primrose Bay. As she waited for Jasmine to pick up, she thought back to the last time she'd called her sister on the landline. A guy she shared the house with had answered and it hadn't taken much for Mia to deduce he was high on something. She'd felt a momentary rise of panic before reminding herself she couldn't fix everything. Jasmine had denied the guy was high on anything apart from life and Mia had let the issue go, but she'd stuck to iPad FaceTime calls after that. Her relationship with her younger sister already had a tension that had built up since they were little and hadn't lessened any before Jasmine left for London two years ago. Jasmine's disordered life baffled and frustrated Mia, and the tension between them continued to bubble away unpredictably, often wavering near the surface, threatening to spill over.

When Jasmine's face appeared with a smile not completely devoid of trepidation, Mia cleared her throat. She skimmed over the preliminaries: How are you? How's work? Since her parents' announcement, which had happened before the lunchtime rush in the café came to its conclusion, Mia had been trying to deal with her own feelings before she could even think about spreading the news to her siblings in England and America. But unfortunately, the longer she'd sat upstairs and the time had ticked away after the café had closed for the evening, the more she knew she couldn't put this off forever.

'They're what?' Jasmine demanded when Mia finished her recount.

'They're separating, Jasmine,' Mia repeated. 'Mum and Dad are walking away from the café, they're leaving Primrose Bay and getting as far away from each other as they can. They've said the café can shut for all they care.'

Jasmine shook her head and half laughed. 'I'll bet they're arguing again and they're just taking a holiday. I blame Dad's Italian ancestry – feisty bunch those Italians…'

Mia curled her legs beneath her on the sofa in her apartment that sat above The Primrose Bay Picnic Company, the business she'd started from scratch. She adjusted the cushion on her lap so the iPad wasn't wonky and before she'd be accused of not listening, of not paying attention to her needy younger sister, she tried to look as though she really was absorbing Jasmine's every word as her sister prattled on, her image beamed all the way from London where she was bumming around and working in a pub while Mia was left behind to face any crisis that came her way.

Some things never changed, did they?

When Jasmine finally let up on her tirade about her parents and their bickering – Mia sensed it wasn't the time to point out that perhaps she had inherited a slice of that Italian feistiness herself – Mia said, 'They're not taking a holiday.'

'Sure they are.'

'Jasmine, they're not. They're very calm now and very matter of fact. They're separating, they're walking away. This is happening.' Mia wondered what it was with this family, running away whenever they came up against a problem. Why couldn't they stay around and fix it for once?

'They've argued thousands of times before.' Jasmine's dark eyes widened.

'Yeah, well this was different.'

'What was the argument about?'

'I've got no idea.' Usually they fought in full view but this time a lot of it went on behind closed doors. 'I heard Grandma Annetta's name mentioned, so maybe she's got something to do with it.'

Jasmine perfected another eye roll over the iPad, a move she'd mastered as a little girl. 'You'd think she'd stop interfering now she's no longer compos mentis.'

'Jasmine!'

'She always had some peculiar hold over them and she was never very nice to you either. She was indifferent to me and the sun shone out of Will's backside.'

Jasmine always did have a way of telling it how it was. Grandma Annetta had certainly had her favourite over the years – Will – and she wasn't shy in showing it either. Now, she was in a nursing home with dementia and had refused to see anyone for months. Mia tried now and again. She didn't want to give up on her, even though Grandma Annetta had made it clear she didn't approve of Mia's choices – getting pregnant out of wedlock, living the life of a single mother, giving up a place at university, to name but a few. Mia had no idea whether it was Annetta's inane stubbornness or her condition but she'd even refused to see their dad, Tim…her own son.

'I don't think we should speak badly of people when they have an illness,' Mia admonished now. 'The question is, what am I going to do? I don't want the café to close, I think they'll regret it. But I can't manage it along with my own business. I guess the reason I'm calling is that it feels like too big a responsibility for me on my own.'

'So you need backup for any decisions you decide to make?'

Mia didn't miss the defensiveness in her sister's voice, but Jasmine was spot on. What Mia truly hoped was that her parents would cool off after a couple of weeks away, come to their senses, and return. But deep down she suspected it wasn't going to be that simple, and even if her siblings weren't nearby, she didn't feel she could carry this burden completely on her own and she wanted to talk things through with them. Part of Mia knew it was to keep them involved, to keep The Sun Coral Café what it had always been. A family business.

'Jasmine, they're leaving in four days,' said Mia desperately trying, but failing, to keep her cool. 'They're downstairs in the café right now making up a list of contact numbers for me. They've had the accountant in to go through everything he needs to do in their absence and they've passed on the responsibility that I don't want, but have to have, because I'm the only mug still here!'

'Don't start taking it out on me.'

Mia knew one tap on the iPad would end the FaceTime call and she'd be back to dealing with this on her own again. Jasmine could snap just like that. 'I'm not taking it out on you. But I'm panicking. I need to either manage this situation or let the staff go, and close the doors for the last time. I don't know what to do.' The admission didn't roll off her tongue easily. It was rare for Mia to concede she was anything less than capable.

Jasmine turned, presumably to talk to one of her roommates. Mia hoped she didn't zone in on anyone inappropriate or she'd worry more about her little sister all those miles away. But Jasmine's face was back on screen in seconds. 'Sorry about that. Ned's looking for his keys.' She sighed. 'You know, they can't split up, they just can't. They're Mum and Dad.'

Mia mellowed, the feeling of temporary solidarity supporting her and reducing her panic. Her sister looked genuinely upset too and it was hard to feel any animosity towards her. 'I don't think we can do anything to change it.'

'They're destroying any chance of us having the café when they're no longer around,' Jasmine sniffed, 'and they're destroying our memories.'

Mia wondered whether she'd underestimated how much Jasmine thought about the family. Maybe Jasmine worried about them too even though she wasn't close by. Her face definitely looked thinner than when Mia had last seen her, overweight and dispirited most of the time. The only time Mia had really seen her sister smile in recent years was when she was in cahoots with Mia's sixteen-year-old daughter, Lexi – something Mia disapproved of entirely.

'Maybe they're hoping Will gets a flight home to Australia and rescues their livelihood,' said Mia.

'They've said that?' Jasmine looked appalled.

'No, but it wouldn't surprise me if that's what they're thinking.'

'Of course, Mr Golden Bollocks, always Grandma Annetta's favourite. He'll have the café handed to him on a plate.'

Mia sighed. 'I wish you two wouldn't fight so much.' Jasmine's relationship with her brother was tumultuous at best. It had been years since they'd been able to find a kind word to say about each other, even when they lived thousands of miles apart. 'You never know, now you're all grown up at twenty-six and he's an old man at thirty-seven, you may be able to put your differences aside.' Her attempt at a joke went some way to lighten the mood.

Jasmine ignored her sister's dig. 'I really don't understand how they can leave us in the shit like this.'

'No, me neither.' Mia took a deep breath. 'Look, I know us three have had our problems over the years—'

'That's an understatement.'

'I wouldn't ask if I didn't need help,' Mia went on. 'I don't want to make the wrong decision. I mean, should I try to employ more staff? Should I close up for a week or so to sort this out and get on top of things? I just don't know what to do.'

'They're selfish idiots.' The hot-headed Italian streak was never far away with Jasmine. With her striking dark eyes and eyebrows and sleek hair that hung in loopy raven waves down to the middle of her back, she was the wildest of the Marcello children. She just didn't realise it. 'Let's not panic,' she said a little more calmly. 'The café can't close. It simply can't. It's iconic to Primrose Bay, part of the landscape in this part of Melbourne, part of our family. This is mental!' Jasmine threw her hands up in the air and her image juddered when she brought them down against the table her iPad was resting on. 'If I was there, I'd yell at them until they saw sense.'

It was the first time they'd agreed on anything in years. But thankfully Mia didn't have the same fiery temper as her sister. If she and Will had inherited it too, there'd be nothing but fireworks between the Marcellos every time they came within a hundred metres of each other.

'None of us knows the first thing about running a café,' Jasmine continued, 'and there's your new business, you have Lexi to look after. And I'm here, Will's in New York.'

'Jasmine, you're stating the obvious.'

Despite a separation of ten thousand miles, Mia didn't miss Jasmine tense up. It'd been years since the three siblings had all been in the same room as each other and much longer since they'd joined forces over anything. Now, suddenly, there was the need to pull together and save a business, which would require levels of communication she wasn't sure they'd ever been able to manage.

Jasmine leant closer to her screen. 'Hey, do you remember when I was really little and Will helped me set up my own little café that I operated out of the cubby house?'

She did this sometimes. Jasmine brought up only the good memories from their past as though they were the only times that ever existed. Perhaps all the way in London she was worried she'd lost all sense of what it meant to belong. It hadn't always been so terrible. Once upon a time Jasmine had been the cute baby sister and, with an age gap of eight years, Mia was the caring, older sibling. Will was eleven when Jasmine came into the picture and he'd organised them both, bossed them about and looked out for them. Mia could still remember him pushing a pram along Beach Road when Jasmine wouldn't stop crying, just to give his parents a break.

'I've got good memories of that house.' Mia went along with the nostalgic conversation and did her best to focus on the positives of their sibling relationship. 'You were six years old and Will helped you set up the little plastic table in front of the cubby.'

Jasmine grinned. 'He helped me make and decorate cupcakes to sell, homemade fruit punch too, and then he organised the chaos when the neighbourhood kids came round with their ten cents to buy a cake.'

'He was very good at keeping order.' Mia smiled, more in memory than in the present moment.

The house on Wattle Lane was sold when Will, Mia and Jasmine had begun to follow their own paths and their parents had moved into the apartment above the café with views across Port Phillip Bay. But Mia still remembered the house they'd been so happy in, with its winding pathway all the way up to the front door, the smell of garlic from cooking that seemed to linger on a permanent basis, the generous garden out back where their dad had built the cubby that made all their neighbours' kids jealous.

Will and Jasmine had got on back then.

'We have to keep The Sun Coral Café going,' Jasmine announced as though reminiscing had enabled her to work through the problem in her own mind. There was an unwavering determination in her voice and Mia was taken aback but impressed. 'Keep the staff and do as much as you can to help out. What about Lexi? She's always after some extra cash.'

Mia closed her eyes. The mention of her daughter reminded her of the strain between the two sisters. Already her mind was racing at a rate of knots. Did Lexi need money for something? Had she discussed it with Jasmine already? Was that why Jasmine was suggesting getting Lexi to help? Lexi and Jasmine were close in age, less than a decade apart, and Mia always worried that the friendship would have a negative effect on her daughter. 'Lexi has her school work.'

'Oh ease up, Mia. The girl has some spare time. It'll keep her out of trouble.'

Mia's mind went into overdrive again. Was Lexi having issues? She didn't think so. She seemed the same happy-go-lucky sixteen year old as ever. Or was Jasmine hinting at the trouble Mia got into, becoming a single mum at the age of eighteen?

Jasmine chewed the corner of her mouth, the mouth that usually had red lipstick on it. Jasmine had put on a lot of weight before she left the bay, but she'd always been gorgeous. Mia had felt uncomfortable watching her around her ex, worried she was flirting with Lexi's father, Daniel. Sometimes she felt as though Jasmine's friendship with Lexi and interest in Daniel were just ways of trying to grasp hold of whatever her older sister had.

'I'd better go,' said Mia abruptly, picking up the iPad. 'I need to call Will and then get downstairs to talk some more with Mum and Dad.'

'I'll come home,' said Jasmine before Mia could end the FaceTime session.

Mia nearly dropped the iPad. She hadn't been expecting Jasmine to take any actual action, at least not physically. 'What about your job? And your house share?'

'It'll be fine. And I'd better go now or I won't have a job to take leave from. I'll be in touch, Mia.'

When the call had finished, Mia set the iPad down on the kitchen benchtop in the two-bedroom apartment she shared with Lexi. Jasmine coming home to help? It was unexpected for her baby sister to step up in a crisis. Had she meant it? Would she really book a flight or would she call in a couple of days to say she'd changed her mind?

Mia had no idea. She took the lid from the jar of teabags and dropped one into the sky-blue polka-dot cup waiting on the bench. She'd almost made herself a cup earlier but hadn't been able to relax with the thought of the impending calls she needed to make. At least one was out the way.

When her mobile rang and the caller display said Tess, she snatched it up, glad of the reprieve. They'd known one another since Grade Three and had become inseparable until Tess had moved to Sydney for a promotion with her job when she was twenty-three.

'That doesn't sound like a happy 'hey',' said Tess after Mia greeted her.

Tess had been there to support Mia when she had Lexi and she'd recently returned to Melbourne after landing a job running a travel agency in the city. She was a good listener as Mia filled her in on everything that had been going on.

'It sounds like hell,' said Tess. 'You know, my parents went through a difficult time, do you remember?'

She did, but there had been no walking away from responsibilities, no leaving the business to sink or float all on its own. 'Your parents are different.'

'They worked through it but it was unpleasant for a while.'

'I know.' She remembered many a night when Tess would come for a sleepover at their house because she couldn't face listening to her mother talking about how she was going to leave her father, move away.

'I was fourteen years old and I still remember it two decades later. It was shit. Have you told Jasmine and Will?' Tess had spent so much time at the Marcellos over the years, she'd almost become a part of the family.

'I've told Jasmine and was about to call Will when you interrupted me. Thank you for doing so, by the way.' Her brother had shunned her for almost two years when Mia got involved with his best friend, Daniel, and fell pregnant, and it had been the most painful time of her life. Even now there was still so much that had gone unsaid that every time they were in contact their relationship was like a well-presented, firm topped crème brûlée. Everything was as it should be, the cooked sugar covered the surface, but one bash too hard and it would shatter, never to be put back together again.

'It's time to face your fears, Mia Marcello. And we'll get together for Prosecco soon.'

'You're on. I'll need a truckload by the time I see you.'

With a heavy sigh but feeling a whole lot lighter from a chat with her best friend, it was time to try and contact Will again and tell her older brother what had been going on in Primrose Bay. Despite their differences and their history, Will was the big brother she'd always looked up to, until she'd almost destroyed their relationship. She'd messed things up and she would always be sorry. With Jasmine there was an invisible strain between them but with Will the fight had been open, loud and there for all to see. Since he'd left the bay neither of them had mentioned the blow-up again and they even managed civil conversation now they were in different countries.

Cradling her cup of tea in one hand, Mia propped the iPad up against the kitchen splashback with her other and then perched on the pine wooden stool.

'Mia, to what do I owe the pleasure?' Will's manner towards Mia had softened over the years he'd been away from the bay. It was as though the physical distance between them both had diluted their issues and they faded away like a rubber band paling as it is stretched further and further. The problem was, the rubber band was about to be let go, about to spring back into place, and Mia already knew it wasn't going to be pain free.

Will's image bumped up and down with the movement of his iPhone, his puffy coat zipped up to his chin. 'You look freezing!' She smiled. The weather in

Melbourne right now was sitting comfortably in the high twenties and refusing to dip.

'What can I say? It's February in New York City. Of course it's bloody cold!'

She wished they could banter on like this for longer. It was easy, lacked problems, reminded her of what they once were. 'Where are you?'

'I'm almost at work. Give me five minutes and I'll call you back.'

Mia hung up and true to his word he was back quickly enough. This time he was inside an office and he'd taken off his hat to reveal the trademark Marcello dark hair, now fashioned in a crew cut that suited him with his blue eyes and deep olive skin. Darker than his sisters, he only had to yell the word 'sun' and his skin would get a no-lined, all-over tan. Mia's friends had been besotted by him at school. Her brother was good-looking, with a heart of gold. She supposed it wasn't his fault their parents always let him take charge.

Will sat in a high-backed leather office chair, suit and tie showing now rather than the winter coat. 'I'm all yours. What's up?'

Usually they had quick calls on the telephone but mostly survived via text messages, which were quick and easy for busy lives especially when geography played a part. Mia was always trying to save money too, which was where the FaceTime app came in handy. She sometimes wondered why they bothered having a landline at home but she'd had one installed out of worry that there could be an emergency and she wouldn't be able to get reception on her phone or any other electronic device. And worry was something she'd always done well, particularly since Lexi was born.

Mia recounted the same sorry story to Will. She told him how at lunchtime her parents had been bickering and when she'd confronted them in the kitchen and asked them to tone it down a bit, her Mum had admitted that the original plan had been to do this in six months to give them time to make proper plans for the business. And when Mia had asked what they were planning to do, they'd told her they were separating.

'It's a postponed mid-life,' said Will, safely tucked away in his own office in New York City where he worked as an IT consultant. 'I knew when he bought that bloody sports car Dad was having the mid-life crisis he'd forgotten to have when he was in his forties or early fifties.'

'Will, you're not taking this seriously.'

'Oh come on, it's Mum and Dad. They fight. It's their thing. It's the Italian blood.'

'It's different this time. They weren't just angry, they looked upset. They looked defeated.'

'When did they say they were coming back?'

'They didn't.'

Will's expression turned serious. He got that crease in the middle of his forehead. Just like their dad. 'You're not joking, are you?'

'Will, I've got my own business to run, a teenage daughter…how much time do you think I have to dedicate to winding people up?'

'Not much I'm assuming. So what, they're taking off and don't give a toss about the business they started from scratch? I find that hard to believe.'

'It's the truth. It's an open-ended holiday. They're both going off their separate ways – him in his blue BMW convertible, her in the Mini Clubman – and that's all they've said.'

The pair were quiet for a while, both thinking.

'Here's what we'll do…' Will rubbed a hand across his jaw.

Usually it frustrated Mia when he stepped up as the head of the household in a crisis, but not this time. She didn't want the entire responsibility for once, and at last it seemed both siblings were willing to pull together with her.

'I'll fly home in the next couple of days,' said Will. 'I'm due to have a bit of time off anyway.'

'Mum and Dad were disappointed you didn't come home for Christmas.'

'I already told them, I'd come home next year. And Jasmine didn't come home either, remember that.' He'd used the excuse of wanting to stay and experience the cold festivities in New York again but Mia hadn't bought it for a second. He was avoiding his family, no doubt about it. She wondered why when he'd had the easiest run out of all of them. Jasmine hadn't made an excuse, she'd simply said she wasn't coming home and nobody questioned it. As usual, being the youngest, she'd got away with whatever she wanted.

'We'll keep the business on its toes,' he went on, 'until they come to their bloody senses. Pain in the arse, but we can't let them lose it. It means a lot to all of us.'

Mia gulped. It was true. The café meant a great deal to all of them even if they didn't always show it. Mia for one couldn't imagine the bay without it. It would be like a butterfly without wings, a heart without a beat. They'd all been so little when their parents started The Sun Coral Café, but all of them knew the sacrifices that had been made.

'I'd better get on and look at flights,' said Will before asking, 'How's Grandma Annetta?'

Mia shrugged. 'Still refusing to see anyone, but no real change.'

'I suppose that's good.'

Mia wondered what Grandma Annetta would make of all this. She was a woman with traditional values – Mia had watched her encourage Will to be the man of the house, virtually ignoring the girls at times as though they weren't anywhere near as important.

'Jasmine is coming back to the bay too.' Mia had always felt like the buffer between her brother and sister, the referee and mediator to ensure they could have some semblance of a sibling connection. Not that it had ever worked. They barely spoke and Mia was pretty sure they weren't in contact unless it was via another member of the family.

'Why?'

'She wants to help.'

Will's eyebrows knitted together. 'So it'll be us three together again.'

Mia didn't say anything and Will made his excuses before they ended the call with an uneasiness that hadn't been there in a long time. She picked up her cup of tea, took a sip and pulled a face. It'd gone cold as she and Will had discussed their plight. She poured it down the kitchen sink and then with a deep breath left her apartment and took the stairs down the outside of the building to street level. Mia ran The Primrose Bay Picnic Company from the small premises next door to her parents' business, and outside as the evening air cooled around her, she walked in to the café and prepared to face the music.

She was surprised but glad her siblings were coming back to Australia. She needed them this time, and that was what siblings did wasn't it? Pulled together in times of strife?

Mia just wasn't sure how the three of them were going to tolerate each other being in close proximity. It could spell trouble. It could open up old wounds and end up making things so much worse.

Chapter Two

Jasmine

Jasmine wiped down the bar top in The Crown & Shilling, the pub where she worked in London's West End. It'd been a long shift tonight, covering for Stella who'd phoned in with a tummy bug. Jasmine knew it was far more likely Stella was having too much fun shagging that rogue boyfriend of hers, but she didn't mind. Stella was a good friend and had covered for her on the handful of times she'd had job interviews elsewhere rather than the claimed 'flu' excuse she'd used.

The truth was, Jasmine's time at The Crown & Shilling, whilst it had been fun, was becoming a strain. There were only so many times you could ignore the owner Pete's accidental-on-purpose brushes past her. On more than one occasion she'd felt the shape of what was in his trousers against her rear as he'd squeezed past her in the cramped confines of the bar. Her boyfriend in the loosest sense of the word, Ned, had offered to come and sort him out as he put it, but Jasmine liked to take care of herself. Call it too many years of being mollycoddled, or stifled – whatever – she much preferred to stand on her own two feet.

Pete had finished cashing up and Jasmine threw the soiled cloth into the tub at the end of the bar ready to be taken away for washing. She always made a point of getting out from behind the bar and never being the very last to leave, and today her colleague Josh was still working away so she knew Pete wouldn't try anything.

'I wanted to ask you about the time off,' said Jasmine.

Pete barely looked up as he polished a few of the optics and got rid of the sticky liquid that liked to collect around the nozzle. 'What time off?' he grumped.

'I mentioned it earlier, at lunchtime, when I got here.'

'Oh that. Yes, you can have holidays.'

'Fantastic.'

'But not for a while. You're my best bartender, Jassie.' She hated it when he called her that. 'And we're busy. Maybe in a couple of months if I can get Stella to do some extra shifts.'

She moved closer to him, not something she did very often. 'Pete, this is a family matter and I really need to be home.'

'Sorry.' He shook his head. 'No can do.'

'Then you leave me no choice.'

'What's that supposed to mean?'

'I quit.'

Josh's head shot up. 'Are you crazy?'

Pete looked at her now. 'I'd listen to him if I were you.' He looked so smug as though he'd backed her into a corner and she couldn't wriggle away. 'Jobs like this are hard to find.'

He wasn't wrong there. She had flexible hours, was paid more than the average and she got on with all the staff apart from when Pete fancied himself as a Lothario. That was why she hadn't managed to find an alternative position – nothing else had been enticing enough for her to take the leap, although the more time marched on, the more she realised she would have to do it at some point. She'd studied a Bachelor of Business (International Hospitality Management) at Melbourne University, a degree designed to prepare graduates for all sorts of careers including international hotels, restaurants and catering. As a little girl Jasmine had dreamed that one day she would follow in her parents' footsteps and run The Sun Coral Café, perhaps expand the premises, even open up others in Melbourne and beyond. But her family had little faith she could do anything, let alone run a business. Not like her elder sister Mia who, by all accounts, was flying with her new venture into picnics. And certainly not like Will who never lost control of a situation. So Jasmine had taken herself off to London for that reason as well as others, and this pub job was a start. One day she'd be running her own business, anywhere in the world. She just knew it.

'I need the holiday,' she said again.

Pete relented. 'Josh, give us a minute would you?'

Jasmine wished Josh would stay but he valued his job too much and scarpered, leaving her alone with her boss.

'Jassie, I can give you a week but nothing more, not right now. You understand, don't you?' Pete put an arm across her shoulders.

She took a step back but not so suddenly it would cause offense. She didn't like the way he was but right now she wanted him on her side. 'Australia is on the other side of the world – I'll need at least three weeks.' She wasn't even sure how much use she was going to be back in Primrose Bay. Mia was so damn capable, and Will too. She wondered whether she'd just be in the way, but she was a part of the Marcello family. There were three Marcello kids not just two and sometimes she needed to remind them of that.

Pete moved closer again and put his arm back round her shoulders. He looked as though he was taking her request seriously, thinking about the situation to figure out a solution. But when his hand gradually traced its way down her spine and fell to the small of her back, moving further still, she knew he was thinking about anything other than her need for time off.

'Pete, get off!' She backed away but she was trapped against the bar.

'Oh come on, Jassie. There's a connection between us.' He put his hands on either side of her body and pinned her against the wooden surface. 'Don't tell me you can't feel it too.'

'The only thing I feel is disgusted.' She couldn't move anywhere and willed Josh to come back and see what was going on. 'I could have you done for this you know.'

And then before she knew it he'd planted a kiss smack on her lips.

She slapped him across the face.

'What the fuck?'

But she didn't stop there. She grabbed the only thing to hand, a sopping towel she'd used earlier to wipe up a spill on the floor, and she threw it in his face. She almost laughed when it stuck to his skin, its grimy contents leaving a residue near his hairline. 'I'll be reporting you!' She yelled at him and shoved him away.

'To who?' He wiped his face and mouth with the back of his hand. She'd never seen him so angry. 'Josh has gone. It's your word against mine.' He watched her go out back.

She grabbed her coat and looped her scarf around her neck, and fired up by his effrontery, she went back through to the bar area. She'd never have thought anything like this would happen today, not when she'd woken up this morning, but suddenly it all became clear and she knew exactly what she wanted to do. 'I can't work with you any longer,' she told him, not wavering in the slightest. 'But if you pay me six weeks' wages I won't make any fuss about what happened here tonight. I won't report you.' Her heart beat faster at the demands she found herself making. Like he said, it was her word against his.

'Oh god.' He laughed. 'What happened here was nothing worse than we see every Saturday night. A man trying it on with a girl who pretends not to be interested.'

Jasmine put a finger to her lips deep in thought. 'Well maybe we should ask what Safe Workers think about that?' She was sure she'd got the name right. 'Not to mention all your followers on Facebook and Twitter. I could always post a photo of the Valentine's card you sent me, complete with its explicit details inside.' His face fell. 'That's right, I kept it, and I'm sure your wife would be interested in seeing it. I could always post it through your door at home.' She shrugged to convey her nonchalance, but really she was bluffing. She had no idea what would happen if she reported him, or even how to make a complaint, and she didn't really want to publicly tell people about him letching on her, but she wasn't going to leave without a fight and her words seemed to be working.

'So you're leaving, just like that.' He had the good grace to look put out.

'I have to go, Pete. And I think after what happened tonight it's in both our interests that I look for other employment.' Her heart beat even faster. No matter how gutsy she could be, she knew she was alone with this man and he could do anything. She could've underestimated him but she forced her voice to remain steady. 'That's the deal. Take it or leave it.' She turned to leave. 'I'll be in touch to sort out the necessary paperwork.'

By the time Jasmine reached her shared house not far from Mile End tube station she had finally calmed down. She had Pete's word that six weeks' worth of pay would be deposited into her account via internet banking tonight, and she'd told him she would be in to see him if he didn't stay true to his word, but she already knew he wouldn't want any bad publicity so she had little doubt he'd do as she'd asked.

She turned the key in the lock of the house she shared with three others. And for the first time in almost a year Jasmine realised how much she actually missed her home, the bay. She wanted to go back to Australia more than ever. She wanted to see if her relationship with her siblings was salvageable. She'd left at the point where she'd felt as though she was suffocating. She'd had to get out, away from everything that was family. All the comfort eating she'd done over the course of five years, since the real cracks in her relationship with her siblings had started, had left her unhappy and seriously overweight. That was how Will and Mia still thought of her now because she'd never hinted otherwise. But when she'd arrived in London it had been a chance to sort herself out, and it had taken a great deal of dedication, new friendships and the self-assurance she finally found being alone and out of the grips of the Marcellos, to reach the point she was at now. She never sent many photos home and when she used the iPad it was only her face and shoulders that showed up on the other side of the world, because she'd wanted to keep a part of herself just for her, at least for a little while longer.

Once she'd taken off her layers and hung up her coat, she pushed open the door to the lounge where Ned was with Felicity and Malcolm, her other housemates. They all had 'normal' jobs with sociable hours so were her usual welcoming committee.

'You look like you've had a hard day.' Ned glanced up briefly from his game of Grand Theft Auto. 'Whoa! That was awesome!' His eyes firmly back on the game rather than her, his on-off girlfriend for the past five months, he didn't lose focus.

Jasmine sighed. She'd come back to the house wanting to spill everything about tonight but what with the weight on her mind of Mia's phone call that morning, her parents' marriage and the business that could crumple in their absence, not to mention her sheer exhaustion and a pervert boss, she couldn't be bothered to tell Ned or anyone else anything right now so she made her excuses and went up to bed. No doubt Ned would be in much later if the cans of beer in the lounge and the half-smoked spliff in the ashtray were anything to go by.

She took off her lipstick, the foundation and eye makeup she was accustomed to, but eyes wide open she knew she wouldn't be able to fall asleep. Her head was buzzing. Instead she took her iPad from the floor where it was charging and brought up the website she'd last used to look into flights home. She hadn't been back to the bay for Christmas in the end, and she knew Mia had been seething about that. No matter what hassles the family had, her sister seemed to have taken it upon herself to make sure they always shared that one special day. But Will had skipped Christmas with the Marcellos too, so at least they had both been the focus of Mia's disapproval.

She scrolled through airlines and prices of return airfares. She had a bit of money saved and the six-week payment from Pete would come in very handy. Of course, she'd need to be careful if she was to manage until she could find another job.

But thirty minutes later, Jasmine had a different plan in her head entirely. She'd made a decision – a rash one, but one she felt okay with. And she'd tell Ned and the others about it in the morning, as soon as she knew Pete had refunded the money. Knowing how fast social media worked, she needed to be careful, because if he got a whiff of her intention to fly one way to Australia without a planned return, he would likely rescind the agreement. After all, if she wasn't going to be in the country anymore he'd know it was highly unlikely she'd bother making an official complaint. She needed to tie up paperwork with him of course, but she was sure Pete would comply with whatever she needed in that respect, because as much as he groped other women, he wouldn't want his marriage to end. He was one of those men who didn't have the balls to go it alone. She felt guilty that perhaps she was stealing money by blackmailing him but quickly decided she'd worked hard enough for him and put up with his ways, so this was the least he could do. She hoped it would discourage him from doing it to someone else. Maybe it would teach him a bit of a lesson. And besides, she knew he pocketed all the tips from customers too, something she and the rest of the staff begrudged. He probably owed her a hell of a lot more if you sat down and worked it all out on paper.

Within the hour Jasmine had booked a flight home in two days' time. She had to be a part of what was going on in Primrose Bay. She had to be there for the business, for her parents. Maybe after she'd settled in, she would try to visit Grandma Annetta too. Perhaps the woman would decide to see her youngest grandchild, who'd been away in London. Grandma Annetta was settled in

Appleby Lodge, a residential care facility out in Melbourne's Dandenong Ranges, where she'd been for the past three years. It was a bit of a drive from Primrose Bay but it was the best facility according to her dad and, despite their differences, he'd always given his mother whatever he could. Perhaps that was what the rows had been about. Maybe their mum didn't agree with spending all that money on Grandma Annetta when there must surely be care facilities closer to the bay. But was that really enough to come between them and make them walk away?

Jasmine looked around the double bedroom in the terraced house now, at everything she'd accumulated that would be unlikely to fit in one suitcase. Her wardrobe contained a modest collection of clothes, slim fitting and nothing like the chunky, oversized outfits she'd worn last time she'd been in Primrose Bay – to hide the weight, to hide the unhappiness that had taken hold of her. London had been her life for the past couple of years and it was an orderly life, one in which she was Jasmine, not one of three kids, a life where she made her own decisions and her confidence blossomed. She'd become her own person. But that was about to change. She was about to be reunited with her siblings and she'd be staying in her parents' apartment with Will, the only person she got on with less than Mia.

When she returned to the bay, could she really be the Jasmine Marcello she was here, away from it all? Or would she go back to being the unhappy girl who'd left the country in the first place?

Chapter Three
Will

Will Marcello stared out of the window of his office on the twenty-fifth floor with a view over the East River in New York City. It was done. He'd booked the flight and in less than seventy-two hours he'd be boarding a plane to return to Australia, the bay, and the family he knew worked better when there was distance between them all.

With his dad's height, at six foot three, he'd chosen not to squeeze himself into economy class this time. And besides, he was missing a ski trip in order to go and sort out the mess that was his family. He'd been ice climbing in late November with a colleague from work, tackling climbs like the Stairway to Heaven, and this year the same colleague had tempted him with tales of Aspen – the town that sparkles when it's buried under a fresh dump of snow, making its ski slopes there for the taking.

Business class was a rare treat but right now Will didn't care about the added expense. Not with the approaching storm back in Primrose Bay due to hit when he met up with his sisters. No, for that he needed proper china, stainless-steel cutlery and his drinks served in genuine glasses.

'Lunch?' Max, colleague and friend at the global financial services firm where Will had worked for the last eight years, leant around the doorjamb.

Will spun his chair away from the window, glad of the distraction. 'Sure.' He unhooked his jacket from the back of the door. 'Have to eat in the cafeteria today I'm afraid. I've got back-to-back meetings this afternoon.'

'No problem.'

The staff cafeteria was pleasant enough as long as you prepared yourself for jacket potatoes with rock-hard bits lurking in the centre threatening to dislodge a tooth, tapioca pudding that tasted a bit like grandma's slippers, and the odd peculiar pasta bake that didn't warrant too much investigation into its ingredients. But today's menu had the lasagne, which wasn't half bad.

'So, I hear our days are numbered,' said Max. 'You're returning to Oz.'

They took the remaining spare table alongside the floor-to-ceiling glass window. Good job Will didn't mind heights. 'I'm not sure how long for but, yes, there are some things going on at home that I need to sort out.'

'I'll have nobody to share these romantic interludes with.' Max pulled a face as he scooped up a bravely generous first forkful of meat and pasta. 'What's happening with your contract renewal?'

Will had been contracting with the firm so long it was like he was a permanent employee. 'They offered one, but with all the crap going down in my family I've put it on hold.'

'See, this is why I live on the opposite side of the country to my folks. They're there but out of sight, definitely out of mind.'

Will twisted the top from a bottle of mango juice. 'Sounds like the perfect arrangement.' Distance had been something Will craved, an antidote to the poisonous sibling relationships he seemed to have with both his sisters.

'You're coming back to New York though, aren't you?'

Max was a great guy despite his table manners. Will tried to ignore the lasagne churning around in his mouth. 'I don't see why not.'

‘They’ll offer you another contract as soon as you’re ready,’ said Max, who had already moved on to a fresh-fruit salad having hoovered up his first course. ‘They wouldn’t want to lose you. You should up your rate. I’ve heard murmurings about coping while you’re away.’

‘Good to know I’ve made myself indispensable.’

‘What are you doing with your apartment?’

‘It’ll stay empty while I’m away.’ Will had thought about subletting it. There were always notices on the board outside the canteen – other workers who wanted their own place, fed up with inconsiderate flatmates. ‘I’ve got enough cash for now.’

Will spent the rest of his day in meetings trying to tie up loose ends before he left. He loved his life here, he loved to travel and discover new places. He’d done a stint in Perth, Australia, before his relationship with long-term girlfriend Paige crumbled around him, then he’d worked in London and lastly headed to the Big Apple on a six-month contract at the ripe old age of twenty-nine. New York was fast-paced, alive, and it ran on adrenaline. Will had loved it from the moment he landed, it was such a contrast to his old life. This, for him, was hassle free and without stress. The city and his life here were about him. He didn’t have to think or take care of anyone else.

The Marcello family had lived in Primrose Bay for all of Will’s life, in a period Californian bungalow on Wattle Lane. The house was from the same era as every other house on the street yet each was unique. Theirs had a huge veranda out front where they had two wicker chairs with cushions that were tatty from three kids clambering all over them with sandy feet or playing games jumping from one to the other. The house itself had beautiful high ceilings with period detail and the living area, which opened up onto the rear garden, was bathed in sunlight most of the afternoon. Will still remembered coming home from school and sitting outside on the back steps, icy pole in hand as his red cheeks cooled from another scorching Melbourne day.

But those days were long gone. They were simpler times.

The one thing that had really made Will take pause about his move to New York City was leaving Grandma Annetta behind. But she hadn't been sick back then and she'd encouraged him all the way. When he was a young boy she'd watched him play in the garden for hours every afternoon. She'd laughed, face animated and kissed with sunshine, and told him he'd make a brilliant business man one day. They'd talk about travel too. They spoke about Italy: the olive orchards in Volustra; the village located above Manarola where she grew up. She told him all about the house she'd lived in with its periwinkle-blue façade, and they invented a backyard restaurant where Will served make-believe slices of tiramisu, the dessert his Grandma made without so much as a glance at a recipe.

Will had always been close to his Grandma, right from when he was a little boy. He didn't know whether it was because he was the only son or because their personalities simply complemented one another; but when he'd visited the bay four years ago for a friend's wedding, she'd shown signs of deterioration and it'd scared him. They'd been out walking, taking a stroll along Beach Road, nodding hello to locals from the bay, soaking up the sunshine. When they'd returned to her house his dad was there fixing up the front fence and Grandma Annetta had invited them all in for a cup of tea. But she'd struggled to open the front door with her key and when Tim tried to step in and help she'd hit out at him. Will had been shocked but by the look on his father's face, this hadn't been the first time something like that had happened.

'What's going on with Gran?' Will had asked his dad when they were back in the café later that afternoon.

'She's not well, Son.'

Why did he have a feeling he was about to be punched in the guts?

'I think you'd better sit down.' And on the stools out the back of the café in the kitchen, while the rest of the world hurried around them, ordering coffees, visiting the beach, going about their everyday lives, Tim told his son that his Grandma Annetta had been diagnosed with Alzheimer's, still mild, but nevertheless present. For now they were managing it but it was time to look at getting her into a residential care facility.

Will still remembered his last conversation with Grandma Annetta. It was two months before she'd gone to Appleby Lodge and her house had been put on the market and subsequently sold. They'd talked on the telephone for almost an hour and he'd been convinced there wasn't anything wrong with her at all. She was so lucid, not an iota of confusion in her voice. They'd talked about New York – Central Park, the Statue of Liberty, all the tourist landmarks for which the city was so famous. She said she was too old to ever come and visit him but she expressed regret she hadn't done it sooner. They both thought the same way, both had a thirst for finding out more. And he knew that if Grandma Annetta couldn't travel now she was older, then she'd do it in her dreams. She'd be back in the tiny Italian village where she'd lived as a girl and had always wanted to return to. Will had overheard enough conversations to know Grandma Annetta resented his mum for being the woman to stop Tim Marcello leaving Australia and returning to Italy. She was forward thinking in many ways, certainly when it came to her grandson, but with her own son she seemed blinkered and refused to listen when he said Australia was his home.

The only sign she wasn't herself was right at the end of their conversation that day. Once they'd covered memories of his childhood, teenage years and talk of travel, she said her goodbyes. At first he thought he'd been mistaken, but it had told him how real her illness was becoming when she'd said she needed to go to sleep now, to climb in bed alongside Nicholas.

His grandfather, Nicholas, had been dead for more than forty years.

*

The New York winter had set in but flights were running on time and on schedule. Will had checked the latest report moments ago, part of him hoping he'd be stranded and unable to leave, the other part of him willing the flight to go ahead so he could go and untangle the mess his parents had left them to clear up.

He looked out the window of the cab as they travelled towards the airport. Snow blanketed the city but not the sort of snow that shut everything down. It was the kind of snow you saw on postcards, in perfect lives, ideal worlds. Not a splash of colour against it, nothing to upset the pristine white. For the first time in more than fifteen years he was about to take an open-ended break from the corporate world and it felt strange, but in a good way. He'd saved up a decent amount of money with work being his main focus. But how did the saying go? You should work to live, not live to work? He knew he was guilty of the latter; maybe it was time to think of the former. But quite what that entailed, he had no idea.

He thanked the cab driver and hauled his suitcase from the trunk of the car, or 'boot' as they'd say in Australia. He laughed, shook his head as he walked in to the airport. He'd have to get used to a whole lot of different sayings again, returning to his home country. Not that he didn't still sound Aussie. He did, he was forever getting ribbed about it, but he'd also picked up the odd Americanism along the way – sidewalk instead of pavement, candy instead of lollies.

Will read a book – the latest Stephen King – as he waited for his flight, and as the plane took off on its angled way into the sky, leaving Manhattan behind, he had a strange feeling in his belly, because as much as he'd settled in to New York, something that was all about him and nobody else, he was finally going home.

Once the plane levelled off after its ascent and the big city was already a memory behind so many people on board, the cabin crew brought meals around to the passengers. Will looked out of the window at the blue skies that reminded him of home, of the happy memories he had in Primrose Bay rather than any memory that made him tense up and had put power behind his legs to get away. It was a contrast to the grey skies that would be lurking when he arrived, at least metaphorically.

'Can I get you a drink, Sir?' the flight attendant offered after serving Will's meal.

'I'll have another VB please.' Victoria Bitter, the taste of home. It was just a shame his Grandma Annetta wasn't there to welcome him with a familiar smile, for him to wrap his arms around. Apparently she'd refused to see everyone else and he wondered how he'd feel if she refused to see him too.

Will grinned at the lack of foil containers squeezed on to a tiny tray. In economy class it was like eating in a doll's house, squished in from all sides, your meal in your face and drinks jostled as the person in front selfishly kept their seat back even though they'd been told to put it upright out of consideration for the passenger behind. Business class was something else. A high before the inevitable low he'd be facing in about twenty-four hours. He'd ordered a taxi to meet him at Melbourne airport and take him to the bay, even though Mia had offered to come and collect him. She was picking Jasmine up when she arrived from London, but Will had expected nothing less. Of course it would be too much to ask their little sister to arrange her own transport. As usual she'd be relying on someone else to do it for her.

He sipped his beer and tucked in to the beetroot salad followed by pan-fried blue-eye fillet. He finished off with a seasonal fresh fruit salad and a posh chocolate that tasted slightly minty. Here he was, heading back to the bay and back to the drama he had no interest in. But the café had been in their family for a long time and he was invested in looking out for its future. Mia had her own business to run so her focus wouldn't be on the café, and Jasmine…well she was a different person entirely, unable to organise much apart from getting herself out of bed in the mornings.

It was time to sort this mess out. He wasn't about to let his parents throw away the family business because of some inflated, hot-headed row that sent them running off around the country. And he wasn't going to let his sisters ruin anything either. He needed to be back in the bay and take control of the situation, even if part of him wanted to run the other way.

Chapter Four

Mia

'If you could both come over here, this won't take long.' Mia used her most authoritative voice as she herded the staff, Briony and Cally, into the kitchen at the back of the café. This wasn't for the customers' ears. Her parents had already briefed them on their impromptu leave of absence but Mia felt she needed to say something herself. The staff weren't happy and there were rumblings of the café shutting down and putting them out of a job sooner rather than later.

'As you know, Mum and Dad are going to be away for a while as of today, so I'll be stepping in until we can sort out a more permanent arrangement.' Mia hovered in the kitchen doorway, keeping one eye on the café.

'We know that already.' Briony was never one to go easy if she felt she'd been wronged. 'Today is the day we all leave.'

'Whatever makes you think that?' Mia asked.

Briony stood tall. 'I thought they were going away indefinitely, leaving the café and selling up.' Briony had been working in the café for five years and she'd always got on with every member of the family.

Mia looked her in the eye. She knew this woman had a family to support and was only worried about her job. 'Nobody has said anything of the sort. They'll be away, but I intend to keep the café up and running. The Sun Coral Café has been a part of my family my whole life. I don't intend to let it go until my parents have decided that's really what they want to do.'

‘And you think you and your siblings can do that?’

Mia was surprised Briony didn’t roll around on the floor laughing; Cally too. They both knew what the Marcellos were like. The whole of Primrose Bay knew they couldn’t be in the same room together without all hell breaking loose.

‘The business will continue as normal for the time being.’ Mia hoped her voice was laced with an irrefutable air of confidence to mask the doubt simmering away inside her.

‘Don’t you have your own business to run?’ Cally asked.

‘I can oversee both for a while, don’t worry.’

No sooner had she said her spiel and left to return to her own premises next door, than she felt the overwhelming urge to curl up in a ball and cry with the enormity of it all. She left the two staff in charge and told them to come next door to get her if they needed help, and she didn’t crumple until she’d shut the door to The Primrose Bay Picnic Company. She wished she’d told the staff to go and yell at her parents, who were upstairs right now, but it was almost as though they’d washed their hands of the café they’d spent decades nurturing and Mia could hardly bear to watch.

The Sun Coral Café sat on the opposite side of the road to the beach. It had a sea-blue frontage and stood out to anyone passing by. Customers ranged from morning cycling enthusiasts, the locals and their children, to school kids from the high school, set three streets back, as they came down for a post-school saunter, girls flirting with boys, boys pretending to be anything but interested. The Sun Coral Café was as much a part of the bay as Mia herself. She’d been there her whole life. Thirty-four years, and she’d raised her own daughter here. It was a place she never wanted to leave.

Mia had gone to the local comprehensive high school and graduated with results that had well and truly pleased her family. It had been the second biggest thing she'd ever told them. The first had been to tell them during Year Twelve that she was pregnant.

Will was the clever one with his aptitude for maths and computing, and his marks had come as no surprise. He'd always been focused too, but Mia had never really known what direction she was headed in. She'd never had much guidance when it came to her career aspirations and had found herself swept along in the subjects she chose and in the path she followed. After she'd fallen pregnant she was determined to show that she could manage her situation, show she hadn't ruined her life. But despite her marks that surpassed expectations, she wanted to be a hands-on parent to daughter Lexi. Mia's own parents had worked so hard to establish their business and they hadn't been around as much as Mia would have liked. She'd always had her siblings – not always a good thing, given how much they clashed – and their grandmother had been a good stand-in. But she still would've liked to see more of her own mum and dad. She didn't want the same to happen to Lexi and so she threw herself into motherhood as a single mum and made sure Lexi saw as much of her and of her father, who amicably remained a big part of his daughter's life, as possible.

After high school Mia's parents had encouraged her to apply for university, build a career for life, try to get into law perhaps. 'I don't want to do law,' she'd told them, 'I couldn't imagine how bored I'd be.'

'Bored?' her mother had laughed. 'I don't think you'll be bored. There are many types of law you could specialise in.'

'Well there isn't much call for a lawyer in Primrose Bay,' she'd said, sterilising bottles ready to make up the feeds for the day. Lexi was three months old already and although her parents were supporting her at the start, Mia was determined to do things her way eventually.

'Melbourne is down the road, a tram ride away.' Her mother plugged the steriliser in as Mia was busy searching for problems with the unit, which wouldn't work.

Mia rolled her eyes. 'See, I've got mummy brain. I don't think I'd get in to any uni to study law.'

'You won't always be this way. Having a baby is a big deal. I did it three times remember?' She smiled fondly at her middle child.

'Did it get easier?'

She shrugged. 'In some ways I suppose it did.'

They both looked at the baby monitor as the lights flashed to indicate movement in the baby's bedroom. Lexi had been asleep forty-five minutes and rarely went on after the short sleep cycle. She had two measly forty-five minute naps in a day, but Mia was rewarded with a long stint at night when Lexi slept from seven o'clock right round to six thirty, and for that Mia would take whatever her daughter threw at her in the day.

'I think I'd like to take some time before even thinking about university and pursuing a full-on career,' said Mia. 'I've got Lexi to consider now.'

Her mum stopped focusing on the accounting books she'd returned to and looked up.

'I'd like a job close to home,' Mia continued. 'I want to walk Lexi to school when she's little; I want to be there when she comes home.' All the times you weren't there for me, she wanted to say, but didn't, because her mum had only done it to build a family business, to give Mia, her brother and sister the very best she could.

'What do you want to do?'

Despite the struggles and sacrifices Rachel Marcello had made alongside her husband and the successful business they'd built together, Mia's mother had always seemed to steer her children well clear of ever doing anything similar to what she'd done. In fact, both Mia's parents talked of traditional careers for their children. They pushed for academia rather than imagination and creative flair, almost as though trying to shape their children into the total opposites of them.

'I think I'd like to start my own business,' Mia bravely announced. She'd rehearsed this speech for when she found her moment, adding in all the right words to convince her mum that it was a good idea. She even had the comparative business figures to back up her ideas. She'd put together a business plan and now she pulled it from the bottom drawer in the kitchen, where she'd hidden it under a pile of clean tea towels.

Mia put the folder on the table and slowly took her mum through the idea she'd been developing in her mind since before Lexi was born. It was a job that would allow compromise, a way to work in an industry that would utilise business skills in a traditional way yet allow for her creative side to shine. In short, Mia loved the bay and had no intention of leaving it, and this was the ideal way to do that. She wanted to bring Lexi up beside the beach, beneath the sun, to have a childhood almost like the one she'd had, except with both of her parents involved as she grew up.

And now, with her parents' departure and the imminent arrival of her siblings in the bay, it was time for Mia to focus her attentions on her own business again. She'd started The Primrose Bay Picnic Company a little over three years ago, right before Grandma Annetta went to live in Appleby Lodge. She was glad she'd been able to show her grandma that despite her single motherhood, which she clearly disapproved of, Mia hadn't made a total mess of her life. She had a growing business, a daughter who was happy and doing very well at school. She could do anything she put her mind to. And it didn't matter if her family rarely commended her on anything. So what if she wasn't noticed? Sometimes she wondered if she'd get more attention if she jetted off to live on the other side of the world.

Mia's parents had always owned the space Mia now used for her own business, but it was only ever used as surplus storage, and so Mia had put her proposal to them that she clear out the area and use it. With its own front entrance that opened out onto the street, there was also a tiny kitchen out the back, a modest preparation area, a store cupboard and a bathroom. She'd painted the walls rose pink with bright turquoise and lilac sea shells stamped at intervals. Daniel had installed drawer units for her, which she'd painted and were now covered in delightful daisies – she and Lexi loved anything flowery and arty.

Mia's plan had begun with how to make money right from the start. And even her mum hadn't been able to protest at the way Mia integrated her business plans with how she intended to raise her daughter. She'd found a job working from home as a data-entry clerk when Lexi was a baby. It wasn't the most interesting job but it could be done while she was at home with a young baby. It'd meant many nights working into the evening, often past midnight, particularly in the early days, but she earned enough to pay board in her parents' house for a time, and then rented the apartment next to theirs, above the café, for a nominal sum. She had enough to spare for the basics, to keep herself and Lexi safe and fed. Her parents had loaned her the initial cash to get the picnic business up and running, and after seven years of saving, putting in more hours once Lexi started school, Mia had eventually launched The Primrose Bay Picnic Company off the ground to what it was today.

Mia put the finishing touches to a posh picnic. The client had requested a 'Proposal Picnic', and when Mia had a visit from him four weeks ago she'd been as excited then as she was now. Proposals were always cause for excitement, even the one she'd found herself on the receiving end of and turned down. She took out a large, wicker, double-handled basket from the storeroom and out the front of the shop tipped it upside down to make sure there was no debris from the previous picnic. She cleaned them thoroughly each time the baskets came back but she always liked to do an extra check before filling them once again.

It was another hot day with the summer heat of February upon them and Mia filled an enormous esky with ice packs from the freezer, then packed the food she'd been making since five o'clock that morning, way before Lexi had gone off to school. Unable to sleep with thoughts of her parents deserting her and her siblings on their way back to the bay, Mia had hand rolled sushi with tuna, spinach and radish; she'd prepared a vinaigrette for the fresh tomato and bocconcini salad she'd assembled; she'd shelled and prepared Australian tiger prawns together with a homemade dip, and she'd put together a fresh fruit combination with cherries, grapes and watermelon.

With just under two hours before delivery time, she added the chilled bottle of champagne to the esky, where the rest of the food was safely tucked inside Tupperware containers. She pulled two bottles of water from the fridge too, as per the list she had in her hand of what she'd agreed with the client.

Her storeroom was meticulously organised. It had to be. It was tiny and so everything was labelled. She took out a blanket from the plastic drawer marked 'blankets', then a tablecloth from the appropriately labelled drawer beneath and, along with two large embroidered napkins she'd hand-stitched herself in beige with intricate red hearts, she took out the heavy-weighted silver cutlery and two champagne flutes. She slotted cutlery and plain white plates – in two different sizes – into the special leather buckles on the inside of the lid and did the hamper up before nipping next door to the café to check everything was running smoothly.

But when Mia arrived in the café she walked straight into a heap of trouble.

'What do you mean you're leaving?' She'd overheard Briony, who hadn't seen Mia until the customer she was handing a takeaway coffee to stood to one side.

Briony waved goodbye to the floppy-haired surfer dude. 'I know we discussed longer hours, but I'm worried I'll be out of a job before long. I've got children to consider, Mia. I need a regular wage coming in and so I had no choice but to put the feelers out. There's a café in Brighton looking for staff, and I've been offered a position. I've loved working here, Mia, you know that. But I have to look after myself.'

Mia let out a sigh. Everything she'd just said was fair enough. 'When do you leave?' It was time to get practical.

'Today.'

'Can't you stay a few more days?'

Briony shook her head. 'If I don't take the job effective immediately they'll offer it to the next person. They're desperate.'

Yeah, and so was she.

Mia put a reassuring hand on Briony's arm. She wasn't happy with this latest development but she guessed Briony had little choice. 'Listen, I've got to go, but is there any way you could cover up until seven o'clock tonight? Lexi has a swim carnival at school and I promised I'd be there.' That was another thing she was determined to do. She wanted to be home for her daughter, there to help with homework, and she wanted to show up to every event at the school. She wanted Lexi to have all the things she'd missed out on.

'Of course I will.' Briony smiled. 'It's the least I can do.' A kind woman, it wasn't her fault she was the proverbial rat deserting a sinking ship.

'Mia, before you go…' Cally spoke up.

'Can we talk when I get back? I'll be here briefly before I have to be at Lexi's school.'

Cally shuffled one flip-flopped foot back and forth and watched the ground. 'It's just that I'm leaving too. Same place as Briony.'

When Mia looked over, Briony avoided her gaze. 'When?'

'I start tonight.'

Great.

*

Mia left Primrose Bay with the boot of her blue Toyota filled. The empty champagne bucket, the fresh hamper and the esky all slotted in nicely and it was only her determination that was brimming over. She could already feel her chest tightening, her breathing shallow. But she wouldn't be defeated by this, by the loss of staff, her parents turning their backs. She wasn't about to let The Sun Coral Café close down. Her siblings would be here soon, and then they'd sort it all out, pull together until her parents came to their senses. They could put all their petty grudges aside for that, surely? Or was she, as usual, being far too glass-half-full?

She stopped at the service station and bought a bag of ice, which she dumped in the passenger footwell on top of a couple of old towels and drove the rest of the way. She parked up on the hill not far from the main entrance to the Royal Botanic Gardens on the south bank of the Yarra River near Melbourne's central business district and waved over at her client, Doug, who was already there. He looked nervous but she'd chat with him as they walked and hopefully he'd calm down as he helped her carry everything down to the central lake, his chosen location.

They chatted until they reached the lake and she waved away his offer of more help. This was her thing and she did it well. 'What time's your girlfriend coming?' She unfolded the picnic blanket and placed shiny grey pebble weights at all four corners to stop it from blowing away – even though the air was still and the day beautiful, you had to be prepared for Melbourne's renowned four seasons in one day.

'She'll be here in thirty minutes. She's walking with her sister.'

'I'm sorry I had to enlist you to help.' Usually she asked Lexi if it wasn't a school day, or either of her parents if it wasn't the busiest time in the café, and sometimes she could manage everything herself if the parking was close by, but not today.

'No worries.'

She waved him away again. 'This is my job. You relax.'

'Easier said than done.'

Mia opened up both ends of the picnic hamper and took out the flowers she'd wrapped and laid in there along with the carefully stowed glass vase that would sit next to the picnic hamper on the blanket. She poured water from a spare bottle into the bottom of the vase – she liked to think the newly engaged couple would be able to take the flowers home with them and enjoy them for days afterwards as they remembered their special moment. Oriental lilies, tall, long-stemmed pink roses and sweet-smelling palm went into the vase. Next, Mia unloaded the esky and arranged the food on plates, covering each with cling film before she stacked them neatly inside the hamper.

Doug did the honours with the bag of ice and tipped it into the awaiting champagne bucket before stashing the bottle of Veuve Clicquot inside at an angle. Mia took the hand-embroidered napkins and rolled them, then fastened each one with a white satin ribbon. She slotted knives and forks into the ribbon and then took the two violet freesias she'd wrapped so delicately and placed inside another Tupperware container, and slotted one in next to the cutlery and the napkin to complete the look.

Admiring looks came their way and Mia knew people assumed they were a couple going all out for a romantic picnic. The knowing smiles from passers-by told her they had no idea she was a single mother with not even a sniff of a love life these days and that this was all a beautiful creation for another girl.

'Thank you, Mia.' If it were possible, Doug looked even more nervous than before. 'I don't know what to say. It's truly beautiful. It's just what I wanted.'

She patted him gently on the arm. 'You're most welcome. And I'll see you in a couple of days when I come to collect everything. Just shove it all in the hamper apart from the ice bucket. Would you mind if I take a few photos and put them on my website? All helps with the promo, you see.'

'Of course not, go ahead.' He stepped aside and she took a few shots with the lake in the background. Proposal Picnics were just part of her repertoire at The Primrose Bay Picnic Company, but they were by far her favourite. She got to play a part in the most magical moment of some lucky girl's life – like Cupid, except instead of arrows she had sushi, fresh salads, pasta dishes and hand-sewn linens. And Doug had chosen a beautiful location as many of her clients did. Here, on the bank of grass looking out over serene water in the deepest of sapphire, broken only by shadows of the palms and surrounding trees, it was the perfect place for dreams to come true. She'd delivered Proposal Picnics to the beach in Primrose Bay, beside the lake in Albert Park, a penthouse in the city with the most exquisite rooftop garden you'd ever seen, and to a boutique vineyard on the Mornington Peninsula.

Mia walked back to the car. Stunning locations for one of the most memorable days of her clients' lives always made her reflect on her own relationships. It was times like these when she wondered whether if she had accepted Daniel's proposal they'd have been happy together.

As Mia drove back to Primrose Bay and reality she was glad she only had the one delivery today. Sometimes she thought about trading in her car for a more practical vehicle, like a van, for the business. If she had more than one delivery to make she could just about get away with it by folding down the back seats, but if she had more than two picnic deliveries she'd be toing and froing from the bay for sure. February to the end of April were always her busiest months and tomorrow she had three picnics booked. And more than that, it was the day her parents were leaving so she didn't have long to get her head straight.

Mia hadn't quite expected her siblings to drop everything and come back to the bay so quickly, but now that they were, it was time to think about how they were all going to co-exist in such close quarters. Both Jasmine and Will had left Primrose Bay without looking back and they'd built their own lives in other corners of the globe. The bay had always been too small for them. And for both of them together? Well – that was a recipe for disaster.

Chapter Five

Mia

'I'm glad you could make it, Daniel.' Mia stood on tiptoes and kissed him when they met in the school car park that evening. Funny, he was Lexi's father and they'd split up before she was even born, but it had taken Mia a long time to drop the 'ex' description whenever she spoke about him.

Very tall, blond and muscular, Daniel was certainly a looker. He kept his physique and fitness with a vigorous addiction to surfing, often heading down to lengthy sessions at Bells Beach on the southern coast of Victoria whenever he could, and when he wasn't doing that he worked as a senior financial adviser in the city. Lexi's father was sophisticated yet down to earth, friendly and handsome. He was the perfect match on paper, and Mia knew some people thought she'd been crazy to let things end between them. But it had been mutual. The initial attraction had been there, obviously, as it had resulted in Lexi, but when that fizzled out, something between them simply didn't connect. He'd done the right thing by her and proposed when Lexi was still a tiny baby, but even as he was down on one knee and Mia had almost lost herself in the romance of it all, they'd both realised he wasn't doing it for the right reasons.

Daniel had also been her brother's best friend and the beginning of the end for her strong sibling relationship with Will. Mia often asked herself whether that was what kept her apart from Daniel. Daniel had told her he'd never go for a mate's sister again…or cousin, or even friend. If he did, it'd have to be for keeps. He said there was no point upsetting everyone when it wasn't even going to last. Had external forces made it impossible for either of them to see a future in the relationship? Mia wasn't sure. All she knew was that the effects of their brief fling had been felt for a long time and had still never really gone away.

'I wouldn't miss this for the world,' Daniel said now, the kind smile that had captured Mia in the first place playing on his lips. She didn't miss the approving glance from one of the teachers as she linked his arm and they went inside the building that housed the indoor pool. Today the doors all along one wall were opened out onto the field at the back and an early evening breeze licked around the inside along with the smell of chlorine and the giggling students.

'Who'd have thought?' He nudged Mia as he waved at Lexi, who grinned and returned the gesture. 'Our daughter, racing in a swim carnival. She hated the water once upon a time.' Daniel had enrolled Lexi in the baby and parent swim classes when she was still in nappies. She'd been terrified of the water at first, digging those little fingernails into Daniel's shoulders. The whole experience had been stressful but not once had he suggested giving up. He'd taken her week in, week out. His younger cousin had drowned in a backyard pool when he was only seven and the pain still lived on in his family, something Daniel was determined would never be felt again.

Always embarrassed by her mother grinning and waving like a looney, Lexi didn't seem to mind Daniel doing the same, Mia noticed. Her friends were even waving over to them now. Mia had overheard Lexi's friends talking about Daniel once, asking if her 'hot dad' would be at her birthday party, or coming to watch the school production. Daniel was thirty-seven, just like

Will, but could easily pass for someone in their late twenties, especially in a wetsuit at the weekend when he went from corporate Daniel to surfer Daniel.

'She loves her swimming,' Mia enthused. 'I'm glad she stuck with it.'

'Is she still going to swim meets with the local club?'

'Yes. I'd tell you if she wasn't.' Mia swore he asked every time they met up. The relationship between the two of them may not have worked out, but Daniel's relationship with his daughter was solid. And if there was a Good Father Award, Mia knew he'd be first in line to receive it.

'We don't want her getting bored,' he said, finally looking at Mia now his daughter and her friends had scurried to the other end of the pool where their teachers were briefing them. He scooched up the bench as other parents arrived, some wearing suits having come straight from the office, others with small kids in tow, bribing them to put up with the heat and the boredom of an event by pushing icy poles in their faces or packets of chocolate-coated biscuits.

'Definitely not. If she gets bored she'll end up having the type of fun we had.' Mia winked at Daniel. They'd started seeing each other when Mia was eighteen and her interest in boys was barely noticed by her parents, who were busy with the café. Mia had no extra-curricular activities – they'd fallen by the wayside when Grandma Annetta had no longer been able to take her – and with her proficiency at completing her school work well and on time, she'd found herself with enough spare time to get into trouble.

'We definitely don't want that.' He pulled a face. 'Has she had a boyfriend before? She's never mentioned anyone.'

'You're her dad, she's not likely to talk to you about boys,' Mia teased. 'There was a boy in her class a few years back. He came over a couple of times.' She laughed at Daniel's face. 'I can assure you they stayed in the lounge room at all times and I made sure I interrupted on a regular basis.' She thought for a moment. 'After that, when she was fourteen, came Aidan Miller. I saw them kissing on the beach one evening.' She didn't share with Daniel that Jasmine had seen them first and left them to it. Her sister was a bad influence, even back then.

'Now that you mention it, I vaguely remember her mentioning a boy called Aidan, but I didn't think anything of it. What happened to him?'

Mia shrugged. 'You know what teens are like. Relationships don't last as long as a loaf of bread.' She smiled and gave a thumbs up to her daughter, who stood on the blocks ready for the off. Lexi nodded at her. She may be embarrassed by her mum sometimes but she still needed her when she was unsure of herself. And, secretly, Mia loved that.

The starting gun fired and Mia and Daniel turned their attention to Lexi, calling her name as she ploughed skilfully through the water. She made good time in her lap of the relay and the next girl off the blocks was even faster, and by the time the fourth did her final lap Lexi was on the sidelines with her mates cheering the girl on and they came in second place, missing the gold by a mere two seconds.

Mia loved how Lexi channelled her energies into swimming and her friendships with girls at the private school Daniel had enrolled her in the day she was born. Mia had wanted to send her to the local comprehensive, the same school she went to, but Daniel insisted. His grandma had left him some money when she died and it was enough to cover the tuition for the first couple of years' schooling. The rest he'd make up from savings once he got a job, and he was confident he had plenty of time to do so. He wanted Lexi to have the best. Mia wondered sometimes whether it was guilt that made him do it; even though they'd mutually agreed to split, she knew he looked at his daughter and sometimes only saw what they'd failed to give her – the stable family with two parents at the helm. But, as Mia had told him, her parents had been at the helm but they'd also been battling in the water the whole time and she knew she and Daniel could give Lexi so much more – and they'd probably do it better apart than they would together.

The next race up was freestyle but Lexi was sitting this one out. She'd be further down the schedule in the 100 metres backstroke and then after that the 100 metres breaststroke, so Mia and Daniel gave her a wave when she looked up and Mia pointed to the outside and mouthed the words 'we'll be back'.

'How's business?' Daniel asked when they'd escaped the heat building up in the crowd as parents vied to see their offspring.

'It's going well.'

'Plenty of orders?' He led the way to the grass outside and the small bank that sloped up from the swimming hall to the grand entrance of the school that wowed any visitor or prospective student.

Mia talked about the Proposal Picnic that morning, the big order she had in for the school too. When she'd first started the business the school had let her put an advert in the community bulletin that went out to parents each week and orders had trickled in slowly but surely, and built even further as word got around.

‘I’m doing the staff picnic in a couple of weeks.’

‘Not in school time, I hope. That’s not why we pay our fees.’

Mia smiled. He loved having so much input in Lexi’s life, financially and emotionally. Lexi lived full time with Mia but they’d never been through any courts to decide that time with her father was equally important. So from when Lexi was a baby and the first time Mia had taken her and all the baby paraphernalia over to his apartment on St Kilda Road, Daniel had shared as much of the care as he could. He’d taken her when Mia was sick, he’d come over to the bay if Lexi was unwell or it was school holidays and Mia had work commitments. When it came to Lexi they shared the load and despite the tension in her relationship with Will, Mia was glad this was one relationship that had worked out, even if it wasn’t in the traditional sense.

‘No, it’ll be at a weekend. I’m catering for sixty staff.’

‘That’s huge. Have you got enough picnic baskets?’

‘It’s massive, and no, I don’t have enough.’

‘Do you have enough anything?’

‘Not right now, but I’ve already found a catering company to loan me crockery and cutlery. I’ve known about this for six months so over time I’ve made all the napkins—’

‘You hand-stitched them all? You’re crazy!’

She nudged him in the ribs. ‘I like doing it. It’s relaxing. And besides, I’m hoping this big commission is the first of many. Who knows, one day I may even find bigger premises or at least a storage facility somewhere and expand. But that’s a long way off.’

‘I have contacts with a firm to lend you all the glassware you’d need. The contact comes with a nice discount too and they'd deliver to me at work – I'll bring them to you.'

'Perfect, that's another thing I can tick off my list.' She smiled.

Daniel lay back and pulled his shades over his eyes. It was after six o'clock in the evening and even though the sun still shone above them, the heat of the day was slowly settling down with a breeze brought in from Port Phillip Bay. 'I can always loan you the money if you want to expand sooner rather than later.'

She lay next to him, face tilted to the sun too. 'I know you would and I appreciate the offer.'

'But you won't take it.'

'Nope.'

'Stubborn.'

'That's me.' She'd paid off her parents' loan that she'd used to start her business as soon as she could. This was something she wanted to own in every sense of the word and she'd even made them agree on a sum for her to rent the premises rather than use it for free. She smiled and turned onto her tummy, glad she was wearing a black shirt and denim shorts…cool, and forgiving when it came to any spills from her job preparing and delivering picnics, or grass stains that could result now without a blanket to lie on. 'I've already arranged for the plates etcetera to be delivered directly to here and then I'll come and check everything before the day, so all I have to do is worry about the food.'

'You sound like you've got it all sorted.'

She sat bolt upright. 'Fuck.'

'Excuse me.' He looked at the two schoolboys passing by. 'Sorry about her, can't take her anywhere.'

'What's up?' he asked Mia as the boys grinned and carried on their way.

'Mum said she'd help me with the food for the school picnic and she won't even be here.' Lexi had already filled her dad in on the developments in the Marcello household. Mia had called him shortly after they'd dropped the bombshell and Daniel had taken Lexi back to his apartment for the evening. They'd gone out to Lygon Street for Italian, her favourite, to take Lexi's mind off her grandparents and how stressed out her mother was.

'Is there anyone else who can help?'

Daniel didn't know the rest of the story. He knew her parents were taking off but what he didn't know was whom Mia had called to come to the rescue. As far as Daniel knew, Briony and Cally would run the café until her parents returned or they had to face the inevitable; selling the place and having The Sun Coral Café taken on by new owners.

Still oblivious, Daniel went on. 'Lexi will help for sure. Earn some extra pocket money. And if the café is quiet—'

'The café is never quiet.'

'No, it's the star of the bay.' Daniel smiled.

Mia's bottom lip twisted and she bit the corner. 'The other staff quit today.'

'Oh shit.' He turned on his elbow to face her. 'When do they finish up?'

She put her sunglasses on top of her head and something about the look on her face made him sit up tall. 'Don't tell me they've walked out already?'

'Briony hasn't.'

'Thank god for that. She's your top worker.'

Mia looked at her watch. 'She'll be there for about another hour before she leaves too.'

‘Christ, Mia. How on earth do you intend to run the café and your own business? You can’t do it. You’ll have to shut the café until you can find suitable people to run it. God, your parents have a lot to answer for. Do they know what they’re doing to you?’ Not only had Daniel had the café in his life since he’d befriended Will at age twelve, but he’d also had plenty of time to experience the Marcello family, and he knew it wasn’t always a happy environment.

‘I’ll have a bit of extra help,’ she said.

‘Who?’

She waved at her daughter’s friend, who, having just finished the front crawl, seemed to be heading off to another activity given the way her mother was rushing her out of the grounds.

‘Will and Jasmine.’

Daniel laughed. ‘Yeah, right.’ And then he looked at her. ‘Oh My God, you’re serious.’

‘They’re both coming back to the bay.’

He whistled through his teeth. ‘Well, that’ll be interesting. You Marcellos don’t believe in doing things by halves do you?’

Mia’s head swirled with the magnitude of it all: the café, her parents’ marriage, the sibling tension that was about to explode with all three of them in the same hemisphere, the massive job she’d taken on with the school picnic. She rested her head on her knees and tried to remind herself that only a certain amount was in her control. It wasn’t up to her to solve every single problem in this family and it wasn’t for her to stress about what everyone else did.

‘Come on, let’s go cheer Lexi on.’ Daniel stood and brushed the back of his trousers in case of grass stains. ‘I’d tell you it’s all going to be okay, but I’m not looking forward to seeing one of your siblings myself.' They began to make their way back into the building. 'In fact, you may be seeing a lot less of me over the next few weeks.'

Mia nodded. 'I'd figured that would be the case.'

Chapter Six

Jasmine

The flight was as crappy as she'd anticipated. Economy class was a squash, even for a five-foot-three-inch woman who was still young enough to contort herself into any position that meant she'd be able to get a wink of sleep. The angst about going home didn't help either. She'd been away for two years, and although part of her was looking forward to being back in the bay – if only to ensure she claimed what was partly hers – the other part of her was hesitant and would prefer to still be in London with its buzz, its anonymity and her boyfriend Ned, who may be interested in computer games more than her but was at least a comfort, an escape.

At Melbourne's Tullamarine airport Jasmine leant in and hauled her enormous rucksack from the carousel. Back when she was hideously overweight she'd have struggled, but now she did it with relative ease. She spotted her tartan suitcase emerging amongst the rest of the plane's cargo and when she'd grabbed that she hoisted her rucksack onto her back, before pulling up the handle to her case and wheeling it to the entrance.

It wasn't even six o'clock in the morning but Mia had insisted she collect her sister from the airport. Jasmine would've been just as happy catching the Skybus to the city and then a connecting train, followed by a walk to Primrose Bay. But then again, the last time she'd been in the company of the Marcello family she'd relied on them for everything. It had become a habit. The day she got a puncture riding her bike home from the city having somehow forgotten the puncture repair kit, she'd gone into the house to get what she needed and by the time she came out Mia was fixing it for her. And when she bought a new desk chair for her bedroom before she started exams in Year Twelve, she'd taken out the contents from the new box as soon it was delivered but Will had taken one look at her with instructions in hand, lining up screws into groups, and he'd taken over, fixing it together in a jiffy. Her family thought she was useless. And, in turn, Jasmine had begun to think she would always be dependent on someone. Until the day came when she'd had as much as she could take, bought a one-way ticket to London and, without a job or a single other person, over she went, across the seas.

And you know what? She could do plenty for herself.

Jasmine had almost reached the doors to the front of the airport when Mia ran towards her, arms outstretched.

'Jasmine!' Her sister flung her arms around her, almost knocking her over with the weight of the rucksack on her back. 'Welcome home!'

Mia was surely overcompensating. This enthusiasm was a far call from how they'd left things when they'd said goodbye. It'd been the briefest of hugs then, neither of them particularly putting much heart into it.

It was then that Mia stepped back and took a good, long look at her sister in the way a parent would appraise their offspring after they'd been away for Schoolies, as though trying to work out from their face exactly what had been going on while they'd been away.

'Jasmine, you look great!'

Jasmine hadn't expected anything less than astonishment. She'd lost a lot of weight and, aside from the odd photo on Facebook, hadn't sent much evidence home to Australia. Losing weight had been something she hadn't thought much about until she'd left the bay and the change of lifestyle, the freedom away from her siblings, had meant a fresh start in more ways than one. The weight loss had been a pleasant by-product of being happier within herself and once it started coming off, there was no stopping her. She took control, she changed her eating habits, she refused to let it beat her. And, slowly, she'd started to change and in parallel had felt her whole life evolving to something new and exciting. She felt like a snake who'd shed its skin; she finally got to exist in her own brand-new form.

Mia's hands still gripped her sister's arms. 'You've lost so much weight!'

No matter their differences, it felt good to see Mia again, and the way she was smiling at her right now made Jasmine wonder whether she'd been worrying about nothing. 'I've lost a lot,' she said. 'Sixteen kilograms in total.' The fitted tracksuit pants and T-shirt showed off her new figure beautifully.

They made their way out of the airport and over to the car park, where Jasmine tried to pay for the parking but Mia wouldn't have it and so she watched her sister pump the machine with coins until it was satisfied and had disgorged the validated ticket.

'This heat is amazing.' Jasmine was already sweating and they'd only gone from the airport terminal to the car. 'I'd forgotten what a good old Aussie summer was like. Bump up the air con would you?'

'It's been in the forties for the last couple of weeks. This is the cool change,' Mia joked as she pulled out of the car park and followed the curved ramps down and out, back onto the freeway.

'I guess I'll get used to it.' She hadn't thought about her home city much during her time away. She hadn't let herself. She'd wanted and needed to get away both in body and in mind, and London had let her do exactly that.

'How long are you staying?'

'I'm not sure yet.' Jasmine looked out of the window at the car passing by on their left – you wouldn't get away with undertaking in the UK; it would be a definite road-rage-inducing behaviour! – and a sky bluer than she'd seen since last summer. She turned to Mia, sunglasses firmly in place over her eyes and the air con starting to cause goosebumps to appear on her arms. 'Tell me, what's happening at the café?'

'Well we've got no staff now.'

'Not even Briony and Cally?'

'They both quit.'

'What?'

'I can't blame them. They've witnessed enough of the Marcello temperament over the years to know that this 'glitch' could be much more. Mum and Dad may not come back, we may not be able to cope. Does that sound like the sort of place where you'd want to work?'

'So what do we do now?'

'We'll keep it going the best we can. I'll open up as soon as we get back.'

'If you let me have a little Bo-Peep first, I'll help you out,' Jasmine sniggered.

'What?' Mia drove on as the city came into view.

'Bo-Peep, sleep.' She was still laughing, she couldn't help it. Her conservative sister had barely set foot out of the bay in all her thirty-four years, let alone been to a different hemisphere. She wondered if Mia would've liked to have travelled had Lexi not come along so quickly, but it wasn't her place to ask what her sister would've done if she didn't have a child. She could see Lexi was her sister's world; she was the girl she let in to her life when she pushed her sister out. Mia and Jasmine rarely talked since she'd left the bay and the fact they'd been thousands of miles apart for a couple of years was probably the main reason they were able to be civil to one another right now.

'So are you still Mandy Dingle?' Jasmine asked, glad of the absence of tension she'd been expecting. With her siblings it was very much a case of living in the moment and you took the easy moments when you could get them.

'Jasmine, I'm too tired for games.' Mia sighed as she overtook a truck on the freeway.

'It's Cockney rhyming slang for single. There was something about it in the newspaper the other day, about how modern Londoners are confused by it. London's like Melbourne, multicultural, so some people think Cockney rhyming slang's fading away. But we still get the odd punter in The Crown & Shilling who'll use it. One of my regulars taught me some great phrases, had me in stitches. Then he challenged the bar staff and every punter in the pub to talk using cockney rhyming slang for the rest of the night and if we did he'd buy a round for the house.'

Mia seemed interested, enthusiastic even, that her sister had learnt something new. 'Tell me some more phrases,' she begged.

'Well, you're my skin and blister.'

'Sister?' Mia took the turning off the freeway that would eventually take them down towards the beach. 'Am I right?'

'Uh-huh.'

'Okay, more.' Mia was smiling now as she kept her eyes on the road, negotiating the traffic.

'I can't wait to get home and see your teapot and lid.'

Mia sniggered. 'What the hell is my teapot and lid?'

'Work it out!'

Mia's frown deepened. 'I really don't know.'

'It's easy. Just make it rhyme with something.'

'I don't have a clue.'

'What would I want to see, of yours, when we get back to the bay?'

'I've no idea. Just tell me!'

'I want to see something of yours…before she goes to school.'

Mia pulled another face. 'Kid! Teapot and lid is kid!'

Jasmine heaved a sigh of relief. 'Finally.'

'Go on, I'm getting the hang of this.'

They were getting closer to the sea. Jasmine could see Port Phillip Bay in the distance. 'Kane and Abel,' she said.

It took Mia a few moments. 'Table!'

'Yep. Tea-leaf…'

'Thief!' The response came back quicker this time. 'I've heard that one before.'

Jasmine sat forward in her seat, distracted as the ocean got closer. She gulped. Now that it was all laid out in front of her she realised how much she'd missed being here in Melbourne, but part of her also felt the pain and loneliness she'd experienced always being an outsider in her family, the youngest sibling who seemed in the way. When the plane had touched down on the tarmac and she'd felt the first waves of the Australian heat as she'd walked through the tunnel connecting the plane to the inside of the terminal, insecurity mixed with excitement rumbled through her. But now, with Port Phillip Bay stretched out lazily in front of her, she suddenly couldn't speak.

'You okay?' Mia negotiated an already busy Beaconsfield Parade with cyclists out in force to enjoy the sunshine.

Jasmine smiled at the sight after having the London winter wrapped around her for the last few months. 'I'm fine. Just weird, being back, that's all.' And she hadn't even seen Will yet. 'Mind if I open the windows?' It was one thing seeing the bay, but to smell the salty sea air would be something else entirely.

Mia turned off the air conditioner. 'Go for it,' she said.

Jasmine felt like a puppy on the rest of the drive back to Primrose Bay, through St Kilda, Elwood, on through Brighton, with her head almost hanging out of the window as she let the salt-tinged wind blow her raven hair until it was a mass of tangles around her face.

'The sign looks great.' Jasmine spotted the frontage of The Primrose Bay Picnic Company just before Mia turned off up a tiny side street and came to a stop. The sign hadn't been there when she'd left, but now, on a white background, the business name was written in loopy ocean-blue lettering.

Mia parked next to the side entrance that led up to her apartment. 'I wasn't going to have a sign,' she said, 'but it's a way of advertising. If people know I'm there, they may pop in on the off-chance and I can give them a leaflet with all the details of types of picnic, events I cater for.'

'You seem to have it all sorted.' Her sister usually did, so really it shouldn't come as any surprise.

Mia turned off the engine and climbed out. 'Mum and Dad will be gone in a few hours. I think they're both desperate to get away, but they wanted to wait around to see you first seeing as it's been so long.'

Jasmine had known the dig wouldn't take too long to rear its ugly head. 'Hey, they were free to come and visit.'

'They have – or is it had? – a business to run. You know they couldn't.'

'If they'd really wanted to…there'd have been a way.' The sisters locked eyes across the roof of the car. 'And I had a job I didn't want to lose, a house I was paying rent for.'

Mia shook it off as though her problems could all go away with a simple movement of her head. 'I don't want to fight about it now.'

The top window from Mia's apartment flew open. 'Jasmine!'

Jasmine looked up. 'Lexi-Lou!' Jasmine was the only one to call her that. Louise was Lexi's middle name and most people had never heard it but Jasmine had called her that as a toddler and the name had stuck. Lexi had once described the nickname as 'kinda cool'.

The window was left open and less than sixty seconds later the side-entrance door flew open and Lexi catapulted into her arms. With only ten years separating them, they were more like sisters or best friends than auntie and niece, and Jasmine knew it rankled with her sister.

'You've lost a *ton* of weight, Jas!' Lexi enthused.

'I've lost weight from my body, not my name.' Will and Mia had called her Jas for years and all it had done was reminded her that she was the youngest, the one they didn't see as being able enough to do anything without their help.

'Sorry, forgot you hate being called Jas.' Lexi covered her mouth as though stopping it from making the same mistake again. 'But I'm serious. You look absolutely fabulous.' She took Jasmine by the hand and practically dragged her inside.

'It's okay, I've got these,' said Mia, hauling the luggage out of the boot.

'Wait a minute, Lexi-Lou. I'll help your mum. Here, give one to me, Mia.'

'Nonsense, up you go.'

'Mia, just give me the case, or the rucksack. I don't mind which!'

Mia wouldn't do anything of the sort and Jasmine gave up trying to tell her otherwise. She followed Lexi up the stairs, glad of the reprieve from seeing her parents just yet. What on earth was she supposed to say to them? She'd called them before she'd left for the airport but neither had given her much of a clue as to what had happened to lead to the sudden announcement that they were splitting up and, worse, leaving their pride and joy of a business to go their separate ways.

'School,' Mia said to Lexi the second she joined them in the apartment. 'You leave in an hour.'

'Okay!' Lexi dragged Jasmine to her bedroom.

'Wow, look at all these posters!' Jasmine sat on the bed and looked around, admiring everything a sixteen-year-old girl would have stuck to her wall. 'I know who *they* are.' She pointed to a photograph with a newspaper article alongside. 'The Vamps seriously came here?'

'They were in Sydney…Dad took me to see them. It was so awesome!'

'I'll bet.' She wasn't surprised that it had been Daniel taking her and not Mia. Of the two parents, he was definitely the least uptight and the one more willing to go with the flow. 'Does your mum mind you putting them on the walls?' From memory Mia was always particular about her apartment, especially when she'd painted Lexi's room a beautiful shade of white. Up until then Jasmine hadn't realised there even *was* more than one shade of white but apparently this was white with a natural hint of violet. At the time Lexi wanted something grown up but was nowhere near ready to give up a bit of colour.

'No, she's relaxed lately. That, or she's so busy she hasn't got time to obsess about the little things.'

Jasmine leant up against the wall at the side of the bed and Lexi sat beside her. 'So what's the goss, Lexi-Lou? Any boys to speak of? You emailed to tell me about Aidan. Did he never get in touch after he moved back to America?'

'He emailed me a few times but then it fizzled out. He's probably met someone. And besides, we're too young to be getting into anything serious.'

Lexi was nothing if not sensible. Mia had raised her well. She was an independent girl with oodles of confidence that her mother had never had. Not in an arrogant or standoffish way, but in the sense that she knew who she was, where she was going. Perhaps as an only child that was one of the advantages. You never had to fight for your place in a family, you didn't have to prove yourself as an equal.

'So tell me all about your life in London,' said Lexi, teenage eyes and ears ready to absorb what it was like to be out in the big wide world, creating new memories, being independent.

Jasmine looked at her watch. 'Don't you need to get to school?'

'We've got ages yet. Oh come on, it'll give me something to daydream about in maths class today.'

Jasmine laughed. 'Don't you let your mother hear you say that. She'll think I'm a bad influence.' As if Mia needed any more reason to think so.

Jasmine and Lexi gossiped about London, what it was like working in a pub – Lexi was yet to set foot in one – and Jasmine's boyfriend, Ned. Lexi wanted to know everything about him. She'd telephoned the house once and Ned had answered the phone, and Lexi, being a fifteen-year-old girl, no matter how sensible, seemed to have developed a bit of an unspoken crush. It seemed Mia's determination to keep her daughter blinkered to the opposite sex still wasn't working. She'd been livid the time Jasmine had seen Lexi kissing a boy and had left them to it. She'd raced down there and poor Lexi had been mortified. She'd told her so afterwards when Jasmine managed to get a moment alone with her. That was the thing with Mia. If she thought there was any risk, she'd guard her young like a swan protecting its cygnet. Perhaps occasionally the cygnet needed to get a dose of reality.

'Do you think Ned will wait for you?' Lexi asked. 'You know, while you're in Australia.'

'It was never serious between us. We're more good friends really.'

'With benefits...'

Jasmine gave her niece a playful poke in the ribs. 'How do you know about benefits?'

'Some girls were chatting at school the other day. It's called a fuck-buddy.'

Mia chose that exact moment to walk in. 'Lexi Marcello!'

'What? I didn't say it, they did.'

'Whatever.' Mia wasn't impressed, and gave Jasmine a look as cold as liquid nitrogen, capable of freezing her sister on the spot. 'It's time to put your lunch in your bag, Lexi, and go to school, where I hope your language vastly improves.' Jasmine didn't miss another disapproving glance Mia gave her before she jostled Lexi out the door.

When Lexi had gone Jasmine filled a glass of water from the tap. 'I guess I'd better get this joy over with.'

Mia stacked Lexi's plate from her toast in to the dishwasher. 'And what joy is that?'

'Mum and Dad.'

When Mia said nothing and wiped down the benchtop before opening the window above the kitchen sink to let some air in to the place, Jasmine said, 'Is there something wrong?'

Mia turned to her. 'You've been here ten minutes and already you're having sex talks with my daughter.'

'Sex talks!'

'I've never heard her say fuck-buddy. Never in my life!'

'And you think I taught her the phrase? If you'd come in seconds before, you'd have heard her say the girls at school were using that phrase.'

'Well she never told me.'

Jasmine muttered, but not quietly enough, 'Yeah, well she wouldn't, would she?'

'And what's that supposed to mean?'

'Would you have ever discussed fuck-buddies with our mother?'

'Oh stop saying fuck-buddy!'

'I think you see my point, Mia. You're her mum but she sees me as more of a friend.' When her sister didn't say anything and pulled that face of hers – a slight pursing of the lips, ever so subtle, a widening of the eyes – she asked, 'Is there a problem with that?'

'Yes.'

'I knew it! All these years and you still hate the idea of me having a relationship with Lexi.'

'Jasmine, I'm glad you like my daughter. But it's my job to worry about her.' Mia picked up an apron from the hook on the back of the door. Jasmine hadn't noticed it at the airport, in the car on the way here, but her sister looked exhausted, like she was ten years older than she really was.

'Are you're worried about Lexi spending time with me?' Jasmine asked.

'Quite frankly, yes.' She looped the apron over her head and wound the ties around her waist. 'I worry she'll see you, all the excitement in your life – London, men, no responsibilities, no real job – and she'll want to morph herself into you.'

'Way to make me feel good about myself, Sis.'

'I wasn't having a go at you. I'm just saying—'

Jasmine held up her hand. Yes, Mia was just saying…she was lecturing her in that subtle way of hers that came more from the look accompanying the words than the actual words themselves. 'I think I'd rather go and face Mum and Dad,' said Jasmine. 'This is about as pleasant a homecoming as I was expecting. Well done.'

She'd expected this level of disapproval from Will, but not quite so much from her sister. All of a sudden she wished she had a TARDIS to whisk her back to London and the carefree life she'd had there. But, then again, if she did that she wouldn't get a look in when it came to the café, and that was something she wasn't willing to let happen.

Chapter Seven
Will

Will breathed in the salty sea air of Primrose Bay for the first time in years. The sun had crept below the horizon, casting a soft golden glow across the sands marked with footprints and trails from beach buggies or surfboards. Seagulls squawked as they lorded it over the almost free sands when the last of the beachgoers had left for the day.

The taxi had dropped him off ten minutes ago. Despite the luggage with him, Will had asked to get out a few hundred metres before The Sun Coral Café and had found a familiar place to sit and look out over the ocean. He'd sat on this same bench many a time contemplating the complexities of the Marcellos' lives, and he'd wanted a moment before he returned to all that.

When he'd had his ocean fix, he knew it was time to face the music. Or rather his family.

He hauled his luggage to the door of the café and was about to push it open when his niece, Lexi, came rushing out, letting the door fall shut behind her. She must've seen him coming.

'Uncle Will!' She leapt into his arms. He adored his niece, now. As a baby he hadn't had much interest in her at all but as she'd grown up he relaxed, stopped resenting her presence and, ultimately, blaming her for the reason his friendship with Daniel and relationship with Mia had broken down, and they'd developed a closeness that helped him feel as though he was still connected, in some way, to Mia's life.

'Lexi, you grow more every time I see you.' He smiled down at her. 'You'll be overtaking me soon!' He doubted it, but she was already taller than her mother, so you never knew. 'How's the swimming going?'

'Great! We were second in the relay at the carnival yesterday and I came first in the backstroke.'

He held up a hand for her to high-five.

'You're so lame, Uncle Will.'

'Do it anyway.' He winked as their hands met mid-air. Laughing, he put a hand out to push open the door to the café.

'I wouldn't go in there if I were you,' said Lexi. 'World War Three just started.'

'Don't worry, I've seen it all before. Where our family is concerned, any world war would be pretty tame. I'd take a legitimate battlefield any day.'

'Well don't say I didn't warn you. I'm going up to the apartment – homework.' She grimaced.

'Oh I don't miss those days.'

'I'll bet. Sometimes it really sucks. Are you staying in the bay for long?'

'Long enough to catch up with my favourite niece, I promise.'

Lexi went off happily enough and Will prepared to brave whatever was playing out inside the café. He pushed open the door and it was as expected, exactly as Lexi had warned him.

There were no customers in sight but, just in case, Will turned the sign on the door to Closed. If the locals came along wanting an evening coffee or late-night snack, he'd deal with it when the time came.

Mia was at the coffee machine. Steam was pouring out as she tried to do something. Obviously she wasn't doing it right because Jasmine was shouting at her, interspersed with yelling at their mum.

‘I just don’t see why you can’t wait a week or two before you bugger off!’ Jasmine yelled, and Rachel Marcello immediately dug her heels in more. The Italian side of the family brought fieriness to the Marcellos, but Rachel brought her own ingredient in the form of recalcitrance.

‘I’ve spent the best part of thirty-eight years raising three children,’ said Rachel. ‘I’ve worked my fingers to the bone in this business.’

‘But it’s *your* business.’ Jasmine screamed back at her mum. Only Mia had looked up long enough to realise their brother was standing right in front of them.

‘Will.’ Mia smiled and came around the other side of the counter, wiping her hands on a tea towel. ‘Welcome home.’

He put his luggage down and hugged his sister, the girl he’d got on with right up until she’d met Daniel and things had changed completely. ‘I ran in to that daughter of yours outside.’

‘She’s been desperate to see you.’

‘She’s getting taller and more beautiful every day.’ He held her gaze until his mum noticed him.

‘Will!’ She rushed over and wrapped him in an enormous hug. And, for a moment, being back in the bay didn’t seem half as bad. ‘You’re here. Oh, and you walked in on a big argument. I’m sorry.’

Nothing new there, he wanted to say.

His mum wrapped him in a second hug as though she was afraid he’d disappear again. He towered over her slight frame and short stature now but they were clearly mother and son, with their deep olive skin and blue eyes. She looked almost the same as she had the day he’d left for New York except, while his dad had got a sports car for his mid-life crisis, Rachel Marcello had added a shade of red to her hair to disguise any greys.

'Hey, Jasmine.' He'd pulled apart from his mum and lifted a hand towards his younger sister, who looked very different – although he couldn't put his finger on exactly why. She had her hands full with a tray of coffee mugs, something he felt sure she would've done on purpose rather than give him a hug. Eleven years his junior, they'd never got on and he doubted they ever would. 'How are things? How's London?'

'It was great, really love it there. How's New York?'

When she put down the tray he could see why he'd thought there was something different about her. At first he'd wondered whether her hair had been styled another way, or was her makeup applied in a new fashion? But now, without anything obscuring his view, he could see that the difference between this Jasmine and the one he'd seen when he was last in the bay was that she'd lost a ton of weight.

And she was still looking at him now for an answer to her question.

'Good. Cold,' he stammered.

'London was the same.'

London had obviously been witness to great change with his sister. She looked healthy, vibrant, confident.

His mother took him by the arm and made him sit. At least it stopped him wondering whether to say anything to Jasmine about how much better she looked than the last time he'd seen her. When he'd been in the bay for his friend Jacob's wedding, he and Jasmine had clashed in a big way. She wasn't working, she'd gone from job to job never holding one down, and she was out until all hours with her friends. She'd come home unusually late one night and had been completely unapologetic to his parents, who'd been worried sick about her, and he'd given her a real piece of his mind. She'd basically bawled her eyes out, told him to mind his own bloody business. He'd wanted to take her aside and shake some sense into her – at least metaphorically – because she was a mess. She had no job, no focus, she was constantly angry at everyone, she never took responsibility for herself, and she was beginning to let her health slide.

'You must be shattered after your journey,' his mum said to him now.

'It wasn't so bad.'

'So come on.' Rachel's eyes danced as she talked to her son. 'Tell me all about it, life in the Big Apple.'

'Mum—' Jasmine interrupted.

'Jasmine, I've listened to stories of London, now I want to hear about New York.'

'I know, but seriously. You're leaving tomorrow and we still don't know enough about running this café to look after it ourselves.'

'She has a point,' said Will, putting a hand across Rachel's. 'I can't believe you and Dad are splitting up. What the hell happened?'

'We've been unhappy for some time.'

He shook his head. He'd had a bit of time to try to understand it but he was still nowhere near. 'Why not stay another week, show us what to do? I don't understand why all of this is so rushed.' He watched Mia busying herself wiping down tables, slotting napkins back into their holders, in control as usual.

Rachel took a deep breath. 'As I explained when I telephoned, your father and I have reached a crossroads in our lives and—'

Tim Marcello came through from the kitchen. He'd probably scarpered out there when his wife and daughter launched into their row. He hugged Will and took a step back to look at his son. 'New York life must agree with you.'

'It's not so bad. So come on, maybe you'll tell me what on earth is going on here.'

Tim looked to his wife. 'I believe you've been filled in already. We need to do this, Son, and if the café has to close, so be it. What is it they call it? Collateral damage? We're trying to do this as smoothly as possible, but staying isn't an option. Maybe we haven't planned this as well as we could have, but we're at breaking point.'

When Will looked more carefully at each of his parents, he could see the signs now, the indication of strain, of weariness that hadn't been there on the surface as they'd welcomed him home. His mum's smile didn't reach her eyes as it had in days gone by, and his dad lacked the usual vibrant energy that surrounded him so well.

Will looked around the café. It felt as though he'd stood in this space only yesterday. It had all the signs that this was more than a business to his family. The shells in a 3D frame hanging from the wall on a piece of old rope, the distressed wooden bench by the front window where people sat to enjoy a takeaway coffee, the chalkboard with the name of the café etched on the curved top.

'It's time, Son. We've explained to Mia that we are happy for the café to shut indefinitely and we'll either pick up or sell up when we return.'

'Stupid,' said Jasmine, loud enough for everyone to hear, before adding, 'It's a ridiculous thing to say and I don't think either of you have thought this through.'

'Jasmine, don't talk to your father like that, please.' Rachel admonished her youngest daughter, who pulled a face back as if to ask why she was being told off when she was only voicing her opinion. 'This is what we're doing. Now we've been through as much as we can with Mia.'

Will looked over at Mia, who by this time had finished stacking up the last of the dirty crockery from the corner table. She looked older than the last time he'd seen her. Not age-wise, but as though her face and body hadn't quite caught up with the exhaustion and plague of family issues inside. But then she thrived on this, she loved taking control, solving everyone else's problems. He wondered whether the weariness had something to do with her inability to fix their parents' marriage, her inability to fix the café with one instant click of her fingers.

'Oh this machine is useless!' Jasmine added a few expletives until Rachel went over to help her daughter. 'I can't get the coffees to look like they should.'

'It takes practice, Jasmine,' said Tim, his voice so soft Will didn't miss the fed-up undertones. 'And time.'

'Well we don't have a whole lot of that now do we!'

Only Jasmine could get away with yelling at their parents. Another perk of being the youngest he guessed. He was pretty sure he'd never spoken to them like that. Ever.

'Right, that's it.' Rachel Marcello planted both hands firmly on the counter at the front of the coffee shop. 'Enough.'

When a customer peered in Tim scurried over to the door, opened it and apologised but said it was an emergency family meeting. Things certainly had changed here on Walton's Mountain. There was a day when his dad would never turn a customer away. A customer one day was a customer for life he always said.

‘Sit down, all three of you,’ Rachel instructed. ‘Come on, Mia. The washing up will wait.’ She stopped her eldest daughter before she disappeared out back and even though they were all grown up now, Rachel’s tone had that don’t-you-dare-disobey-me hint about it and they all did as they were told.

‘Your father and I are separating. End of.’ Her voice didn’t waver. ‘We have said, time and time again, in emails, phone calls and discussions with all three of you over the last couple of days that we are happy for you to shut the café. Keeping it open was something Mia insisted on doing. And I’m assuming you are all in agreement.’

Will and Jasmine reluctantly nodded and so did Mia, even though she’d made the decision in the first place.

‘So,’ their mother continued. ‘Without Briony and Cally you’ll have to somehow manage it together. Mia has a business to run, Will, you have a life in New York and, Jasmine, you have a life in London. But if this is what you all want then you have to lead the way from here.’

Rachel Marcello paused and let out a long sigh. ‘Remember, The Sun Coral Café isn’t the be-all and end-all for any of us, so in our absence do as you see fit. Close down, stay open, we don’t mind. And when we both return to the bay we will make some long-term decisions.’

Will already knew from emails and what Mia had told him that his parents would be contactable only in emergencies. The accountant would come and do the books, Mia knew how to use the reordering system for the café supplies and in the short term this was entirely manageable.

Will didn’t really want to think about the long term.

'Mum—' When Will put his hand on hers she pulled it away and he saw the tears in her eyes, the first sign she was having doubts or was finding this at all difficult. Mia had the same determined streak.

'Now if you don't mind,' she said, as though he hadn't reached out to her at all, 'I'd better get back to packing. Will, the spare room is made up for you. Jasmine, our bedroom is all yours.'

'How long will you be gone?' Will asked his dad, but it was his mum who answered. He found himself wondering whether this separation had been more one-sided than he'd thought.

'I've no idea,' she said. 'As long as it takes.'

'Any hints as to where you're going?' Jasmine planted her hands firmly on her hips. 'It'd be nice to be kept in the loop.'

Why couldn't she ever speak to her family with a hint of concern? Her demands always sounded as though they were only ever about her.

'I don't really know yet,' said Rachel. 'I'm driving up to Batemans Bay in New South Wales to see my friend Sara. Remember her?'

'Isn't she the one who went all New Age and runs a yoga retreat now?' Will wouldn't have picked Rachel as a yogi. Women at his work did yoga in their lunch hour, off in their multicoloured stretch pants and tight tops, coming back with smiles on their faces as though they'd had an erotic massage rather than an exercise class. He couldn't understand the attraction himself. Give him adrenalin any time.

'That's the one. She's very successful and people come from all over Australia to be at her retreats.'

'I bet she wouldn't shut up shop and bugger off for weeks on end,' said Jasmine, riling her mother as was her way.

Rachel Marcello chose not to answer the question and Mia had already gone over to try her hand at the coffee machine while there were no customers. She looked as though she had about as much clue as Will how to use one.

'I can't get the coffee to look or taste anything like it's supposed to,' Mia called out before too long, as they were all still digesting the law that had been laid down in the last few minutes. 'I'm worried we'll scare customers away.'

'Come on, let's start again.' Tim ushered Mia out of the way. 'Let me show you some basics.'

It'd take more than that, thought Will.

'So where to after Batemans Bay?' Will asked his mum, eager to build up more of a picture of how this would all pan out.

'I really don't know. I'll see. Maybe I'll become a devout Yogi and stay there in my spiritual haven.' She laughed and, despite the situation, Will was glad to hear her make a joke, albeit a rubbish one.

'And what about you, Dad?' he called over to where they were standing at the coffee machine. 'What are your plans?'

'First stop is the New South Wales Golf Club.' Even by his voice Will could tell his dad was into this. He wanted this. Now Will had no idea which of his parents had instigated the separation and the walking away from their business. Perhaps it was just as they'd claimed: a mutual decision.

'Do you remember Perry?' Tim asked.

'Isn't he the guy whose wife left him for her caddy from the golf club?' Mia piped up, still trying to perfect a latte. 'A female caddy?'

Will couldn't help but let a laugh escape.

'Yes, it's true,' Tim admitted. 'Perry's wife Joanna left him for Felicity, the caddy who'd been by her side for the past ten years while all along her husband thought she was learning the sport to spend more time with him.' He rolled his eyes at the absurdity.

Will shook his head. 'Poor Perry. He's a decent guy.'

'He is,' said Tim. 'Anyway, I'll be spending a week playing golf every day and thinking about nothing else. First stop will be the pro shop for a new driver – mine's seen better days.'

'And after that?' Will asked.

'Like your mother said, we haven't made plans. We will be emailing you all here, to answer any business queries you have, but our details are only for emergencies. This is about each of us and the next stage of our lives. We both need this time away.'

Will wondered what the next stage would involve for those his parents left behind.

*

By nine o'clock that night Rachel and Tim Marcello were packed. Tim loaded up his single suitcase, a holdall and his bag of golf clubs into his BMW convertible, parked out front on Beach Road, and Rachel loaded her two suitcases and a flowery holdall into the boot of her Mini Clubman, the car she'd acquired a few years ago; it had been brand new at the time, an anniversary gift from her husband. They said their goodbyes, promising to be in touch soon but requesting they be given enough space to sort through their own problems first. They reiterated that it wouldn't do any harm to shut the café indefinitely in their absence and that the kids weren't to hesitate in doing so if that's what they decided was best all round.

'Can I interest anyone in a coffee?' Mia asked after they'd waved their parents off and gone back inside the café.

Will grinned. 'Are you making it?' He was glad they'd called an unspoken kind of truce for now, the burial of any ill feelings while they sorted out this mess. He locked the door to the café behind them. He'd lock up properly when Mia returned to her apartment and put the alarm on when he and Jasmine went upstairs to their parents' apartment. 'I'll give the coffee a miss, actually. I'm shattered and I want to sleep as soon as my head hits the pillow.'

'Didn't you sleep much on the plane?' Jasmine asked. She too was being far more polite than he'd expected.

He'd slept very well in his business-class seat on the plane, the seat that fully reclined into a bed. He knew his sister would have flown back from London in the squished economy class, so he wasn't about to rub her nose in it. Maybe later, if she annoyed him enough.

'No, too much going on in my mind,' he lied. 'I still can't believe they've gone.'

'Not gone,' Jasmine corrected. 'Buggered off.'

'You're right. They have 'buggered off'.'

At least all three of them could agree on something.

Jasmine smiled. She was much friendlier when she did that. The sister he thought of when he thought of the bay as he sat at his desk in New York usually had one hell of a scowl on her face.

Mia brought over two coffees – one for her, one for Jasmine. Will wasn't sure what kind they were. Usually he could spot a cappuccino, or a latte, or a macchiato straight off, but not this time. Mia would need a lot more practice or they'd have a lot of unhappy customers. And he was pretty sure neither he nor Jasmine would be able to do any better.

'Lexi told me she did well in the swim carnival yesterday.' It was too late to talk any more about their parents or the café. Will decided all the shit would still be there in the morning.

'We were so proud of her,' said Mia. 'She's a great swimmer.'

'Always has been from what I remember.'

'I can't take the credit. Daniel insisted she learn from an early age and he put in the hard yards when she didn't want to get in the water. I think I'd have gone crazy taking her in a pool screaming her head off.'

Will bristled at the mention of Daniel's name. He'd been his best friend at one time, but their friendship hadn't taken the strain of a sibling's failed relationship and unexpected pregnancy. His younger sister had been eighteen at the time, her whole world ahead of her, but ended up with no control over what happened next. She'd been forced to follow one definite path in her life and Will had never been sure whether she'd ever been truly happy. And he blamed Daniel in part for that. His parents had been far more accepting than he had. They'd even told him how supportive Daniel was, how much he was there for Mia even though they weren't together, but all Will had seen was Daniel going about his life with the same ease as before. Will had distanced himself from the both of them, given up on the travel plans he'd had with his mate, and as soon as he'd found a job he'd gone to Perth – a good four-hour flight away from the whole situation.

'He's even taken her for a few surf lessons,' Mia continued. 'Down to the Mornington Peninsula for a weekend.'

Daniel was a great surfer. They'd done plenty of it as teenagers but it had never hooked Will in the same way as it had his friend. Daniel was a master at the barrel, power carves and had even conquered the aerial – that impressive surf manoeuvre where a surfer hits the crest of a wave and flies through the air. When they were teenagers Will had wondered whether Daniel would go on to compete, but he'd only ever done it as a hobby. Over the years Mia often talked about Daniel going surfing before he went to the office. Of course he'd only heard this via his sister, because by that time Daniel was the father of his sister's baby rather than a friend of Will Marcello's. He sometimes wondered whether her references were merely to keep the peace between her brother and the father of her daughter, or whether she was trying in some odd way to make him forgive and forget. But he couldn't. It wasn't that easy.

'He said he'd teach me too.' Jasmine sipped the coffee from Mia and if it didn't taste right she was obviously on her best behaviour and not mentioning it.

Mia seemed on edge. 'When did he say that?'

'Last time I babysat – the time you had flu and Lexi was staying with him and he had a business meeting. It was ages ago, but I remember.' When her sister pulled a face she said, 'Oh relax, we're only friends.'

Mia's wasn't such a ludicrous assumption. For a moment, Will had wondered the same about Jasmine and Daniel himself. But Jasmine wouldn't do that, would she?

'Anyway,' Jasmine continued, 'I'll learn eventually. He's probably forgotten all about the offer anyway.'

'Too cold in England?' Will asked in an attempt to engage his youngest sister in civil conversation. He still couldn't get over how much she'd changed, at least on the surface.

'Not enough sea in the capital city,' she answered.

'There are some great surfing beaches down in Cornwall.'

They launched into a conversation about New York, about London, about the people they'd met, the places they'd been. It wasn't until they'd been talking for quite a while that Will realised Mia was cleaning up around the coffee machine having slowly drifted away from the conversation. Staying in the bay all her life meant she was probably excluded from most of what they talked about and he wondered whether she'd be doing anything different had Lexi not come along.

When the conversation came to a natural pause Will went over to Mia and took the tray full of cups through to the kitchen, stacked them in the dishwasher and pressed the button to start the cycle.

'So how is Daniel?' He asked her now.

'He's fine. Happy enough.'

'Is he with anyone?'

'A girlfriend? No. There was someone a while back but I'm not sure what happened there.'

'Does Lexi see plenty of him?'

'All the time.' She smiled. She knew her brother too well. Even though they rarely talked these days, she'd know he was always going to make sure the man who was permanently linked to their family did the right thing. And it sounded as though he had no worries on that score.

They cleared the kitchen and Mia locked the cash in the safe, running through the process with him and

Jasmine for cashing up at the end of the day, and by the time they locked up and alarmed the premises Will was too exhausted to care that he was back in the proximity of his sisters after all this time. Back to the Marcello way of life.

As the saying went, tomorrow was another day.

Chapter Eight

Mia

If her sister had a go at her one more time, she'd scream.

'I'm doing my best,' said Mia through gritted teeth as she tipped away the supremely awful macchiato she'd tried to make for a customer. She looked once more at the notes she'd made after first Briony had taken her through the process briefly and then, yesterday, her dad had done the same: avoid bubbles in the foam, it said; only pour a little bit of the frothed milk into the espresso or it'll turn into a cappuccino. So far Mia had bestowed on the beverage more bubbles than a child's bedtime bath and she'd managed to pour enough foam in to make the entire drink into what she could only describe as froth with a hint of coffee.

Today, all day, it'd been like having toddlers let loose in the kitchen. And they had only just reached lunchtime. There were cups and spillages everywhere because they'd not managed taking orders, fulfilling orders and clearing up simultaneously; the dishwasher needed emptying; and cups should've been left on top of the coffee machine to warm through. And, to top it all off, they'd run out of raisin toast. Mia had sworn then, so loudly Jasmine shut her in the kitchen so as not to terrify the customers. It didn't help, either, that Will had been chatting for the past thirty minutes to his mate Leo, arranging a catch up in the city that evening. Did he have any clue how important it was to get this right, before they lost customers and they wouldn't be choosing whether to shut the business? If they weren't careful, it'd be a foregone conclusion.

Mia was jumpy and the familiar feeling of something stuck at the back of her throat had reared its ugly head again. It happened occasionally, particularly when she was under an emotional strain. The first time it had happened was when she'd launched The Primrose Bay Picnic Company. She'd had many a sleepless night panicking that her business would flop, that she'd have to go back to data entry to support herself and her child. And the feeling in her throat had kept her awake, night after night. Apparently it was a common symptom of General Anxiety disorder, but she started to worry it was more. She went to see the doctor, had an endoscopy to check nothing was amiss, and got herself into an even worse state worrying she had a disease that would claim her life and take her away from Lexi altogether.

Of course, the endoscopy came back clear and after several follow-up appointments with her doctor and discussion of her other symptoms all he could put it down to was stress. 'Stop trying to manage the world,' he had said to her, his familiar kind smile firmly in place in the middle of a dark beard that would fade to grey as the years went on. 'You simply cannot control everything, Mia.'

Ever since then, whenever she got stressed out about anything – a huge order at the picnic company; when Lexi had come home in floods of tears in Year Nine after being picked on; when she thought about the relationship she'd lost with her brother since the day she'd told him she was pregnant; and a couple of days ago when her parents announced they were splitting up and The Sun Coral Café was basically being left to its own devices – she got the same feeling, as though she'd swallowed a piece of bread and it hadn't gone down properly.

The feeling was back now and she tried to zone out and calm down, although it wasn't easy when the customer waiting for the macchiato was beginning to get impatient. She couldn't blame him. He wanted takeaway so was most likely on his way somewhere else. He didn't need to watch three siblings bickering as one of them attempted to use the damn coffee machine.

'Do you want me to have a try?' It was Will beside her now.

'No, I'm doing fine.' She tapped the sides of the jug to rid the foam of bubbles and then, with a fresh espresso shot waiting for her in the takeaway cup, she poured the frothy milk she'd made using the espresso machine. As she came to the end of the pour she lifted the little jug containing the foam and wiggled it from side to side and lo and behold it formed a shape on the top. Ha! There! She'd done it. Ok, so it wasn't quite the same heart or tulip shape she'd seen her parents do with ease so many times, but it was a near-perfect macchiato. The perfect shot with the perfect froth.

She took a takeaway lid and fitted it onto the cup. 'I'm so sorry, sir.' She handed it to the customer and then lifted the lid from the jar of cookies on the counter. With the tongs she took out a dark-chocolate cookie with white-chocolate chips, placed it onto a napkin and handed it to him. 'On the house, with my apologies.'

She took payment and one happy customer left the café with a smile replacing the scowl that had begun to form as he waited.

'I hope you don't give out free picnics all the time,' Jasmine scolded. 'It's no way to turn a profit.'

'I'm just trying to keep our heads above water at this stage,' Mia quipped. She looked over at Will trying to get to grips with the coffee machine and having no luck.

‘Will, why don’t you take the orders and I’ll make the coffees?’

He held up his hands. ‘No, no. We’re all in this together. If you show me, I’ll do it.’

Mia peered into the cup he had just made. ‘What is that?’

‘It’s a skim latte.’

‘Give me a taste.’ She took too big a gulp and pulled a face. ‘There’s barely enough coffee in there, it’s like warmed milk, and the consistency is all wrong.’

‘But it says in your notes that a latte is supposed to be milky.’

‘It’s supposed to be a ratio of one to one. See.’ She pointed to the line she’d scribbled, which had the ‘1:1’ beside it.

‘Well I couldn’t read your writing. It’s scrawl.’

‘Whatever,’ she snapped, and went out back to get more coffee granules to fill the grinder. But the change of scene did not have the desired calming effect and her voice bellowed out, ‘Who left the lid off the container of coffee beans?’

‘Oh chill out, Mia.’ Jasmine came in, rolled her eyes and put the lid on herself.

‘It’s too late. If the beans aren’t fresh the coffee tastes crap.’

‘Oh bollocks. Nobody will notice.’

‘They will! It’s like making up a fresh sandwich with day-old bread. Believe me, they’ll know. God, Jasmine. Just think next time would you?’

‘Actually it was me, sorry.’ Will, who had evidently given up perfecting his latte, came into the kitchen. ‘We’ve been so busy I forgot.’

Mia counted to ten, took a deep breath, willed any dizziness to stay away – it was another symptom of her stress that she refused to give in to.

Jasmine went out front but came straight back to summon her brother. 'The customers at table two are still waiting for their drinks.'

'So make them then.' Will leant against the industrial fridge. 'The order is next to the coffee machine.'

'You said you were doing it! You've been hogging the bloody machine for ages in your quest to take control. As per usual.'

'And what's that supposed to mean?'

'You're so judgemental. I can't do anything right!' Jasmine's voice had gone up three octaves by now.

'Someone has to be sensible and work through the mess. And I doubt that person is going to be you!' Will matched his sister's volume.

Mia went out front and, ignoring the catfight in the kitchen between her brother and sister, attempted to make a latte, two hot chocolates and a strawberry milkshake for table two, who were waiting patiently and doing their best to act as though they couldn't hear a thing. Thankfully they weren't locals, although sometimes that was worse. Imagine if they went home to wherever they were from and told everyone they'd been to the worst café ever in Primrose Bay. They could be featured in travel guides for all the wrong reasons.

When Mia finally fulfilled the order, grateful it was only the one coffee, she went out back again. 'This has got to stop.' Her voice authoritative, in true disapproving parent mode she stood the other side of the kitchen door with it open only a crack so she could keep an eye on the front of the shop. 'We all want the same thing, am I right?'

'And what's that?' Jasmine huffed.

'We all want the café to be a success, to keep its position in Primrose Bay and to keep loyal customers and at the same time attract more.'

'Get to the point, Mia.' Will's face looked as though it could explode at any second. She'd seen that look on him many times before – when Jasmine had taken his tennis racket without asking and had dropped it in the road on the way back from the courts in the next suburb so a car completely crushed it; when he wasn't able to go and hang out with his friends after school because his parents needed him to mind his baby sister. And then – Mia couldn't help shuddering at the recollection – when he had found out that she was pregnant by his best friend.

'We need to start interviewing staff,' Mia went on. 'I've got my own business to run and it's a quiet day today but most of the time I'm rushed off my feet. I won't always have time to be in here.' The only good thing about being overly busy was that she hadn't time to think about her parents' crumbled marriage, she hadn't time to think about what she could've done differently to make things easier for them so they wouldn't have ended up separating.

Will took a deep breath and exhaled. Ever practical, he seemed keen to move things forward too. 'Do you have anyone in mind?'

'There's a short list at the back of my notepad…if you can read my scrawl, that is.'

Will retrieved the notepad from beside the coffee machine out front. 'What's that number?' He pointed to one of the contact details.

'It's a two!'

'Could've fooled me.'

She rolled her eyes. Why did he have this incessant need to antagonise her? Sometimes, when she wasn't as busy as normal, when she got to sit back and read a book or take a walk along the beach, she thought about her brother all the way over in New York, and she missed him. After they'd fallen out over Daniel there had been an unspoken truce and they'd started at least to be civil to one another, but they'd never got back to the relationship they'd once had. Sometimes it made her sad. Other times she accepted it was the inevitable.

'Mum has had those details for a while, but give each person a call,' said Mia. 'And we'll start interviews.'

'How about a poster in the window?' Jasmine suggested.

Mia waved her hand. 'We don't have time to wait for someone to saunter past and see it. We need help, now.'

Jasmine tutted, and not quietly either. 'It's how I got my bar job in London. I was on my way to the jobcentre and happened to walk past The Crown & Shilling. There was a sign in the window, and I went in to ask about the position and started two days later.'

Mia refilled the dispensers on two of the tables with more napkins when she noticed them running low. 'Put up a poster if you think it'll help.'

'Why do you never believe in me?'

Mia turned to say something but Jasmine had already left to stomp up the stairs, presumably to find paper, pens and Sellotape to make the sign.

'I'll go and phone these people,' said Will. 'Mind if I go next door to the picnic shop?'

'What, you can't be in the same apartment as your sister?'

'I shared a place with her last night, didn't I?'

'You want a medal for it?' He and Jasmine had shared the space last night and Mia wondered how that had gone. She hoped they would've both been so jet-lagged they hadn't had time to start bickering.

'Look, can I go next door or not?'

Mia fished the keys from her pocket. 'Let's hope we find someone, and soon. Then we can all get back to our own lives.'

The rest of the day passed in a whirl, and not a pleasant one. As soon as her siblings returned and the sign was in the window and interviews had been scheduled, Mia bickered with Jasmine, and Will battled with both of them. Mia had seen her brother at social occasions often enough – weddings, twenty-firsts, sporting celebrations – and he had the gift of the gab with most people but here, in the café, customer service didn't seem to interest him at all. The only thing he seemed happy to do was keep the kitchen out back as tidy as possible, which Mia knew was better than him sitting around doing nothing.

Back in the picnic shop that afternoon, when it was quiet enough for her to leave the other two in charge, Mia checked her website for emails and responded to those she needed to. She added the photos of the Proposal Picnic she'd taken yesterday. The rich green of the lawns contrasted against the shimmering depths of the Central Lake, and the added colours from the picnic blanket stood out while the silver champagne bucket glinted in the sun. As she went about her own tasks she felt a sense of calm settle across her shoulders. Away from her brother and sister, away from the noise of the coffee machine – the grinding, the tamping, the hiss from the steam wand – she was happy. They just needed to manage this until their parents returned. They could do that, couldn't they?

*

'Tell me, Hermione, what experience do you have of working in a café?' Mia was interviewing the first of three candidates Will had contacted. Eighteen years old, with legs up to her armpits, she knew her brother would've probably taken her on without even asking her a single question. That was why she'd left him to interview the short, chubby fifteen-year-old boy with an unfortunate stutter.

'I've worked at cafés all over: Elwood, Brighton, St Kilda.'

'Great, so you're familiar with a coffee machine.'

'Definitely.'

'You can teach all of us.' Mia laughed and ticked her sheet next to 'coffee skills' but when she looked up she didn't miss Hermione looking over at her brother.

Mia pulled Hermione's attention back to her rather than Will and asked her further questions: why she wanted to work at The Sun Coral Café, what she knew about them, what sort of wages she was expecting.

'And why did you leave your last job?' Mia asked.

Hermione's lips twisted as she thought of an answer. Mia wondered if she was contemplating making something up. 'A customer was incredibly rude to me and my boss didn't stick up for me.'

In her peripheral vision Mia could see Will still ogling Hermione. With long blonde hair down to her waist, a sizeable chest neatly encased in her fitted T-shirt, along with denim shorts that could rival Kylie's gold hotpants, she was an attractive girl. But Mia wasn't interested in her appearance. She needed someone who could do the job, which meant making the coffee for a start – and showing them all how to do it.

'So what happened?' Mia asked.

'The customer was getting impatient because I hadn't filled his order – I was busy making a sandwich for another customer.'

'And did you try to resolve the conflict yourself?' She'd read up about what sort of questions to ask prospective employees before today, worried she would employ someone unsuitable and be stuck with them.

'I threw a jug of milk all over him! I wasn't standing for that. The arrogant tosser.'

And just like that Mia's hopes of finding the perfect employee in this candidate faded. She couldn't add another feisty person to the mix. There were already three Marcellos and they needed someone level-headed who could tone down the madness. Mia finished the interview by asking a few further questions, more out of politeness than anything else, then told Hermione they had other people to interview but she would be in touch if they wanted to talk further.

'What was wrong with her?' Will asked when he'd finished with his candidate who was no good because it turned out he could only work weekends. Why he'd not told them that in the first place when Will had called, Mia had no idea.

Mia explained the reasons Hermione had left – or rather been fired, as Mia assumed was really the case.

'She sounds like a live one.'

'Oh put your eyes back in their sockets. Yes, she was gorgeous but, no, we don't need someone like that.'

'Right, next candidate,' said Will.

They both sat down with the third candidate, who turned out to be no good either. She could work a coffee machine but she interrupted constantly, didn't want to listen when Mia was trying to explain the process – 'Oh, I know all that,' she'd dismissed. And at one point during the interview she'd boldly excused herself to answer a call on her phone! Will had laughed at that point and Jasmine, watching from the table in the corner where she was wiping down, couldn't help but snigger. Mia had ended up stifling a giggle and as soon as the girl had left they all ended up walking sedately out to the kitchen, where they'd fallen about laughing once they were out of sight of the customers.

'Who does that?' Jasmine exclaimed. 'Who even has their mobile on during an interview, let alone answers it?'

'Gen Y, that's who.' Will shook his head. 'Where do these people learn their life skills? That's what I want to know.'

Mia poked her head out of the kitchen. 'Customers,' she said to the others, but when she asked what she could get for the lady, most likely in her late forties, with kind eyes and a sensible hairdo rolled up in a French pleat out of the way, the woman said she'd seen the sign in the window and was looking for work.

Jasmine was out of the kitchen like a shot. 'Do you have time to chat now?' she asked.

'Of course.'

Jasmine showed the lady, Monica, to the empty table at the side of the café, away from the three that were currently occupied.

'Jasmine,' Mia whispered, 'I'll do the interview.' She held up her notepad. 'I have questions.'

Jasmine dismissed her with a wave of her hand. She beamed a smile to the latest person to come in and when

Mia turned she saw it was her daughter. Was it that time already?

'How was your day?' she asked when Lexi followed her back to the counter, where she refilled the jar with chocolate-chip cookies after Will brought a fresh tray through from the kitchen.

'It wasn't bad.'

Mia's sixth sense – her parent antennae, as she called it – told her there was something else going on. 'Come on, out with it.'

'Can I have a smoothie?'

'Nice try. Not until you talk.'

Lexi sighed one of those teenage sighs accompanied by a roll of the eyes, an action that told you she thought no parent could possibly understand anything that was going on in her life.

'It's school, that's all. It's full on. I think I'm just tired from the swim carnival. It was a lot of pressure, you know.'

Mia nodded. 'You worked hard and you deserved to do well.' She took down a glass and started to make the smoothie. She didn't need to ask what flavour as it was always the same: strawberry and mango. Mangoes had been Lexi's favourite fruit as a little girl. Mia would cut the messy fruit into chunks and while she was arranging them all on a plate, Lexi had already picked up the rectangular core and was making sure she got every last bit of it, slurping as the juice ran down her chin.

Mia sliced banana and a handful of strawberries and dropped them into the blender. She added Greek yoghurt, a scoop of vanilla ice-cream and a good measure of milk, before whizzing all the ingredients together. This was something she could do in her sleep. Not like the blessed coffee machine. She cut a fresh strawberry from its pointy tip almost to its stalk and then gently pushed it onto the side of the glass.

Lexi grinned. 'Thanks, Mum. You're awesome.'

Mia watched as her daughter drank the smoothie. For a moment she looked just like she had when she was five years old and had first started school. Every afternoon she'd come home and have a glass of ice-cold milk with a cookie on the side and tell Mia everything about her day. Now, even with the lure of a smoothie, Mia barely got so much as a grunt out of her.

'Who's that with Jasmine?' Lexi looked over her shoulder to where her auntie was sitting.

Mia crossed her middle finger over her index finger on both hands. 'I'm hoping it's a new employee. God knows we can't go on like this.'

Lexi sat at the counter drinking her smoothie and Mia and Will worked around her. When Jasmine finished the interview, she left the lady at the table and came over to Mia.

'She's perfect.' Jasmine kept her voice low. 'Go over and have a chat, but I think we've found her. And she can work up to four days if we need her to, long hours if required.'

'I'll go and have a talk with her.' Mia started to walk away but turned back to face her sister. 'And Jasmine…'

'Yes?'

'It was a good idea putting the poster in the window.'

Jasmine shrugged. 'I know it was. I wouldn't have suggested it otherwise.'

Monica turned out to be the perfect candidate, just as Jasmine had said. She was older, had a sense of reliability about her, hadn't thrown anything at anyone on her last job, and she lived in the next suburb so could come in at short notice if needed.

‘Where’s Lexi and Jasmine?’ Mia asked Will once she’d finished the interview. Thankfully the café was in a lull following the post-school-day rush.

He shrugged. ‘Dunno. They disappeared upstairs ten minutes ago.’

As though talking about them conjured them up out of nowhere, Jasmine and Lexi came through the door that led up to the apartment above. Giggling and laughing they were, and Mia felt a pang of jealousy. She should be pleased they were close, she really should, and she’d thought her jealousy over their friendship had gone until she’d walked in and overheard their conversation the other day about ‘fuck-buddies’. It had only highlighted to Mia that her daughter was sixteen years old – only two years younger than she’d been when she got pregnant – and was venturing into that unknown, experimental, exhilarating yet terrifying world where relationships with the opposite sex started to matter, and she could get her heart broken. Or, worse, history could repeat itself and she could fall pregnant.

‘Where did you two get to?’ Mia tried to sound more nonchalant than she really felt.

‘Never mind that,’ said Jasmine, still grinning. ‘What did you think of Monica?’

Lexi waved to Jasmine and then Mia and disappeared through the door to the café as she went back to their own apartment.

Mia tried not to think how happy her daughter was after she’d spent time with Jasmine, did her best not to obsess about what they’d been discussing up there. ‘She’s perfect. She starts in the morning.’ When Jasmine rolled her eyes and shook her head, Mia asked, ‘What’s the look for?’

‘Because.’

'Because what?'

'Because I told you the advert in the window was a good idea.'

'And I agreed to let you do it.'

'Exactly. You agreed. You *let* me do it. I don't know, Mia. When are you guys going to have a little faith in me?' She didn't wait for an answer. She went back into the kitchen and, by the sound of it, Mia knew her sister was taking out her frustration on the innocent crockery.

'Jasmine, I'm sorry.' Mia followed her out back as soon as she'd made the chocolate milkshakes for two teenagers who came in with sand all up their legs and in their hair. Her parents had never moaned about the ocean being brought to them in this way. 'It's a beach café,' they'd always said; 'it makes it more authentic,' her mum had laughed, picking up the broom for the umpteenth time. Mia found herself wondering where they both were right now. Was her mum doing downward-facing dog and chaturanga poses by the bay? Was her dad chasing the elusive hole-in-one on the golf course? And were either of them thinking about the three siblings they'd left at the helm of their lifelong baby, the business they'd built from scratch?

'Jasmine,' Mia said again when her sister ignored her. 'I'm sorry I doubted you. It's just…well it's been a while since either you or Will have been here and you know how I cope, I—'

'You take over. You think you have to solve the world's problems.'

'That's not fair.'

'Maybe not. But it's true.'

Jasmine was pretty accurate in her assessment of course. Her doctor had told her as much when she'd been diagnosed with GAD. 'Stop trying to manage the world,' he'd said. But it was in her nature and letting go wasn't easy.

'So Monica will be in at eight o'clock tomorrow morning,' Mia offered in the hope a change of tack would rectify the tension.

'I'm taking the day off.' Jasmine turned and held up her index finger to tell Mia to wait. 'I've enrolled myself on a barista course. One of us needs to. Monica can show you and Will everything she knows tomorrow, but this will be formal training that I think is necessary. Mum and Dad both did it a few years ago to make sure their skills were among the best in the business.'

'I remember them talking about it.' Mia smiled at the memory of her parents' togetherness. 'I think they had a lot of fun. Dad even thought he'd be able to enter the World Latte Art Championships one day.'

'It was a lot more than fun.' Jasmine pointed to the wall and the framed certificates that had been there for years.

The certificates had been there right in front of her eyes for so long that Mia hadn't really looked at them closely before. She thought they were much like the certificates Lexi had received numerous times in assembly. Each child had been awarded certificates at least twice during the year and it was exciting for them, they felt they'd achieved, but it was also a fun way of encouraging them. Her parents' barista certificates had become part of the wallpaper in the café, disguised by the surrounding sea shells, pictures hanging from old rope, the huge blackboard on the wall for a menu.

'They're professional accreditations,' said Jasmine. 'They're what help to make this café what it is.'

A few days ago Daniel had muttered something about a voucher he had for a similar course but Mia hadn't listened to any of the details because she was far too busy to swan off for part of the day. She'd turned him down flat. Maybe if Jasmine messed this opportunity up, Mia could still go on the course if she made room in her schedule.

'I'll go and get the training,' Jasmine continued, 'and you and Will, and Monica, can hold the fort here. I'll decide whether we need anyone else trained up. I guess it depends.'

'On what?'

'On how much my siblings are willing to let me teach and show them what I know.'

Had Jasmine read her mind? She felt guilty for doubting her, but she was used to her little sister messing up and for everyone else to come to the rescue. It was the way it had always been.

When another customer came in and Jasmine greeted them with a warm smile she didn't always show to Mia, Mia wondered whether her sister was right. Did she and Will doubt her too much? Did they assume she couldn't do things as well as they could? Was that what had made their sibling rivalry evolve into more of a sibling envy as the years had worn on?

And, if so, where did they go from here?

Chapter Nine
Will

Will hadn't seen much point in hiring a car during his stay. It would work out stupidly expensive and the public transport in Melbourne was pretty good. He also wanted to enjoy the sunshine as much as possible, breathe in the ocean air he'd missed without knowing it.

That afternoon he walked from the café in Primrose Bay along the foreshore, taking in deep lungfuls of the sea air to rid himself of the family tension and noise in the café he wasn't used to. Sitting at a desk in his office in New York was a complete contrast to here, where there were constantly simmering tensions between him and his sisters. He walked beside the ocean for as long as he could and then cut through the streets of Brighton, made for the station and caught a train into the city.

When he arrived at Flinders Street a huge smile crept across his face. There really was nothing like coming home. He found himself humming a rendition of 'I Still Call Australia Home' until some girl looked twice at him as though he were a few sandwiches short of a picnic. It was the same look Mia sometimes gave him, as though he was in her territory now and she was the one making the rules. Funny, Jasmine had the cheek to call *him* the control freak, when her sister was doing a much better job of it than he was.

Will found his friend glued to his iPhone screen on Degraves Street, sipping a beer as he waited for him.

The men shook hands. 'Great to see you, Leo.'

'Likewise, mate.' Having got the waitress's attention already with his dirty blond hair and tanned, muscular arms, Leo ordered a beer for his friend. 'You're looking well,' he told Will. 'New York must agree with you.'

Leo had a flash job as a cameraman for a major Australian television network. They'd met through Will's ex, Paige, and had been mates ever since. They were both into sports – Leo had joined him skiing in Aspen one year – and they'd spent many a day after Will's breakup with Paige, scaling the spider wall and negotiating large overhangs and chimneys at the indoor climbing centre in Perth.

'I'm not doing too badly.' Will thanked the waitress for his drink. 'You look like you've taken to Melbourne life pretty well. Not tempted to return to Perth?'

Leo shrugged. 'Maybe someday, but the work's here for now.'

'Are you still keeping fit?'

'I am. I found an awesome climbing gym just down the road.'

'I'd love to go. I need somewhere to work off the tension.'

'Great. How's tomorrow evening sound? Can you get away?'

'I'll make sure I do.' His sisters couldn't object if it was near closing time for the café. Most of their trade was done during the day or after school and by seven o'clock it usually trailed off to next to nothing, except for a few stragglers not wanting to give up the sun and the sea, couples out for an evening stroll, or locals stopping in for a cup of coffee they hadn't had to make themselves.

Leo grinned. 'You're pushing forty. No sign of the middle-age spread yet, but you wanna be careful.'

Will laughed. 'You're not far behind me, so I wouldn't mock.' It was good to see his mate again. Leo was easy to get along with, a good laugh and there wasn't much they couldn't talk about.

They chatted more about each of their jobs, what they loved about them, what they hated.

'I work with some great people,' said Will, 'and some not so great.'

'Tell me about it. I work with a cameraman who honestly farts more than a bloke after a night on the curry and the turps.'

'Sounds pleasant. Not sure what's worse, that or the guy I sat next to for a while until they moved me to my own office.'

'A farter?'

Will shook his head.

'A throat clearer?'

'Oh yes, we have a couple of those too. Bloody annoying. This is worse, though, way worse. I was eating my lunch at my desk one day, working through to get everything done, and I heard a funny sound. I couldn't make out what it was but when I looked over the partition, the guy in the cubicle next to me had a foot up on the desk and was clipping his toenails.'

Leo's laughter attracted the glances of two twenty-something girls walking past and Will smiled back at them. It'd been forever since he'd had a date, let alone a relationship, and kicking back in the heat with the sunshine doing its best to creep along the tiny lane filled with cafés spilling out on to the space outside, he needed some action soon. Maybe not with those girls though – they were barely older than Lexi.

'Reckon that's worse than the farting.' Leo shook his head and ordered two more beers from the passing waitress. 'So how's life in the bay since you've been back?'

'Interesting.'

'How's the family?'

'As bad as usual.'

He and Leo had often kicked back after a climb and as they'd drunk rocket-fuel juice – a combo including beetroot, carrot and ginger – they'd often talked about family. Leo had the straightforward mother and father living in the suburbs; dad was an architect, mum was a homemaker. And he had three sisters he got along with famously. Will's family were the flip side of that with their stresses and complexities.

Will filled Leo in on what had been happening in Primrose Bay.

'It's not so bad with Mia,' he explained. 'We get on much better now. The unspoken truce started it and since I've been away and then come home, I'm kind of appreciating what she went through back then as an eighteen year old. I'm not sure I could handle the responsibility, but she's come out on top and Lexi's a great girl.'

'And what about your other sister?'

'Jasmine…' He sat back in his seat, puffed out his cheeks. 'Well she's a different story altogether.'

'I've got sisters so I know they can be difficult.'

He looked at Leo now. 'You're close to all your sisters, so don't give me that.' He grinned and took a swig of beer. 'Difficult? You don't know the half of it. Jasmine is disorganised, erratic, lacks independence. She frustrates me mostly.'

'How can she lack independence when she took herself off to London? She got on okay there, didn't she?'

Jasmine had surprised the entire Marcello clan when she'd gone off to the other side of the world with no job to speak of. But that was just it…she was lucky more than a good judge of a situation. She'd fallen on her feet and found a job and a place to stay quickly in London, but if it had gone the other way, which it could so easily have done, he expected he'd be the one picking up the pieces. His parents would've sent him to sort out the mess, or, worse, she'd have come to New York and moved in with him or something crazy like that. She'd suggested it once, saying she wanted to see a bit of the world and perhaps America was a great place to start. He'd told her he didn't think it was a good idea. 'I have my own life, I don't need my kid sister hanging around.' Brutal, but Jasmine didn't do subtlety. If he hadn't been so direct she would've carried on in her own oblivious way.

'Is she really so bad?'

'Someone always has to be there to help her. Take coming to the bay from the airport for example – I caught a cab; Jasmine had Mia pick her up. And when we've organised joint presents for our parents in the past, it's never Jasmine who takes charge and orders something or collects monies. She partied hard before she went to London too and I know how much it stressed Mum and Dad out. I could hardly stand listening to their woes when it came to my younger sister.'

What Will didn't share was that when his parents had been working so hard to build the business, Will had been called upon to take responsibility for his younger sister. He'd organised her for school in the mornings. Of course, she was never ready. No matter how early the alarm went off he'd always be rushing her out the door, hanging her bag over her shoulder for her to get her moving. Then, when she was in her early teens, he'd had to go and meet her at school so she didn't have to walk home in the dark; he'd had to help her with her maths homework when she was struggling and his parents were worried she wouldn't make her grades. It wasn't as though he didn't want to be a part of the family, but he'd felt at times his role was so much more than an older brother.

'Enough about family,' said Will, unhappy they were plaguing his thoughts even now, away from the bay. 'How's the love life? Has there been anyone since Ruby?'

'Nah. I've steered clear of all women for the last few months. Ruby was enough to put me off for life.'

Laughing, Will said, 'You don't mean that. You'll be back in the game soon.'

Leo shrugged and talk turned to footy as they ordered a bowl of nachos each. Even though the start of the season was way off, they talked AFL teams, Grand Final, the latest scandal with drugs.

'I've missed the G.' Will sighed. 'Even though I caught up on games on cable TV, it's not the same as being there.'

As both men polished off their nachos, they launched into the battle of the teams – Leo was a West Coast Eagles supporter, Will's team was the Melbourne-based Hawks, and neither would concede the other team could possibly take out the premiership.

'They're close on the ladder,' said Leo with a raise of his eyebrows, 'but that could change any time.'

As Will reached for his beer he locked eyes with a girl coming his way dressed in a navy pinstriped skirt with a crisp white shirt and heels that did nothing to detract from the tanned legs leading up beneath the material. As soon as she noticed him, she beamed a huge smile his way.

Will stood. 'Tess?' Moving away from the table, he pulled her into a huge bear hug. 'Tess Anderson! I don't believe it.'

Tess hugged him back. 'Will Marcello, I thought you'd said goodbye to the bay for good. But Mia told me you were back. Sorry about the circumstances.'

'Thanks.' He only broke the stare when he realised how rude he was being. 'Sorry. Leo, this is Tess, a friend of Mia's.'

Leo's chair scraped back as he half stood to shake Tess's hand. 'Nice to meet you.'

'So what are you doing here? Where's work now?' Will's eyes were firmly back on his sister's best friend. He hadn't seen her in more than a decade. Back then she'd had a sharp razor-cut bob, but now her blonde locks were wavy and hung down her back with some cascading over her shoulders.

'I'm the manager at the same travel agency I worked for before I left for Sydney,' she explained. There's a lot of sideways movement in my line of business.'

You could say that again. She'd gone sideways and upwards, breaking out of the mould from a shy, unsure girl with braces in her late twenties after refusing them all her life to a stunning, leggy blonde with curves in all the right places.

'Let me buy you a drink,' Will insisted.

'I'd love to, but I'm meeting friends over at the casino tonight. But I'll see you again soon. I'll be in the bay to see Mia. I think she needs a few drinks to de-stress.'

'I think we all do.'

She reached out and touched his arm. 'I'll see you soon, yeah?'

When she walked away he watched her for a while and when he turned back Leo was laughing.

'Put your tongue back in,' said Leo.

'What?' Will shook his head. 'No, she's my sister's friend.'

'Yeah, and I'm about to join the priesthood.' He tipped his bottle of beer back to get the dregs. 'And if I'm not mistaken, she didn't look as though she'd fight you off if you made a move.'

'Shut it. Come on, I'll pay for these and we'll go somewhere else. I could use the walk and there's a great Irish pub I know of.'

Leo pulled his sunglasses down from the top of his head as Will took out his wallet. 'Next round's on me.'

'Too right it is.' And as they turned right out of the laneway and up towards Elizabeth Street and onto Little Collins, Will half wished they were going to the casino.

Chapter Ten
Jasmine

'What's up with you?' Jasmine watched her brother tap the portafilter basket onto the knock-out drawer to get rid of the used coffee grounds.

'Nothing.' He wiped the portafilter basket with a cloth.

'Rubbish. You had a skinful last night with your mate, didn't you? Tut tut, that's no way to run a business.'

'I thought you were going on a coffee-making course or something. Hadn't you better leave?' he suggested through gritted teeth. 'And where has Mia got to?'

'My, my…we are brusque today!' Her teasing earned her another dirty look. 'Keep your hair on, I'm leaving in about half an hour, and Mia was in first thing this morning but has her own business to run. She's next door doing her thing but I'm sure she'll be back in soon.'

Monica stepped in to help Will, whose brain obviously wasn't in gear this morning. She poured beans into the coffee grinder and fixed the portafilter basket beneath the spout.

'Where did you go?' Jasmine asked him as he took out a jug and poured milk into it. 'Come on, what was your poison?'

'I can see it'll be easier to just tell you than ask you to be quiet.' He put the jug beneath the steam wand with the tip fully immersed just as Monica had shown them only moments ago. She'd told them if the wand touched the bottom it would make a god-awful noise, and Will wouldn't be able to handle that with his hangover. They also knew now that if the wand was too high in the jug it would make so many bubbles it would look more like washing-up liquid than coffee.

'We started at a café,' Will explained, 'then went on to The Irish Times, followed by a rooftop bar that I can't even remember the name of. And I would've stuck with Guinness but for some reason the sun went to my head and we went on to the whisky.'

'Ouch. Whisky is the worst. I saw too many punters wasted on it to ever be tempted to touch the stuff.'

This was the most Will had spoken to her since they'd started sharing their parents' apartment. They'd kept their distance as much as they could up there, been polite and coexisted because they had to. As Jasmine had climbed into bed that first night, she'd lifted up the photo in the silver frame on the bedside table. It was a photo of all three children. Mia and Will sat next to one another and Jasmine was on Will's lap, laughing away with her brother's arms around her. When had it all changed? When had the sibling rules been rewritten and turned them from three happy-go-lucky siblings to a brother and two sisters with an ongoing pernicious relationship?

'Should I do the pour?' Monica asked Will now.

'Thanks.' He managed a smile. 'I'll go and unload the dishwasher.'

'Done it.' Jasmine rolled her eyes. She could see her brother was suffering but it was his own silly fault. 'Do yourself a favour, Will. Try to show up sober tomorrow.' When Will went out back muttering to himself, Jasmine lent Monica a hand until a new customer came through the door. She smiled and spoke over the noise of the coffee grinder. 'May I help you?'

'I'm looking for Will.'

‘He’s out back, I’ll go get him.’ She had to hand it to her brother when it came to his friends – first Daniel and now this one; her brother seemed to have no shortage of good-looking male company. She went out the back to get Will and by the conversation that ensued when Will came into the café, she realised this was the man her brother had been drinking with last night.

Will did his best to ignore his sister until good manners came to the fore. ‘Jasmine, this is Leo, a friend from Perth.’

She nodded. ‘Nice to meet you, Leo.’

‘Likewise.’

‘What brings you to the bay?’

‘We’re filming down the beach this morning.’

‘The volleyball comp?’

‘That’s the one. It’s an all-day event so I’ve come for some sustenance. Caffeine is the only way I’ll stay alert.’

Jasmine took the order for a cappuccino and as she gave the steam wand a purge and the boys moved aside, Mia came back from the picnic place next door.

‘Shouldn’t you be going?’ Mia asked, checking her watch.

Jasmine filled a jug with milk. Trust Mia to be on her case about time management when she was more than capable of organising herself. ‘I’ll just make this for Will’s friend over there, then I’ll go.’

Mia barely glanced their way. ‘What sort of coffee is it?’

‘A cappuccino. Takeaway.’

Mia ushered Jasmine away from the machine. ‘That, I can manage. Go on, you don’t want to be late. We’re relying on you to bring lots of hints and tips for this place.’

Mia must've had a good session in the picnic place. She was in a good mood and for once Jasmine accepted the bossing around. It'd give her time to enjoy the city she'd been so far away from for so long.

Jasmine lowered her voice. 'Monica is due a break soon so when you've made that for Will's mate, perhaps let her have fifteen minutes before we get busy again.' Aside from a group of walkers licking at ice-creams, they'd been quiet this morning.

'I'll make sure she gets one before I go back next door.'

'You're not staying?' Jasmine hooked her bag over her shoulder and kept her voice low. 'I don't think Will is in much of a fit state to be managing the place when Monica goes on lunch.'

'Well he'll have to. I can't let business slip, no matter how manic it gets in here.'

'He's got the hangover from hell.' Jasmine grinned and, if she wasn't mistaken, the corners of Mia's mouth tugged at the sides a bit too. They'd probably both enjoy knowing their brother was suffering a little rather than being his usual tower of strength. 'But you might want to tell Monica to be vigilant with him today. We don't want complaints for poorly made coffee or burnt toast. Do you know he burnt three rounds of raisin bread yesterday? And he's left the lid off the coffee grounds more than once, which ruins the—'

'…taste. Yes, Jasmine, I know. I told *you* that.'

'And I have remembered ever since.' That was what Mia and Will didn't understand. If Jasmine was shown or told the right way to do something, she was pretty quick on the uptake. 'I just want to say that the smell of lightly toasted raisin bread draws people in, you know it does. But the smell of burning toast will send them running in the opposite direction.'

'Jasmine, you've made your point.' Mia took out a broom from the cupboard near the kitchen door and swept the area around the coffee machine.

'I'll be back later before you shut for the day.'

Jasmine escaped into the salty air, walked to the station and caught the train to the city. She was early enough that she had time to head over to Federation Square, where she bought a takeaway caramel macchiato – made the way it was supposed to be – and sat on the steps out front watching the city go by. The green and yellow trams dinged their bells before whizzing off to their next stop, she watched crowds emerge from Flinders Street Station and cross over at the junction, and she sat back, tilted her head to the sun and let the feel-good endorphins rush into her body for the first time in days. With all the stress of the café since her arrival she'd even found herself texting Ned late last night, wanting a taste of the familiar, something that reminded her she was more than this person in Primrose Bay whose siblings saw fit to boss her about. It'd been nice to chat to him but the texts weren't anything beyond a usual friendship and she felt strangely okay with that.

She soaked up the sun, finished her coffee and dropped the takeaway cup into the bin before making her way towards the venue. Since she'd gone over to London on her own, found a job and a place to live, Jasmine had proved to herself, and she hoped everyone else, that she could manage her own life. Every little achievement – catching the flight, navigating a city she knew nothing of, starting a job in which she had no experience – was another notch up in her confidence. When she'd started working at The Crown & Shilling she'd had no idea what some drinks even were, she'd not had a clue how to pull a pint, and when the landlord had asked her to draw a shamrock on the top of a pint of Guinness she'd laughed in his face. But she'd gritted her teeth, determination had kicked in and she'd learnt everything she needed to do to be a valued member of staff. Just a shame she wasn't so valued that she was above being groped. But she hadn't told her siblings anything about that. Knowing them, they'd see it as something else she'd been unable to do. They'd roll their eyes and say it was typical: typical Jasmine, irresponsible, no proper job, and somehow she wouldn't be the girl who took a stand against her boss, it would be turned around and made out to be her fault. As far as Will and Mia knew right now, she still had a job to return to in a few weeks.

Walking in to this new place today, Jasmine knew she could do this and, more than that, she needed to. It was a brand new environment, just like London had been, and that gave her a buzz, a sense of confidence. They were in over their heads at the café and while Monica had been a great help this morning, they still needed to learn themselves in case Monica moved on too, or if she was sick. Will in particular was a problem. He wasn't used to an active job. He spent his days sitting on his butt at a desk. And now, in the café, he was continuously burning milk and getting combinations completely wrong – lattes with barely any milk, macchiatos that were nothing like they should be. And Mia, although doing better, was still making a lot of mistakes and every time they got the beverage wrong they were pouring money literally down the drain. Jasmine didn't need a degree in accounts to work out that it didn't made sound business sense to keep going as they were.

Jasmine chatted with some of the other attendees gathered in the reception area at the venue. There were two backpackers who hoped to find work in cafés around Melbourne and its surrounding suburbs before they moved on; there were a couple of newlyweds who had received a top-of-the-range coffee machine as a wedding gift and wanted to know how to use it properly; and there were two guys who seemed very serious and didn't appear to want to chat. And then, when Jasmine turned, she smiled at the familiar face.

'Daniel?' She stepped forward and hugged her sister's ex-boyfriend, her niece's father. 'It's great to see you!'

Holding her arms he stood back and appraised a very different Jasmine from the one she knew he would remember. 'Look at you, you look fantastic!'

'I've lost some weight.'

'I'll say.'

She grinned. 'What brings you here?'

'Probably the same reason as you.'

'What, you have a business that could fail if the three people running it don't buck their ideas up?'

'Not quite. I'm here because of my love of coffee.' He made a flamboyant gesture with his arms.

'Honestly?'

He shook his head. 'The course was a Secret Santa present from someone at work and I hadn't got round to using it until now.'

'Wow, you must be at the top of your game. Secret Santa presents at the pub were less than a tenner and consisted of chocolate body paint, a mug with the words 'I'm a twat' written on the bottom and a keyring in the shape of a penis.'

'Crikey, were those all for you?'

She slapped him on the arm playfully. 'Cheeky. No, but I did buy one of them.'

'Let me guess, the keyring?'

'Nope, the mug. It was for my boss. A plain white mug but when you picked it up and drank, everyone around you would see the words 'I'm a twat'. I thought it was perfect for his morning coffee.'

'And was he?'

'Was he what?'

'A twat.'

Jasmine felt her cheeks pink up. 'He was a bit.'

'Care to elaborate?'

'He made a pass at me, and not a subtle one.'

'What did you do?'

'I quit.'

Daniel whistled through his teeth. 'Well done. But you probably didn't have to. There are all sorts of laws protecting workers.'

She shrugged and didn't elaborate with the whole story. 'Could you do me a favour? Don't mention it to Mia. I haven't told her or Will anything about it.'

'Consider it our secret.' He tapped the side of his nose conspiratorially. 'You know, I offered to let Mia take my place on this course.'

'You did?'

He nodded. 'I thought she'd make good use out of it but she's too busy with her own business, too stressed to take any time out.'

Jasmine was relieved Mia had said no, because she was glad to be doing this and doing it alone. It felt like part of the control, part of showing her siblings what she was made of.

The organisers came in to the room and the conversation stopped. When all the participants were perched on stools lined up in a semicircle, the focus shifted to the intensive training program they were on for the next five hours. They were to learn about coffee making, milk texturing, free-pouring techniques, and etching, and it wasn't long before the practical side began.

Given they'd been told it usually took three to four months for baristas to master the art of free-pour, Jasmine was pretty pleased at the skills she'd learnt and developed after the first few hours. Everyone in the class had their own equipment and Jasmine was working at an espresso machine with two group handles, one for her, the other for Daniel, whom she'd paired up with.

'You're not doing too badly.' Daniel watched Jasmine finish off the latte with the classic rosetta design they'd been shown. 'I can't seem to get the hang of it at all.' He looked down at the latte he'd made and the non-existent artwork on top.

The instructor was making his way slowly round the class but Jasmine gave Daniel a quick lesson in the technique. 'You need to start high so the milk from the jug goes underneath the espresso.' She waited for him to make another latte. 'That's it, and as you pour, move the jug to the back of the cup, then rock the jug back and forth, wiggling, then cut through at the end and finish.'

'You make it sound so simple.'

'Here, I'll do it with you.' She made another latte with her machine and then lifted her milk jug to a certain height, waited for Daniel to copy, and showed him the technique she'd only learnt that morning too.

'You're a natural.' It was their instructor, Marco.

'Can you show me another fancy design?' She was eager for more, much more.

Marco explained how to form the tulip on the top of the latte, which involved a first pour, then a pause before another pour, and then a third pour, cutting through from one side to the other to form the stem. Jasmine tried a few times but this one was trickier and would take a lot more practice.

When the course had finished, Jasmine and Daniel removed their aprons and emerged into the Melbourne sunshine. 'I'll have to show Lexi some of those designs,' said Jasmine. 'She's very arty.'

'I'm sure she'd like that.' Daniel pulled his shades down over his eyes at the same time as Jasmine positioned her sunnies and they moved out of the way of passers-by to the edge of the street, where the sunlight managed to reach from between the tall buildings dominating the city.

'I'm not sure Mia would.'

'What makes you say that?'

'She thinks I'm a bad influence.' Jasmine shrugged. 'Oh come on, don't tell me she's never said anything to you.'

'She hasn't said anything, I swear. We're good friends still but she's never been one to talk about her siblings.'

'Figures.'

'Listen, I know we've had a lot of coffee today – I for one am buzzing – but how about a beer to wash it all down? My shout.'

Jasmine knew she should probably get back to Primrose Bay but right now, with the sun warming the back of her neck, she could use a nice cold beer. She didn't drink anywhere near as much as she used to. The last time Daniel had seen her she'd been very much into boozing with her friends in a big way. She'd down shots

– Cowboys were a favourite with their sweetness of butterscotch schnapps and Baileys – add beers to the mix and always end the night back at someone else's place with a takeaway of some description. It was a roller-coaster life she was unable to step down from and the more she ate and drank the more weight she put on and the more miserable she was. The comfort eating was only ever a reaction to her unhappiness but she didn't have it in her back then to sort herself out. Changing her ways and her life had only happened once she'd been away from her family.

Nestled in a curved booth in a bar in the city centre, Jasmine tucked in to the sandwich Daniel insisted she needed. She'd gone for tuna and cheese on rye, no mayonnaise. Since she'd been back in the bay there'd been a couple of occasions where she'd almost caved in and gone to the dark place she'd been in for years, eating to dull the pain and stress, but her resolve had kicked in each time and she'd risen above it. Some people suggested having an old photograph of your former self pinned somewhere to stop you ever wanting to lapse and be that way again, but Jasmine didn't need photographic evidence. The images and the feelings that had come with her appearance were etched in her mind forever.

'So tell me…' Daniel had gone for the pizza. He could probably get away with it, with all the surfing he did. 'Why do you think Mia doesn't approve of you?'

'Because she's told me before.'

Eyebrows raised, he said, 'Really? I mean, I knew you weren't best friends, but I never realised she disapproved of her own sister.'

'She's worried I'm a bad influence on Lexi.'

'But you've always got on with Lexi.'

‘Exactly. We’re only ten years apart and Lexi’s at that age where she sees me as cool Auntie Jasmine. She’s even been talking about going and working in London, taking a gap year before university.’

Daniel put down his beer.

‘Oh shit, now you’re angry with me.’ Jasmine exchanged the sandwich she’d been eating for a few mouthfuls of her beer.

‘I’m not angry, but she’s my daughter. Of course I’m concerned about anything she has planned for her future. I thought she had her heart set on uni. Why have I never heard anything about this?’

‘Oh Daniel. I really think it was a fleeting comment.’ God help her if he ever found out what the latest topic of conversation was with his daughter. Even when she was in London, Jasmine had been Lexi’s go-to person when she had anything bothering her. Texts and emails made communication so much easier and more instant. And now, Jasmine was the confidante Lexi told *everything* to. Jasmine had wondered whether she should be telling Mia what they’d discussed recently, but if she did that she’d lose Lexi’s trust for good.

‘Maybe I’ll ask her about it,’ said Daniel.

‘I wouldn’t worry too much,’ Jasmine assured him, ‘especially now I’m over here and not there. I think she saw my Facebook posts with photos of London – not that there were many –and started to wonder what it was like, started to realise she had the option of leaving the bay. She hasn’t learnt that from her mother, that’s for sure.’

‘Hey, I’m no longer with Mia, but I do care about her. Just because she hasn’t ever left the bay, it doesn’t make her a bad person, or clueless.’

‘Oh god, no. That’s not what I’m saying at all. What I mean is that Lexi sees one side of life from Mia. She sees a woman running her own business, a woman who loves being where she is. But with me she sees the side she’s never known about.’ Jasmine finished off her sandwich but declined the offer of a second beer. Her sister would definitely have something to have a go at her about if she went back to the café reeking of alcohol.

Daniel tucked in to another slice of pizza. ‘I see your point. And you’re a good auntie.’

‘Thanks.’ She only wished her sister saw it that way.

‘Anyway, enough about Lexi.’ Daniel changed the subject. ‘I want to know all about *you*. You took off for London two years ago and you did it all so quickly your family barely had time to say goodbye. And you’re looking great now, by the way, so come on. What happened to you since we last saw each other?’

Jasmine hadn’t talked about this with anyone before now. Nobody knew what a state she’d been in when she’d decided to up and leave, nobody had delved into her reasons after she left, and the simple physical transformation of her former self was praised and envied upon her return. Yet the reason why she’d been so miserable in the first place and let her life spiral into those depths of despair were something nobody had ever addressed.

‘I was miserable,’ she told Daniel now. ‘I left because I couldn’t stand being here any longer and I knew my life needed to change.’ She took a deep breath. ‘Are you sure you have time to hear this?’

Daniel relaxed back into the leather seat. ‘Take as much time as you need.’

Chapter Eleven

Mia

Monica was a godsend in the café. But with only four days covered, it left another three during which the Marcello children would be left to their own devices, and that worried Mia. She had a big picnic order today, so it would be up to her siblings, in her absence, to ensure The Sun Coral Café ran smoothly for the next few hours.

Yesterday, Jasmine had returned from her barista course brandishing her accreditation certificate and blathering on about something known as milk texturing and latte art. Apparently she'd bumped into Daniel there too and Mia realised he must've used the voucher he'd offered her a few days ago.

It had felt weird hearing about her ex from her own sister and it had been slightly unnerving, especially when Jasmine blithely announced they'd been for a beer afterwards. But Mia reprimanded herself. There was no need for jealousy – Daniel wouldn't do anything. Not with her little sister…would he? Then again, if Jasmine made it clear she was interested, maybe he would.

Oh god, stop it! Mia scolded herself.

She put the finishing touches to the picnic foods for thirty people this lunchtime. There was a rowing competition down on the Yarra River with crew and coaches celebrating afterwards, and Mia had been in the kitchen at five o'clock that morning making fresh mini bread rolls, which had now been fashioned into delicate bite-sized pieces with brie and cranberry chutney; there were portions of a creamy buffalo ricotta salad with orecchiette pasta; Australian tiger prawns with a lemon and dill dip; a selection of summer fruits; and dark-chocolate brownies with thickened cream to go on the side.

Mia took the last five Tupperware tubs from the fridge and loaded them into the awaiting eskies, added an extra ice pack on top to ensure the journey from Primrose Bay to the Yarra River in the heart of the city wouldn't let anything spoil, and clipped each lid in place. She took the eskies out to the car one at a time and, with the seats already folded down, everything slotted in nicely and she closed the boot.

She was about to leave when she saw Lexi strolling along towards her. 'What's wrong? Why aren't you in school?'

'I'm home for lunch, that's all.'

'You don't usually come home for lunch.' Mia reached out and took her daughter's hand momentarily, until it was shaken off and she was dismissed as a helicopter parent. 'Are you sure everything is all right?'

Jasmine, who was wiping down a table inside the café, tapped on the window and waved to Lexi. She only turned round to continue what she was doing when Mia shot her a look.

'Everything is fine, Mum. I'll go and say hello to Jasmine first.'

'She's working.'

Lexi peered in the window. 'It doesn't look too busy.'

'Just make sure you get back to school on time.' She hugged Lexi and turned to go back to her car. There was a fine line between taking an interest when it came to her daughter and interfering, and if she crossed that line there was the danger of never getting to the bottom of anything. But as she drove away from Primrose Bay she wondered how much more Lexi had told Jasmine than her own mother.

As a rule, Mia wasn't a big driver. She hated new places – the time she'd been to Sydney with friends back when she was new to the roads had put her off for life, driving with drivers who knew exactly where they were going and were unforgiving if you didn't. But she loved driving in and around Melbourne, windows down, soaking up the atmosphere. This was her home city, one she was wholly familiar with, and even the hooked right turns didn't faze her. She'd tried to explain them to Grandma Annetta, who had lived in Melbourne for years yet never driven in the city. 'It's so the trams can travel down the centre of the road, Grandma,' she'd said. 'You keep left and pull away from the traffic and when the lights change you turn right from the left-hand lane.' Grandma Annetta had never grasped it, and Lexi had always hated them. She'd closed her eyes as though they were on a fairground ride just waiting for something awful to happen. It didn't bear thinking about that in a year or so Lexi would be able to get her Ls and then her Ps and then freedom. Another part of control would slip from Mia's fingers and the thought terrified her.

With no hook turns to keep her amused today, Mia took the familiar route towards the Yarra River. She followed Boathouse Drive and when she'd found a parking spot – not an easy feat – and fed the meter, she called the boat sheds to send down a few volunteers to help her with the baskets and eskies. The client had offered – apparently there were a lot of keen club members watching the competition who would be only too happy to participate in getting the food ready for their heroes – and he sent enough helpers that they only needed one journey from car to boathouse, which was lucky as the event had drawn huge crowds to both banks of the Yarra as well as a television crew. Boats were coming in and out of the sheds as the races continued and the whole scene was manic.

Mia's client was in one of the sheds towards the end but luckily Mia had her helpers to guide the way and someone else to open doors before she took the stairs up and into the clubhouse. There she was given full rein over the kitchen. There was a long table, on which she placed the five separate hampers and opened them up. She unloaded the eskies and put everything onto plates and covered each with cling film, arranged hand-sewn napkins with cutlery, and added bottles of Prosecco to each hamper. The races were coming to an end soon and then, according to the girl in the zoot suit who'd greeted her at the door, the rowers would take these picnics to enjoy on the river-banks further up, where they already had a space reserved. They had the perfect day for it too. The temperature wasn't too high – mid-twenties, which was pleasant compared to the stifling heat they'd already experienced this summer – and there was a gentle, welcoming breeze.

When Mia was done she stacked up the eskies. She could easily take them one by one back to her car but her volunteers sprung up as soon as she emerged from the kitchen and before she knew it they'd left the sheds and everything was back in the boot ready for the off. She took a deep breath and leant against her car, sunglasses down, enjoying the sounds of the crowds now that the final race had finished. The mood was light and jovial and down here, watching the gentle ripples in the water as a single scull went by – she must've been waiting on standby for the race to finish, desperate to get to her sport – Mia's problems lifted away from her shoulders with ease. Down here there was no café, no siblings bickering, no parents with a falling-apart marriage, no daughter keeping secrets from her. Down here it was just her and her thoughts.

Anxious to savour the escape, Mia made a spontaneous decision. She went over to the meter and fed it with more coins. She took out a tartan blanket from the back of the car – she always had spares just in case a client wanted them – and took it down a bit further to where the banks of the river had quietened as people dispersed after the race. She laid out the blanket, weighting one side with her bag and the other with the Birkenstocks she'd kicked off her feet. She lay down, half-shaded by a tree behind, and let the breeze whisper across her face, the distant chit-chat calm her mind.

A deep voice caught her on the brink of nodding off. 'Mia?'

She sat upright. She had no idea who the man was until he bobbed down to her level.

'We met the other day.' He held out a hand. 'I'm Leo.'

'Ah yes. It's nice to see you again.' She shook his hand. Whoa, did he have a handshake on him!

'Sorry, too strong?'

'I'll survive.' She grinned. Strong men had always been appealing and she didn't mind the lingering pressure in her fingers. 'What brings you down here?'

He hooked a thumb back over his shoulder. 'I'm with the TV crew, getting in everyone's way. We were filming the races, the aftermath, interviews with the rowers. May I?' He indicated the blanket.

'Of course. I was just taking some time out before I head back to the bay.'

'Good idea. From what Will says, it's pretty full on.' He unhooked the small cooler bag he'd been carrying on his shoulder, opened it and pulled out two cans: a Diet Coke and a Sprite. 'Take your pick. I usually have a supply of drinks when I'm working. I've drunk all the water so now it's onto the good stuff.'

Mia chose the Sprite and flipped open the top. It gave a satisfying pshhhht and she sipped the bubbly liquid. She watched Leo, his tanned arms, the tendons showing strength probably developed from lugging a camera and equipment around everywhere, the muscles in his shoulders, the strong neck and sun-kissed skin. He had dark blond hair, trimmed at the sides but floppy on top. She hadn't noticed him much at the café the other day – she'd been distracted by other things and the stresses surrounding the Marcellos – but now she noticed, and she watched as he opened the can of Diet Coke and took a few thirsty gulps.

'So what brings you here?' he asked.

Glad she could hide her embarrassment at watching him, behind her sunglasses, Mia explained about the picnics, the client at the rowing sheds.

'Ah, I think that's where I just finished filming. I went upstairs and filmed a couple of the rowers doing an interview – navy- and lavender-coloured zoot suits. Not that a bloke should even know what colour lavender is!'

Mia laughed. 'That's the shed where I took the picnics.'

'I saw them. Me and the crew were eyeing them up when we left. There's no time for snacking when it's race time and I spotted the bottles of bubbly and some tiny bread rolls and was almost tempted to steal something.'

'I'm glad you didn't!'

'Who else do you make picnics for?'

They shuffled the blanket back a little more into the shade as the sun crept across the sky and out from behind the branches of the nearby tree. Mia reeled off a list of types of picnics, clients she'd had in the past.

'It sounds impressive,' said Leo. 'I'm in awe. I've only ever been able to work for a boss or a company. I don't think I'd have the nerve to go into business on my own. It must take a lot of guts.'

She appreciated the understanding. She'd never once heard that from Will. Sometimes she wondered whether he thought her picnic business was just a nice little hobby she was indulging in. 'It's going well now. I've had some bigger clients lately; I'm even thinking I may need to hire a helper, at least for the deliveries. I can handle the cooking and the preparations at the moment, or at least I can if the café is in good hands, but I keep having to rope clients in to help transport eskies, picnic baskets and the like. It seems rude when they're paying for a service.'

'I'm sure the picnics themselves more than compensate.' He looked around them. 'You should've made yourself an individual picnic and enjoyed it here by the river. It's such a nice day.'

Clouds meandered across the pale-blue sky and a double scull glided through the water. A river ferry cruised on by in the opposite direction and Mia and Leo waved back to a group of schoolkids.

'Tell me about your work. I've bored you with mine after all.' Mia spoke to stop herself staring at Leo and thinking of him in ways she probably shouldn't. Being immune to his charm and attractiveness was easier said than done.

He grinned. 'I can genuinely say I love my job.'

'Not many people can say that.'

'You must though?'

'Of course. I wouldn't do it otherwise.' She had a passion she couldn't explain to other people, a drive and determination that refused to falter. 'When it's your own business you have to love it or what hope do you have?'

'I get that. It wasn't always the way for me though. I started out my working life as an accountant and it bored me senseless, sitting at a desk looking at numbers all day. Every day was the same. I kind of fell into it but managed to climb my way out. I ended up with an apprenticeship so I learnt on the job and now no two days are the same.'

Leo talked some more about the news-gathering he did, the joys of spending many of his working days outside. 'It's not all basking in the sunshine by the river though,' he concluded. 'Sometimes it's pouring with rain, in the winter it's freezing and we're still there filming. Sometimes I'll be filming news outside the Supreme Court in the city and quite often we'll wait around for hours for people to emerge.'

'Hence the suntan?'

He glanced at his arms. 'You could be right.'

He looked like he should be at the beach, salt water clinging to bronzed forearms dusted with golden sand.

She cleared her throat to dismiss the image. 'So how do you know my brother?'

'We met in Perth, been friends ever since.'

Mia remembered now. 'You met through his ex, Paige.'

'That's right.' Leo talked about Will's breakup with Paige and it gave Mia a fresh insight. Conversations with Will had never been that in-depth, especially after the fallout over Daniel, but hearing it from another source made her realise what he'd been through. He must've had his heart ripped out by the sounds of it. Paige had upped and left one day, her only excuse being that she wasn't ready for a long-term commitment. The next thing Will knew, she was engaged to a man ten years her senior and pregnant with their first child. According to Leo, Will had felt as though their whole relationship was based on lies and he hadn't wanted to get seriously involved with another woman since.

Mia groaned when her mobile rang but she knew she had to answer it. It was Will, and he wasn't happy. The café was manic, Monica had food poisoning so they were down a person and Jasmine was wasting too much time perfecting patterns in the coffees to really do any work. At least that's how her brother described it. When Jasmine was born he'd idolised her in a way Mia had thought was tender, sweet, the true quality of a big brother. He'd been eleven years old at the time and had taken to changing nappies, feeding the baby, comforting her when she was sick. But maybe that was where it had all gone wrong. Will had been approaching his teens and whilst his friends were beginning to get the freedom you only dreamed about once you reached double digits, there was Will, pushing a pram up and down Beach Road when Jasmine wouldn't stop crying, putting meals on the table for his sisters, ensuring everyone was happy. It'd all gone onto his shoulders and he hadn't complained once. Perhaps it was his silence that had eventually come between them.

'I'm sorry, Leo,' Mia said now. 'I really have to go.'

'Duty calls?' He stood and shook out the blanket for her.

'Unfortunately it does. The café is manic and my brother is having a hissy fit.'

‘Well it was nice to see you again.’

‘Thanks for the refreshments.’

‘It was my pleasure.’ He carried the picnic blanket to the car and she opened the boot so he could push it in on top of everything else. ‘I hope to see you again.’

‘I’d like that,’ Mia replied.

As Leo walked towards his truck, a black Hilux, he called over his shoulder, ‘Say hello to your brother for me.’

‘I will.’

But when she climbed into the driver’s seat she wasn’t sure that was such a good idea. Will’s friends and his sister didn’t mix. She’d found that out the hard way and they’d only just established neutral ground where they weren’t exactly close, but at least they didn’t despise one another the way they had a few years ago. She couldn’t go back to feeling that way – powerless to mend a broken trust. What she really needed to do was get a grip and never let herself think of this man as anything other than a friend of her brother’s. Otherwise, it could rip her family apart once and for all.

Chapter Twelve

Mia

Despite yesterday's hectic morning down at the rowing sheds followed by an even more manic afternoon back at the café, where Monica's absence meant the Marcello children all had to pull together more than ever, Mia was chirpy this morning and humming away. She put it down to relaxing in the sunshine on the banks of the Yarra yesterday, and a decent night's sleep because she was so tired, but deep down she knew part of her high had been meeting up with Leo. She hadn't truly admitted it to herself, though, until five minutes ago. When she'd heard Will talking on the phone to Leo, arranging another climbing session, her heart had shifted up a gear.

It had been the same when she met Daniel. She was eighteen years old and had known Daniel for years but they'd never socialised together. Daniel had a huge bash for his twenty-first birthday, held at his family's home in Brighton East with close to fifty guests – mostly testosterone-fuelled males – and had invited Will. Daniel had extended the invite to Mia, presumably because he'd known her for years, and she'd taken best-friend Tess along for moral support. That night was the first time Mia had seen Daniel in a new light.

'Sorry if our behaviour's a bit too much,' he'd said to her as a few of the boys had wheelbarrow races. Those words were the most her brother's friend had ever really said to her. Usually it had been a kind smile or a wink as he walked past her bedroom on their way out the door.

'It's fine, it's a party.' She smiled and carried on watching the race. Whoever lost, or collapsed midway, had to down the tall glass of spirits that had god knows what in it. Mia had already seen people pouring vodka in, another adding a shot of Pernod, a glug of beer. Revolting. 'And anyway, you've just turned twenty-one, you should be getting wasted.'

Will was up next with another bloke holding his legs in the wheelbarrow position. He looked like he wouldn't make it off the start line – let alone all the way to the table set up at the other end of the garden upon which was the potent forfeit. 'Will certainly doesn't seem to be holding back,' Mia sniggered. 'Sorry, I've just never seen him this drunk. It's quite a new experience to see the responsible one all over the place.'

Daniel perched on the grass next to her. It was a wonderfully cool autumnal evening after the hazy days of summer. 'He needs to let off some steam. Uni is full on this year.'

Mia didn't doubt it. She'd seen Will cooking the books, much more so than at school. 'Are you on the water?'

'Got to pace myself.'

'It's your party,' she admonished. 'Let me get you a beer.' She went to stand but he pulled her arm so she wasn't going anywhere.

'I have to be careful. I'm a diabetic, and getting dehydrated after a night on the booze sent me to hospital once before.'

'Really?'

'I got carried away doing the same thing all my mates were doing, ended up drinking a stupid amount and vomiting my guts up. I got so dehydrated and had abdominal pains and irregular breathing.'

'It must've been scary.'

'I think the word you're looking for is stupid.' He returned her grin.

'So what happened to you?'

'My parents took me to hospital – I fought them every step of the way of course, told them they were making a fuss.'

'And were they?'

'Yes, thank goodness, because we found out I was suffering from alcoholic ketoacidosis. I was given fluids via an intravenous drip and the ketones in my system and my blood sugar were monitored until they'd reached acceptable levels. Then I got to go home.'

Mia took a deep breath. 'Your parents must have been terrified.'

'They've never let me forget it.' He looked over to his mates. 'And they shouldn't. It was a wake-up call, let me tell you. I can still have a few drinks but I don't go crazy, not like your brother.'

Mia looked over to where Will was doubled over laughing after dropping the legs of one of his mates in the wheelbarrow race.

'In all the time I've known you, I never realised.' Mia had seen Daniel share countless family dinners and she'd never had a clue. She sipped her vodka orange suddenly grateful she didn't have anything so serious to worry about.

'I kept it discreet, still do. I'm not embarrassed but I'm a private person; I hate drawing attention to myself. At school around exam time my teachers would make such a fuss – I was allowed extra rest breaks if I needed it, a drink and a snack midway if I felt myself having a funny turn.'

'Doesn't sound all that bad to me.'

'I wanted to be like everyone else though. Being different is hard. My diabetes was considered a disability.' He put the word disability in air quotes and Mia got it.

'See this…' Daniel leant closer and turned over one of his surf bracelets, the one in black leather with a small, silver square fixed onto it with a peculiar symbol that looked like a snake on a stick. She'd seen it enough times over the years, the single bracelet on his left wrist, separate from the cluster on his right wrist – one of brown-chocolate leather twisted with fawn, another a tan rope bracelet.

He pointed to the insignia. 'This is the international medical alert symbol. And these…' (he turned the bracelet over so Mia could see the underside) '…are my personal details. In a medical emergency doctors can access my records using my first and last name – anyone can see I have type 1 diabetes and am insulin dependent, and right here…' (he pointed to a phone number with the word 'Mum' beside it) '…is my emergency contact.'

Mia shook her head. 'I honestly never knew. You seem normal to me.' When he nudged her playfully the heat of his skin sent goosebumps up her arm.

'That's because I'm your brother's mate and we do our best to avoid annoying little sisters,' he teased.

She'd never talked to Daniel much, she'd never been up this close to him. She was eighteen and he was twenty-one but that night they chatted like they'd never done before.

The next few times she saw him it had been different between them. The atmosphere had changed since the night of the party. Mia had only had one boyfriend, when she was sixteen, and she was flattered by the attention Daniel was giving her – the fact he was older made her feel grown up, sophisticated and in another world. Daniel started texting her and before long they were messaging one another late into the evenings, even a couple of times during the night. Texting led to meeting up occasionally. They'd go for walks around Albert Park Lake, they went to Luna Park, Daniel holding her hand on the roller-coaster as they giggled away, they ate ice-creams and strolled along Brighton Beach, and the first time Daniel kissed Mia she thought she'd died and gone to heaven. This boy, this man, interested in her! It was something else. But more than that, he felt like a truly good friend. She had Tess, but Tess had a boyfriend at the time and rarely came up for air.

The day Will found out about Mia's budding relationship with Daniel was horrendous. Up until then they'd constantly debated when would be the best time to tell him, but they'd continued to put it off.

'I don't think he'll be happy,' said Daniel. 'We should've told him from the start.'

'Why? It's our business.'

'Yeah, but this is my mate who I plan to go travelling around the world with.'

'Really?'

'America, Europe…we've been talking about it for ages. Hey, we'd come back to the bay.' He'd kissed her then, reminded her of how he felt. 'But it's not only women who tell one another everything. Will and I have always talked about girls in the past, what we've done—'

'Have there been many?'

Daniel's laughter echoed around his back garden. They often went to his parents' place because they were out all day every day and they could have privacy here. 'Not too many, I'm no Jack the lad.'

'Good. I wouldn't want to be another notch on the bedpost.' She'd rolled on top of him then and they'd kissed, his dark-blond hair highlighted in the sun and her thick ebony locks falling across his face.

'Talking of bedposts,' he said, 'do you want to go upstairs?'

They'd fooled around before, plenty of times, so Mia led the way. She'd confided only in Tess when it came to Daniel, but the rest of the world knew nothing, and their clandestine relationship made this exhilarating, addictive. But when they got to the bedroom, sun-kissed from an afternoon lazing on the grass without a care in the world, they went beyond where they'd been before. It was Mia's first time and Daniel had been gentle, attentive, everything she could've asked for.

But the world came crashing down around them when, after so long spent worrying about when to tell her brother, Will found them together and it was a fait accompli. He'd focused his anger on her, yelled at her that he never wanted anything to do with her ever again, called her a little bitch, his words dripping with disdain.

Will's voice now, in the café, brought Mia out of her daydream. 'Are you happy for me to knock off by four o'clock?'

'What? Oh, I was hoping I'd have cover until seven. Monica still isn't back and with it being a Friday we're often busier than usual. I still need to sort out the mess of picnic hampers from yesterday and I have online messages and orders to respond to.'

'Oh come on, Mia. I've been in here all day so far.'

'I know, and this is what happens when three kids get lumped with a business when their parents skip town. I'm sorry, but it's the way it is. And I know that when you bugger off back to New York and Jasmine buggers off back to London, it'll be me holding the fort. So, for now, just suck it up.'

Will bristled. 'For a start, don't talk to me like that.' He lowered his voice so the customers at the far-corner table didn't overhear. 'And, furthermore, stop swearing – it's not ladylike.'

'Oh fuck you!'

'Seriously, Mia.' He shook his head as the little bell above the café door tinged. 'I'm going at four o'clock and that's that. Work around it, find a way, you're used to solving world problems.' And with that he turned to serve the next customer and left Mia glaring at him and muttering under her breath.

Mia, Will and Jasmine worked flat out for the next couple of hours. The bay had somehow attracted more visitors than ever that day, or at least that's how it felt.

When the bell above the door tinged again, Mia glanced up to see Daniel making his way towards the counter. Before today he'd avoided any risk of running into Will and he looked so awkward when he spotted her brother wiping down a table in the far corner. He nodded a hello to Will and then looked to Mia to be rescued.

'I'm here to collect Lexi.'

'Thanks, Daniel.' Mia knew how hard it was for him to come face to face with Will again. 'With the café and the picnic company I just don't have the time today.'

'No worries. I'll take her to her friend's house. I'm happy to do it.'

Mia smiled. 'I know you are, and she'll probably appreciate you taking her more than me.' Lexi was so excited about the school dance and had insisted she go over to a friend's house and sleep over so they could make a real night of it. The friend lived in Brighton East and Mia didn't want to have to put her in a taxi.

‘Helicopter parent,’ Lexi had called her, tongue in cheek, or at least so Mia thought. But it wasn’t that she didn’t trust her daughter. She just didn’t trust other people.

‘I’m a novelty, she sees you all the time.’ Daniel waved over to Jasmine, who was clearing a table by the window.

Will finally came over to the counter and Daniel turned to face him. ‘It’s good to see you.’ The atmosphere was palpable when Daniel held out a hand for Will to shake. It was the first occasion in a long time that the men had seen each other. With Will out of the country, Daniel’s visits to Lexi and drop-ins to the café had been straightforward.

Will had the grace to return the gesture and make small talk. He asked Daniel about the surf, his latest trip down to Bells Beach. Mia served the next customer and did her best to eavesdrop, willing them to keep it civil.

Getting pregnant to Daniel hadn’t happened that first time, the time Will had walked in on them, it had happened on one of the handful of times afterwards. The times they’d been together discussing how hideous this was – not only the embarrassment of being caught in the act but also the fact they’d lied. Will tolerated a lot of things, but dishonesty definitely wasn’t one of them.

‘Is she ready?’ Daniel asked Mia, clearly as uncomfortable as he looked. ‘I knocked at the door to the flat but there was no answer.’

Will disappeared into the kitchen. The washing up was all done, the dishwasher was mid-cycle, and Mia knew he was doing it to avoid any more conversation with either of them.

Mia pulled her phone from her pocket. It was too busy in the café to go round to the flat herself so she’d text Lexi.

'If you're looking for Lexi…' said Jasmine, a pile of dirty plates resting along one forearm, three glasses clutched between the fingertips on her other hand as she paused at the counter on her way to the kitchen, '…she's upstairs at Mum and Dad's.'

'What's she doing there?' asked Mia.

'She wanted to borrow some lipstick and my blush-pink cross-strap heels. And then I suggested she use my fancy Jo Malone bath oil and relax before the big event.' She grinned, more at Daniel than her sister. 'Your daughter is very excited, and very persuasive.'

'Go on up,' said Mia distractedly to Daniel.

Jasmine dumped what she was carrying in the kitchen and moved on to making coffees for another customer, perfecting the latte art every time, and fifteen minutes later Daniel came down with Lexi.

'You look stunning already.' Mia smiled at her daughter, who had her midnight-blue dress in a see-through carrier hooked over one arm and Jasmine's heels dangling off one hand. Lexi, with her baby-blue eyes and long, wavy dark-brown hair that had a hint of Daniel's lighter colour when the light shone on it, wore subtle makeup that enhanced her natural features; she was a gorgeous mixture of both her parents. Sometimes Mia couldn't help staring at her, an action sure to get her in trouble with her daughter.

'Take plenty of photos of you girls in your dresses.' Mia pressed the palms of her hands together. 'Please.'

'Oh, Mum, we will. You know what Carla is like with her selfies.'

'True. But no posting any inappropriate pictures…anywhere.'

'That goes without saying.' Lexi let her mum hug her and hold her for longer than the usual two seconds.

‘And don’t let anyone do anything they shouldn’t,’ Mia went on.

‘Mum.’ Lexi rolled her eyes. ‘Stop worrying.’

She couldn’t help it. It was her job. Having a child was the biggest responsibility you could ever have and the worrying never ended. When they were babies you worried they were still breathing as they slept – many a time Mia had stood beside the cot in the middle of the night and held a finger beneath Lexi’s nose to feel her little breaths on her skin – then when they were toddlers it was worry about whether they’d fall from the monkey bars and break their arm, when they were at school you worried they’d be bullied, then when they got to Lexi’s age it was worry about the big wide world and all the dangers it held. Both she and Daniel had been concerned about diabetes too, the condition they knew could be hereditary. And Mia still fretted now, if ever Lexi was unwell, even if the symptoms were barely matchable to those of diabetes. But so far, so good, and Lexi didn’t have any health concerns at all.

‘Stunning.’ Jasmine approved the lipstick. ‘And look after those shoes. They weren’t cheap.’

‘I will, and thanks, Jasmine. It’s great we’re the same size.’

‘Great for who?’ But Jasmine smiled at her niece and Mia felt a stab of jealousy. She’d never lent her daughter shoes – they were completely different sizes. It was another part of her daughter’s life to exclude her, yet a part that let Jasmine in.

‘Have a wonderful time,’ said Mia as Daniel ushered Lexi along. ‘I’ll see you when you get home. And thank you, Daniel.’

‘I’m off.’ Will emerged from the kitchen as soon as Daniel escorted his daughter out of the café and the coast was clear.

Mia looked at her watch. ‘It’s not quite four o’clock yet. We kind of need you here.’

‘Tough.’ He didn’t look at her. ‘I’m meeting Leo and I don’t want to be late.’

‘You know it wouldn’t hurt you to be more polite to Daniel. He was your best friend once upon a time.’

Will stared at her. ‘Yeah, he was. Once upon a time.’ And with that he ignored her protests and left for the day.

Chapter Thirteen
Will

Will had tackled the Stairway to Heaven climb a handful of times. In the San Juan Mountains of Colorado, the snow sparkling in the sunlight and the blue staircase of ice flow ready for the taking, he'd felt unstoppable. To tackle the climb and succeed, not to mention come away from it alive, he'd worn a helmet in case of ice falling from above; he'd had concerns about whether his bolt anchor would hold, whether the snow was stable enough. It had pushed him to all kinds of limits – a mental game in which his body would scream at him to stop and he'd be pushed through by his love affair with adrenalin, the beauty of the mountains, and his determination to achieve anything he wanted.

Inside the climbing gym in Melbourne's city centre wasn't quite the same environment but it was still the release he needed. Climbing up and across artificial rock structures was demanding and risky, required strength, agility and mental focus. It was good exercise and got Will's head away from his family and the business.

By the time he had taken off his harness Leo was waiting for him. They'd arrived at the same time and climbed many of the same walls, but Will's focus had been intense as the feel-good endorphins kicked in, and he'd climbed far longer than his mate.

Now, he changed out of his climbing shoes and back into a pair of runners and they walked over to a café to grab a bite to eat and a coffee.

Will grinned when the waitress put a macchiato in front of him and he took his first sip. 'This coffee is way better than any of my own attempts.'

‘Not calling yourself a professional barista yet then?’

‘Far from it. I should pay customers to drink what I make rather than the other way round.’

‘That bad?’

‘Worse. But Jasmine seems to have got the hang of it.’ His sister had surprised him, first by having the nous to enrol on a barista course and then by being able to execute her skills in a live environment and pass the practice on to her siblings. Not that he’d let her help him more than was necessary. A brief overview and he’d insisted he could manage just fine. Except he knew that wasn’t true.

Leo tore the top from a pack of sugar, poured it into the latte and stirred. ‘How’s she finding it? Being back in Australia?’

He’d never even asked her, even though they were sharing the apartment above the café. He knew how it felt for him to be back from New York – it was weird, it felt alien almost but at the same time he had regular flashes of nostalgia. Like when Daniel walked in…a reverse kind of nostalgia as he remembered the friendship that had altered because of Mia. ‘I think she’s settling in.’

‘Will she return to London?’

He shrugged. ‘I don’t know.’

‘And how’s Mia?’

‘In control. As always. Worrying. As always.’

‘I saw her the other day.’

‘You did?’ She hadn’t mentioned it to him.

‘I told her to say hello to you but she must have forgotten.’ Leo elaborated on the day beside the river when she’d been catering and he’d been working and Will wasn’t sure but he thought he noted something in Leo’s voice, an approval, a need to know more, and when he asked his next question Will knew his mate wasn't asking after his sister out of politeness. 'Does she work in the café every day?'

There it was. Leo's subtle way of placing where Mia would be, in case he wanted to cross paths with her again. Will prickled. The fling between Mia and Daniel had happened more than sixteen years ago when they were all so young, yet still it rankled. Now, he and his sister were fully fledged adults. It shouldn't matter to him who she chose to spend time with, who wanted to spend time with her. But it did. All it reminded him of was how his siblings had the power to impact his life without even trying. One of the reasons he'd left the bay was to escape the suffocating feeling he felt when he was with his family. He'd been moulded into a shape that didn't fit, but in New York he'd started over and got to know exactly who he was.

'She has her own business,' said Will, 'but she's putting in a lot of time at the café too.' Heaven forbid she entrust it to anyone else.

They talked more about the picnic business and Will realised Leo knew as much as he did. It must've been more than a passing hello he'd shared with his sister, and yet she'd not said anything. Then again, she'd be afraid to, given past events.

They talked more about work – Will's and Leo's – and Leo told Will about some of the climbs he'd tackled here in Australia: Mount Buffalo and the Grampians.

'We should head to the Blue Mountains,' Leo suggested.

'Good idea. I overheard the girl behind the desk talking about it. There's a great range of climbing – over fifty different crags.'

'Let's do it.'

Will was just about to suggest another coffee when Leo's phone rang and by the sounds of it he was going into work tonight.

'The joys of being a news-gathering cameraman,' Leo confirmed after he hung up.

They parted ways and Will ventured towards Flinders Street Station, but a voice stopped him as he reached the steps out front. He moved to one side, out of the way of the crowds that had just crossed the road and were rushing to make their connection. 'Tess?'

She pulled her sunglasses onto the top of her head so they nestled comfortably in her hair. 'Where are you off to?'

'To Brighton,' he said. 'Then I'll walk to Primrose Bay. I enjoy the exercise.'

Still two steps below, she smiled up at him. 'I'm off to Brighton myself.'

'I didn't realise you lived there.'

'I live in Hampton East but my parents are still in the area and I'm looking after their house and cats, and dog, and goldfish, while they're away.'

They began making their way towards the barriers. 'So you're a regular pet sitter.'

'Something like that. But my car is there so I'm happy to give you a lift home to the bay.'

Will grinned. 'Screw the exercise.' He patted his bag. 'My legs are killing me. I've been at the climbing gym.' He didn't add that he'd powered round there, fuelled by frustration, resentment, whatever else he had bundled up inside of him thanks to his family.

They each fed the barrier with a train ticket and, through the other side, made their way to the appropriate platform. Space on the train was sparse and Tess took the last seat while Will stood next to her and they chatted as much as they could in the crowds. He surreptitiously looked at the heels she wore, the navy fitted office dress, the red lipstick on heart-shaped lips. She'd never been like this when he'd seen her with Mia years ago. If she had been he would've had trouble keeping his eyes away, his mind otherwise engaged. But it wasn't just her appearance, it was the way she chatted and laughed, with the air of assuredness that made her beautiful in every way.

When the passenger next to Tess got up for his stop, Will sneaked in to the vacant seat.

'Mia never mentioned you were a climber,' said Tess as Will squeezed his bag in to the space between his ankles.

'I love it.'

'We'll have to go sometime.'

All of a sudden he had a rush of very non-climbing adrenalin through his body. 'You climb?' He could imagine her lithe body, her hips adjusting as her feet found the footholds and she progressed up a wall, her upper body and feminine contours as she moved, the blonde hair as she completed her descent and freed it from a ponytail.

'I only started because my niece had a climbing party and wanted me to join in. I was the belayer at first but my sister encouraged me. She had the perfect excuse, being pregnant with her fourth, but her husband belayed and after a quick introduction from the staff I did my first climb.'

'Did you make it to the top?'

'I did. And I signed up for a beginners' course for the following weekend. I'd been looking for another way to keep fit and I was bored with the gym so climbing came along at the right time. I haven't been in a while as the block of lessons finished.'

His heart pounded. 'It's addictive isn't it?'

She held his gaze before he leapt up, realising it was their stop and the doors were about to shut.

As they walked back to her parents' house for her car they chatted more about climbing, a subject Will was relaxed with and, while not showing off, could impress her with. She was fascinated by the sound of some of the outdoor climbs he'd tackled, particularly the ice climbs.

'I'd be too scared to do it,' she declared when she pulled her car off the driveway and they made their way to Primrose Bay. Will did his best not to watch her legs as her feet operated the pedals. Her dress rode further up her knees each time she moved.

'It's terrifying the first time,' he said, 'especially if you think about everything that could go wrong. There's the risk of avalanche, ice falling on your head, the thought of your bolt anchor not holding. But it's a rush like no other. When you're out there in the freezing cold, the beauty of the mountains, you get higher and higher and it makes you believe you can do anything.'

She was watching him, he could tell, at least as much as she could while concentrating on the road.

'My mate Leo and I have been discussing the Blue Mountains,' he told her. 'I've not climbed there yet.'

'It'd be amazing if I could do something like that one day. You know, put all my skills into real practice.'

She slowed as they approached the café and Will noticed the lights were on inside, which was strange so late in the evening. Maybe his sisters were up late perfecting their latte art. He focused on Tess once again. 'You should promise yourself you'll do it one day.' He almost added that he'd take her but managed to stop the words tumbling out.

When they stopped she left the engine idling and turned in her seat and smiled. 'I suppose there's no reason why I can't.'

'You've got the right attitude. You need that to climb.'

Tess nodded and there was the uneasy moment, almost as though they'd been out on a date and neither knew the best way to say goodbye.

'Thanks for the lift home,' said Will.

'Oh, here.' She took out her phone. 'Tell me your number and I'll text you so you have mine. Then, if you want to go to the climbing gym let me know. I've finished lessons but I know I need to go more regularly if I want to keep fit.'

When she smiled Will tried to dismiss all thoughts of ways he could possibly keep her fit. And none of them involved climbing up a wall.

'It'd be good to be with someone else, belay for each other,' she said.

'Yeah.' Unable to say much else apart from his phone number, he took out his phone. He felt like an awkward teenager as he waited for her to text so he could save her number in his contacts.

Will climbed out of the car fuelled by even more endorphins than he'd had during tonight's climb, and waved to Tess as she drove away. He was about to go round the back entrance when he heard yelling coming from inside the café, and when he knocked on the door Jasmine let him in.

'What's going on?' he asked as Mia continued to yell.

'I'm in trouble, that's what,' Jasmine mumbled.

‘It’s my job, as a mother, to worry about you!’ Mia shrieked at Lexi, who sat on a stool in the café taking it all in.

‘You were spying on me!’

‘I wasn’t at all!’ Mia’s and Lexi’s voices were at fever pitch and Will’s ears were ringing already. ‘The party finished at ten o’clock and when you still weren’t home at eleven and not answering my calls, I tracked your iPhone.’

‘Exactly! Spying on me!’

‘Why were you at Jasmine’s?’ Mia, hands on her hips, demanded an explanation.

Will spoke in hushed tones to his younger sister. ‘Why was she at your place?

Jasmine tutted and whispered, ‘she needed my advice.’

Mia turned her anger to her brother and sister. ‘Stop whispering, you two!’ But immediately after the rebuke she focused on Jasmine alone. ‘Didn’t you think you should let me know where my daughter was?’

Jasmine tackled her sister head-on, their faces inches apart. ‘I assumed she’d already told you where she was. And to be honest, I don’t know why you’re getting so riled up. Lexi was safe at home, with me, upstairs, where she’s been a thousand times before. Clearly it was an oversight not to make sure she’d told you her whereabouts, but jeez, Mia…’

‘Jeez, Mia, what?’ Mia spat.

‘You need to stop worrying! About Lexi, about everything else. Stop worrying the world’ll crumble around you unless you hold it up yourself. Stop worrying something bad is just around the corner. Stop worrying people are out to get you. Just…stop worrying full stop!’

‘Oh fuck off, Jasmine.’

Even Lexi raised her eyebrows now and Mia asked her to go home, wait for her there.

'I don't think there's any need for that,' said Will.

'And you!' Mia's anger came his way. 'Was that Tess I saw outside dropping you off?'

Busted. 'You were spying on me too?'

'No, I wasn't 'spying' on you. I heard a car engine outside and quickly locked the door in case they thought the café was open. I pulled back the blinds to see who it was and I saw you both.'

'What, you saw us chatting?' If Tess had wanted to do anything else he'd have been the first to agree, but he wasn't about to admit that.

'So what is it, Will? Is this payback for Daniel? Are you trying to do to me what I did to you?'

'Oh now you're losing it. Don't judge everyone by your own vindictive standards.' He looked at Jasmine. 'You're right, she does worry too much.' He turned back to Mia. 'And you also poke your nose in where it's not wanted or needed.'

'You want something that is mine!' Mia shrieked.

'What?' He was inches apart from his sister now. 'That's ridiculous.'

'Is it? You both do. You and Jasmine. You want this café when I'm the one who has been here in the bay helping out when I'm needed, making sure I pick up the slack.'

'Mia, you called us,' Jasmine pointed out.

'I needed a sounding board; I didn't expect you to both come running back.'

'Didn't you?' Will asked. 'Well what did you expect? Did you think we'd leave you to do it all yourself?'

'I don't know, but I think the only reason you two came running back from your little corners of the globe was so you wouldn't lose out financially. You see this café as your birthright and that's the only reason you don't want it to fail.'

Jasmine shook her head. 'You have a low opinion of us both.' When Mia didn't answer she carried on. 'And nobody asked you to manage it all alone. So quit being so self-righteous, would you?' Jasmine was calmer than Will was used to hearing her when confronted by either of her siblings. Usually she unleashed the inner Italian and nobody stood a chance. Usually Jasmine was like a grass fire ripping through a dry field, unstoppable, threatening and unforgiving.

'We're all here to help,' Will asserted, knowing he'd have to be the peacemaker. 'And I'm sorry if you feel we're treading on your toes, but that's the way it is. If we don't all pull together the café will go to pot. It's not just about the money side of the business, it's about the café itself. It's about what Grandma Annetta would want and it's about protecting what Mum and Dad worked so hard for. They're clearly not thinking straight right now and I'm pretty sure they'll regret it, but personally I'd like to see this place still standing when and if they ever come back.'

'What, you think it's the magic glue that'll hold their crumbling marriage together?' Mia was incredulous. 'You old romantic.'

She was upset. Will did his best to ignore the dig. 'You never know.'

Mia harrumphed. 'Yeah, well maybe you should take over, Will. It's what you're good at!' She pulled off her apron, took out her keys to the café and dumped them both on the counter. 'There you go, Will Marcello. If you want the café business yourself, then go ahead. I'm done. I have my own business to run.'

Had he been naïve not to see that coming?

'I won't be setting foot in here again, so go to hell,' she yelled. 'And you,' she pointed to Jasmine, 'stay away from my daughter!'

And with that, Will watched Mia stomp out of the café, slamming the door shut behind her.

'Now that's what I call a good dose of sibling rivalry,' said Jasmine in her wake. 'And why does she assume the café is all up to you. Why doesn't she ever see me?'

Will didn't have an answer to that. All he could think about was that he had just been handed the reins to a business he wasn't sure he had any genuine passion for. Was it ridiculous to think that pulling together and saving this café would save his parents' marriage and see them live out a Happy Ever After? Or would it be better for all three of them to cut their losses now and accept what was happening?

Chapter Fourteen

Jasmine

Jasmine locked up and Will set the alarm for the café before they both went upstairs to their parents' apartment.

'Will…' Jasmine turned in the doorway to face him before he had the chance to disappear into the spare room. 'Can I ask you a question?'

He sighed. 'I'm tired, Jasmine. I need a shower after the climbing gym – can't it wait?'

Ignoring him, she continued. 'Do you really think that by saving the café we'll save Mum and Dad and get them back together?'

He leant against the doorjamb. 'I really don't know anymore. I half expected them to change their minds and I'd be on the next plane back to New York when they decided they weren't going to go through with their plans.'

She mirrored his actions and leant against the doorjamb of her parents' bedroom. 'Mia thinks we're being naïve.'

'She probably knows more than us. She's the one who's been here the whole time,' he admitted.

'A fact she likes to remind us of.' The eye roll made her brother smile. 'I just can't imagine them not being together.'

Her words hung in the air until Will spoke. 'It's more than their marriage that I think about.' When Jasmine looked at him he said, 'The bay without The Sun Coral Café is like a cappuccino without froth or a doughnut without any sugar. Both are perfectly all right that way, but the froth and the sugar are what make them both shine. The Sun Coral Café is iconic to Primrose Bay. It's featured in guidebooks, it's talked about.'

Arms folded, Jasmine looked at her brother. 'Can you honestly say you want to stay here running it when you've been working in New York, living a completely different life?'

He shook his head. 'When has it ever been about what I wanted?'

His words took her by surprise. They were laced with something but she didn't know what. Gone were the days she'd tried to understand her brother. 'Mia is clearly over it and walking away, so that leaves me and you at the helm. But if you want to jump ship, just make sure you give me plenty of notice.'

He stared at her. 'What, you think you can look after the place on your own?'

She glared at her brother because, yes, that's exactly what she thought. 'Just keep me informed of whatever you intend to do. Don't do a Mum and Dad and leave with barely any notice.' She knew that with a bit of warning she could cope. She'd get her own staff, run it the way she saw fit, and there'd be no bickering like there was now, which surely took up most of their energies.

Before Will turned to leave she said, 'I tried to see Grandma Annetta.' Her words stopped him.

'When?'

'The day after I returned to the bay. She refused to see me. She won't see anyone. What, why are you looking at me like that?'

Will shook his head. 'It surprises me, why you bothered.'

'Why, because you're her favourite?'

'No, because she refuses to see everyone, even Dad.'

Over the years, their dad and Grandma Annetta had had their fair share of slanging matches, but Jasmine had no idea what they were about. She'd been busy with her own life and had wondered whether riling people was just Grandma Annetta's way. Her dad had always tried to please his mother, to gain her approval, but, from what Jasmine knew about her grandmother, that approval had been something Annetta rarely gave.

'I wanted to know what she thought about Mum and Dad, how they've left their own business without so much as a backward glance.'

Will shrugged. 'Even if she agreed to see you, I hardly think she'd be an expert in our parents' marital problems. The impression I got is that she was most likely the cause of a few of them.'

'Maybe she was, but I had this faint hope she'd be able to give us advice on the café – where to go from here.'

He pulled a face. 'Highly unlikely. And you're sounding like Mia. Stop worrying about everything.'

'I do worry! You go sauntering off to see your mate, you don't put the café first. Someone has to!'

'Oh here we go. I suppose after your job as a barmaid you'd be the expert in all things catering, would you?'

'I did a lot more than work behind the bar, Will.' Was there any point in arguing? He'd made up his mind about her and he'd decided she was incapable of having a business and running it efficiently. 'I'd do a better job than you. You say you can't bear the thought of the café disappearing from the bay, but you've no interest in running it. Come on, be honest.'

'I've got my own life,' he snapped. 'And I won't apologise for that.'

'I'm not asking you to!' She was merely asking him to see her, to open his eyes and realise she was a grown adult rather than his annoying little sister. All their lives he'd been the one in charge, but he didn't care enough about the café – not in the same way she did. But trying to explain that to her older brother who'd never cared much for her opinion was next to useless.

'Maybe Mum and Dad are right,' he said. 'Perhaps it's time to cut our losses and walk away from this place.' He tugged a hand through his hair. 'And I've had enough arguing for one night.' He turned and disappeared into the spare room, shutting the door behind him.

Jasmine went into the kitchen and filled a glass of water from the tap. She heard the pipes groan as Will took a shower and seconds later she'd opened up the pantry and rifled through its contents: a bag of Doritos lurking at the back, half a loaf of sliced fruit bread, one lonely flapjack in a Tupperware container, and a four pack of Kit Kats. She grabbed the chocolate – her fingers were poised, ready to pull in opposite directions and open the red-and-white wrapper, devour the dark chocolate treats inside.

But she stopped. She wouldn't go there. She wouldn't do it to herself again.

She put the packet back where it had come from and shut the pantry door, leaning against it so everything was safely trapped inside. She grabbed a banana from the fruit bowl to satisfy her need to eat something, anything. Years ago she would've eaten all those Kit Kats in response to a run-in with her sibling. She would've barely tasted the remaining flapjack as she'd shovelled it in, and she would've probably washed it all down with a sugar-laden can of Coca-Cola. But not this time. She was no longer the weak Jasmine who'd left the bay unhappy and gone to London sixteen kilograms heavier. Now, she was in control of her own life and ready to take whatever her family threw at her.

As Jasmine ate the banana she thought about her sister and her niece instead of the discussion she'd just had with Will. She was close to Lexi, as close as a best friend and much closer than her own mother was to her. Over the years Jasmine had thought it would be something that made Mia happy, something her older sister would approve of, that would show her as a valid member of this family. The teenage years were hard enough and without anyone on your side, they could be unnecessarily painful, yet here was Jasmine, a best friend for Lexi, and Mia couldn't show the slightest bit of gratitude, only jealousy. The bottom line was that her own sister didn't trust her. Mia had never trusted her.

When Jasmine heard the water from the shower turn off she quickly threw her banana peel in the bin and escaped to the confines of her bedroom. She'd have to spend all day with Will in the café tomorrow, and she didn't want to even see him again tonight, let alone talk to him. What she wanted was a good night's sleep to give her the determination to ignore the undercurrent of emotion and prove she was just as competent as anyone else.

*

Mia kept good with her threat and was nowhere to be seen in the café the next morning. Jasmine was up ridiculously early and the first thing she did was to turn off the alarm system. She was eager to prove, from this moment on, that it wasn't only her physical appearance that had changed. She wanted to show that she was so much more than the sibling who got in the way, the sibling who needed to be watched over.

With another sunny February day there was no need to use the downlights in the café when she started her day at five o'clock. The whole place had a soft glow through the blinds still in place over the windows. The food display cabinet was empty – they emptied it every evening once the café was shut, having monitored its levels well enough all day to ensure there wasn't too much wastage. Jasmine looked at the laminated list on the wall in the kitchen, the foods that needed preparing each day and the reason she was up so early: fruit salads, banana bread, pear-and-raspberry bread all needed to be made from scratch. You never knew who was going to ask for what – if she made the banana bread first, her first customer of the day would want pear and raspberry. If she made pear-and-raspberry bread, the first customer would want the banana. It was always the way. With a sigh, she checked the recipe and switched the oven on to preheat. She opened the side door to the cafe to get some fresh air circulating but left the fly wire shut. With no direct sunlight into the kitchen, at least it was cool at this hour and not too unbearable to work.

She washed her hands again and, following the recipe for the pear-and-raspberry bread, set about weighing ingredients, enough to make four loaves. The instructions were for two but they had four tins and it made sense to make more. If she froze one as soon as it had cooled, she'd be able to get it out of the freezer as soon as they ran low. She'd make this variety now and then wash the tins so she could make the banana bread straight after.

Once the loaves were in the oven it was time to get the cash boxes from the safe. When she opened it she spotted the red cash bag still lurking in the back. She'd need to do the banking today and she scribbled a note on the whiteboard in massive letters so they wouldn't forget, and then slotted the cash box into the till at the front of the shop, emptying a plastic bag of ten-cent coins and another full of one-dollar coins so they'd have enough change for the morning. She'd not had many emails from her parents but they always reiterated the need to be strict when it came to the financial side of the business. They should bank takings regularly and pass the information on to the accountant. For two people who'd walked away, Jasmine guessed she should be thankful for every morsel of information they shared.

Thankfully, the café was clean now. Long before Lexi had shown up on Jasmine's doorstep and Mia had had her meltdown last night, Mia and Jasmine had performed the end-of-the-day ritual. Floors had been swept and mopped, all the tables were sparkling clean, sugar pots were refilled, napkins slotted into their dispensers, table numbers wiped and straightened on their polished chrome stands. The dishwasher had been stacked, emptied, re-stacked and emptied again, and all crockery was put away in the appropriate place. Mia had put out the rubbish and even cleaned the inside of the windows to free them of sticky finger-marks that showed up all the more in the sunshine. It was always the way at the end of the day. There was never the plea: I'm-so-tired-can't-we-do-it-tomorrow? Because tomorrow it'd be straight on to the next task.

With the loaves cooking away, Jasmine felt calm, collected, ready to tackle what was thrown at her next. She even smiled to herself. She could do this. More than that…she *was* doing it! But she didn't have much time to reflect before a knock at the fly screen and a call from the milk delivery company had her scurrying out to the kitchen to take the crates of milk inside and unload into the fridge. Flustered because she had no idea where the company chequebook was, she signed for delivery and when the man went on his way realised they must have ordered and paid for it already. But who dealt with the company? Who dealt with reordering? Was it automatic?

She felt a flush of annoyance. It was all well and good Mia stomping off. But the fact was, she needed to come to the café and at least brief her sister on what she knew. She'd been the only one to have any sort of handover from their parents after all.

Jasmine took her frustration out on the fruit as she chopped it ready for the fresh fruit salads that would go into the chilled display cabinets. They weren't a big seller first thing but come morning tea time, especially on a hot day like today, lots of people craved them – especially with a good dollop or two of Greek yoghurt.

When Will breezed in twenty minutes before opening time she said, 'Nice of you to join me.'

'We don't open till seven thirty.' He poured coffee beans into the grinder, took a cup down from the top of the machine and reached for the nearest jug.

'Who's that for?'

'Der…'

She snatched the cup from his hand and he almost sloshed milk all over the countertop as he lifted it to pour into the awaiting jug. 'What's your problem?'

'I've been in here since five o'clock!' she shrieked at him. He didn't need to know how much she'd enjoyed taking on the responsibility, assuming the control.

'What, you want a medal for it?'

'You can't waltz in and expect everything to be ready. Your idea of running a café is so way off the mark.'

'You sound like Mia.'

Before she could think of an appropriate comeback the oven timer pinged. She put on oven gloves and lifted out the loaves, springy to the touch and filling the kitchen with the intoxicating fresh-baked-fruit smell. She'd need to leave them to cool in the tin for ten minutes and then turn them out, let them cool some more and slice them into thick wedges.

By the time Jasmine turned back, Will had the milk measured out and before she had a chance to speak he ground the coffee beans to drown out any conversation. Fuming, she went through to the café and opened up all the blinds. Sure enough there was a customer waiting already.

'Come in,' she welcomed. She took a deep breath to calm herself.

The man, dressed in a suit, ordered a takeaway cappuccino from Will, who was at least pleasant to the customer if not to her.

Jasmine checked the supplies of raisin bread – two loaves left – and took one from the freezer. 'Are these on automatic reorder?' she asked Will as he made the coffee. She wasn't sure how good a job he was doing. He looked like he was doing it the way she'd explained, but he hadn't been the best at listening to her instructions.

'No idea.'

'Or do we go to the local shops and buy them?'

'No idea.'

'Come on, Will,' she hissed under her breath as he fitted the plastic top onto the takeaway cup.

When the customer left he turned to her. 'Jasmine, I have no idea how things run in here. I know as much as you. Don't always assume I know everything just because I'm the oldest.' He stalked off to turn the sign on the door from Closed to Open.

Jasmine wondered whether any of them had really grown up at all in the years since their childhood.

Huffing and puffing, but mostly frustrated, she texted Mia. She wrote, rewrote, deleted and wrote her reply again, over and over. In the end she didn't attempt to make any peace, she simply said they needed to know things and needed her to do a handover before she left them to run the place.

A steady flow of customers ensued, those walking along beside the bay and taking the opportunity to grab a snack and refreshment, others on their way to the main hub of Primrose Bay and the offices or shops that sat a short distance from the beach. And then before Jasmine knew it the mothers' groups were in with tiny babies still in the pram, little ones who weren't yet old enough for preschool.

'Any word from up high?' Will asked.

'What?'

He pointed to the ceiling, but to the left to indicate Mia's place.

Jasmine took out her phone and there was a message waiting. She'd been so busy she hadn't had a chance to check. She shook her head. 'Says she'll have some time later but right now she has her own business to run.' Clearly her sister was out to prove a point. Jasmine pulled a face and put her phone back in her pocket.

Will greeted the next customer, a woman whom Jasmine had definitely seen in here before and who had two lively kids by her side. 'Jasmine, where's the banana bread?'

Jasmine looked in the back of the counter and then her breath caught as she realised her oversight. 'We don't have any. I forgot to make it.'

'Fantastic,' he muttered. 'We always have it.'

'Sorry, I got waylaid doing every bloody thing else around here.'

'Don't get bolshy, I'll tell the customer, but next time we need to make sure everything on the menus is actually available.'

'Tell her there's pear-and-raspberry bread, I'm sure that's fine.'

But as Jasmine emptied the drip tray from the coffee machine and cleared the table next to where the lady was sitting, she heard the youngest of the two children start bawling his eyes out as Will explained that they didn't have what he wanted. The next thing they knew, the kid was lying on the floor spinning round in crazy circles like he was about to take part in some kind of breakdancing competition. She guessed this was a toddler tantrum. Talk about an overreaction.

Jasmine left the kid screaming and Will trying to talk to the mum about what she wanted and went out to the kitchen and emptied the dishwasher, something that had to be done regularly to keep the cycle going – dirty cups, plates and everything else in, then empty and restack, load dirties, run again, then repeat.

Will looked none too impressed when he came out back. 'My ears are ringing. Who knew a small kid could make so much noise.'

'Should I make up the banana bread now?'

He tutted. 'Bit late for that isn't it?'

'Yeah, well maybe you could get up at a reasonable time and actually…I don't know…help!'

Will rubbed his face with his hands, and then with a quick check of the front of shop he turned to Jasmine. 'The only way this is going to work is if we come up with some kind of system. We need to know who should be doing what, and when.'

'Well that's the first good suggestion you've made since you returned from New York.'

Exasperated, he said, 'I'd better go and serve.'

He left Jasmine annoyed but all the more determined to succeed. She wasn't going down without a fight. This was another challenge she was going to win.

*

By the time they closed up that afternoon Jasmine and Will were at least in the swing of things and the bickering, for now, had stopped. They took turns and instead of running around like headless chooks, one of them manned the coffee machine and dealt with beverages while the other cleaned tables and served any food requested. Jasmine had no idea why they hadn't done that sooner. It was common sense but both of them, with their need for one-upmanship, had focused on doing everything themselves and being the best rather than actually running the café properly.

When Jasmine's phone pinged she pulled it out and saw a message from Lexi. She was with Daniel at the Jam Factory in South Yarra, about to watch a movie, and she wanted Jasmine to join them afterwards for food. Jasmine almost typed back that she couldn't, it would only anger Mia, but why shouldn't she go? Why should Mia always get her own way? She had a relationship with her niece, a good one, and her niece confided in her. The last thing she wanted was for Lexi to have to bottle everything up, keep it all inside, the way she'd done herself. What she'd told Jasmine last night was a typical teenage problem, but if Mia knew exactly what had upset her daughter and sent her running to her Auntie Jasmine in the first place she'd surely hit the roof.

Jasmine left Will to lock up and alarm the café and treated herself to a taxi over to South Yarra. It was a bit of a splurge but it was only the once, and after the day she'd had she needed some relief. When she looked up to Mia's apartment window as the taxi pulled away from the curb she couldn't see a light on. Mia was probably already in bed, asleep, without a care that she still needed to do a handover for the café. Well, tomorrow, Jasmine decided, she'd bang the door down if she had to and get all the information they needed.

The taxi dropped Jasmine right outside the Jam Factory and she found Daniel and Lexi inside, tucking into late-night sushi.

'Help yourself.' Lexi gestured to the sushi. 'Dad ordered loads as usual.'

'It's true,' Daniel admitted. 'I ordered for a family of eight, not two!'

Mia helped herself to what looked like a teriyaki chicken California roll and used the plastic knife to spread on a little wasabi. 'You're usually full up on popcorn after a movie, aren't you?'

There was Lexi's infamous eye roll. She'd perfected it to a T and it was a dead giveaway that she was related to Jasmine because she'd always done it too. 'That was when I was little, Auntie Jasmine.' She put an emphasis on the word Auntie.

'She's more sophisticated now,' Daniel teased.

They laughed and chatted easily here and not once did Jasmine feel guilty. Lexi was family and at sixteen years old she was heading towards adulthood – certainly old enough to decide who she could and couldn't see.

'Oh, there's Charlotte from school.' Lexi waved over to a girl with blonde hair tied in a high ponytail. 'Would you mind if I went to say hello?'

'Sure.' Daniel proffered the tray of tempura prawns to Jasmine.

She took one. 'I didn't realise how hungry I was.'

'Is the café that busy?'

'I don't know how my parents did it, you know. Day in, day out, usually seven days a week with rarely any holiday time. It's exhausting.'

'Do I detect a glow though?' He grinned.

'What do you mean?'

'You love it, don't you? I can tell.'

'How?'

'It's like when I'm tired and I've committed to friends to go down to Bells Beach for a surf. I drag myself out of bed, bitching and moaning it's too early, it's cold, I'd rather not go. But I know that deep down there's a rumbling, a passion that will only take a little bit of ignition beneath it and off it'll go.'

Jasmine smiled then. 'Weird analogy but, yeah, I suppose you're right. Before I went away to the UK I dreamed of running the café single-handedly but it seemed completely out of reach. My family would never think I could do it – Will and Mia certainly don't – but it was what I'd always wanted.'

'Did you ever tell anyone?'

'My brother or sister you mean?'

'I was thinking more about your parents. Did you discuss it with them?'

She bit into the last piece of prawn tempura and discarded the tail in the plastic container with the others. 'They were always too busy.'

'Have you heard from either of them?'

'Only the bare minimum. I emailed to ask for a couple of contact numbers for suppliers but they take forever to respond.'

'Where are they now?'

'God only knows. One is probably on the East Coast, the other on the West.'

'And you didn't see it coming?'

Jasmine shrugged and nodded to Daniel's offer of water from the jug filled with ice and lemon. As he poured some in to a glass for her she said, 'Looking back I should've done, but when I left for London I had my own issues.'

After the barista course in the city that day, Jasmine had told Daniel a bit about her unhappiness and her comfort eating. He was almost like the big brother she'd never had and he'd certainly been a lot nicer to her and a lot more willing to listen than her own siblings. She'd told him all the things she used to eat when she was on a spiralling binge. One day she'd been so upset after a row with Will – to this day she couldn't remember what it was about, but she knew they'd yelled so much their Grandma Annetta had thrown a bowl of ice-cold water over them to make them take notice of her – she'd got the tram into the city and had lunch with friends, gorging herself at a Chinese restaurant with everything from prawn crackers and duck pancakes to egg fried rice and gooey sweet and sour chicken. She'd washed it all down with a few glasses of wine and then stopped at a bakery where she'd had a cream cake, moved on to a coffee shop where she'd had a hot chocolate and a muffin, and on the way home she'd cried as she'd eaten a caramel slice. She was disgusted with herself at the time but powerless to stop it. Eating gave her a rush that helped her cope, a pleasure that was hers alone.

'I was tempted to overeat again last night,' she admitted. 'After a run-in with Will.'

'And did you?'

She smiled, proud of herself. 'I pigged out on a banana.'

'Whoa, steady on.' He laughed with her. 'What stopped you going for the bad stuff?'

'Years ago I overate because I was unhappy. It was an unhappiness that didn't stem from one single event but from a lifetime build-up. Years and years of never feeling good enough, of being looked down on, of never being encouraged.'

He reached out and touched her hand, urging her that it was okay to go on.

'What stopped me last night was that I've changed. I went to London, a place where nobody knew me, nobody had a preconceived notion of who I was, and I took charge of my own life for once, in a better way than ever before. And just because I'm back, doesn't mean I've lost that sense of control. Part of the learning curve was to realise I couldn't be upbeat all the time and that I had to be my own person. I stopped letting others' actions impact me so powerfully, to the point where I'd let my own life fall apart.'

'I can't believe you never told your family about any of it.'

'You haven't mentioned it to Mia, have you?'

'Of course not and I won't. But I know Mia and I think she'd be upset if she knew how you felt back then, what had made you go.'

‘I’m not ready to tell anyone. As far as they know, I’m just slim now instead of fat. End of.’

‘Okay.’ He patted her hand. ‘It sounds as though London was just what you needed.’

A sudden pang of nostalgia for those early days in the city made her smile. ‘In London I was Jasmine the barmaid, the Aussie girl who liked a laugh with her new friends. I wasn’t the youngest Marcello girl, Will’s sister or Mia’s sister, I was simply…me. I’d been really unhappy with my weight, obviously, but I’d been in a rut and never did anything about it. The worse I felt, the more I ate, and the more I ate, the worse I felt. The vicious circle was difficult to step out of.’

‘So what changed?’

He was so easy to talk to, she ended up telling him everything. ‘One day, about three months after I’d arrived in England, I was moving into the shared house and grabbed an old pair of jeans. I pulled them on easily, but there was no way they were staying up without a belt. The last time I’d worn them I’d only just been able to do up the button. After that, I braved looking in the mirror and I could notice things were changing. My stomach was still big but not bulging out so much, my boobs had gone down in size—’

‘Thanks for that visual.’ He grinned.

‘Sorry. I just like reminiscing about those days because I see how far I’ve come, how much I’ve changed. I don’t ever want to go back to how I once was. In the house share we started to cook meals together and I was lucky because the others were a pretty healthy bunch and we all had budgets to adhere to. We’d make big casseroles, or shepherd’s pie, or baked potatoes. And I started going to the markets and buying heaps of fresh fruit and vegetables. It was a lifestyle change as well as weight loss and I don't think I could've done one without the other. I needed to realise what I was doing to myself, pigging out on doughnuts, iced buns, chocolate, crisps.

'I started to realise I could still eat a lot, but if I had a lot of the right stuff, it was good for me. My tastes had already started to change by then – in the mornings I'd reach for an apple or a banana instead of a Mars bar, for lunch I'd have a jacket potato with salad or baked beans instead of a couple of slices of pizza, for dinner I loved cooking with the others so rather than having Chinese or Indian takeaways, we'd have home-cooked meals.'

'It sounds as though you really sorted yourself out,' said Daniel. 'You know, much as Will and I haven't seen eye to eye in a long time, I can't imagine he wouldn't be on your side if you told him any of this. Maybe the reason you three bicker so much is because deep down you actually give a shit about each other.'

'You're kidding. This would just be more ammunition for the other two.' She felt herself welling up. 'It's another part of me that didn't live up to their expectations.'

'Oh come on, whatever makes you think that? What makes you think you need Will or Mia's approval anyway?'

'I know I don't.' She sniffed. 'But sometimes I'd really like it.'

As Lexi came wandering over, Jasmine dabbed her eyes with the tissue she'd pulled from her bag.

'What's wrong?' Lexi asked.

'Daniel was making me cry with laughter, that's all.' Thankfully Lexi didn't ask what the joke was as Jasmine would've had a hard time concocting something.

'Dad, do you mind if I go back to Charlotte's place for a while? Her mum said she'd run me home afterwards.'

Daniel looked over to Kerry, Charlotte's mum, and waved. 'I'm sure that'll be fine. But home by eleven o'clock please, or your mum'll have me hung, drawn and quartered.'

Jasmine wondered how daft her sister was not to want Daniel. He was good-looking, had a good job and a lovely apartment, he was the best father you could wish for and he was so kind. Jasmine had had a huge crush on him back when he and Mia first started seeing each other. She'd been almost eleven years old and just starting to be aware of boys. And Daniel wasn't even one of those, he was a man.

'I know, I know. I'll be home before curfew.' Lexi kissed her dad and Jasmine and scurried back to her friend.

'Won't Mia want to know exactly who she's with and whose mum is bringing her home?' Jasmine asked derisively.

'I'll text her, and she knows Kerry well so it won't be a problem.' Daniel picked up his phone and did just that. 'Mia's a worrier, but she's not an ogre.'

Jasmine waved over to her niece. 'I can see both you and Mia in her.'

'Well, she gets all the best bits from me of course.' He winked. 'Come on, I'll take you home. I'm not parked too far away.'

Jasmine hooked her bag on her shoulder and scooped up the red cardigan she'd brought in case the temperature deigned to drop tonight, but it was pleasantly warm outside so she looped it through the bag's handles. She pulled the tie from her hair and ruffled it to let it blow in the wind. Feeling the warm night air brought it home to her how much she'd missed this city. London had the wow factor for sure: Big Ben and the Houses of Parliament lit up at night; the buzz of Leicester Square that carried on late into the evenings; crowds of shoppers on Oxford street; green spaces that stretched for miles, juxtaposed with the great city at its heart. But there was a feeling of nostalgia here in Melbourne that transported all of that excitement, the joy of the unknown, and knocked it back in an oddly settling way.

'You look deep in thought,' said Daniel, his suit jacket looped over his arm.

'Just appreciating the city, that's all.' Her hair whipped across her face in the warm winds that were typically Melbourne.

'How about we appreciate it some more?' They walked along Chapel Street as a green-and-yellow tram cut down the middle. 'We could have a quick drink in Bridie O'Reilly's.'

'Yes! I haven't been there in years. Gosh, I remember some shocking nights doing Cowboy shots in there with a friend. It was incredibly wild and very messy.'

'That settles it. I'll have Coke as I'm driving, and you can get sloshed and forget all about your brother and sister.'

'Sounds perfect to me,' said Jasmine as they came to the pub in question.

People sat outside enjoying the evening warmth and one of them called out to Jasmine to tell her she'd dropped something as she walked towards the front door. She turned back to pick up her cardigan that had somehow unwound itself from her bag handles. It was only as she laughed with Daniel and he tied it on her bag extra hard that they both looked across at the car waiting in the queue by the lights – or, more importantly, the person inside, who was staring at them as though they were both married to other people and had just been caught cheating.

'Mia,' Jasmine mouthed.

But her sister did nothing more than give them a filthy look and drive on.

If Jasmine had wanted to add fire to the mix of sibling rivalry, she'd certainly managed to do that tonight. In a big way.

Chapter Fifteen

Mia

Mia muttered to herself as she drove away from Chapel Street – anything to stop herself from whacking her foot on the accelerator and driving on until she hit something. She'd delivered a last-minute order to a house in South Yarra for a Proposal Picnic and after leaving there with a smile on her face, a feeling of positivity, she'd seen Jasmine and Daniel: her sister and her ex.

First Lexi and now Daniel. Was there nothing of hers that Jasmine didn't want for herself? She was even taking control of the café when Mia had been the only one of the three of them who had stuck around to help their parents when they needed it, the only one who cared about the bay. She may have told Jasmine and Will to run the place themselves, but seeing it happen without any control over it herself was a different matter entirely.

Livid, Mia parked up in Primrose Bay and let herself into her flat. She'd already had Daniel's text to say Lexi would be home by eleven as she was with a friend, but he'd failed to tell her who he was with instead. It dawned on her then that Jasmine must've been with Lexi too when she'd expressly told her to stay away from her daughter.

Getting pregnant at eighteen had been a disaster when it had happened but the moment Lexi was born Mia hadn't regretted a single thing. Lexi was hers, she was there for her daughter night and day, they were each other's best friend. At least, until Lexi had hit the teenage years. When her daughter was thirteen Mia noticed more and more that she was beginning to idolise her Auntie Jasmine. Jasmine was in her early twenties, out every night and partying with friends from the local school. She didn't have many boyfriends, but she certainly caught the boys' attention with her long ebony hair that hung almost to her bottom. Lexi started to try dressing like her – her first little black dress when she was fourteen, just like Jasmine; racy red lipstick, the same shade as her auntie wore; she even began styling her wavy hair in the same way with the centre part. The only thing she didn't do was dye it black. Thank goodness she kept her beautiful dark-brown wavy locks, lighter at the ends and a mixture of Mia's dark and Daniel's blonde shades.

Mia stood, hands on the kitchen sink, looking out the tiny window. She leant in to inhale the scent of the Strawberries & Cream hydrangeas, the deep rosy-red flowers nestled in the terracotta pot with their white and pale-pink buds in the centre of glossy dark-green leaves. She filled a small glass of water at the tap and gently lifted the leaves so she could feed the plant. As a little girl she'd loved playing in Grandma Annetta's garden, a place of serenity filled with hydrangeas just like these. She'd been allowed to pick some and had pressed them in a flower press she'd got for Christmas, and in the hallway of her apartment now sat the glass-framed posy tied with straw-coloured ribbon. Every time she looked at them, still beautiful all these years later, it reminded her of simpler times. Of when they'd been a busy but content family, back when sibling rivalry was all about who got the first ice-cream when the van sang out its tune and crept its way down Wattle Lane.

It was close to eleven when Mia heard keys in the door and she thought back to the last time they'd fought, when Lexi had been at Jasmine's and she'd been worried sick. It still rankled now that whatever they'd been talking about that night was something she, as Lexi's mother, wasn't a party to.

Mia picked up a cloth by the sink and pretended to wipe down the kitchen work surface.

'You're up late.' Lexi dropped her keys on the table and came over to hug her mum.

Mia breathed in the scent of her hair – a new, more expensive shampoo than she'd used before, but one she'd bought with her own pocket money. It smelt of salons, of grown-ups, not of her little girl anymore.

'I had a job delivering a Proposal Picnic,' said Mia. She didn't mention that it was in South Yarra or that she'd caught Daniel and Jasmine together. The last thing she wanted was for this to blow up in her face tonight, not with Lexi anyway.

Lexi plugged her phone in to the charger on the kitchen benchtop. Mia had the rule of no iPhone in the bedroom after nine o'clock. She'd heard too many stories of nasty girls bitching and bullying in cyberspace so she kept the bedroom as the one sanctuary.

'Did you enjoy the movie?'

'It was great.' Lexi filled a glass of water from under the tap. 'Charlotte was in the same cinema but I hadn't noticed. I went back to her place for hot chocolate.'

'And marshmallows?' She knew her child's weakness.

'Always.' Lexi smiled. 'Dad says hi by the way.'

Yeah, she bet he did. 'How is he?'

'He's good, working hard.'

She waited to see if Lexi would mention anything about Jasmine but she already knew if she waited she'd be old and grey before anything came out of Lexi's mouth.

'Goodnight, Mum.'

'I'll be going to bed soon,' said Mia, blowing Lexi a kiss. 'I need to nip down to the picnic shop, I left my diary there.'

Lexi rolled her eyes and giggled. 'I'm telling you, Mum, you're the only one that uses a Filofax anymore!'

'No I'm not,' she quipped, 'they wouldn't sell them if it was only me.'

'Goodnight, Mum.'

'Goodnight, Lexi.'

Mia opened the drawer and took out her Filofax, which bulged with notes and Post-its. She'd put it on the table when she came back so it looked like she'd been telling the truth. When she heard a car pull up outside the café she peeked through the curtain and it was no surprise to see Daniel's car disgorging her little sister out onto the pavement. Mia watched Jasmine wave at Daniel and cross over to the café before disappearing down the side to the entrance of her parents' apartment. And then Mia locked up and went next door.

'Can I come in?' Mia didn't wait for an answer. She barged past Jasmine the second she opened the door.

'Er…I think you already are in.' Jasmine shut the door behind Mia and followed her up the stairs to the apartment.

'Have you got something to say to me?' Mia stood, arms folded tightly across her chest, glaring at her sister. 'Well?'

'What do you want me to say? Is this because you saw me with Daniel?'

She harrumphed. 'You're so blasé about it, aren't you? Typical Jasmine – off in her own little Jasmine world, doing her own thing, not giving a toss about anyone else.'

'Where the hell did you get that idea from?'

'I asked you to stay away from Lexi for a start!'

'I know you did, but I still don't understand why. I thought you'd appreciate someone looking out for her. Lord knows she can't talk to you.'

'And what's that supposed to mean?'

Will emerged from his bedroom. 'What's all the noise? Some of us are trying to sleep. You know, so we can get up early and help out.'

'Oh put some ear plugs in then!' Mia yelled at him. He muttered a few expletives and retreated back into his room and his music clicked on, presumably to drown out the noise of the catfight between his sisters. Usually good at managing situations, Will had obviously had enough, and refereeing a sparring match didn't appear to be high on his agenda tonight.

'Lexi does talk to me, and I'll thank you not to poison her mind against her own mother,' Mia spat.

Jasmine, hands on hips, almost mirroring Mia's stance, screamed back at her. 'I am her friend.'

'Well, that's just it. You're not supposed to be her friend, you're supposed to be responsible, the adult.'

'That's your job. You're the one who got knocked up when you were just out of nappies.'

'Oh shut up!'

'No! It's about time someone told you what they thought. You're not so perfect, Mia. You make out you are, but even you make mistakes. You're so stuck in your own world where everything has to be structured and ordered that you don't even see what's going on in your own daughter's life.'

'And what do you know about parenting?'

'I may not be a parent but I know enough about relationships, I've lived with you and Will my whole life and it was stifling. To be living alongside such perfection was nauseating.'

Mia leant against the table, her knuckles white she was so angry. This wasn't about her parenting skills. 'What's going on with Daniel?'

'Nothing is going on with Daniel.' Jasmine smiled as though she was enjoying this.

'You looked pretty cosy to me.'

'That's your paranoia talking again.'

'Is it?'

'Yes. Daniel happens to be a friend. I babysat when Lexi was tiny and we used to talk and talk. We even messaged each other on Facebook when I was in the UK.'

Mia knew her sister was divulging details just to rile her and she wouldn't rise to it.

'Look, Mia. My friends have all left the bay, done something with their lives, and it's nice to be able to catch up with someone who sees me the way I am.'

Before she could really think about what she was saying, Mia blurted out, 'Do you want everything that I have? Is that it? Are you so jealous of me that you want my daughter to side with you and become your best friend, and you want my ex to become yours? Maybe you want to have his baby too!'

'Oh my god!' Jasmine shrieked. 'I don't know why I bother sometimes. You're sick!'

Will emerged again. 'That's enough, you two. You're both being petty and ridiculous and for two grown adults it's embarrassing.'

'Don't you start bossing us about,' said Mia.

'Yeah, you've always done that,' Jasmine joined in. 'The man of the house,' she said, putting the phrase in air quotes. 'Golden bollocks.'

He made a disapproving sound. 'Go home, Mia. Sort this out another time.'

'Nothing to sort out, Will. Jasmine knows my feelings now and she may be running the café with you but that's the extent of how much I want her involved in my life.'

'Suits me,' Jasmine snapped, and with that stormed to her bedroom and slammed the door so hard Mia could feel the vibrations underfoot.

'Did I hear Daniel's name mentioned?' Will was more awake now and filled a glass of water at the tap. He glugged it down and turned to his sister.

'Stay out of it, Will.' She headed for the door. 'You've both been away from the bay and I've been quite happy. You're back five minutes and all hell breaks loose. What does that tell you? And as for the handover, work out how to run the café on your own or email Mum or Dad. I'm done helping. I've got my own life and I like it. What you do with yours is your choice.'

She matched Jasmine's slam when she left the apartment, but she lingered long enough to check the glass in the frame of the door after the almighty bang to ensure she hadn't broken it.

*

'I feel mean not doing a handover,' said Mia. She was sitting opposite her best friend Tess in a café in the heart of the city.

'Like you said, they're old enough to go it alone.'

'Why do I sense a 'but'?'

Tess tore off another chunk of her blueberry muffin. 'There's no 'but'.'

'Oh, come on, I've known you long enough to know when you're holding back.'

'Can I ask why you kept the café up and running in the first place?'

'What do you mean?'

'What were your reasons behind it?' Tess stirred her cappuccino. 'Did you want to take over one day? Did you want to make it a success so it's there when your parents get back? Were you trying to prove you're better at this stuff than Will or Jasmine?' She held up a hand. 'I'm not having a go at you. I'm trying to work out what you were thinking.'

Mia sighed and scooped the froth from the top of her own cappuccino. 'I don't want the business; I never did.'

'Right, that's a start.'

Mia thought some more. 'I don't think Jasmine is the right person for it either. Will could be, but not her.'

'And why not?'

'She's always been flighty, never stuck to one thing. She's always been the one we've looked after, Will and I, bailing her out of one scrape after another.' Tess had already heard many a saga when Jasmine was younger, especially in her teen years, and her older brother and sister had sorted out various predicaments: the time she'd gone to a party she'd been forbidden to attend down by the Yarra River and called Will after someone had spiked her drink; when she'd been stranded in the city without the money for a taxi home because she'd spent it all at a restaurant with her friends – Mia had rescued her that time and given her a huge lecture all the way home; and the time Jasmine was bridesmaid for a school friend and had fooled around with the groomsman and ripped her beautiful sky-blue silk dress before the official photographs had even been taken. Mia had been there in an instant with her sewing kit, her thoughts more on the bride who wanted this day to be perfect than her little sister who had screwed up yet again.

'Mia, you know I'm your friend and I'm on your side.'

'But…'

'Do you ever wonder whether Jasmine really needed you every single time?'

'Of course she did.'

Tess thought for a moment. 'How did Jasmine get from the airport to Primrose Bay when she arrived?'

'I picked her up, you know I did.'

'And how did Will get to the bay?'

'He got a taxi of course.'

'Did you ask Jasmine if she *wanted* a lift, or did you insist on picking her up?' Tess shrugged. 'Look, she's not my sister, but I do know you very well. I know you're a worrier and you'll do anything for anyone.' She gave her friend a kind smile. 'Perhaps Jasmine never stood on her own two feet because she was never allowed to…or never forced to.'

Was she right? Did they assume Jasmine was incapable and did they make it worse by rushing to her aid every time?

Tess finished her muffin. 'How's the other sibling?'

'Will?'

Tess nodded, her mouth full.

You'd know, she thought, but she made a conscious effort not to spoil their conversation with an accusation. 'He's fine. Much easier to handle than Jasmine.'

'And do you think he could run the café?'

'It's certainly what our Grandma Annetta always hinted at. She spoiled him all the time. Will this, Will that. Like neither of us was ever as good as he was. Maybe she had old-fashioned views and wanted him to be the man of the house so all we were good for was playing and being good little girls. But I don't think Will even wants the place.'

'Do you think he'll move back to New York?'

'I really don't know. We're not close, not like we were once upon a time, before Daniel.' Tess had been Mia's lifeline back then, when her life was falling apart. 'The café is special to all of us, our whole family, but I can't see Will running it – his heart wouldn't be in it. When I started my own business I worked my butt off —'

'I know.' Tess smiled. 'I barely saw you and when I did you talked about it non-stop.'

'I had to though, don't you see? To get a business off the ground you have to make it your life.' She'd worked night and day promoting, advertising, preparing packaging, designing menus, networking, and she'd been exhausted but had revelled in the excitement of *her* business. She wanted to make it a success and she swore her drive and passion was what had made it so.

'Did your parents intend to leave it to the three of you eventually?' Tess asked.

'I don't think they'd thought that far ahead. Over the years my family doesn't seem to have done much forward planning at all. It's been the busy here and now – so much so that Mum and Dad reached breaking point and left. Without direction, it all fell apart.'

Tess thought for a moment. 'Why do you think Will is back in the bay if he isn't interested in the café?'

'As much as the café has never been in his heart, family has. Even when he pushes me away, or Jasmine, even our parents, he was always the golden boy. Grandma Annetta doted on him and when he went off to New York she gave him her blessing. I don't think she did the same for Jasmine when she went to London, or for me when I announced I was pregnant. She's always held something back with us, given her all to Will. I think some of her attitudes have rubbed off on him. And the café, although not his passion, has memories. I think that deep down he believes the café being in one piece when Mum and Dad return will help them get back together.'

'It's very loyal.'

Mia shrugged. 'I think sometimes he wishes he'd stayed in New York.' She told Tess about how he and Daniel had come face to face and there was tension between them still.

'You'd think they would've both moved on,' said Tess.

'I think too much was said back then, too much nastiness, and neither of them knows how to let it go.'

After they'd finished their coffees they walked along the banks of the Yarra. Mia loved it down here next to the water, boats chugging past or rowers out to enjoy the summer's day, caps pulled down to cover part of their face, sunglasses firmly in place as their craft glided through the water.

'I think you need to go home and talk to them both, Mia,' said Tess as they moved out the way of a cyclist. 'Especially Jasmine. You told me all about Lexi and I really think she's just trying to put her niece's best interests first.'

'You think I should be glad they're friends?'

Tess pulled a band from around her wrist and gathered her long blonde hair up into a ponytail, relief from the heat of the day. 'I think you should take a step back.'

Mia pulled her friend's arm so they came to a stop. 'Do you think I'm jealous of their friendship?'

Tess pulled a face that gave Mia her answer. 'It's only natural. For so long it's been you and Lexi on your own and up until her early teens you were best friends, closer than even you and I were, in a different way. You have an incredible bond but Lexi is now at an age where she's forming new relationships, new friendships.'

'Lexi's hiding something from me, I know it,' said Mia. 'She was so upset the other night and ended up with Jasmine, most likely telling her everything. It kills me not to know what's going on in my own daughter's life.'

Tess put an arm around her friend's shoulders. 'I know it does, Mia. But you have to let her find her own way a little bit. I don't have kids but I'm sure it's the best thing in the long run. And isn't it better she has your sister to turn to than some unknown person who could be a really terrible influence?'

'You're right.' Fear of the unknown was always what had undone Mia.

'Of course I am. So you'll talk to Jasmine about all this?'

Mia nodded. 'When I get home I'll talk to her and sort this out once and for all.' It was the only way she could see herself not being ostracised from her own daughter's life.

Chapter Sixteen
Will

'I'm not sure about this.' Tess was harnessed up and standing at the foot of one of the climbing walls. With Will belaying, they'd gone for one of the more challenging climbs.

'You don't trust me?' Will asked, and even he detected the flirt in his voice. He'd been kidding himself that this was friendship and nothing more, because the sparks flying off both of them as the chemistry mixed told him it was so much more. He pushed the word 'hypocrite' from his head and recollected himself. 'I've belayed hundreds of times before, Tess. It's all safe.'

'I know I'm being paranoid. I didn't realise I'd be this nervous.' Tess covered her face with her hands, shielding those swimming-pool-blue eyes and apple cheeks. All he could see were the heart-shaped lips he'd thought about kissing a million times. She took a deep breath. 'Let's do this.'

They locked eyes. 'That's the girl.' He watched her tighten the buckles to adjust the leg loops on her harness; he tried to calm any physical reaction as he checked her harness was on properly, at her request. Every time he stepped closer to her he swore those pheromones leapt out the top of her head and made straight for him.

Will clipped his carabiner to the ropes and when Tess stepped forward he clipped hers there too, and for a moment their bodies were so close he could feel her breath against the skin of his arms. 'Ready?' He swallowed hard when she looked up into his eyes.

Tess nodded. 'Ready. Just don't let me fall.'

'I promise I won't.' He cleared his throat and turned technical instead of sounding like a love-struck teenager or a sap out of one of those cheesy romance novels. 'My job is to take the slack, hold you if you slip off any of the footholds, and safely lower you down at the end. I promise to do all those things. Scout's honour.' He locked his thumb and little finger on his right hand against his palm and held up the three fingers in the middle, pointing them to his temple.

'Were you ever a boy scout?'

He shrugged. 'Not the point.'

She grinned and shook her head. She put her hands on the farthest footholds she could reach and her right foot on the foothold half a metre up the wall, and began climbing. Will pulled the live rope every time it went slack as Tess progressed up the wall scattered with the colourful footholds and he kept hold of the dead rope at all times. The first time someone else had belayed for him he'd been nervous too but after a while you knew to trust the person looking out for you. It was the same on any climb, whether it was in an inside climbing gym or out there in the Colorado mountains.

Tess looked down at him once and when he smiled up at her she carried on right to the top. He heard a 'woohoo' and then she held up one thumb to signal she was ready to come down. She did as she'd been trained to do, leant back and bounced her feet against the wall as Will released the rope slowly, bit by bit, to lower her back to safety.

'That was fantastic!' Tess was beaming. 'I was so nervous! Can I go again?'

'The same wall?'

She shrugged. 'Yep. A few more times and then I'll move on to another.'

'Off you go.'

As Tess climbed and Will belayed he wondered what Mia would have to say if she saw them now. He knew Tess hadn't mentioned anything to his sister because he'd asked her when they'd arrived at the climbing gym. And he'd already seen Mia lay into Jasmine and really didn't want to be on the receiving end of one of her tirades. There was enough tension in the café and he didn't want to add to it, especially now Mia was refusing to do any sort of handover as though she enjoyed holding the cards and wanted to watch them squirm.

He thought about his friendship with Daniel and how it had suffered when his best mate had become involved with his sister. He'd seen red then. He had been livid that Mia was taking away a part of him, because all through his life he'd had to share everything with his sisters. He'd stayed in a lot when his mates had had the freedom to go out – the café was so busy his parents had relied on him to babysit or 'keep an eye' on his sisters and he'd resented them for that. He was angry at Daniel for having sex with his sister full stop – there were some things you just didn't do as a friend and that was one of them – so how would Mia react to this?

'Will!' Tess was at the top again, frantically giving him the thumbs up to come down. How long had she been up there while he daydreamed?

He fed the rope through as she gently progressed back down to ground level.

'You were off with the fairies.' She was out of breath now, having done one climb after another in quick succession. Tiny beads of sweat had formed on her chest just below her collarbone.

‘Sorry about that.’ He unclipped them both from the set of ropes so they could tackle another wall, a higher one this time.

‘I’m not sure I’m ready.’ She looked up at the wall Will had led her to. ‘It’s a bit high.’

‘Don’t know until you try,’ he said, already clipping on his carabiner and hers.

‘You’re a persistent guy, Will Marcello.’

His lips twisted into a smile. ‘I have my uses.’

He wasn’t sure but he thought she’d blushed before she turned to make the climb, and he did his best not to watch her butt as she climbed further and further up the wall, his eyes on her the whole time.

Tess was truly exhausted after she managed to do the wall no fewer than five times, making it right to the very top on her last attempt. And after they’d changed out of their gear they walked down to Southbank and to Ponyfish Island, the floating bar beneath the pedestrian bridge.

‘Now you know you can trust me.’ Will pocketed his change after buying two beers and they sat on stools overlooking the water with the city skyline lit up behind them.

‘I’m still in one piece,’ said Tess with a raise of the eyebrows. ‘You should’ve climbed for longer yourself, I wouldn’t have minded.’

There wasn’t much that got in his way when there was a wall to climb, whether rock or ice, but this girl had and he didn’t mind a bit. He’d wanted to finish up and go for a drink, get to know her more, so he’d climbed a handful of times with Tess belaying and that had been it. ‘I’ll be there with Leo again soon enough.’

‘Do you lead climb?’ she asked.

'I do.' And I concentrate far more than you caught me doing tonight, he thought to himself. 'There are twenty-something walls I think, up to sixteen metres, so by the end of a session I'm spent.'

She sipped her beer, no trace of the lipstick she'd worn when he'd first seen her that day in Degraves Street. 'Tell me some more about ice climbing.' She turned on her stool so she was facing him.

'There's nothing like it.' His mind went back to New York, to his escapes to Colorado, and he told her all about his first-ever ice climb – the fear, the exhilaration.

'I don't think I'd be very good in the cold.'

'It's pretty damn freezing,' he agreed. 'Sometimes it feels as though you'll lose your fingers it's that cold, but then you're at the top and the scenery is spectacular; the adrenalin that got you there gives way to euphoria.'

When they fell quiet, Tess asked him how things were going in the café.

'As well as can be expected.'

'I wondered whether it was better with only two of you in charge now.'

So Mia had already told her she'd jumped ship. 'Actually, Jasmine is doing better than I ever thought she would. She keeps surprising me.'

'In what way?'

'I was shocked she went to London, let alone managed to find work there and a place to live. And her physical transformation is nothing short of amazing.'

'She's lost a lot of weight, I hear.'

He pulled a face. 'I knew how unhappy she was in the bay. I should've asked her about it then.'

'Maybe. I've been talking about her with Mia.'

'Jasmine is not Mia's favourite person right now, what with her friendship with Lexi.'

'I think Mia will try to talk to her.'

'Really?'

Tess smiled. 'We had a good chat yesterday and I think for Mia it's been hard having you both back. It's not that she doesn't want either of you here – she phoned because she needed her brother and sister, needed them to be a part of what's going on – but she also knows she worries too much. She takes the weight of the world on her shoulders, tries to sort out everyone else's problems. And when you three clash, it makes that task very hard.'

Will pulled at the label on his beer bottle.

'She mentioned Daniel.' Tess held her hands up in defence before Will could speak. 'All she said was that too much has gone on between you both and neither of you seems to know how to move on.'

'So she wants us to kiss and make up?' As defensive as he was, sometimes even he was unsure who he was really angry with after all these years, or even why. But every time he saw Daniel he couldn't take the leap to resurrect anything.

'Anyway, enough about my sisters and me,' Will swiftly changed the subject. 'It's too nice a night to talk about all my sad little problems.'

Tess's giggle was music to his ears. 'What do you want to talk about instead?'

He locked his gaze with hers. 'You.'

The breeze lifted the blonde ringlets she'd freed from her hairband. When he'd seen her years ago, in her early twenties and nothing more than a friend of Mia's, she'd been unsure of herself, almost as though she hadn't quite let go of those teen years yet. But now her inner confidence exuded sex appeal. And that spelled trouble.

They talked about her family, her life in Sydney since she'd moved away, the bay, and her job as the manager of a travel agency.

'You must travel a fair bit yourself,' said Will.

'I've done a lot of Asia travel – Singapore, Malaysia, India, Vietnam, Sri Lanka…oh, and the Maldives. But I haven't done much of Europe or the Americas.'

'Have you done any?'

'I've been to Scotland – for a wedding – England, Belgium, Spain, and Vancouver. It's having the time really. I get a huge discount from work, but if I go somewhere I'd like to do it properly, you know. Experience everything – its culture, the people – more than I think I could take in in a few weeks.'

'I know what you mean. A quick visit to New York is nothing like living there. Living in a country gives you access to all the hidden parts tourists never discover, means you can revisit places over and over again and their familiarity becomes a part of you – it gives you a sense of belonging.'

'Exactly.' She rested her chin on a scrunched-up fist, her elbow on the bar as she looked at Will. 'Do you think Mia would be angry if she knew about us meeting up like this?'

He blew out his cheeks and shook his head. 'I think she would, yes. Did you mention anything?'

'No, I couldn't. She was ranting about Jasmine and then you and Daniel, and she needed a friend. She didn't need me to add to the upset.'

Will reached for Tess's other hand then, which had dropped away from the discarded beer bottle. He covered her fingers with his own and they both looked at their skin, suddenly making contact. 'You know we should tell her sooner rather than later,' he said. 'That's if you want to see me again.'

Sheepishly, she nodded. 'I do.' She squeezed his fingers in her own. 'She won't thank us for keeping this from her.'

'I feel like a hypocrite.'

'After Daniel?'

He nodded.

'I don't think you are. She was eighteen when they got it together and he got her pregnant pretty quickly. Sorry,' she added when his face fell, 'but he did. And at the time, a guy three years older was a big deal. It's nothing now we're all older and Mia is no longer just your little sister. She's a woman with her own business. She's a mum.'

'She's certainly changed.'

'Since you went to New York?'

He shook his head. 'Not just that. Since she had Lexi. I could barely be near either of them when Lexi was little, I was too angry with Mia and Daniel, and as much as I knew I was being ridiculous, I never wanted to back down. As Lexi got older she blossomed into this impossibly cute toddler and Mia took control in a way I'd never seen and I started to admire her and how adept she was at taking control of her life.'

'Did you ever tell her any of this?'

'What do you think?' He returned her smile. 'Siblings rile each other, rub each other up the wrong way. They rarely give one another compliments.'

Tess shifted forward on her stool. 'I think you probably regret that you didn't. I don't know what's wrong with you Marcellos, you're all so great individually but thrown together it's like a pack of unexploded fireworks and we all need to run for cover.'

‘Must be the Italian influence from Dad’s side.’ Will laughed but only for a moment until he realised he was still holding Tess’s hand and their faces were inches apart.

‘We should talk to Mia,’ Tess whispered.

‘We will,’ he whispered back, and his hand reached up to those blonde ringlets, held the back of her neck, and he leant forward until his lips met hers. The kiss was tender, soft, but those fireworks she’d mentioned were going off in the night sky all around them.

When they pulled apart he knew there was one person he had to tell before this went any further.

He couldn’t afford for anything else to come between their family.

Chapter Seventeen
Mia

'I can't believe you got me the job.' Mia grinned over at Leo, who was standing in the doorway of the picnic place. He'd come over to give her the good news in person. The crew making a new show – some dating programme with a twist that was under wraps for now – wanted picnics for the set. Out in the country at a big old homestead in the Yarra Valley, she would be required to provide picnics for twenty people on each of the consecutive five days she'd scored the contract for, and, even better, three well-known magazines had agreed to do write-ups.

'I said I knew someone,' said Leo, looking all handsome, his blond hair shimmering in the sunlight, his shades nestled in the top as he leant on the doorjamb and chatted to Mia. 'I also said I'd only arrange it if they assured me they'd feature your business in the magazine too.'

Mia stopped mid-roll of prawn tempura Californian rolls, the bamboo rolling mat poised beneath her fingers. 'You're kidding.'

Leo shook his head, grin firmly in place. 'This will be great for business.'

'It certainly will.' She finished rolling and wiped her hands on her apron. To have her business mentioned in magazines was publicity she could only dream of with her limited advertising budget right now. 'Leo, I don't know how to possibly thank you. This is incredible.'

'I've told them your picnics are amazing – based on the minimal amount I saw of them at the rowing sheds that day – so all you need to do is prove me right.'

‘I’ll do my best.’ She’d have to get planning. The event wasn’t for a couple of months yet but she didn’t want it to creep up on her. She wanted to know exactly what she was doing. This would call for an exquisite menu, new hand-sewn napkins, perhaps a few new picnic hampers. If she was going to appear in national media, she wanted everything to be perfect.

Deep breath, Mia. Deep breath.

‘Are you okay?’ Leo moved towards her.

Mia waved a hand in front of her face. ‘I’m fine. Just a little overwhelmed. But be assured, I can do this.’

He reached out and when his hand met her upper arm she calmed beneath his touch. ‘You can definitely do this. I wouldn’t have recommended you otherwise.’ She held his gaze until he said, ‘Here, check out these photos of the homestead.’ He handed her his phone from his back pocket and scrolled through images.

‘It’s gorgeous, a real getaway location.’ She marvelled at the sprawling accommodation that looked like the ultimate escape, the place to really get away from it all and forget your troubles.

When the oven timer pinged Mia stopped dreaming and took out a tray of falafel balls she’d made earlier.

‘They look and smell good.’ Leo moved closer and Mia did her best not to get flustered and drop the entire tray before she pushed it onto the work surface. Being attracted to a friend of her brother’s was not good news. Not good at all.

She put a falafel onto a piece of kitchen towel. ‘Here, you can taste test for me.’

Leo blew on the morsel until he decided it was cool enough and tentatively took a bite. ‘I wouldn’t turn your back if I were you,’ he said. ‘These will be gone in seconds. They’re damn good.’

Mia grinned and inspected the rest of the falafels. They were golden brown, dry to the touch but springy when she pressed gently on the top with her fingers. 'I'm serving them with pitta pockets,' she told Leo, 'so the kids at the picnic will have a great time filling the pitta with the falafel, tzatziki and strips of cucumber.'

'It's a kids' picnic?'

'It's an eightieth birthday so guests of all ages – grandparents, parents, kids – with eighteen people in total so I'll make three picnics all together, each serving six.' She took out a few cucumbers from the fridge. 'Sometimes it's a bit like feeding the five thousand.'

'You look like you enjoy it.'

She wished he wasn't staring so intently at her right now but she was glad of the task in front of her.

Leo and Mia giggled their way through the next half an hour as Mia sliced, peeled and chopped, and put falafel into Tupperware, wrapped wedges of brie in cling film, filled pots with red onion chutney and mixed up a basic lemon dressing to accompany the salad. By the time she was ready to load the eskies, Leo had offered to help.

'It's really not necessary,' said Mia. 'I have a system.'

'What, you put one esky on your back, one on your head and the other under your arm?'

She smiled. 'No, I park up as close as I can – in this case as close as I can get to the beach – and then I get someone or a few people from the party in question and they help me.'

'Mia, use me. I'm here, I'm ready and if there's any issues parking at least I can unload for you until you find a space somewhere. It saves traipsing all the way from wherever you end up leaving your car.'

'Don't you work?' She had one more attempt at keeping some distance between herself and her brother's friend.

'I'm on a late shift today so it'll be hours before I start.'

She met his gaze. 'Well thanks, I appreciate the help.'

The question was, would Will appreciate the interaction if he saw them?

Out at her car, which was parked in front of her business premises, Mia put the back seats down. Sometimes she wondered why she didn't just leave them that way given how many times she had to do this.

'Right, what's first?' Leo was poised, hands rubbing together, ready to do whatever was asked of him. Nice guy. Shame he knew her brother.

'First, we'll load up the four eskies. Oh damn—'

'Problem?'

'I haven't put the bags of ice in the top yet.'

'You'll need those. It's roasting out here today.'

'You wait here, if that's okay, with the car and the eskies and I'll grab the bags of ice. They're in the huge chest freezer in the kitchen at the café – couldn't fit them in my tiny freezer – won't be a sec.' She ran off before he could suggest helping.

'I'm here to collect my bags of ice,' she told Will, who was taking payment at the front counter. She smiled warmly at Monica and then disappeared into the kitchen and opened up the chest freezer.

He finished up serving and followed her. 'You're not here to tell us how the place runs then?' His voice had an edge. 'Of course not, because that would make this too easy.'

'Not now, Will.' She pulled out each of the three bags of ice. 'I've got my own business to run.'

'I know, you've told me enough times.'

Two bags slipped from her grasp, to the floor, and she picked them up again.

'Don't you think you're being unreasonable?' Will continued as she gripped hold of the bags and made her way through the café again.

'I'll do some kind of handover, Will. Just not now.'

'Tonight then,' he insisted.

'Okay. Oh, no, not tonight…' This time she rested the bags on the ground voluntarily. They weren't the lightest of things. 'I'm seeing Tess. She's coming over and we're off to the movies.'

'What time?'

'What?' She didn't bother picking the bags up yet. They were too heavy to hold while she stood here talking.

'What time is she coming over?'

'Why do you care?'

'Then I'll know what time you can spare us five minutes of your precious time, won't I?'

'She's coming at seven o'clock. The movie starts at nine. If the café is quiet around six, we'll do it then. Okay?' She gritted her teeth this time and picked up the bags of ice but in her haste dropped one on her toe. 'F—'

'Don't say it, it's not ladylike. Come on.' Without giving her a chance to stop him, Will lifted up the bags with ease, opened the front door and walked towards her car. 'I'm not sure you should've left the picnics on the pavement for anyone to help themselves to.' His laughter stopped when he saw Leo resting on the base of the car boot. With the boot open, he hadn't initially seen him.

'Hey there.' Leo put his phone back in his pocket.

'What are you doing here?'

'I'm helping out your sister.'

'Why?'

Leo looked taken aback at the way the question had been asked. 'I was around, don't have to work until later, so it would've been rude not to.'

Mia kept her head down and lifted the first esky into the boot before placing the bag of ice inside the top. She couldn't look at her brother right now but he seemed to soften when Leo, ignoring any tension, told him about the job with the TV show he'd managed to get for Mia.

'She'll work on location and have a great time.' Leo smiled in her direction and Mia caught the grin. She couldn't help smiling back. 'It'll be full on but the publicity alone will be worth it. You should be proud of your sister.'

Mia wished Leo would stop now. He'd already talked her up so maybe it was time to give it a rest. He lifted the other two eskies into the boot for her while she disappeared back in to the picnic company for the three wicker hampers she'd already filled with cutlery, hand-sewn napkins, fresh flowers and crockery. Before she braved the open air again she watched Leo and Will through the small window at the front of her business premises. They had started laughing about something or other, which was odd. She'd assumed Will would be fuming. It was quite obvious there was an undercurrent of attraction between her and Leo – even the least observant of people would be able to see that – but her brother didn't seem in the slightest bit bothered.

Why not?

She took the hampers outside one at a time and then locked the door to the premises behind her. 'Ready,' she said to Leo as she hopped in the driver's side.'

In the corner of her eye she'd noticed the men shake hands and when Leo climbed in beside her she was surprised when Will appeared at her window, resting one arm on the roof of the car as he leant in to talk to her.

'I'll see you tonight then,' he said, 'and we can go over some of the inner workings of the café.' And with that he tapped the top of the car, nodded to Leo and practically skipped back in to the café.

Will being nice to her was oddly unsettling.

'Ready?' Leo asked.

Mia shook herself to attention. She'd been staring at the closed door of the café a moment too long. She did a U-turn when the coast was clear and headed along Beach Road through Brighton, Elwood, St Kilda and Albert Park. She chatted with Leo about some of the bigger jobs he'd had in his career as a cameraman. He'd covered major sporting events that a lot of guys would give their grandma away for if it meant they got to attend; he'd been at the court-house when big cases were the talk of Melbourne. He thrived on the variety and Mia wished they were driving on further so they could keep chatting.

'Here we are.' Luckily for her there was ample space to pull up near the playground area. The family party had agreed to meet on the beach just down from here so Mia called to say they had arrived and when two strapping teenage lads came to help carry everything down to the sand, Leo organised everyone and between them they took everything in one go.

On the sand Mia was glad for the gentle sea breeze to ease the summer temperature and was even happier that it wasn't a strong wind that would blow sand into all this lovely food. She laid out blankets and weighted the edges down with polished rocks. She opened up hampers and unloaded the eskies into each – she'd slotted a menu in to each too so the guests knew what to expect – and then she shut the tops to keep the sand out and the coolness from the ice blocks in until the party was ready to eat.

Leo and Mia took the eskies and walked back the way they'd come and when they stepped off the sand they turned to watch the party. The family were gathered around the hampers like big kids unable to wait a moment longer. The star of the show, eighty-year-old John, looked enraptured having all his loved ones around him, never mind the food. Mia stood and stared.

'Are you okay?' Leo placed a hand on Mia's arm and she looked down at it against her golden skin.

'I'm fine. It's just…' She pointed to the family as their whoops of joy and laughter filled the air. 'I don't remember ever being like that.'

They walked back towards the car and dumped the eskies in the boot.

'Hang on,' said Leo. 'Let's not go yet. Sit down for a while.' He nodded over to a palm tree with welcoming shade beneath and Mia followed him. When she'd sat down he said, 'Do you mean it?'

'Mean what?'

'That you were never like that as a family. I find that hard to believe.'

'That's because you're not a Marcello.' She brushed the cotton of her ruby-red shorts to rid them of sand that was lurking in one of the creases.

'You must remember happy times, surely.'

Mia leant her back and her head against the trunk of the tree and took her sunglasses off. 'Of course I do. We were always cared for, never wanted for anything, but what I also remember is that we never had enough time.'

'Enough time for family?'

'Mum and Dad worked so hard and of course we are all grateful for that. It's what fed us, clothed us, put us through school. And it taught us the work ethic. I knew before I started my picnic business that it would be bloody hard work and it was, still is. I think I'm more focused because I learnt from them.'

'Why do I sense there's a 'but' coming?'

'I have Daniel, my ex, so I'm not a single mother – far from it, in fact. But one of the things I was determined to do with Lexi was have her experience the kind of home life that I never had. We were always with our grandma and when Will was old enough he looked after Jasmine and me. My parents worked seven days a week, long hours too. The café became their lives, they let it take over. I kept wishing for them to get old so they wouldn't be able to stand up for so long, so they'd be forced to hire extra help, so I'd finally get them at home and we could be a family.

'Even in the winter, out of season, the café was steadily busy. The businesses who operate all year round want their coffees, their snacks from somewhere and because the café's close enough to the main street of the bay, we never ever shut.' Mia nodded back towards the beach. 'We never packed up the car and went off to the beach all together like that. We went out, of course, but either it was rushed as they couldn't leave the café or else Mum or Dad had stayed behind to run the business.'

When Leo nodded Mia said, 'Oh would you listen to me, going on and on.' She closed her eyes. Even in the shade the air was warm against her face. 'Bet you wish you hadn't offered to help now.'

'I don't mind, not at all. But I am going to have to go.'

She opened her eyes. 'That's a shame.' Designer stubble grazed his chin and the sides of his face, his hazel eyes didn't leave hers and her breath caught as they looked at one another.

He stood up and held out a hand to help her to her feet. 'Come on, take me back and I'll pick up my car. I'll be late for work at this rate.'

Mia let him help her to standing. Still beneath the palm tree, her eyes were level with his collarbone and when she looked up he was staring down at her. His face inched closer towards hers and she could feel the heat from his skin.

What was she doing? She pulled away and put her sunglasses firmly back in place. 'We'd better get going, don't want you to be late.' And with that she scurried towards the car.

*

Mia thought about Leo all afternoon and kept repeating over and over in her mind that he was a no-go zone. She couldn't do it again. This family was fragile enough, but no matter how dysfunctional they were, this family was the only one she had.

She busied herself with another birthday picnic, this time for two people, so easy and quick for her to transport to St Kilda at four o'clock, and then when she saw Jasmine and Will working in the café as Monica left for the day, she went next door to see them. Maybe she could do a handover talk now. It was one way of sounding out Will's reaction to the run-in with her and Leo, and it was better than worrying about it over and over – wondering whether he was angry and the smiles and amiability earlier had all been an act so Leo wouldn't think he was a complete arsehole. And besides, she'd talked about this with Tess. She needed to make amends with Jasmine because deep down, Mia knew that it was better and safer for Lexi to confide in a member of her family than a stranger she knew nothing about.

'So this TV gig sounds like a winner,' said Will, surprising Mia again with his friendliness.

She instantly bristled and wondered what his hidden agenda might be. 'It's a good opportunity.'

'Nice of Leo to put a word in for you.'

She watched him and tried to gauge his temperament but if he was annoyed, his anger must be running as an undercurrent because she couldn't see it on the surface.

When Jasmine walked in she avoided Mia's gaze. She immediately put on an apron and got on with serving the next customer. Mia watched her empty the used coffee grounds into the knock-out drawer then wipe out the portafilter basket. She filled it with fresh coffee grounds and followed all the procedures she'd been a novice at just a few days ago. Jasmine looked the part; she even seemed to be enjoying it. Had Mia underestimated her sister?

When Jasmine had served her latest customer and the café rush lulled, Mia took her brother and sister through some of the things her parents had discussed with her. She handed them a laminated sheet that listed all the jobs to do every morning, with timings for each. The list wasn't set in stone but it would help them to get to grips with the running of the café. Mia knew her parents usually just went with the flow but she'd insisted they take her through the daily routine, piece by piece, so she could build up a picture in her mind. It was the only way the café would be able to survive in their absence.

'Sometimes you might not stick to the list I have here,' she explained to Will and Jasmine after Will had served a banana muffin to a teenager and sold a can of lemonade to another. 'But it's a guide. It'll stop you forgetting to make something, it'll help you to be organised. And this other list here,' she handed Will the piece of paper, 'this is a general overview of the busiest times so you can monitor staffing. Both of you will need some time to yourselves, you can't work twenty-four seven, but at least this will show you when it's the best time to aim to take a break. You can work out a better schedule with Monica rather than calling her up at the last minute because you're rushed off your feet.'

'Would you mind showing me some things on the computer?' Jasmine asked. 'I'm not sure about the spreadsheets or the stock reordering. I'm sure I'll pick it up but it'd be good to have some tips.'

'Sure.' Mia looked at Will. 'Does that apply to both of you?'

Will hesitated and then surprised Mia when he said, 'I'll leave it up to Jasmine. I'm happy for you to teach her and she can pass the information on.'

Clearly Jasmine was taken aback too, going by the look she gave both her brother and her sister.

When Monica walked in Mia took Jasmine upstairs to go through the computer side of things that her parents had shown her. Jasmine made two cups of tea as Mia fired up the laptop and opened the spreadsheets, and over a cuppa and a Tim Tam biscuit, Mia taught Jasmine everything she'd been told about the business.

Tea finished, Mia said, 'And that's it. Mum and Dad took me through as much as possible – I wasn't letting them go anywhere unless they did.'

'You always did worry.' Jasmine smiled at her older sister.

'Well in this case I think it was necessary. And things seem to be going well now.' She took the empty cups and plates over to the sink and put them on the draining board. ‘You and Will seem to both be on the same page – you haven’t scratched his eyes out yet.’

‘As if I would!’ Jasmine feigned innocence. ‘I love my older brother.’

‘I know you do.’ More seriously Mia said, ‘I wanted to apologise about going off at you about Lexi.’

‘Really?’

Mia sat back down at the table opposite her sister. ‘Yes, really. I overreacted and I know it’s good she has someone to turn to. I can’t pretend I’m happy when she keeps secrets from me, but I suppose I should be grateful she has another adult to confide in.’

‘I’d never lead her astray, Mia.’ Jasmine tugged at the ends of her hair that had swung over her shoulder and down her chest. ‘We’re so close in age that she’s like a friend, but I’ve never forgotten that I’m her auntie and I have a responsibility.’

Mia nodded her appreciation. ‘Is she okay though?’ She waved a hand before Jasmine could answer. ‘I’m not asking you to tell me what the two of you talk about, I just want to know if I should be worried.’

‘She has concerns but they’re no worse than those of any other girl her age,’ Jasmine assured her. ‘She’s a lovely girl – you should be proud of her.’

‘I am.’

‘And believe me when I say there’s nothing going on between me and Daniel.’

Mia looked to Jasmine.

‘Honestly, Mia. We’re friends, he’s really easy to talk to. Like Lexi, sometimes I need that too.’

Mia wondered how she’d grown up with a sister who’d become her daughter’s confidante and her ex’s friend yet was so far away from her emotionally that they may as well be strangers.

'Eurgh,' said Jasmine. 'Dating Daniel would be like dating my own brother.'

Mia giggled. 'He's not that bad.'

'Not at all – he's very good-looking. I often wondered why you two never lasted, but he's been a part of this family ever since I can remember. Will's friend, then your boyfriend. Oh god, no. It'd be wrong on so many levels for me to be involved with him.'

Mia was relieved to hear the words from her sister and she truly believed her. 'Well I'm glad we've cleared the air.' Maybe she'd misjudged Jasmine after all, completely overreacted to the friendships she had with the people close to her.

'Me too. And thanks for doing the handover. Will and I were managing okay down in the café but really it was a lot of guesswork and the information you've given us will help us to get more organised.'

'I'm glad.'

Jasmine perched on the edge of the kitchen table, her bottom neatly poised on the wood. Mia still couldn't get over how much weight her sister had lost, how much happier she looked even when they'd been rowing. 'Have you heard from Mum and Dad again?'

Mia shook her head and ran water into the empty cups in the sink. She hadn't had a chance to empty her dishwasher yet. 'They've really gone AWOL.'

'It's almost like they're trying to punish us,' said Jasmine. 'Maybe…'

'Maybe what?'

'Maybe Dad has lost his marbles…you know, like Grandma Annetta. They say Alzheimer's, dementia…well it can run in families, can't it?'

Mia genuinely laughed. 'Sorry, I'm not laughing at the prospect of any of us getting dementia. I'm laughing because I'm pretty sure Mum and Dad still have all their faculties.'

'But they used to be so in love, so together. Their shouting matches came out of passion not hate, and now they're walking away – from everything.'

Mia came and sat next to her sister, a strange sense of calm between them now they'd talked about Daniel and Lexi. 'It completely floored me when they left.'

'Really?'

'What, you think I'm immune to it all?'

'But you've been so organised.'

Mia shrugged. 'That's me. But I'm a worrier too, you know I am. And if something like that blows up in my face the first thing I want to do is find a way to straighten it all out.'

'So does Will. That's why he came home from New York.'

'He's always been responsible.'

'He doesn't want the café long term though.'

'Are you sure? He's the son, after all. And Grandma Annetta never lost sight of all of those traditional values – you know, the man of the family goes out to work and all that. Maybe that's why she never really warmed to Mum. Perhaps she disagreed with Mum putting her whole life into the café.'

'Sometimes I wished she hadn't.' Jasmine spoke tentatively.

'You wish she hadn't focused on the café?'

Jasmine nodded. 'She was always too busy for us. Don't think I'm terrible or selfish, Mia, but I really wish we'd had a more traditional upbringing. It would've been nice to come home to her in our kitchen rather than frantically racing around the café. Grandma Annetta was brilliant but it wasn't the same. Do you think us kids ended up driving her insane?'

Mia couldn't help but giggle. 'She's not insane…and no, we didn't drive her to it. Of course we didn't.'

'It would tip me over the edge, minding three children,' said Jasmine.

Mia turned to her sister. 'You don't see kids in your future?'

'I haven't thought about it much really. I'm only in my twenties. Maybe the thought will kick in when I'm ancient like you, in my thirties.' Her cheeky grin told Mia that although their relationship had almost broken, perhaps they'd found a way out.

Mia checked her watch. She had time to empty the dishwasher before Tess turned up for their evening out, and then at least that was another task done. 'So you're happy with the stuff on the computer I showed you?' She wanted to be sure. Even if she'd more or less told her siblings to get on with it without her, she still worried. 'You don't need me to go over it one more time?'

'Don't stress, I've got it. And if I have any questions I know where to find you.'

Mia stood on tiptoes to put the clean mugs away in the top cupboard. It felt good to be needed, to be the older sister she hadn't really been when Jasmine had taken off to London. They'd chatted every now and then but their relationship had never been a close one.

As Mia stretched and pushed the last cup onto the shelf in the cupboard she glanced out of the window and noticed Tess's car parked down below. She was way too early.

'I'd better get back to the café, or at least help Will to clear up.' Jasmine's voice had Mia turning away from the window. 'I'll run him through everything you showed me. And Mia, thanks. Thanks for trusting in me, thanks for giving me the benefit of the doubt.'

Mia nodded. 'You're welcome.' And she resisted adding anything along the lines of 'Don't let me down.' It didn't need to be said so she would keep quiet for once and maybe her relationship with her sister could start to bloom from this moment on.

Mia hurriedly changed into a cornflower-blue silk top and a fresh pair of jeans, anticipating Tess's knock at the door any minute. But when Tess still hadn't appeared ten minutes later, and Mia had even had a chance to brush her hair and spritz on a bit of perfume, she sent her friend a text. Maybe she'd arrived early and knowing how manic Mia's life was these days, had taken off for a quick walk along the beachfront. But the text came back soon enough to say she was waiting in the café and had got chatting to Will.

Mia closed the window in her bedroom and the one in the kitchen, then locked up and went down the stairs, outside the building and around to the café herself. She gave her best friend an enormous hug when she got there.

'He's not bad at making coffee,' said Tess, with a cappuccino in front of her. She was busy scraping off the froth Will had sprinkled with chocolate powder. 'I was a bit early so I thought I'd give you a chance to get ready.'

With the café quiet, Mia sat with her friend at the table by the window looking out over Beach Road towards the ocean. They chatted about Mia's picnic business and Tess swapped stories about her day, her dreams of doing more of the travelling she was selling to others.

'I'd love to do Europe properly,' said Tess. Her eyes sparkled as she spoke. 'Greece with its whitewashed buildings, go to Provence when the lavender is in full bloom, visit Italy and drink red wine as the sun goes down.'

'You sound like an audio travel brochure.'

Tess giggled. 'I do, don't I?'

They talked some more about Italy and Mia's family roots, her Grandma Annetta's desire to return there some day.

'It must be hard to settle in another country and not yearn for the one that you grew up in.' Tess thanked Will when he took away her empty cup and Mia wasn't sure, but she thought she saw something pass between them. Nothing concrete, but a look: a look that spoke of closeness or an exclusion. She tried not to let it bother her.

When Tess excused herself to go to the bathroom, Mia surreptitiously watched Jasmine working the coffee machine as though she'd been doing it her whole life. Mia smiled inwardly. Perhaps this was what was known as turning a corner, the moment they would collectively begin to move forward. Their parents were…well, wherever they were, they weren't here, and Mia felt sure now that the three siblings could keep the business going until they chose to return.

Ready to leave with Tess, Mia was about to say her goodbyes to Will and Jasmine when the front door to the café burst open and in came Lexi. She was all smiles and holding hands with a boy Mia had never seen before.

'Mum, hi!'

Mia wondered whether her daughter had hoped she'd already be at the movies and that she'd be able to introduce her new boyfriend to her cool uncle and trendy auntie instead of the mother who had, on more than one occasion, been accused of being overprotective.

'This is Harry.' Lexi was still holding this boy's hand.

Mia extended her own hand in greeting. 'It's nice to meet you, Harry.'

Tess rescued Mia from any awkwardness and as she introduced herself and said hello to Lexi, Mia appraised this new person in her daughter's life. He was tall, with curly blond hair cut short at the sides but longer on top, had a suntan that was usually only achieved by living in Queensland or spending an inordinate amount of time on the beach, and she wasn't sure but she thought he had a hole in one ear where a piercing may once have been.

'Mia…earth to Mia.' Tess giggled.

'Sorry, what did you say?'

'We'd better go if we're going to catch the movie.'

'Oh, yes. Well, nice to meet you, Harry.' Mia nodded to him but he was already far too busy being introduced to Jasmine, the cool one. 'Oh damn,' she said to Tess. 'I must have leant up against something on the table. I've got chocolate powder on the bottom of my top. Sorry, I'll just go back out to the kitchen and try to wash it off at the sink.'

Mia left Tess chatting with Lexi, Jasmine and Harry and out in the kitchen she ran the tap and dabbed at the brown patch, used a bit of soap, and the mark lifted out. She'd probably caught it just in time before it stained. She squeezed the material between two sides of a clean tea towel and, feeling much more presentable and glad she didn't have to change – this top was her best smart top that went perfectly with skinny jeans and strappy flat sandals in the same colour – she threw the tea towel in the laundry at the back of the kitchen. Turning round, she accidentally knocked something to the floor.

'Shit!' She looked down to see Jasmine's phone and, picking it up, she prayed the screen was intact. 'Oh, thank god.' The iPhone case had saved the day and the screen looked as good as new. But it was also unlocked. Mia tutted. Not only did it drain the battery, it was irresponsible to leave your phone open to tampering and she'd have to tell Jasmine to be more careful. But instead of putting it back on the bench as she'd intended, Mia's eyes zoomed in on the name at the top of the screen: Lexi.

She looked around her, her heart thumping, because she knew what she was about to do was overstepping the mark. Her fingers hovered because all she wanted to do was swipe her finger in a scrolling motion against the screen and see what kinds of conversations her sister had been having with her daughter.

But she couldn't do it. She put the phone down on the benchtop she'd knocked it from and it was only as she turned to go back to the café and heard Jasmine and Lexi laughing along with Tess and Harry that her curiosity got the better of her. She just wanted to look, to reassure herself that Lexi was ok. That was fine, wasn't it? After all, if it was that secret, Jasmine would've locked her phone.

Mia moved her fingers to scroll up through the conversation and the words she saw made her smile, reassured her even. Lexi told Jasmine, 'I can't wait for you to meet Harry. You'll love him!' The message prior to that was nice too. It was from Jasmine to say she was glad everything had been sorted out and glad she had been there for Lexi. Mia had nothing to worry about. It was basic boy trouble and nothing more that they'd been in cahoots about.

Mia was about to put the phone back when the message above the last one she'd read caught her eye. From Lexi, it said, 'Thank you for coming with me to the doctor. I was so nervous!'

Mia's heart raced. Was her and Daniel's worst fear about to come true? Had Lexi started to feel unwell, was she a diabetic? If she was, it was better to catch it sooner rather than later.

Mia couldn't help herself. She was worried. She scrolled up again to a message that had been sent the day before. She moved up and up through the words until she finally found the one that would tell her why her daughter had been to the doctor, why she'd wanted someone with her for moral support.

Mia dropped the phone onto the worktop with a clatter. What she wanted to do was sling it against the wall, watch it smash into a thousand pieces.

Right now, Mia wanted to buy her sister a plane ticket out of here – back to London, away from the café and the bay, away from Lexi. If Jasmine thought she'd won her over and played the part of the good younger sister, she was sorely mistaken.

This time she'd gone too far.

Chapter Eighteen

Jasmine

'What's up with Mum?' Lexi asked later that evening. Harry had gone home and Jasmine and Lexi had gone up to Mia's apartment after Will volunteered to finish clearing up the café. 'Do you think she's annoyed at me for bringing Harry home?'

'Of course not.' But the thought had crossed Jasmine's mind. She'd thought she had reached a point where she and Mia finally understood one another, but when Mia had left the café earlier that day there was something simmering beneath the surface, something she wasn't sharing with anyone. Even her best friend Tess had looked confused as she'd said goodbye and followed Mia outside to the car.

'I'm sixteen,' Lexi began, 'not that much younger than Mum was when she had me.'

Jasmine smiled at her niece. 'Maybe that's what she's worried about.'

'Do you think so?'

'Probably. But don't worry too much. Harry seems lovely.' She turned to her niece. 'You really like him, don't you?'

'I do.' She let a small smile escape. 'He's different from the other boys my age. Some of them act like idiots but Harry has a softer side. He's in the footy team and swims, and he's one of the lads when he wants to be, but it doesn't stop him having a heart of gold.'

Jasmine hugged her niece. 'It sounds like you're onto a winner there. And I'm sure your mum will come round once she gets to know him.'

‘I hope so.’ Lexi took a can of lemonade from the fridge and cut a wedge of flapjack from the plate on the table. ‘I’d better get on. I’ve got so much study to do and I don’t want to be in any more trouble with Mum than I already am.’

After Lexi left with her snack and her drink to take to the confines of her bedroom, Jasmine wrapped the flapjack Mia must’ve made and although it smelt divine she didn’t break off a chunk for herself. Proud at her determination and strength to resist temptation, she put it inside the cupboard and went to pull her phone out from the back pocket of her jeans – except it wasn’t there. She looked beneath the magazine Lexi had been idly flicking through as they’d chatted, she looked on the ledge by the front door, in the bathroom in case she’d left it there (she was always taking it out her back pocket if she needed to use the toilet because once it had fallen right in when she’d pulled her jeans down).

Damn, it must be back in the café. She called out her goodbyes to Lexi and trotted down the stairs and outside into the evening sunshine, which was milder than earlier but still a stark reminder that the heat wouldn’t take much of a break overnight. She let herself in to the back entrance of the café, which had stairs to access the apartment as well as the café itself. Luckily, Will was still sorting the takings so the café was open.

‘What are you doing back here?’ Will looked up from the safe as he stashed the float in there.

‘You should keep this door locked you know, someone could jump you while you’re holding all that money.’

‘Then how would my annoying little sister get back in when she’d left her phone and her keys behind?’ he quipped, nodding over to both said items.

After they'd locked up and alarmed the café they went upstairs to the apartment.

'No plans tonight?' Will asked. Sometimes she was amazed at how civil they were being.

'No, just the usual TV for me I think. I'm exhausted.'

'I thought you were used to being on your feet at all hours of the day and night.'

She shut the front door to the apartment behind them. 'It must be the emotional involvement with this place.' She was only half joking. 'What about you? Do you have plans?'

'I'm meeting Leo for a drink and a bite to eat in St Kilda. I'll grab a quick shower and then I'll leave you to have the place to yourself.'

Jasmine fixed herself some toast with poached eggs and a side of mushrooms cooked in minimal butter. She added spinach to the side and some grilled tomatoes. It was a quick and easy meal for one and she ate it in front of the TV after Will had left. When she'd scrolled through every television channel, including all the extras from Foxtel, she logged on to Facebook. She didn't use it as much as some of her friends but it was a good way to catch up with what was going on in their busy lives. The whole world seemed to operate at a much faster pace nowadays, or was it just the way she saw it?

Bored with Facebook and in need of a familiar voice, Jasmine made use of her parents' phone line that had a cheap deal for international calls and she phoned the house in London. It was the weekend so she was bound to catch someone for a bit of a natter. It felt weird she was calling a house that wasn't her home anymore, almost unreal, and when Ned answered the phone her face broke into a smile.

'When are you coming back?' he asked in the London accent she'd missed without realising. 'Are you pining after me?' he wanted to know; 'Is the sun shining twenty-four seven?' was his next question.

Jasmine was passed between housemates and chatted for almost an hour, catching up on everything happening in the Northern Hemisphere. If Ned were here in front of her now she'd probably hug him and fall into bed with him for comfort's sake but she knew neither of them thought of the other as their one great love. It was fun while it'd lasted and they'd always be friends but that was it.

'So seriously, when are you coming back?' Ned asked when she'd yawned for the millionth time and told him she'd have to go.

'It's a mess in the café. It won't be running smoothly for quite a while yet.'

'That's not what I asked.'

'Did you rent the room out?' She was worried she'd left them in the lurch and they'd be hard pushed to make up the extra rent even though she'd covered four weeks' worth.

'It's not a problem. My mate Steve is moving in next week.'

Steve was the mate who wore jeans that hung a good ten inches south of his crotch. He was Ned's partner for the PlayStation and someone Jasmine felt sure hadn't had enough daylight since the console was first invented. 'I'm glad you've found someone.'

'You're not coming back, are you?' It was a rhetorical question but one delivered without malice.

'Probably not. At least not for a while.' She still had a tiny niggle at the back of her mind at the dream she'd had for the international business one day. But that dream felt so far off and, right now, the café was all she could think about. Ever since she was a little girl she'd daydreamed about being in charge of it one day, and managing it in her parents' absence was definitely one step closer. 'If I get on to a shipping company in the next few weeks, would you pack up the rest of my things for collection?'

He agreed to help and before they finished the call, Jasmine promised Ned and the others that she'd post photographs of the bay and the café onto Facebook. So far she'd failed to do so but hearing their voices prompted her to get on with it.

She picked up her own phone, which was almost out of charge, and the first thing that hit her was that she'd left it unlocked and in her messages. She was usually careful to close all her apps or it'd drain the power, and she'd lost count of the times Mia had lectured her about putting a password on it, having the screen lock itself after a time delay.

She held her breath as realisation hit.

Lexi's messages were right there in front of her, the screen a perfect display of her idiotic mistake. She knew now that Mia must have seen the texts when she'd gone out to the kitchen to wash the chocolate off her top. She'd seen them, read each one, and that was why she'd been so furious when she'd left the café earlier. It was the only explanation for why Mia had been fine one minute, sitting beside the window watching the ocean, looking over in her direction every now and then as she demonstrated her prowess on the coffee machine, and the next minute, bam. She'd been presented with the shock discovery that her daughter and her sister had been keeping something from her.

Oh this was bad. Really bad. Jasmine knew now that she could kiss goodbye to any relationship they'd salvaged, to any trust that had been built.

In one careless moment, Jasmine knew she'd ruined it all.

Chapter Nineteen
Will

The phone woke Will the following morning after Jasmine agreed she would open up the café with Monica to give him a break. Neither of them wanted to burn out like their parents clearly had and, according to Mia's schedule, Wednesday morning was usually quiet and only took two staff to manage. Luckily for them, Monica was happy to do her share of morning shifts.

'Will Marcello speaking.' He stood in the kitchen and yawned, still half asleep. The sun shone brightly through the window making a play for his retinas and even though he'd been back in Australia for a few weeks now, he still wasn't used to the intensity of it.

A woman from Appleby Lodge was calling on behalf of Grandma Annetta and asked Will if he'd be able to come in today some time.

'She really asked for me?' he probed. 'I'd heard she was refusing all visitors.'

'That's right, she has up until now. But she's lucid enough this morning. She insisted I call you; she even gave me the number.'

'Right.' Will stared down at his bare feet, the cool tiles beneath his skin. 'I'll try to come in today.'

The woman reeled off the best times for him to visit – sooner rather than later was the clear emphasis – and when Will put down the phone he slumped against the doorjamb, one hand rubbing the stubble of his chin. His Grandma hadn't wanted to see anyone for years but now she wanted to see him. That was good news, right? Or was it something else that could come between him and his sisters? They'd always thought of him as the favourite and this latest development could add more fuel to the fire that was almost out for now, but still had embers circulating in the air.

Maybe he should keep quiet, not tell them. He could say he was going for a climb with Leo, or into the city for something. These thoughts and others churned over and over in his head as he ate a bowl of cereal, slurped a morning coffee, took a shower and had a shave. He hadn't seen Grandma Annetta since he'd left the bay and their chats had been infrequent. He stared into the bathroom mirror. Was he really ready to see her now?

Once he was dressed he Googled taxi numbers on his phone but as he did, Tess called. She wanted to arrange another climbing session and he ended up telling her all about his previous phone call. After his relationship with Paige ended this was the closest he'd got to another woman. Some people talked about 'the one that got away,' but he talked about 'the one who broke me.' Things with Paige had been as close to perfect as he'd ever be able to imagine until one day, out of the blue, that was it. It had knocked him sideways, and ever since, he hadn't seen much point in putting in the hard yards with a relationship. He'd wanted the Happy Ever After like his parents had – waltzing around the café after dark when they thought everyone else was well and truly asleep, snatched conversations and private jokes – but when even they had started fighting, long before he moved away to New York, he'd started to wonder why anyone even bothered to fall in love. What was the point when it all turned to shit anyway?

But now, he'd met Tess. And Tess was different. She had a certain something, a quality he couldn't name. But whatever it was, it wrapped all around him and refused to let go. With Tess, he wanted to make the effort.

'Take my car, Will,' Tess insisted. 'A taxi will cost a fortune and it's too short notice for a hire car. My car is sitting on the driveway at my parents' and I'm about to leave and catch the train to work. I'll put the key under the front wheel where nobody can see it.'

'I owe you big time,' he said when she let him get a word in.

'It's my pleasure.'

Even those few words had him grinning from ear to ear. 'I'll be back this afternoon so text me when you're home from work and I'll drive round to you. I could pick you up in the city if you'd like.'

'Nonsense. I'll get the train home. I'm insured for any driver too…you are over twenty-five aren't you?'

'I think we can safely answer yes to that question.'

'That's settled then.' He could hear a smile in her voice. 'And this way I get to see you later.'

'I'd really like that.'

God, he was grinning like an idiot! He put the phone down just before he heard footsteps and the door to the apartment flung open. It was Jasmine, puffed from the stairs. 'Could you help out downstairs?' She tried to get her breath back. 'Mia's schedule is all well and good but we have three mothers' groups in right now and toddlers demanding attention.'

'Sure thing.' He put his dirty dish and cup in the dishwasher.

'Oh. Right. Thanks.' His younger sister pulled a face in confusion at this sudden compliance and Will followed her down to the café.

His enthusiasm to help must've taken her by surprise and there were no arguments as they worked side by side until just after nine thirty, when the café experienced its first lull of the day and he took his chance to leave.

Monica was happy to do a full day in lieu of no shift tomorrow, and he grabbed his wallet and phone and told Jasmine he'd be out for the rest of the day. The best time to visit Grandma Annetta was about eleven o'clock, so he'd have plenty of time to collect the car and make his way to Appleby Lodge. Apparently morning visits were ideal, when residents weren't too tired, when the heat of the day hadn't got to anyone yet. And, to be honest, he wanted to see her as soon as possible now she'd asked for him.

He headed to Tess's parents' place in Brighton and retrieved the car key from in front of the tyre just as Tess had told him. It took a bit of getting used to a different car, especially because the last few times he'd driven it'd been in a left-hand drive on the right-hand side of the road. But once he got used to it and the satnav spewed out its instructions he made his way towards Gembrook, in the foothills of the Dandenong Ranges. Just past the town he turned off and followed a winding road lined with trees until he came to Appleby Lodge.

He gulped as he drove up the sweeping driveway. The woman on the phone had said Grandma Annetta was lucid, she'd begged for him to be contacted. But this still felt odd. She hadn't been in touch for such a long time. He'd written to her when he'd left New York to let her know what he was doing, but even as he'd penned the letter he hadn't expected a response – not after he'd heard she was refusing to see anyone. But he'd written anyway. She was too special to ever stop trying. She'd been there for him ever since he was a little boy and he'd be there for her now.

He parked up under the shade of the tall mountain ash trees and gathered his thoughts. It was a glorious morning with a soft breeze gently swaying the leaves of the branches above so the cool air whispered down onto his shoulders when he stepped out of the car. He wasn't sure what to expect with this care home and as he'd driven here he'd expected a more hospital-like environment, clinical even. But as he opened the double doors at the front and announced his arrival to the receptionist, he got a very different impression.

Appleby Lodge was a grand residence with a sweeping veranda out front equipped with several comfy-looking rocking chairs, side tables and a beautiful view across manicured gardens. The whole place was nestled in amongst the bush and had he not had the help of the satnav he expected he would've struggled to find it.

'She'll be delighted to see you.' Sammy, the same lady he'd spoken to on the telephone, took Will down a long corridor and as he walked his heart pumped as though it wanted to leap from his chest. How could he be nervous? He'd grown up with Grandma Annetta, he had lovely memories. Perhaps it was the fear that she'd forgotten so much of that, and now she wouldn't be the same person. Part of him wanted to run the other way and just remember her how she used to be.

Sammy led him into a lounge decorated in neutral tones. There were round-backed armchairs dotted about. A couple of residents occupied one end – two men, chatting away in hushed voices – and at the other end sat a tiny old lady who was dwarfed by her chair. But he'd know her anywhere. She looked different from how he remembered her, but when she raised her head and his blue eyes locked with those chestnut eyes that had looked at him the same way as a little boy he almost burst into tears. And crying was something Will never did.

Sammy stepped forwards and her voice softened as she crouched down. She held on to both of Grandma Annetta's hands. 'Will's here to see you.'

Please, God, let her remember him. Let her remember everything they'd shared over the years. It'd break him if she didn't.

Will edged forwards. Apparently his dad had got this far, been invited in to see her initially, but as soon as his mother had looked at him she'd panicked and said she didn't want to see anyone, she didn't know who anyone was anymore. His dad would've been devastated – Will knew from the tone of his voice when he'd recounted the story on the telephone. Mia had tried to see Annetta but never got further than reception and Will knew his mum had tried but failed too. Even Jasmine had made the effort, but he doubted she would again. She seemed too fragile, almost scared of rejection.

'Thank you,' said Will to Sammy as she cautiously retreated and he sat down beside his grandma. She was focused on the crocheted blanket covering her knees.

'Are you cold?' he asked.

'No.' She shook her head but wouldn't turn to face him. She'd had grey hair as long as he could remember and it looked no different now. It was wound up into a bun at the back of her head, held in place with a few clips, but he wondered, did she do her hair by herself still? Or was that something else she'd lost the ability to do?

'So why the blanket?' he asked.

'It was a gift.'

'Who from?' At least she was talking.

'Roberta.'

'Is she a friend of yours?'

Grandma Annetta nodded. 'She's Italian.'

‘Ah.’ He let out a laugh. ‘You always could track down one of your own.’ When he’d been little he remembered going to the markets with her and she was forever meeting new people, introducing her grandson with an air of pride. ‘Where’s she from?’

‘Manarola.’

He sat forwards in his chair. ‘No way.’ And that was it, it was like opening the floodgates and they launched into an easy conversation about her home town, the rocky slopes between the hills, the Mediterranean she missed so much, the brightly coloured homes she’d longed to return to one day but had never managed to.

‘You get your passion for travel from me,’ she said, as clear as day, looking at him as though taking in every square millimetre of her grandson’s face, imprinting the image on her memory hoping that this one would stick. ‘Tell me more about New York.’

And so he did. He told her about his job, recounted amusing stories about colleagues. He told her about Central Park and how in the dead of winter, with snow everywhere, it was his favourite time where he’d wrap up warm and trudge through the white stuff as the sun reflected off its surface.

‘But my favourite season…’ he said, marvelling at the animation on his grandma’s face, hoping it would last as long as he was here, ‘…is the fall. Leaves turn from green to deep reds, browns. The red maples shed their red leaves, sugar maples their mix of orange, yellow and red.’

‘It sounds beautiful.’ She reached out to him and he covered her hand with his own.

Anxious not to let the moment slip away he didn’t talk about his family, not yet. Instead he got Grandma Annetta talking about her own childhood, her memories of Manarola, the painted pink house she grew up in. But then, it was time.

'I hear you haven't seen Mum or Dad, or Mia.'

When she looked at him he wondered whether she was going to slip back into a different state, real or pretend, and avoid the confrontation. But her personality of old shone through and she said, 'I get so confused, Will.'

'You're sick, that's why.' He gulped as his voice broke.

'I didn't want anyone to see me like that.'

Will knew her Alzheimer's was still in the early stages, with some days much better than others. When he'd got the call from Mia about his parents' abandonment of the bay it'd almost been a sign he needed to come back before this disease progressed and the woman he remembered as Grandma Annetta would only exist in his memories.

'Would you like to go outside?' he asked, wondering if she ever walked anywhere now. She'd loved to walk when she'd been looking after him and his sisters. They'd moaned a lot of course, especially in the heat of the day, but she'd told them to make the most of what God had given them the ability to do while they still could. Oh how right she'd been.

Grandma Annetta held his arm and they made their way outside. He wanted to pull her into a giant hug but he was afraid he'd break her. Her grip against his skin made him feel close to her just as he had felt all those years ago as a little boy – holding her hand to cross the road, she locking her hand around his smaller one for fear of losing him as they meandered through the busy Melbourne markets.

Sammy had followed them outside and brought two tall glasses of water, both with a slice of lemon in, and after she'd left and they were settled in some chairs, Will knew he had to broach the subject.

'Mum and Dad have taken off,' he said. There, like ripping off a plaster, it was done.

She looked up at him and for a moment he wasn't sure whether she'd heard what he said. 'I see.'

'They've gone. They've walked away from the café, from everything.' When Grandma Annetta fell silent he wondered was this part of the disease? Did sufferers lose interest in what was happening to their own family? 'They told us to shut the café down for all they cared, and left us three to it. Mia phoned in a panic and Jasmine and I returned home.'

He had her attention now. 'Jasmine's home too?'

'Yes. I'm sure she'd love to see you.'

Annetta turned and looked out deep into the bush. She didn't speak for a while and Will sipped his drink as he waited as patiently as he could.

'You three deserved more.' Grandma Annetta turned to her grandson now.

'What do you mean?'

'The café became their only focus.'

'Are you talking about Mum and Dad?'

'I thought I was helping,' she said.

Okay, now she wasn't making much sense. 'Helping with what?'

'The café building. I bought it. I thought I was helping them but sometimes I wished I hadn't.'

Maybe her lucidity was taking a turn.

She took a deep lungful of the country air and smoothed the skirt of her red dress, a dress longer in length than she would've worn once upon a time – Will recalled the red dress she'd worn in the photograph of her with his grandad: they were in their twenties, high on life, smiles brighter than the sun, and that photo had stayed by Grandma Annetta's bedside every day until Will had left the country. He wondered, was it by her bedside now?

A giggle escaped from Grandma Annetta. 'I own it you know.'

'Right.' Was this for real? He had no experience of someone with any kind of dementia and he looked around for Sammy, who could perhaps be an intermediary in the conversation, but there was no sign of her.

'Maybe I could come back and run it,' she continued. 'Mind you, a customer would order a chocolate ice-cream and I may end up giving them a dustpan and brush, or they may order a sandwich and end up with a soggy dishcloth.' Her giggles attracted the attention of another resident who called out a hello and laughed with her even though he had no idea what the joke was.

She wasn't making much sense at all. Will put a hand on her arm as though that would calm her down. 'Are you telling me that you own the business premises, where The Sun Coral Café is run from?'

'Yes! I was left a nice little nest egg from your grandpa when he died and I wasn't stupid – not back then at least!' She let out a full belly laugh and Will decided to go with it. He wasn't sure of her claims but he grappled to find out as many details as he could in case there was an element of truth in what she was saying. Her mood could snap any second like a thin twig underfoot in the bush, unable to survive hefty footfall, and she'd lapse into a different state entirely.

'I invested in property,' she continued, 'so the premises and the two apartments upstairs are all mine. Oh, and a nice little yellow-coloured house in Manarola. I'd have preferred sky blue or a flamingo pink, but you can't be too choosy.'

Oh she'd really started to go now. Owning the café? A house in Italy? There was no way this could be true. He wondered what was best in this situation. Should he talk sense into her and make her see she was imagining things, or should he keep going along with it and give an old lady in a residential care home the joy she clearly craved from her memories?

'You two seem to be having fun.' Sammy passed by and delivered a pack of cards to the two residents at the opposite end of the veranda. A kookaburra had taken up position in front of them and they were both pointing and chatting as though he was an old friend.

When Sammy passed them again Grandma Annetta engaged her in conversation, asking about her fiancé, and from the conversation that ensued Will had a funny feeling his grandma was completely here in the moment and none of this was merely a figment of her imagination.

Will crouched down in front of Grandma Annetta now and looked into her eyes. 'Let me get this straight…you own the café premises, the two apartments above, plus a house in Italy.'

'You don't believe me.' It wasn't a question.

Will rubbed the back of his neck and sighed.

'It's all true, Will. I'm having one of my good days today.' She patted his hand and then reached a hand to touch his cheek. 'Especially now I've seen you.' When he didn't say anything she reeled off her full name, her husband's name and the year he died. 'My son Tim is your father,' she went on, 'and he's married to Rachel. You have two sisters, Mia and Jasmine. Mia has a daughter, Lexi. I remember the day you ran to the ice-cream van and twisted your ankle, your face on Christmas morning the year you got the red bike with white stripes. I remember from your letters that you once climbed to the top of the Empire State Building, you ice-skated in Central Park last year and vowed never again as you were so uncoordinated, and you can't understand why so many people love hot dogs in New York City.

'I remember everything, Will, because it's a good day.'

He looked at her. She really was telling the truth. 'Why did you keep all of this quiet?'

'I never kept it a secret.'

'You never told anyone either.'

'Tim knows, so does Rachel. They wanted to make enough money to buy me out, to purchase the café premises and the apartments. But when they came to me I wouldn't let them.'

Will began to realise this was sounding more and more true by the second. 'Why not?' He grinned. 'You could've bought a flamingo-pink *and* a sky-blue house back in Italy then.'

'Because they're about money, money, money.'

Will didn't miss the note of disdain in her voice and he felt it his position to stick up for his parents. 'They were doing the best for their family.'

'Pah! For what? So they could run the best business in town? They lost sight of what was important in life, that's what they did. They didn't see you kids as the individuals you were.'

Will sat back in his chair. He happened to agree with his grandma but he didn't share her anger, the bitterness that laced her accusations. It was what it was and his parents had tried their best. Had they failed their kids by trying to succeed so much?

'Where have they gone?' Grandma Annetta asked now. 'Have they taken off to spend all those profits because I won't sell them the premises? They'll run themselves into early graves. They won't be around to see their grandchildren grow up.'

Where had all this anger come from? He knew his mum didn't have the easiest relationship with her mother-in-law but how had a bit of tension gone this far?

'Nobody knows where they are,' he admitted. 'They've gone their separate ways.'

'You mean…' She turned to him and her anger gave way to shock and disbelief. 'No, they can't. They can't be ending a marriage. They can't.'

'Annetta, are you okay?' Sammy was by his grandma's side as she began to look frantic. As though she was looking for an escape route, a way to get out of this world she didn't always recognise. It was as though she'd been sitting in the sunshine one minute and darkness had moved overhead creating monstrous shadows every way she turned.

'Grandma Annetta, it's me, Will.' He put his hand over hers again but she whipped hers away and held on to Sammy instead, gripping her forearm, hands shaking.

'I want to go to my room,' Annetta begged. She didn't even look his way despite him saying her name over and over.

Sammy looked at him. 'I'll take her to her room and I'll be back. Please don't go anywhere.'

He sat back down on his comfy chair and stared at the chair Annetta had been in only moments ago before she'd physically and mentally disappeared right before his own eyes. He hadn't realised how much resentment Grandma Annetta had. He wasn't even sure if resentment was the right word – it was hard to read her emotions when he hadn't seen her in so long. Lucid or not, perhaps she hadn't been telling the truth. Perhaps the café belonged to his parents after all and she was off in some fantasy land pretending it all belonged to her. He knew over the years she'd longed to return to Italy. She'd begrudged Rachel because she saw her as the woman who'd stopped her son returning there too. But how could she be angry with Tim? He'd given her three grandchildren and she'd doted on them.

Grandma Annetta had turned from being bitter and angry to incredibly sad the moment Will told her his parents had upped and left, gone their separate ways. Will wasn't sure what to make of it, not at all.

'Will?' It was Sammy. She gestured for him to sit down again and she took the chair next to him.

'How is she?'

'She's sleeping. She was out like a light.'

'I don't know why she suddenly got so upset,' he said.

'It happens. People with the disease often get more confused, restless or insecure as the day wears on. I expect seeing you was a lot to take in and brought out a lot of emotions, some of which Annetta can't always cope with. It was good of you to come though.'

'I'm glad she wanted to see me.'

Sammy nodded. 'It's a first. She hasn't accepted any visitors for a long, long time. Do try again, won't you?'

'Of course. Although I'm worried about upsetting her.'

'Like I say, she may need time to lie down, process, and perhaps another day she'll want to see you.'

'Should I turn up unannounced or wait to be invited?' He returned Sammy's kind smile. 'Maybe I could come up at the weekend.'

'That sounds like a great idea.' She stood to accompany him off the veranda and back to his car. 'And, Will, call any time. She may chat to you and if not we can always update you on her progress. She's a lovely lady.'

Will smiled. 'She is.' And when he got in his car he waited to turn out of the long driveway before he wiped beneath his eyes.

*

'Typical,' said Mia when he told her and Jasmine where he'd been that afternoon. Trust Mia not to see past her own feelings. Will had driven straight back to the bay after visiting Appleby Lodge. To keep busy and not dwell on the visit to his grandma he'd told Monica she could head home and he'd take over for the last hour or so with Jasmine.

'What could I do?' He poured the milk from the jug in the way Jasmine had shown him to make a heart symbol on top of the latte. Mia may have told him and Jasmine they were on their own with the café, but now she seemed to be hovering around as though she didn't trust either of them not to make a mess of what they'd been charged with. 'She asked to see me. I couldn't refuse to go.'

Jasmine took payment for a can of Diet Coke and dropped the coins into the till. 'I can't believe she didn't turn you away.' She plonked her hands on her hips, suspicious that her sibling had some advantage over her. There was a time she'd looked up to her older brother but Will couldn't imagine her doing the same now.

After he'd served the latte and a slice of banana bread he motioned for Mia and Jasmine to follow him into the kitchen. They kept their distance from one another and all eyes were his way.

'So, she remembers you.' Mia pulled a face but he couldn't read her expression. He assumed it was one of jealousy because Grandma Annetta had never asked to see either of his sisters. 'I thought her disease was worsening every day. I assumed she wouldn't see us because she had no idea who we were.'

Will knew he'd need to choose his words carefully. Jasmine had inherited the fiery Italian spirit and Mia was the worrier, but Mia's temper often simmered under the surface and it was the most dangerous type of all.

'I think she has good and bad days,' he told his sisters. 'Sometimes she remembers more than others.' He thought that might placate them.

'More like selective memory,' Jasmine quipped. 'She remembers you because you were always her favourite.'

'Oh for goodness' sake, what are you – twelve years old?' He shook his head. Part of him had already wondered the same, even after he'd said hello to her today, but after she'd looked so confused and bewildered that Sammy had had to take her off to her room for a lie-down he'd realised it was the disease making her do all of this, not intention or spite. She was becoming confused with everything – people, surroundings, her place in the world. And it was heartbreaking.

'If you're interested, she was looking well and strong. Moving around just fine.' There, he'd guilted them in to listening. Mia poked her head around the kitchen doorway to check for lurking customers but, aside from the couple enjoying their coffees at the table in the far corner, the café was quiet. 'She knew who I was and we talked.'

When Mia shook her head he said, 'What?'

'Nothing.'

'Come on, out with it. You're obviously seething about something so why not say it?'

With a heavy sigh Mia said, 'You were always Golden Bollocks.'

He couldn't help but laugh. 'What?'

'You were. Grandma Annetta worshipped you. Mum and Dad thought you could do no wrong. Jasmine and I never got a look in.' She still wasn't looking at her sister and Will wondered what was simmering between them.

But he didn't have time to worry about his sisters' hang-ups from their childhood. 'There's something you don't know.' He leant against the metal bench in the kitchen. 'At first I thought Grandma Annetta was going a bit gaga but it all makes sense now. I once heard Mum and Dad arguing about her and the position she'd put them in. None of it made sense until Grandma Annetta told me about the café…not the business itself but the premises. All this.' He gestured around them. 'It belongs to her. Both apartments belong to her. She's even got a house back in Manarola.'

'What?' Jasmine took a turn to check the café but it was still quiet for now.

'Why would she even want to own this place?' Mia was curious. 'I thought Mum and Dad owned it all, I thought that's why they worked themselves into the ground for it.'

Will had been piecing it all together on his drive home from Appleby Lodge. He'd heard his parents talking on more than one occasion and knew his dad was always trying to prove himself to his own mother.

Grandma Annetta was annoyed he had no interest in returning to Italy and all Will could think was that perhaps she'd believed that if the couple never owned the café premises then she would be able to keep having a say in what went on in their lives. Grandma Annetta had never got on with her daughter-in-law, but doing something so underhand and devious was hard for Will to comprehend. His Grandma Annetta was so kind-hearted, so full of life when it came to family, or at least that was how it had seemed on the surface.

'What's this about the house in Manarola?' Jasmine asked now. 'Mum and Dad never mentioned anything. Sometimes I'd hear them talking about Italy with customers but the way I understood it, their lives were here now, Grandma Annetta's included.'

'All I know is what she told me today.' Will shrugged.

Mia sighed. 'I wish she'd agreed to see the rest of us.'

'Maybe she will,' Will reassured her. It'd been a long time since he'd fought his sister's corner. Ever since Daniel he'd backed off and left her to her own devices. 'She seemed really well and we talked for quite a while. But the care assistant, Sammy, tells me this happens a lot with patients. They can be happy enough one minute and as they get more tired they can get stressed, they want to escape what's going on. I'll go back and see her another day though. I don't think she'll refuse now.'

Curious, Jasmine asked, 'Why now? Why all of a sudden? Why did she ask to see you in particular?'

'I kept in touch when I was in New York. I wrote her letters every month. She never replied, but she got them all – she even referenced some of the things I'd mentioned in the letters.'

'You wrote to her?' Mia didn't sound put out, just surprised.

'She was always there for me – apparently I was her favourite, according to you two,' he raised his eyebrows, '– so I want to be there for her now. I made up my mind when Dad told me she was turning away visitors that no matter what she did, I'd keep trying as hard as I could to keep her very much a part of this family.'

His sisters stared back at him as though he were talking a foreign language, until Jasmine scurried out to the shop when they heard voices behind them.

Alone with Mia, he looked at his sister. 'If she favoured me when we were growing up, you can't blame me for that you know.'

Mia met his gaze. 'I know.'

'Will.' Jasmine's voice carried through the door. 'Tess is here to see you.'

Damn, he'd driven back to the bay and meant to text her to say he'd return the car later. He'd even parked down the road far enough that Mia wouldn't spot the car. But when he'd got to the café his mind was on Grandma Annetta and he'd busied himself in the café, totally forgetting to contact Tess.

A look of confusion flooded Mia's face until he said, 'I borrowed her car.' But confusion gave way to something else as he attempted to explain. 'I needed to get to Appleby Lodge.' She was still staring at him as he gestured to the front of the café. 'I'd better give her the keys back.'

'Hey you.' He smiled warmly at Tess once he'd made his escape. What he really wanted to do was kiss her there and then but that was never going to happen. He took the keys from his pocket. 'I meant to text and say

I'd return the car to you myself. You didn't have to come all this way.'

Tess wasn't in her work attire. Instead she wore shorts and a loose-fitting T-shirt, runners and a baseball cap. Her face was makeup free but she looked even more gorgeous than when she dressed up. He felt a physical reaction stir within him when their hands met as he gave her back the car keys.

'I needed the walk,' said Tess. 'And besides, this way I get to see you. Do you want to join me for a stroll along the beach?'

When he turned he met Mia's gaze and as he moved to the side she looked at her best friend for answers. By the look on Tess's face she hadn't expected to see Mia in here. The last she'd heard, Mia had washed her hands of the café and was coming nowhere near it.

'Mia…' Tess began, but her friend cut her off.

'You don't have to explain,' said Mia. 'It's fine. We're fine.'

Tess touched her on the arm. 'Are we?'

Mia softened. 'Of course we are.' Then she looked at Will. 'But *we* are not. You bloody hypocrite!' The venom and volume of her voice shocked Jasmine, Will, Tess and the handful of customers in the café. 'You're screwing my best mate after the crap you threw at me about Daniel!'

'Keep your voice down.' Will frogmarched his sister through the café and out to the kitchen and left Tess and Jasmine staring after them.

Mia spun around as soon as they were behind the door. 'How could you? You sanctimonious tosser, Will Marcello! And I know your history with women. You love them – or pretend to like them at least – and then leave them. Well I won't let you do that to Tess, do you hear me? She's my best friend. I don't have friends all around the world like you do. I have very few special people in my life and those that I have, I want to keep.' She pulled at her hair. 'What is it with you and Jasmine? Do you want everything I have? Do you want a business in the bay, my friends, my daughter?'

Her voice had gone supersonic and she was almost like Grandma Annetta, as though she'd gone off to a different planet entirely and he wasn't really there at all.

'All my life, I've worked so hard,' she ranted on, 'so hard to be a part of this family, to be noticed, to do something beyond the ordinary, the mundane. And nothing I do has ever been worthy.'

'You're not making sense now.' His voice was calm, much quieter than hers. 'I think you're blowing this out of proportion.'

'Am I?'

'Yes!' He raised his voice now. He wasn't immune to the portion of Italian blood that ran through his own veins. 'You're being melodramatic. Nobody is trying to take anything away from you. And don't forget, you ruined my relationship with my best friend. Yes, that's right!' She had the audacity to look shocked. 'I may be a boy and boys aren't supposed to care about all that stuff but I did. Daniel was my friend, the one thing I had of my own without you and Jasmine being any part of it. God knows I paid my dues over the years with you two—'

'What's that supposed to mean?'

'You were always there, both of you. When my mates were off playing footy or going to the cinema, going to the beach with girls from our year, I was looking after my little sisters. I was making packed bloody lunches for you both – I was ironing for fuck's sake, making sure you both got to and from school okay. And all because I was the eldest, the man of the family! Well let me tell you, sometimes being the man really fucking sucks!'

Mia slumped against the fridge door. 'Why Tess?' Tears began to stream down her cheeks. 'Why my friend? Is this revenge for Daniel? I know what you're like with women, Will. It's been one after another according to Dad. He talked about you as someone who would never go the distance, who wasn't cut out for marriage or even monogamy.'

He must admit he'd said that once to his dad and it was half true. Some days he wasn't really sure he believed in the sanctity of marriage if it all ended up in tatters anyway.

'Are you going to bed her and then toss her aside and bugger off back to New York?' Mia went on, swiping the tears away with the back of her hand. 'Is that the plan? Leave me with no best friend as revenge for what…being too young to look after myself when our parents were too busy?'

How had it come to this? He didn't hate Mia – far from it. But how had all their problems festered for so long until it ended up in a screaming match full of bitter accusations?

When he turned Tess was standing in the door to the kitchen. 'Tess, I…'

'No need to explain.' She held up a hand. 'I'll leave you guys to it.'

'Tess, wait.' But his words fell on deaf ears as she left the kitchen and walked out through the café.

'You need to get over yourself, Mia.' He pointed a finger at his sister. 'This is not revenge for Daniel. Daniel happened years ago and at the time I couldn't forgive you but believe it or not I've matured over the years and moved on.'

'Bullshit. You haven't moved on. You won't talk to Daniel, at least not properly, and you've never apologised for how you were to me back then.'

He harrumphed and shook his head. 'Yeah, well neither have you.'

He was out of the café so quickly he almost knocked the dirty plates from Jasmine's hands. He turned right out of the door and ran in the direction of where he'd parked the car, calling Tess's name all the way.

When he reached her he pulled her to him, wrapped his arm around her and kissed the top of her head. 'Please don't believe what she said back there.'

'It's not true?'

'It was, at one time. It's been a long time since I've contemplated the whole meet-someone-settle-down package. I guess I've been made too aware over the years of how it can go horribly wrong. But I like you, a lot, and if you can see past the reputation my sister seems determined to tarnish me with, I'd like to see what happens between us.'

'I'd like that too.' She hesitated. 'But I don't want to see Mia hurt again.'

'I know. Believe it or not, neither do I.'

'You need to forgive her for what happened with Daniel.'

'What? That's ancient history.' He'd got his breath back by now. 'And I love Lexi to bits.'

'Then for goodness' sake, tell Mia that. Tell her you forgive her for getting involved with Daniel. At the end of the day they were like us – younger, granted, but still like us: two consenting adults. It just didn't work out. But look at what an amazing job your sister has done raising a beautiful daughter, and although she and Daniel aren't together, they're really good friends and are mature enough to put Lexi first.'

He squinted in the bright sunlight as he held her upper arms and looked down at her. 'You're very bossy when you want to be.'

'I have my talents.' She fought a smile but couldn't resist for long.

When he bent down to kiss her lips, not caring who saw now, she stopped him by pulling away. 'Promise me you'll sort this out with Mia once and for all. I won't have this come between us. She's my best friend and always will be.'

'I promise.' He tried for the kiss again and this time she didn't resist.

Chapter Twenty

Mia

Mia let herself out the back entrance to the café. She couldn't face the customers who may have heard the showdown with her brother, or the sister she hadn't yet confronted with what she knew. Jasmine had tried to talk to her earlier but she'd blanked her saying she didn't have the time, it'd have to wait. But she knew she couldn't wait forever.

And now Tess. Or, more to the point, Will and Tess. Since when had they become an item? She'd had her suspicions but she still hadn't expected it. Hearing Tess ask her brother if he wanted to walk along the beach with her had felt like a slap in the face, like he was still trying to find a way to punish her for Daniel.

It all made sense now…this was why Will was so calm about Leo, why Will was going out of his way to be nice to her or at least stop any pettiness between them. She'd thought he was finally maturing, seeing things from her point of view, but all the while it was for his own gain. And did he really expect her to believe that all his bitterness and resentment stemmed from being lumbered with the responsibility of his sisters at an early age?

Mia lifted her phone to text Tess but decided against it. If there was one thing she was sure of in this world, it was their friendship. They'd been best friends for years and she was confident that would never change. Then again, she'd come between Will and Daniel, so who knew what might happen.

A knock at the door startled her out of her reverie and when she opened it Jasmine was standing on the other side.

'Are you okay?' Jasmine asked.

'Sure.' She walked away leaving the front door open.

Jasmine came in and closed it behind her. 'What the hell was all that about back there? Are they together now?'

'I suppose they are.' Mia didn't look at her sister because she knew that if she did she wouldn't be able to control the deluge of allegations that would come from her mouth fuelled by hurt.

'Are you okay with that?'

'Will and Tess can do what they like.'

Jasmine looked around her. 'Is Lexi home yet?'

'How would I know? She doesn't tell me much. I'm sure she tells you more than she tells me.' She locked eyes with Jasmine.

'You saw the text between me and Lexi, didn't you?'

Mia feigned innocence. 'I don't know what you're talking about.'

Jasmine twirled the strands of her hair around her finger. She used to chew it as a girl, a nasty habit Grandma Annetta had hated. She'd do it whenever she was nervous about something going on at school, whenever Will got annoyed at her for being 'under his feet' as he put it.

Mia tried to keep calm but in the end her emotions got the better of her. 'How could you?' She didn't shout or scream; she spoke in a low voice that made Jasmine pale, if that were possible with her olive skin that had darkened in the short time she'd been back in Australia.

'Mia, I—'

'I don't want to hear it!' Mia bellowed. She didn't care that the windows in her apartment were open, that the entire length of Beach Road most probably echoed her voice right now. 'How could you keep this from me?'

'Is that all you're worried about?' Jasmine was incredulous. 'And there I was thinking you'd be worried about your daughter.'

'I am!'

'No, you're more focused on the fact that I helped her out. You're jealous and you always have been. You'll never accept that we are friends, you'll never trust me enough to have her best interests at heart.'

'I wouldn't expect you to understand,' Mia spat. 'You're not a mother so how could you?'

'Yes, yes. I get it! For crying out loud, Mia. We all know you're a parent and I'm not, you've gone on about it enough times. What, are you in some kind of club that excludes people like me from having an ounce of common sense? Lexi came to me for advice and help.'

'So you took her to the doctor's.'

'Yes I did.' She sounded almost proud.

'And you waited for her to be prescribed the contraceptive pill. You don't see anything wrong with that?'

Jasmine shrugged. 'Actually, no I don't. If I hadn't gone with her she would've gone and got it anyway. She texted me for advice after she and Harry got serious and I talked it through with her when I came back to the bay.' Jasmine took a deep breath and her voice softened, but only a little. 'Mia, she's a woman. She's sixteen years old and, yes, she's your daughter, but she's old enough to make her own decisions when it comes to sex.'

‘Don’t you dare condone what you did.’

‘I did the responsible thing, Mia. I went with her. If she’d been able to talk to you she would’ve wanted you there instead.’

‘Oh and you made damn sure that didn’t happen.’ Mia banged the top of the kitchen table with the flat of her hand.

‘What’s that supposed to mean?’

‘Ever since Lexi was old enough to take notice of you, you used it to your full advantage. What I don’t understand is why.’

‘You’re being ridiculous now. I can’t talk to you when you’re like this.’ Jasmine shook her head and turned to leave.

‘You’ve wormed your way in to Lexi’s life,’ Mia called after her. ‘You’re trying to make her like you.’

Jasmine spun round. ‘And what’s so awful about that? Come on, Mia. The gloves are off now, aren’t they? Maybe it’s time you told me exactly how you feel.’

Mia walked towards her sister. She was right. It was time to say exactly how she felt. For too long she’d kept quiet when she didn’t like something, let worry consume her at times. ‘Your partying ways when you were Lexi’s age are not something I want her to get into.’

‘I think you’ll find most people my age – apart from your perfect self that is – did pretty much the same thing. They got drunk, they partied, they enjoyed their youth. When you had a baby your partying days were over.’

‘I never went for it like you did.’

‘We are different people, Mia. That’s why! And neither of us is perfect. You think I partied too much; I think you were dull and stayed at home, safe in the bay, never venturing farther than Melbourne. Maybe I don’t approve of all the life choices you've made but you don't hear me banging on about it.'

'Well Lexi is a good girl, she won't be getting drunk and sleeping around. I won't let you shape her into a version of you.'

Jasmine froze and neither of them said a word for almost a minute until Jasmine calmly walked to the front door. She opened it but then stopped and turned back. 'Mia, have you ever thought that maybe what you're most worried about is Lexi turning out like you, getting pregnant and being tied down? Maybe you're jealous of the freedom I had, the freedom Lexi has. And none of that makes you a very nice person.'

She slammed the door on her way out.

*

Mia heard Lexi come home at about ten o'clock but she was already curled up in bed. The fight with Jasmine and the earlier confrontation with Will had knocked her out emotionally and physically. She felt weak, powerless to control anything. She'd already been asleep for an hour or so but now lay awake as the bay fell asleep all around her. She imagined the waves – the blackness of the night letting them crash invisibly to the shore. If you walked along the sand right now it'd be cool beneath your feet, the dry grains would run between your toes. When you were at the beach nothing else seemed to matter. The sounds, the smell of the ocean lulled you into a sense of calm.

But she wasn't at the beach now. She was here, lying in this bed, and all she could think about was the confrontation yet to come.

Jasmine was right. She'd never ventured far from the bay. Primrose Bay was her home – she'd never yearned to travel like her siblings did, it'd never entered her mind to go and work in another country, experience something different. But Jasmine was also very wrong. Single motherhood hadn't taken anything away from her, it hadn't stopped her. Because she had never wanted to get away, never felt the need. She and her siblings were completely different people and to think that they could pull together and manage this family mess, keep the café up and running until their parents decided to return, seemed ludicrous now.

Mia quietly crept out of bed and to the cupboard in the hallway. She pulled out a holdall and took it back to her bedroom. She packed a few different outfits, she packed her washbag, she packed her phone charger. She left a note for Lexi telling her she needn't worry, but she'd be gone for a few days. She was well aware that this is what her parents had done and she'd berated them for walking away. But she couldn't see any other solution. Staying here was overwhelming, she felt trapped, as though the walls were closing in on her. For years she'd put the family worries on her shoulders and so, for the first time, Mia packed her things, locked up behind her, crept out to the car and drove away from the bay.

For the first time, she didn't deal with a problem. She ran away from it.

Chapter Twenty-One

Will

Last night Jasmine had stormed into the apartment after a run-in with Mia. She hadn't told him much about the fight but Will knew it was the biggest one they'd ever had. Usually Jasmine would mutter under her breath about her sister, curse and complain about her. But this time the anger had been so fierce she hadn't offered any explanation. She'd slammed the front door behind her and made straight for the fridge. Not finding what she wanted in there she'd raided the pantry and eventually pulled out a tinned syrup sponge. It must've been in there for years. She'd struggled with the tin opener, which in the end she'd hurled across the room. Will had ducked and it had landed on the sofa, missing his head by centimetres.

'What the hell is going on?' he'd bellowed across the room.

Jasmine stood at the kitchen bench, shaking. The tin in front of her had only a tiny indentation where she'd attempted to open it. He lifted the tin and peered at the side. 'As I thought,' he flipped open the bin, 'out of date by eleven months.'

Jasmine was crying now, something he hadn't seen since she was a little girl. He wanted to put his hand on her shoulder but for some reason he froze, he couldn't move closer. Two sisters crying in front of him in such a short space of time was setting him on edge and he wished he could handle it better than he was.

'What happened, Jasmine?'

'What did I ever do to her?' Her words were barely decipherable amongst her tears. 'She hates me.'

'Did she use those actual words?' He leant against the kitchen bench next to his sister, who might have changed physically since he'd last seen her but was still the emotional mess he remembered.

And then the whole story came out. How Lexi had a boyfriend and they were getting serious. They'd talked about taking the next step and having sex and they wanted to be careful, wait until they were ready. And once they were ready they'd decided to use condoms and for Lexi to go on the pill.

'She doesn't want to get pregnant like her mum did,' Jasmine explained. 'She'd never say that to Mia but the thought terrifies Lexi. She wants to go travelling, explore the world, end up at university. She wants to have her life pre-children – her words, not mine,' she added, presumably because she wanted Will to know that she hadn't put that thought into her niece's head.

'Lexi refused to talk to Mia about sex. I told her to, I really tried to persuade her as I knew Mia would want to know, but she flatly refused.'

'I can understand why. Mia would probably freak out,' said Will.

'Exactly.' Jasmine wiped beneath her eyes and then plucked a tissue from the box on the benchtop to blow her nose. 'Lexi booked a doctor's appointment and she asked me to go with her. It was all last minute. She hadn't planned on telling anyone but she was worried, she wanted to know what questions to ask. It's hard being sixteen and making such an adult decision, especially if you're too scared to tell a parent. I went along to the doctor's with her and I'd persuaded her that she should tell Mia. She was going to.' Jasmine shook her head and took a deep breath. 'But Mia saw some texts on my phone and found out before Lexi got the chance.'

'You should get a bloody lock on that phone.' When he grinned Jasmine actually smiled back at him, not the sort of moment they'd shared much, at least since she'd grown up. When she was little he'd fallen in love with her smile. When he'd taken her for ice-creams or to play on the swings at the park, sun-hat on her head, giggling away, he'd been besotted with his little sister. But when he'd started to miss out on being a teenager because he had her in tow, he'd not been able to join friends after school because his parents had the café and he had to meet Jasmine from school, slowly but surely the resentment had set in. He'd done his best not to let it but over the years it had got so bad he could barely have a basic conversation or be in the same room as her. His anger and frustration had found its way out, and that was how he coped with it.

Jasmine had gone to take a long bubble bath after that and left Will to contemplate the whole mess.

*

Today, in the kitchen of the café, as he sliced the fresh loaf of banana bread Jasmine had made after she'd slotted the pear-and-raspberry bread into the oven, Will felt as though last night had been a start. She'd talked to him at least, and he'd listened. And it'd been a long while since they'd done that. This morning, her eyes still puffy, Jasmine had told him she'd talk to Mia once she'd had a while to calm down and he knew he needed to do that too. They'd agreed that after the café shut at seven o'clock they'd order takeaway upstairs in their parents' apartment and they would sort this whole mess out. It was about time.

Will took an order for four cappuccinos to go and Jasmine put the banana bread into the glass display cabinet before going out to the kitchen to chop up fresh fruit for the fruit salads. Monica wasn't in today so it was all systems go. It was already busier than usual and when the door opened and Lexi walked in, he instantly knew something was wrong.

Had Mia had a row with her daughter too?

'Hey there,' he said. 'Give me one second. I'll just make this short black and I'm all yours. Coffee?' Lexi shook her head as Will emptied the used contents of the group handle into the knock-out drawer and refilled it with fresh coffee from the grinder. 'Jasmine's out back,' he said as he continued, but when he'd finished making the coffee Lexi was still hovering at the counter.

Will beckoned Lexi into the kitchen where they joined Jasmine. 'What's up, Lexi?' He wiped his hands on a tea towel.

'It's Mum.'

'She's angry, I'm guessing.' Jasmine used both hands to wiggle a big knife through a hunk of watermelon.

'She's gone.'

'Gone where?' Jasmine finally pushed the knife all the way through the flesh and sturdy skin and turned the big piece of watermelon on its side, ready to be chopped into chunks.

'Gone.'

Will looked at Jasmine, then at Lexi, but before he could say anything Lexi handed him a note. It was from Mia, to Lexi.

'She left that for me this morning,' said Lexi. The poor girl looked worried sick. 'It's my fault, isn't it? Because I wasn't honest with her, she's had enough.'

Jasmine was at Lexi's side as Will read the note out loud:

My beautiful Lexi, I need to get away for a few days and sort my head out. As you know, the relationship I have with your Uncle Will and Auntie Jasmine has always been a bit difficult and complicated. Never more so than now, with your Nan and Grandad leaving the bay. And Jasmine and I are not on speaking terms after I found out she'd taken you to the doctor behind my back.

I love you, Lexi, but I'm suffocating here and I can't reason with anything, anyone or even myself, so it's best I get away for a while.

Try not to worry and I'll be in touch soon.

Much love,

Mum x

Will could see Jasmine was biting back the tears at this latest development. Her arms were wrapped around Lexi as their niece sobbed against her shoulder. Sixteen-year-old emotions ran high at the best of times but Lexi didn't need this on top of everything else.

'Lexi, she'll be fine.' Will patted her on the shoulder reassuringly. 'You know your mum better than either of us, and I'm sure she'll be back before we know it.'

Lexi blamed herself over and over but Jasmine and Will were insistent it wasn't her fault.

'Lexi.' Jasmine pulled away from her niece now, her hands still on her upper arms. 'This is not your fault. It's mine and Will's, and our parents'.' She looked to Will for confirmation and he couldn't argue. 'We've made a right bloody mess of this family over the years and Will and I both ran away from it, but your mum stayed here. That wasn't fair on her.'

Will wondered where on earth Mia would have gone and as Jasmine kept talking he texted Tess to see if she had any idea.

Jasmine hugged Lexi tightly. 'Don't worry, she'll soon be back, bossing us about and organising us all.' She looked over to Will. 'Are you messaging Tess?'

'If she's told anyone, she'll have told her best friend.' Although maybe she wouldn't, given how upset she'd been at the prospect of a relationship blossoming with her brother.

'Right, Lexi,' Jasmine declared, 'I'm going to be the embarrassing auntie now and I'm walking you to school.' Will was relieved to hear Lexi laugh. 'No discussion, I'm doing it. Is that okay?' She looked to her brother.

'It's busy but I'll handle the café. This is more important.'

After they left he stood at the coffee machine wiping it down, mopping up any trace of spills and coffee dust around it. When he realised a customer was asking for service, he wondered how long he'd been in his own little world.

*

Jasmine returned soon after walking Lexi to school. Harry had been at the gate waiting for her and Jasmine had handed her niece over to him, glad she wouldn't be wandering around alone even for two minutes.

The café was crazy busy that afternoon and at one point Will had considered calling Monica and begging her to come in, if only for an hour so they could take a breath. But he and Jasmine managed the rush together; they took turns manning the coffee machine, they alternated being in the kitchen when more food preparation was required and they coped with whatever the day threw at them. Lexi came in after school and Will made her favourite smoothie. Harry was with her and when she used the bathroom Will took the opportunity to ask how she was. Harry told Will she was okay but worried. Will guessed worrying was a quality she got from her mum and for some reason the conclusion made him smile.

At closing time Will turned the café sign to Closed, locked the door and drew down the blinds. 'I really thought she'd come back by the end of the day.'

'Me too.' Jasmine stopped sweeping and rested her hands on top of the broom. 'Her note might have said she needed some time away, but Mia rarely leaves the bay and if she does she's back as soon as possible. As far as I know the only time she's been away from Lexi has been when Lexi went on school camps.'

Will pulled out a chair at the table he'd wiped down last. 'Tess said she'd asked Mia to go away a few times – she gets cheap deals because of her job – but Mia was always adamant she didn't want to in case she was needed.'

Jasmine joined him and sat in the chair opposite. 'It's odd though, don't you think?'

'I guess we're all different.'

'But it's weird she never fully trusted Daniel enough either when Lexi was with him.'

'I don't think it was ever a case of not trusting Daniel,' said Will, 'it's more a case of her being afraid of not being there. If something happened, she'd never forgive herself.'

'It's weird.'

Will smiled. 'Yeah, it is weird. But it's Mia. She's always been the same. We could look at it as her being strange, but I'm beginning to think, especially after reading that note with her use of words such as "suffocating", that all along she's just been putting everyone else first. Pretty selfless really.'

Jasmine shook her head. 'What a bloody mess. When she phoned me in London I knew I wasn't coming back to a happy family with a white picket fence and everyone smiling and laughing, but I didn't think I was coming back to this minefield. Mum and Dad thought they were leaving us with a café to take charge of but really they left us with a messy sibling relationship to tackle above all else.' She took the napkins out of the dispenser and neatened them up before pushing them back in. 'It's like someone dropped a grenade on The Sun Coral Café and then stood back waiting for it to explode.'

'Great analogy, Boots.'

Jasmine's head shot up and she gulped. 'You haven't called me that in years.'

He smiled at her across the table. 'I haven't done a lot with this family in years.'

'What happened, Will?' Tears sprung to her eyes. 'With us, I mean.'

His chair scraped back and he said, 'I think we're going to need something a bit stronger than coffee for this, aren't we?' And off he went upstairs to the apartment and came back brandishing a bottle of gin, a bottle of tonic water and two crystal glasses.

'I'll get the ice.' Jasmine was back within seconds and pushed out several cubes into each glass. Will poured the gin and Jasmine added the tonic If only their relationship had always been this easy.

'So…' Jasmine began.

'So…' said Will with a smile. 'I'd better start from the beginning.'

'I guess you better had.'

He took a big mouthful of gin. 'I was a bit grossed out when Mum and Dad said they were having another baby.'

'Jeez, you really are starting from the beginning. Sorry, carry on.'

'I have to start then to be able to explain how I feel.'

'Fair enough.' She quietened.

'At age eleven I knew about the birds and the bees, and the thought of my parents doing that was…to be frank…repulsive.'

Jasmine sniggered. 'Agreed.'

'But by the time you arrived I was excited. You were this beautiful bundle of joy and it was a novelty for me and Mia to have another sibling. You had all this dark curly hair, a big curl that fell in the middle of your forehead, and everywhere we went people would give us admiring looks. We were the perfect little family.

'By the time Mum had finished breastfeeding I loved nothing more than giving you the bottle as soon as I came home from school, last thing at night, first thing in the morning. And I was in charge of course – I wouldn't let Mia anywhere near you.' He grinned at his sister, remembering her as a little girl. 'I was the eldest, it was up to me to look after you. And for a while I was happy to do so. But when I turned twelve, the novelty of looking after a one year old lost its charm. I was becoming more independent, breaking away from my parents. I no longer needed to be met from school, I was ready to move on to the next stage. Except Mum relied on me a lot and that freedom I watched my friends enjoy didn't come my way.'

'I thought Grandma Annetta looked after me.' Jasmine knocked back the rest of her gin, Will took his cue to do the same, and Jasmine topped up both glasses.

'She did. She was always there and she loved having another grandchild to fuss over. But not long after your first birthday she fell and hurt her hip, which meant she was out of action for a while. Eventually she had a hip replacement and with that came recovery time. So the responsibility for you fell on me.'

'That doesn't seem fair at all.'

'It's partly my fault,' said Will. 'I never complained about it. I knew I was the eldest – Mia was too young to be put in charge. It was just the way it was.'

He smiled. 'One day, after Melbourne had had an unseasonal dry spell, it poured with rain non-stop and you begged me to take you out to jump in puddles. Mum had bought you a new pair of gumboots—'

'I remember! They were bright turquoise with giraffes standing tall up the sides. God, I loved those boots.'

'You certainly did. You'd been wearing them inside, around the house, for months on end. You wore them to the shops to get ice-cream, you wore them to the park when everyone else wore sandals. But the day it rained I gave in and took you down to the road around the corner from the primary school—'

'Where there was a driveway with a dip in the road leading up to it and water would pool.' Jasmine laughed. 'That was the best puddle ever!'

'You jumped up and down, squealing with delight.' Will was laughing now. 'You completely soaked me, standing next to you in my waterproof coat doing my best to stay dry. And when you looked as though you'd fall asleep on your feet from all that jumping, I said, "Come on, Boots, let's go home for hot chocolates." And from then on, the name stuck. I called you Boots right up until…' He broke off because he couldn't remember the last time he'd used the nickname for his baby sister.

'You must've really resented the time it took to look after me.'

He shrugged. 'Not at first. And then Dad and I would talk and he'd say, "One day, Son, this café will be yours to run and you'll be glad we worked so hard to get it established." I knew he felt guilty for how much they relied on me and I guess it was his way of showing their appreciation, and that they'd make it up to me. We'd chat for hours after they came home and Mum saw to you and put you to bed. We'd talk about the restaurant business his parents had owned and how they'd worked so hard to get it to be a success. I could see passion in his eyes and I felt proud at how much responsibility he'd be handing over to me.'

'I was always jealous when you'd talk about the café,' said Jasmine.

'You were too little to understand then.'

She shook her head. 'Not when I was really tiny, but as I grew up you always seemed to be talking about it, especially with Dad.'

'Why would you be jealous? I always thought you girls hated the place, how much it encroached on the family's time together.'

'Oh we did, but I wouldn't have minded being more involved,' Jasmine admitted. 'Mia was jealous too. We could see that Grandma Annetta favoured you.'

Will smiled. ‘I think she felt sorry for me and everything I was expected to do. But, like I said, I never learnt to use the word “no”.’

‘So when did you and I stop being so close?’ The gin must’ve given Jasmine the guts to be frank.

‘I think I got to the point where I needed to do exactly what Mia has done today. I needed some distance. I met Paige and moved to Perth to be with her and that’s when the cracks between me and you widened into crevices. You weren’t very old but each time I came back you’d plummeted more and more into the dreaded puberty and I was doing my own thing. There’s quite an age gap and with neither of us making any extra effort, my memories of you really became the memories that had driven me away – the lack of independence my friends always had, the sense of responsibility I thought I didn’t mind when really it was slowly eating away at me.’

‘But none of that was my fault.’ Jasmine crunched on the remains of an ice cube.

‘I know, it’s ludicrous. But it wasn’t only you I was annoyed at. I never told anyone else but before Paige even appeared on the scene, my best mate and I had plans to travel the world before we settled down with the daily grind of a real job. We’d planned which countries to go to, looked into visas. We were all ready to go as soon as uni finished.’

‘You’re talking about Daniel, aren’t you?’

‘Yep. And when Mia got pregnant Daniel said there was no way he could go. He had responsibilities now, he had to find a job as soon as he graduated, because the money he’d been left wouldn’t last forever. He said there wouldn’t be much time for fun, and I’d already waited so long for proper freedom – I wanted to make up for the independence I'd lost, have a ball before I was faced with the responsibility of life I suppose.'

'So yet again one of your sisters had taken something away from you.' Jasmine reached over and brushed her hand against his arm. 'I never saw that until now.' Her voice wavered. 'You must've hated us.'

'Hate is too strong a word, Jasmine. The gin must be getting to you.'

'It's not the gin, Will.'

'I promise I never hated you. But I was gutted when my plans fell apart. And you're right, I saw it as something else being taken away from me. But like a typical bloke I shut up about it, I didn't complain, I just let everyone else get on with their lives around me. I was indifferent to Lexi when she arrived, I was indifferent to everyone really. And Paige's appearance in my life was just what I needed.'

'I liked her,' Jasmine told him. 'She seemed good for you. I'm sorry it didn't last. What happened?'

'I really don't know.' He proffered the bottle of gin again but Jasmine shook her head. He topped up his own glass, determined to get through every ounce of this explanation right now. 'I guess it wasn't meant to be.'

'And Tess. How do you feel about her?'

He thought for a moment. 'Different. I haven't had a serious girlfriend in years but Tess…she feels right. She's gorgeous, of course, but she's kind too, and I suspect she'll never be afraid to put me in my place, tell me how it is. I like that in a woman.' She'd certainly put him in his place about Mia last night. 'She told me to sort things out with Mia, to forgive her about Daniel, and I was going to. But she took off.'

'Do you forgive her?'

He took a deep breath. ‘I was angry for such a long time but when Lexi started to become this impossibly cute niece hanging on to the leg of my jeans every time I visited, I began to mellow. I actually started to admire Mia for what she was doing. Daniel was on hand for her always but at the end of the day she was raising a child on her own without a relationship to fall back on. When she was tired at the end of a day or wanted company, she didn’t have the special person waiting at home for her. I started to see how hard it was for her.’

‘I don’t suppose you ever told her that though, did you?’

He sat back in his chair and swigged his gin. ‘No, I didn’t.’

‘Do you think she’ll ever come around to the idea of you and Tess?’

‘Who knows? I punished her about Daniel for long enough.’

Jasmine shook her head. ‘She won’t hold a grudge, that’s not Mia.’

‘Let’s hope you’re right.’ He sighed. ‘Anyway, enough about me and my love life. What about you? Isn’t there a guy waiting for you in London?’

He listened as Jasmine told him all about Ned, the shared house, the job she’d worked in. And, as she talked, little by little he came to realise he’d underestimated his baby sister. No longer was she relying on anyone else. She’d actually moved to the other side of the world on her own and stood on her own two feet. And she’d survived to tell the tale – something he knew none of them had ever thought she’d do.

‘Can I ask about the transformation?’ he said now.

She grinned. ‘By “transformation”, you mean weight loss?’

'I was being tactful.'

She held her glass aloft. 'Too many of these and it'll all go back on.'

'So what made you make the sudden change?' She was avoiding the question but they were talking now, finally, and he wouldn't be fobbed off.

'Remember last night when I found the syrup sponge in the cupboard?'

He frowned. 'Yeah, when you almost decapitated me with the tin opener.'

'Sorry about that.' She pulled a face. 'But that's what I did, years ago.'

'Throwing tin openers?'

'This isn't a time for jokes, Will. I'm trying to tell you something here.'

'Sorry.'

She took a deep breath in. 'It started in my early twenties. I was out partying all the time with my friends so the weight piled on – alcohol, late nights, takeaways and junk food took their toll. But more than that. I ate to escape.'

'I don't understand.'

'Oh I didn't do it in front of anyone, not if I could help it. And you were away by then, anyhow, in New York having a great time. But, here, Mum and Dad fought all the time, I'm pretty sure Grandma Annetta didn't approve of me at all – she'd seen me fall into the house drunk too many times – and Mia was busy bringing Lexi up and doing her best to keep me away from her.'

'Lexi has always doted on you.'

'I know, but that has always come between Mia and me. Mia always disapproved of how much I partied, but it was my escape and I was in a crowd of friends who were always clubbing, always at the pub after work. When Lexi approached her teens she began to take more notice of me, wanted to mirror the way I dressed, use my makeup and perfume. It was nice in so many ways because sometimes it felt as though she was the only person who saw me. I felt as though I flew under everyone's radar.

'I wanted to be seen as an equal. I wanted to be just as good as you and Mia. But I never was.'

'I'm not sure that's true,' said Will.

'Our parents made you look after me and help out at home, but somehow you've blamed me my entire life.'

Will sighed and rubbed a hand across his jaw. 'All I could see was what was taken from me. I felt like you took all my time, Mia took my mate. I took a lot of my frustration out on you and I shouldn't have.'

'You were the eldest, responsible and in charge,' Jasmine went on. 'Mia was organised and so damn capable. I was always the one you two had to watch and make sure I didn't do anything wrong and that feeling didn't disappear in early adulthood. I felt as though nothing I did would ever make me stand out enough. I began to comfort eat and it took away the pain and the feeling that I would never live up to you two.'

'I never realised.' How could something so consuming be in front of his eyes yet he still hadn't been able to see it?

'You were too busy assuming you'd have to pick up the pieces after me. So I'd let you. I'd let you come to the rescue, let Mia organise me. Until, one day, I'd had enough. Like Mia has today, like you had back then, just like Mum and Dad.'

Will used a serviette to put beneath his glass as condensation ran down his wrist. 'What a family we are. Talk about bailing when the going gets tough.'

'We're pretty lame really, aren't we?' She let a smile escape but then turned serious. 'I ate when I was unhappy, Will. I also ate when I was celebrating and washed it all down with alcohol. Food became something that comforted me and I was in control. But the more I ate the fatter I got and the worse I felt, so I'd eat more to feel better. And the vicious circle continued.'

'Did you change as soon as you were away from the bay?' he asked.

'Once I arrived in London, I slowly began to get my confidence back. Nobody knew anything about me and when I found a job and a place to live I had this kind of euphoria. Doing those things without any of you lot gave me a boost of confidence that seemed to catapult me into action. I had this feeling that I could do anything I put my mind to. The weight gradually came off the happier I got and when I realised it was melting away, it spurred me on. It's only with all the trouble recently that I've even contemplated turning to food again.'

Jasmine started to giggle. 'Imagine if the tin opener had hit you!'

'I'd have thrown it back at you,' he quipped.

Jasmine's laughter filled the café. 'I've no doubt you would.'

When the laughter died down he asked, 'So where to from here?'

'I think we need Mia to come home.'

'And?...' He sensed something else.

'I think it's time to call Mum and Dad and demand they come back. Enough is enough, Will. They can't bugger off and leave this mess. I don't think they've any idea what they've done by upping and leaving. This is their family. Let them deal with it properly for once.'

Will took his phone from his pocket and called each of their parents in turn. Neither of them answered but he left a short, sharp message for each. He told them this wasn't about the café any more. This was about them, all seven of them: Tim, Rachel, Will, Mia, Jasmine, Lexi and Grandma Annetta. Their family. And when he'd left messages he sent them an identical email as well as a text message. He'd covered all bases.

'Do you think they'll come home?' Jasmine picked up her phone and keys from beside the till.

'They'd better,' he said, picking up a cloth to wipe down the table they'd sat at. 'You go on,' he added when Jasmine looked around to see what else needed to be done. 'This is the last of the cleaning and I'll be up when I'm done.'

'Thanks, Will.' She hesitated. 'We had a good day today.'

He nodded. 'We had a good day.' He went out to the kitchen and ran the cloth under the tap but as he turned to go back to the café and wipe up the other side of the counter, he stopped at Jasmine's voice.

'It was when I was upset after Josie Richards called me fat.'

'What was?'

'The last time you called me Boots. It was a few days after my eleventh birthday and puberty had kicked in so I was piling on the puppy fat. I was so upset and when you met me from school you said, 'Come on, Boots, take no notice. We can jump in muddy puddles if it'll cheer you up.'

'I remember.' A simple moment but it brought tears to his eyes now. Tears for all the years they'd bickered or not spoken, for all the remorse he had that they hadn't spoken like this before and repaired their sibling relationship.

'As a joke you jumped in a huge puddle and soaked me from head to toe.' His sister smiled at him, tears prickling the corners of her eyes too. 'I was so angry but I was laughing, I couldn't help it. I looked up to you, my big brother, who would never ever let anyone or anything hurt me. That's the last time I remember you being kind to me.'

'I'm so sorry, Jasmine.' He didn't break her stare and when she stepped forward to hug him he let her.

'I'm really sorry too.'

Chapter Twenty-Two

Jasmine

'How did you sleep?' Jasmine watched Lexi emerge from the bathroom and handed her a plate with two slices of toast and honey.

'I'm not hungry.' Lexi moved past Jasmine and took a bottle of water from the fridge to slot into her school bag.

Jasmine put the plate onto the kitchen table and led her niece to the chair, pushing on her shoulders to ensure she sat down.

'Wherever she is, she's fine.' She put a hand over Lexi's. 'Don't worry too much. And eat this toast, please. Just one slice.' She slid the plate in front of her niece. 'And then I can walk to school with you.'

At least that coaxed a smile out of Lexi. 'I'm old enough to get myself there you know.'

'I know that but humour me, would you? Mia would want me to be with you if you were upset. Well…actually she said she didn't want me anywhere near you, but I've got a feeling that when we eventually talk to her she'll come around.' She crossed her fingers beneath the table, hoping that would be the case.

Last night Jasmine had gone upstairs after her stint at the café and grabbed enough food to cook herself and Lexi a healthy stir-fry. She knew her niece would insist she was fine alone but there was no way Jasmine was going to leave her. She'd cooked them dinner. They'd talked, they'd worried. Lexi had had a long chat with Tess and the more people that reassured her Mia was fine, wherever she was, the more her niece seemed settled. But this morning the worry was there on her face again.

When Jasmine had persuaded Lexi to eat one of the slices of toast, they left for school and then Jasmine joined Will and Monica in the café. She was anxious for news.

'Have they called?' she asked her brother the second she walked through the door.

He shook his head.

'Damn. What are they playing at?' She nodded to the offer of a coffee and filled the jug with cold milk from the fridge while Will filled the group handle and slotted it in place. She took up station by the espresso machine as Will made the coffee.

'I've left messages again this morning,' he said, handing her a latte. 'I even said that Mia has a big catering job coming up at the school but that she's disappeared, which could be putting her business in jeopardy.' He pulled a face. 'I may have sounded a bit melodramatic but Mia has had that contract for ages and she was stoked. Mum and Dad heard all about it so I thought it might help bring them to their senses. When Mia has a busy schedule at the picnic business, she never slacks off. She could have two broken legs and arms and somehow she'd get those picnics to the clients requesting them.'

'They've been good at getting back to us eventually, when we've had queries,' said Jasmine, confused as to why they weren't getting in touch now, 'but you'd think they'd be more on the ball with this. They're too wrapped up in their own problems and it's as though they're happy to forget about us.'

'How's Lexi?'

Jasmine sipped the latte. 'How do you think? She's confused, worried. We all know Mia's sensible, but it'd still be nice to know where she is. I think that's what Lexi can't get her head around. It's very out of character.'

Will served the next customer – two fruit salads and two glasses of orange juice. And after he'd handed the customer her change he turned to Jasmine again. 'I feel responsible.'

'For Mia?'

He nodded.

'Gone are the days, Will, when you were held responsible for me and my sister. She's big enough to look after herself. I texted Daniel again, by the way, but he hasn't heard from her. I was hoping he'd admit to hiding her from the rest of the world – it's the sort of good deed he'd do.'

'They're still good friends aren't they?'

'They are, and it's great for Lexi. She may be raised by a single mother but I doubt most kids in her position would be so grounded and have so much attention from their separated parents.'

Will nodded. 'I think I've royally fucked up.'

'About Daniel, you mean?'

'Yep. I was a tosser really, when you think about it. I mean, what sort of man goes crying about his sister taking away his best friend? It makes me sound like a total girl.'

'Well, when you put it that way…' Jasmine's smile placated him. 'Look, from what you said last night, I suspect Daniel was just the final thing in your life to symbolise us girls messing things up for you, intentionally or not. I just wish you'd had a chance to explain before Mia took off.' She looked into her coffee.

'I feel like something shifted between us last night, Will.'

He nudged her. 'It did. We're good.'

'I'm glad.'

Jasmine finished her coffee and then tied on an apron, ready to throw herself into work. The café was getting busier, even for a school day. The sun was out in full force but the cool breeze outside lowered the temperature and seemed to have brought people flocking to the beach. Toddlers whose older siblings were in school, elderly people making the most of the cool air to take a walk, a group of young adults playing volleyball as though they didn't have a care in the world.

Will, Jasmine and Monica worked full on all day and by the end of the shift Jasmine was exhausted.

'Thanks, Monica, you didn't have to stay so late,' Jasmine told their employee at six o'clock when all three of them looked ready to fall asleep on their feet.

Monica put a hand on Jasmine's arm. 'It's my pleasure. You're having a hard time, I can see that.' She collected her bag from the locked cupboard in the kitchen and before she left she said, 'I hope you have news about Mia soon.'

Jasmine locked the door and turned the sign to Closed. It was an hour earlier than usual but there were no customers inside and today the extra hour would have to be sacrificed. Will pulled down the blinds to block out the sun and any passers-by who might peer in, wanting a coffee, snack or cold drink for their walk along the beach.

'We mustn't do that too often,' said Jasmine, nodding towards the blinds. 'But I'm so glad we're doing it today.'

‘Me too. Are you okay to cash up and I’ll go and see Lexi?’

Lexi had knocked on the window as she and Harry walked past on their way home. But for once nobody batted an eyelid at the sixteen year old taking a boy upstairs to an empty apartment. Lexi was sensible, she knew right from wrong, and Mia was going to have to learn to trust her when she returned. Right now, Lexi needed someone and Jasmine began to wonder whether if she’d had a steady boyfriend herself, when she’d felt so excluded from her own family, so unnoticed, would she have been a happier teen and a more content adult? Then again, perhaps nobody had the magic formula for being happy.

‘Tell her I’ll be up at the apartment in half an hour,’ Jasmine replied. ‘I’m making us tuna niçoise for dinner.’

‘Can I get in on that?’ Will asked cheekily, patting his stomach.

‘Of course you can. I’ll make plenty.’ She was enjoying this new relationship with her brother.

‘Thanks, Boots,’ he called over his shoulder as he let himself out the back way.

Jasmine grinned. And she was still smiling when she took the cash float from the till and locked it in the safe for the night. She threw out the leftover food from the display cabinet, put the dishwasher on and washed up what couldn’t go into it. She wiped down the counter beside the till and allowed herself a moment to lean against the wall behind and look over the café: empty, but still a sight to behold. This was an enormous responsibility and they were actually doing it, running a business. No matter what mess the family was in, there was hope, wasn’t there? Hope that they could all come out the other side unscathed.

She pulled down the flap of the alarm cover and was about to arm the system when there was a knock at the door. She groaned. She and Will had worried that their regulars would object to the early closing. There were several who often stopped for a takeaway coffee on their way home, others who wanted a cold drink after another energy-filled day at the beach.

'We're closed,' she called as chirpily as she could when whoever it was knocked again, but they didn't relent.

She unlocked the door, twisted the handle and pulled it open, prepared to tell whoever it was that due to unforeseen circumstances they'd had to close early.

But instead her shoulders sagged in relief when she saw who was on the other side.

Chapter Twenty-Three

Will

Jasmine hasn't wasted any time running up to tell him who was downstairs in the café after closing time. With his parents back in town, at last, Will gave Harry and Lexi some money and told them to go into the heart of Primrose Bay and treat themselves to an Italian meal tonight. Lexi didn't need to be around for this confrontation and he'd sounded out Harry enough now to know he was sensible and would look out for her. Off they went, promising to be home by ten o'clock, and Will and Jasmine went downstairs to the café to face the music.

Gathered in the café, all four of them tried to keep calm about Mia's sudden departure from the bay.

'You're a dab hand at that,' Tim told Jasmine as she made lattes all round. 'Can you do the tulip?'

'I'm an expert at the heart.' She smiled. 'The tulip will take a bit more practice.'

Tim's dark eyes matched his daughter's. Will regarded him now, the dark hair he'd once had replaced by a rich silver – he looked distinguished rather than old. More than once Will had hoped the genes would carry him that way too when he reached his fifties and sixties.

'Try now,' Tim encouraged his daughter. She did as he suggested. 'Start pouring…that's it…stop halfway and then go again…yep…and a third time…now…' He raised both hands in the air. 'She's a professional. A natural!'

Jasmine had told Will the other night that she'd never felt noticed by this family. Now, he was far more astute when it came to her feelings and couldn't help noticing her melt beneath the praise, revelling in the moment.

'She's taken to it well,' said Rachel to her son. Her hair had hung in a much redder bob in the photographs he'd seen a couple of months before returning from New York, but now, Rachel Marcello looked far more beautiful, with cinnamon brown shades that softened her face and the natural waves she'd let come back rather than attacking them with straighteners when it wasn't tied up as she worked in the café.

Whatever had happened during their time away, both of their parents certainly looked far more relaxed than ever before.

'No thanks to you two.' Will couldn't help it. Playing happy families was all well and good but they all knew what lurked beneath. 'You landed us all in it, you know.'

Rachel turned to her son now as Tim and Jasmine giggled beside the coffee machine, trying out latte art. 'Will, we walked away for our own reasons,' she began, 'and we were happy to shut the café in the meantime. Walking away for us meant exactly that. But Mia insisted she wasn't going to let that happen and, by coming here, both you and Jasmine have shown that neither of you could let that happen either.'

Tim and Jasmine joined them and handed out coffees – Will had the classic rosetta on top of his latte, their mum had the heart, Jasmine and their Dad had the tulip.

'I don't see how you could have expected us to sit back and let the café suffer,' said Will. 'It's our family business. We've grown up with it and I can only assume that one day it'll be handed down to us three.'

Rachel turned to her daughter and reached out a hand to stroke her hair. As she spoke she looked at Will and Jasmine in turn. 'Ever since we started the business it took over our lives – it dominated your lives too – and we both reached the point where we had to get out.'

'So you decided to leave us to sink or swim,' said Will, angry enough to look each of them in the eye.

'As your mother said,' Tim began, 'Mia was the one who insisted the café stay up and running. Over the years we never had the guts to shut the place, not even early one afternoon for a special occasion, never on birthdays, not even on our anniversary. We poured our hearts and souls into The Sun Coral Café and ended up despising each other for it.'

'Why did you come back from London?' Rachel asked her daughter. 'And, Will, why give up a perfectly good job in New York?'

'It would've been wrong to leave Mia to cope with all of this on her own.' Jasmine's voice wobbled as she spoke. 'I thought if we could keep the café going, make it a continuing success, then maybe you guys would stay together.' He didn't know whether it was because Jasmine was a girl or whether it was because she was the youngest, but she seemed the most devastated of all of them at their parents' decision to separate. She looked down in her lap and Will could see how hard it was for her to fight the tears.

'Oh, Jasmine.' Rachel hugged her daughter tightly.

'We've always been brought up to pull together as a family, Mum,' Will said. 'You taught us that. You both did.' He took a big gulp of latte, impressed with his sister's coffee-making skills despite the situation they were in now. 'I think that's where Mia was coming from when she decided to keep the café open. She called me and I knew that if she'd done that, she must need help desperately. So I came home – I didn't see any other way.'

'You always were responsible.' Tim looked at his son.

'I had to be,' said Will, aware his voice had risen an octave. 'You had two younger children. There was no room for me not to be perfect, no room for me to mess up.'

Tim and Rachel Marcello looked at one another but it was his dad who spoke first. 'Since we walked away from the café, your Mum and I have talked a lot about that.'

Will wasn't sure they'd ever understand.

'We relied on you too much, Son. We never realised it at the time but our dedication – or obsession, as I think it became – meant we relied on you to look after the girls, especially when Jasmine came along and your Grandma Annetta got older. At the time neither of us realised it but when you took off to New York and eventually Jasmine went to London, your Mum and I—'

'We took a long, hard look at ourselves.' Rachel's eyes welled with tears but she refused to let them fall. 'You three don't have a very good relationship and we started to blame each other for that. Your father blamed me for assuming you'd mind Jasmine, feed her, change her nappies. I blamed him for never hiring extra staff so we could make more time for us as a family.'

'It takes two.' Tim smiled at his wife now as he sat in a chair opposite.

'We could see what a mess we'd made of our family,' Rachel added. 'We wanted to raise children to understand the work ethic, but we wanted a family too. Sometimes I was angry at myself that I'd got these three beautiful children yet I didn't feel I had a close relationship with any of them.'

'Mum, that's not true.' Jasmine's tears fell freely.

'I was close to Mia when she had Lexi.' She toyed with her coffee spoon. 'I tried to be there for her like Grandma Annetta had been there for me, but when she announced she wanted to start her own business I knew it was because she wanted a different upbringing for her baby.' When she gulped, Will knew all these admissions were hard to say out loud. 'She never told me so, but I could read between the lines. She gave Lexi all the things I couldn't give you three. She gave her security, comfort; she showed her not only how to have a work ethic but how to have a balance between a job and a family.'

'Wait a minute…you said you have both talked since you left the café. When?' Will rubbed a hand across the back of his neck. This was all getting very confusing. 'And how come the both of you arrived here together tonight? I thought you'd gone your separate ways.'

Jasmine sat forward, anxious to hear an explanation too. 'What's going on exactly?' she demanded.

When Tim and Rachel smiled at one another, the whole story came out. They had indeed gone their separate ways but almost forty years of marriage had clearly gelled some of their ideas together because, two weeks in to the breakaway, they'd both ended up down the Great Ocean Road.

'It was pouring with rain.' Rachel's voice came alive. 'And I hadn't sorted out anywhere to stay. I was living a different life, in which I didn't plan anything, so I'd decided to drive until I was tired and find a bed and breakfast.'

Tim cut in. 'I'd booked my accommodation already – couldn't help the organised side of myself.' Will laughed at that because his dad had forever been making lists, planning, making sure everything ran as smoothly as possible. ‘I was staying in a lovely bed and breakfast in Apollo Bay for four nights but a thunderstorm completely hampered my plans to go for a beach walk one evening. Instead, I decided to sit in front of the fire in the communal lounge. I had the place all to myself, cupping a glass of the finest brandy—’

‘When I walked in,’ Rachel finished for him, looking at her husband the way they’d looked at each other once upon a time, many years ago, when the kids were all so much younger. ‘We started talking and found ourselves actually managing to laugh together. For most of our married life we hadn’t had a night apart except for when I had a hospital stay with each of you children. We’d worked together, lived together, done everything together. But that night, well, it almost felt like a date. I hadn’t admitted it to myself until then but I’d missed him.’

Tim’s head tilted to one side with affection as he looked at his wife. ‘I’d missed her too.’

‘Marriage is hard work,’ Rachel told Will and Jasmine. ‘The rewards are great but you have to earn them. And sometimes you have to uncover them when they become buried in everything else, buried from what goes on in everyday life. With us, there was no respect left, no friendship, and we both felt we had failed you kids. We had failed each other as a result, and in the end the business meant nothing if we weren’t together.’

Tim stood and put both hands on his wife’s shoulders. ‘We talked before we left too, before we went our separate ways.’ He looked at each of his children in turn. ‘When Mia said she’d refuse to let the café suffer and she’d take charge, we knew it wouldn’t be long before she called you both and we decided that, the way things were with you three, this would be make or break time.

Either you'd iron out your differences or you'd end up hating each other more. When you were all in different countries there was no hope of reconciliation so we had to rely on this being the answer.'

'You played us,' said Will.

'We did, Son.' Tim waited for a rebuke but it didn't come from his son. Will almost approved of this part of their plan. Without it, he doubted he and Jasmine would ever have managed to sort out their relationship.

'I don't think we ever hated each other, Mum.' Jasmine spoke softly.

'I'm very glad to hear that,' said Rachel.

'Your mum and I are back together now,' Tim began tentatively, ready to take on whatever reaction Jasmine and Will threw at him.

'For good you mean?' Jasmine didn't hide the hope in her voice. 'Or just until Mia turns up?'

'For keeps,' said Tim, and Rachel repeated the exact same words. 'Son?' He looked at Will for a reaction.

'I'm pleased for both of you and I'm glad you've sorted out your differences.'

'You don't sound all that pleased.' Rachel patted her husband's hand, still resting on her shoulder.

'Well, aside from the fact that Mia is still out there somewhere and nobody has any idea where, what I want to know is what part Grandma Annetta played in all of this.'

His parents' faces fell.

'I went to see her,' Will explained.

'She saw you?' Tim sat down again as though the information was too much. 'But she refused to see any of us. She wouldn't see me.'

'I've been writing to her ever since she went into Appleby Lodge.'

'You have?' Rachel was surprised but smiled across at her son. 'You were always very close.'

'I knew she might not know who the letters were from, I knew she might just tear them up or throw them away, but I had to take the chance. She was always there for me when I was younger and I never felt her support wane, ever. I wanted to do the same for her.

'It took me a while to have the courage to go up there and try to see her,' he continued. 'I didn't want to be turned away as I knew it'd hurt. I'd heard the hurt in your voice enough times, Dad.'

Tim nodded and gave a small knowing smile.

'But then I had a call from the nursing home and they said she'd been asking after me.'

Tim brightened. 'She must be doing really well.'

'I think she was that day, but I think each day is different. We had a long talk, even some laughs, but by the end she practically ran away from me.' That had hurt. Even though he knew it was the disease and not him, it'd been painful. Not once in the years Grandma Annetta had been by his side had she ever turned him away and sometimes he wondered whether escaping to New York was as much about getting away from the bay as it was about avoiding her disease and everything it brought with it.

'She told me some things about the café.' Will looked at his dad and then his mum. 'She told me she actually owns all this.' He looked around him, at the walls that held memories with every slight chip in the paintwork, with the tables set out as they'd always been, the smell of freshly roasting coffee constantly in the air as it had been for so many years.

‘What I don’t understand,’ Will continued, ‘is why us three children never knew. I can’t see why you all felt the need to keep that information hidden.’

Tim got up and wandered to the coffee machine he’d stood in front of every day for years and made another round of coffees for all of them without even asking. They’d grown up with an appreciation of the stuff and the only time they strayed from habit was to try a different variation from their usual.

‘Your grandma loved you,’ said Tim when he returned to the table. ‘All three of you,’ he reassured Jasmine. ‘Like I said, we relied on her a lot when you were all little.’ He cleared his throat and toyed with the handle of his own cup as Rachel delivered the rest of the coffees to the table. ‘She was also behind your mum and me one hundred per cent when we started the café. We couldn’t afford to go it alone and with the sale of the family restaurant she’d already bought the premises in Primrose Bay long before I was married. I’m not sure why she bought them – perhaps she wanted to put her money into something, anything, in case her plans to return to Italy never came to fruition.’

‘She longed to return there, didn’t she?’ Jasmine delivered a rhetorical question and Will knew they all felt a pang of sadness that Grandma Annetta had never got her wish.

‘She was desperate to return,’ Tim confirmed. ‘But her desperation only became apparent when I met Rachel. Rachel’s parents had a café business in Tasmania that they were happy for us to run but I know my mum wanted me to stay close to her. Ever since Dad died, I was the man of the family, and I don’t think she ever wanted that to end. I was happy to be with her but Rachel and I had no money to start the café we dreamed of. Then Mum came up with the idea that we pay her rent for the premises she owned. We'd pay each month and eventually make up the capital to buy it from her. We could make it our business in the meantime.'

'That was generous of her,' said Will, glad his grandma had done the right thing.

Rachel harrumphed and shook her head but she let her husband tell the story.

'Mum made out she had no money for house repairs, bills, and so we paid a bit more rent than we thought she'd have charged us each month. But we were happy to go along with it because it meant the café could be up and running, and eventually the capital would be paid off sooner anyway.'

'We always wanted to save enough to buy her out,' Rachel added. 'I for one didn't want to be in her debt.'

Tim patted his wife's hand and Will saw the signs of the strained relationship his mum had had with his maternal grandmother. He watched his dad grip hold of his coffee cup, the liquid inside untouched.

'Your grandma had a dream,' Tim continued, 'to return to Manarola, where she grew up, and the dream grew after my dad died. She never made a secret of her desire to return, and for a while I let her believe that I'd go too. But that was before your mum and I got serious.'

'Surely Grandma Annetta knew you were committed to each other?' said Will. 'You had a business together – it doesn't get much more serious than that.'

Tim shook his head. 'I think she thought, and hoped, we wouldn't last. She thought the business would probably be too much of a struggle for us, being novices, and it'd go the way a lot of new businesses were going at the time. Thinking back, it's probably why she encouraged us to get the café up and running in premises she owned. That way we had no financial ties. Nobody to answer to if we had to walk away.'

Jasmine frowned. 'But once you married and started having kids, surely she let up on hoping you wouldn't last and you'd return to Italy?'

Tim sighed long and hard. 'Things definitely improved although I never forgot what she'd been like to Rachel in the early days. Giving my mother grandchildren placated her a little and she threw herself into helping us, most probably out of guilt.'

'I still don't understand why you kept all this from us,' said Will. 'It doesn't make any sense.'

Rachel put a hand on his. 'We ended up having a huge row with Annetta a few years ago. In all the times she's refused to see either of us I've wondered whether it was really the disease or because she was still so angry.'

'What was the row about?' Jasmine probed.

'She admitted the only reason she'd let us have the premises was because she didn't want us to go off to Tasmania. It turned out she has a house in Manarola too—'

'You know about that?' Will asked.

'I bet she painted an idyllic picture.' Rachel couldn't help letting the anger escape. 'I knew she'd always hoped Tim and I would split up and she'd be able to have her son with her, back in Italy. And even when I gave her grandchildren I know part of her wanted us all to up sticks and go there.'

'But our whole lives were here, how could she expect that?' Jasmine was incredulous.

'I know that, your dad knows that, but Annetta didn't care. And the night we had the row she'd announced to us that she was selling the premises as she wanted to leave – get out of Australia and back to her roots. At the time she hadn't shown any signs of being unwell – it was long before we realised there was a problem. Oh, we had an almighty row that night. Shouting and screaming at the tops of our voices. She told us she'd give us back all the money we'd paid so far, but she was going to sell it to the first buyer she found. We were still a good way off being able to afford it ourselves, so what could we do?'

'Do you think she would've sold it out from under you? Couldn't the law help you with that?'

'We never drew up a proper contract.' Rachel looked to her husband and Will wondered whether that had been a bone of contention over the years. 'We would've had to find new business premises and it wouldn't be the same. There's nothing else suitable in the bay and the café's position has become an iconic part of Primrose Bay, right opposite the ocean.' Her voice faltered, showing Will how much of her heart and soul she'd poured in to the business over the years.

'Do you really think Grandma would've left?' Jasmine asked. 'I always thought she wanted to return to Italy but could never imagine her doing it without her family.'

'I don't know,' Tim admitted. 'All I know is that with the threat over us it created a tremendous strain.'

Will wasn't going to let his question go unanswered. 'I still want to know why you kept this all quiet. We're grown-ups, we could've even spoken with her and tried to make her see how unreasonable she was being.'

Rachel dropped her head in her hands and began to sob. 'We ruined this family – it's all our fault.'

And neither Will nor Jasmine could argue.

Chapter Twenty-Four
Jasmine

'Lexi's home safe and sound,' said Jasmine, rejoining her parents and brother in the café. When her mum's tears had started, Jasmine had taken the chance to check on her niece and ensure she'd met her curfew. It wasn't that she didn't care how upset her mum was, it was that they were all upset and, knowing what their family was like, it could almost be time for World War Three. 'She's upstairs in the apartment and Harry has gone on his way.'

'Who's Harry?' Tim asked.

'He's Lexi's boyfriend,' Jasmine explained.

'I'll bet Mia's anxious.' Rachel was calm and collected once again. 'She's a wonderful mother but she was always such a worrier. She was naturally going to be more protective too, given her own situation with Daniel.'

'She'll drive her away if she's not careful,' said Will. 'But then who am I to judge? I can't hold down a relationship let alone start a family. Mia is a worrier, but she's a great mum – we all know that.'

They all looked at one another, contemplating the absent member of the Marcello family. Jasmine checked her phone again, but nothing – no news from Mia, no update from Tess, and Daniel had texted to say he'd not heard a thing.

Jasmine looked at her mum, face awash with worry. 'Mia will be fine.' She covered her hand with her own. 'I'm sure of it. Don't cry.'

Rachel Marcello pulled out a tissue and dabbed beneath her eyes. 'I'm not crying because of Mia. I'm worried, yes, but she's got sense – I know she'll be ok.' She looked at her husband and then Will and Jasmine too. 'I've made such a mess of this family.'

Jasmine almost opened her mouth to say something but she couldn't. She couldn't deny it. She wasn't angry or bitter – this family was what it was – but she was grateful they were finally all together, because running away wasn't the answer at all.

Will went out to the kitchen and returned with a half loaf of banana bread. 'We need to eat,' he said simply when they all looked at him. He sliced it up and divided it between four plates.

Tim couldn't bring himself to eat anything. 'We let you kids down.' He looked at the floor, shook his head.

'What, by working your butts off in the café?' For weeks she'd wanted to lay the blame right at their feet but straightening things out with Will had helped Jasmine to rationalise a situation better. 'Excuse the phrasing, but that's what you mean isn't it?'

Tim nodded. 'Parents are supposed to do it all. They're the breadwinners, the organisers, the family glue to hold everyone together. They're there through every up and down in their own lives and yours.

'It was only after the confrontation with your Grandma Annetta that we realised what mistakes we'd made.'

'Your father and I…' Rachel began. '…Well, we had an even bigger fight after the one with Annetta. We were angry at each other and ourselves. We'd raised three amazing children and it broke our hearts to see you three pulling apart in different directions.'

Jasmine looked at Will and they both stayed quiet.

'Jasmine, I could see how very unhappy you were when you were overweight,' Rachel said matter-offactly. 'I tried to tell myself you were young, having a great time, and of course there wasn't anything more serious, but I'm right, aren't I – you were miserable?'

Jasmine gulped. This time it was her eyes filling with tears and when her mum put an arm around her shoulders the tears fell.

'I felt like I was in the way,' said Jasmine between sobs.

'How could you possibly feel like that?'

'I was the little kid sister who everyone was too busy to notice and I was lumped with Will, who didn't want me.'

'Boots—' Will began.

Jasmine looked at him and then her mum. 'Will and I have talked, a lot, and we really have sorted things out between us.'

'You have?' Relief washed over Rachel's face.

'I think from now we will be just fine. I can't promise we'll never bicker, but we've worked through our differences.'

Tim rubbed his face with both hands. 'God, what did we do?'

'You did what you thought was right,' Jasmine told them. 'I doubt there's a parent rulebook to follow to the letter, but you were right, Mum. I was really unhappy before I went to London. Will was the eldest, the strongest and the most responsible – the leader of the pack. Mia was capable and strong; she even made single motherhood at eighteen look like a walk in the park. And then there was me. I went unnoticed.'

Rachel gripped her daughter's hands in hers. 'You were never unnoticed. Is that really how you felt?'

Jasmine shrugged. 'You already had two children, you had a business and life was crazy busy. I assumed it was how all children feel a lot of the time but then when it felt as though Mia and Will were both against me too, I just…I couldn't…I couldn't cope.' She looked to the ceiling and willed the tears to stop while she put her point of view across for the first time ever.

'Did you really think Mia and Will were against you?' her dad asked.

Jasmine knew the only reason she was able to explain now was because she'd had a long talk with her brother and they understood each other more than ever. 'Will had his own reasons, as you've said. Being a babysitter, nappy changer, school-drop monitor and packed-lunch maker is enough to tip any teenage boy over the edge.' Her words at least raised a laugh in the room. 'But the resentment ran so deep and Will was used to being responsible. He carried on thinking he had to bail me out every time, even as I got older. The resentment spiralled.' She looked at her brother. 'The thing is, I didn't always need rescuing. Maybe sometimes I should've been allowed to make my own mistakes like everyone else in this family. It's part of the reason why I went to London. To do something on my own, where nobody could come and rescue me. My success or failure was all down to me.'

Rachel looked fondly at her daughter, a hint of regret in her smile. 'I always thought you'd be happy with siblings to talk to rather than me. How did I get it so wrong?'

'Mia and I had our problems too,' Jasmine went on. 'Her defences went up as soon as Lexi and I started to become good friends.'

'You are so close in age,' said Rachel, 'and she's overprotective, but why would she worry about Lexi being around you?'

'Don't you see? I'm the bad influence, the party-goer, the girl who would lead her daughter astray. She never, ever trusted me with Lexi and she made it pretty obvious. I felt in the way, not a real part of this family; I felt untrusted and unworthy – and so I left.'

Tim came over and wrapped both his arms around his daughter, and Will gave the three of them some time. He disappeared out to the kitchen and Jasmine knew he'd be frantically leaving messages on Mia's voicemail or texting her. Despite their differences they were still a strong family and it was a sobering thought.

'Neither of us ever meant to make you feel that way,' said Tim.

'I guess you were so busy with the café, and us three were supposedly grown-ups, so you had no reason to doubt we were fine.'

Will returned with a bottle of wine. 'I figured we're not going to be going anywhere tonight so we may as well.' He smiled. 'And besides, we've had so much coffee we're in danger of running out, and then what would our customers do?'

This time, rather than resenting him for taking over and controlling a situation, Jasmine felt admiration for her brother – the man she'd thought never had a care in the world yet had had the weight of responsibility on his shoulders for too long. She watched as he retrieved four wineglasses and poured them all a glass of red with no preamble, no enquiries as to who wanted one.

'Part of the tension in our marriage,' said Tim, wineglass in hand, 'and we only realise this now after having time away and talking, a lot, was that we knew we'd failed our kids. We'd taken away a part of Will's adolescence by making him shoulder too much responsibility; we blamed ourselves that our eighteen-year-old daughter had got pregnant and ended up a single mother; and we blamed ourselves that you were so unhappy, Jasmine. We buried our heads in the café as though everything was fine, and it was wrong. We blamed each other, silently most of the time, and let everything come to a head.'

Jasmine leant her head against her mum's shoulder and let her hug her tight. She'd wanted this out in the open for years and the overwhelming relief now was almost too much.

'Do you think we are the reason Mia walked out this time?' Tim asked. He'd already finished most of his glass of wine as they sat around the same table in the café, the lights dimmed, the blinds shut.

'I think we're all to blame,' said Will. 'We've always seen Mia cope with whatever life throws at her, including a baby. She handles everything as though it's only a slight bump in the road.' He shook his head. 'The way I treated her when it came to Daniel was unforgivable.'

'Son, you had your reasons – I'm sure Mia knows that.' Tim frowned. 'But it was years ago; surely you're not still angry with her?'

'I tried to tell myself I wasn't, that I'd moved on, but I know that's not true. We had a huge fight before I left for New York.'

'This family…' Rachel topped up her wineglass. 'Why do we fight so much?'

Will explained his feelings about Daniel and how he'd treated Mia over the years and Jasmine decided it was best to come clean about the fiasco with Lexi and the doctor's appointment to get the contraceptive pill. With Mia missing, they needed to know everything – they all did. They needed to understand Mia for once.

Will also told their parents about Tess and how he'd seen her a few times and it was starting to feel like it was going somewhere.

'I'll bet Mia has something to say about that,' said Tim, his fingers planted either side of the base of the glass.

'And so she should,' Will affirmed. 'I gave her hell about Daniel and here I am, doing the same.'

'We should never have left her to hold the fort,' Rachel berated herself.

'You didn't,' said Jasmine. 'You told her to shut the place.'

'She's right, Mum.' Will waited for his mum to meet his gaze. 'And regardless of all the turmoil between us three, our priority now is to find where she is and get her home.'

There was a knock at the café door and Jasmine peered out from behind the blind. 'It's Daniel.' She looked at Will.

'It's fine, let him in,' said Will.

'Has she been in touch?' Jasmine asked straight away, standing aside to let him set down the cardboard box he was carrying.

He shook his head. 'I was hoping you'd have heard by now.' He touched a hand to Jasmine's arm but when he spotted the Marcellos sitting there at a table he smiled, stepped forwards, shook Tim's hand and kissed Rachel on the cheek. Despite his not being a fully-fledged member of their family they were incredibly fond of him and respected the ties he now had. 'Are you back because of Mia?' he asked them.

'It was time we came home,' said Tim, although Jasmine knew it was down to their frantic messages.

'What's in the box?' Jasmine peeked in the top.

'It's for Mia. I have some contacts through work and was able to get a huge discount on extra wineglasses for the big picnic job she has coming up at the school – you know what she's like – these posh picnics of hers have all the trimmings, nothing fake. I had them delivered to work rather than try to tee up a time with Mia when she'd be around to accept delivery. I thought I'd bring it all here while I had the chance – she'd kill me if I forgot.' His smile faded when nobody else smiled back. 'I really thought she'd be back by now. I can't believe she hasn't been in touch.'

'We all did,' said Rachel. 'When's the picnic job scheduled?'

'I can't remember,' said Daniel. 'But I think it's soon.'

Jasmine picked up the box. Mia wouldn't let this job slip through her fingers, surely. It was too important to her. 'I'll take it through to the picnic place.'

Tim took the box from his daughter. 'Let me help. You go and get the spare key and I'll wait with this until you're back.'

Jasmine headed upstairs to retrieve the spare key for The Primrose Bay Picnic Company, the business her sister had single-handedly built up from an idea scribbled on a piece of paper. She popped her head around Lexi's door to find her niece fast asleep. For a moment Jasmine leant on the doorjamb and watched her sleeping form, the duvet gently rising up and then down with each breath. She was probably exhausted from the worry. When Jasmine spotted Lexi's phone still in her hand she gently prised it from beneath her fingers and set it on the bedside table. This girl was Mia's world and even though Lexi didn't always want to confide in her mum Mia was her world too.

With the key in her hand, Jasmine went downstairs and let herself and her dad into the picnic place. She flicked the light on in the cupboard at the back and made room for the box of glasses and then shut the cupboard again.

'She's made this place quite something.' Tim ran a hand along the white laminate surface, stained in some places from the usual daily hive of activity. 'It's her pride and joy, just like the café was ours. But she never let it stop her being who she was as a person.'

Jasmine looked around the tiny space that Mia had done her best with and by the time she looked at her dad again his hand covered his eyes.

'Dad…' She put a hand on his shoulder and he covered it with his own hand, gripped hers beneath it.

'She's a grown woman,' he said desperately, 'she's perfectly entitled to take off for breathing space, but it's so unlike Mia.'

'I know,' said Jasmine. She spied the red Filofax on the wooden shelf above the work surface and took it down, flicked through the diary pages in case there was anything there. Her mouth fell open when she zoned in on this weekend's activity.

'What is it, Jasmine?'

'Shit. It's in two days' time.'

'What is?' Her dad looked at the diary entry. 'St Bartholomew's,' he read. 'Does Lexi have an event at school this weekend?'

'Lexi doesn't,' said Jasmine. 'But Mia does. It's the picnic job we've been talking about.'

Mia had drawn a heart around the figure '100' too because it was the school's one hundredth birthday. The kids were having celebrations all next week with activities and sports events. These later school years could be full on and Lexi and her friends were already looking forward to a more lackadaisical environment. The teachers had planned a weekend picnic for all the staff and their partners, plus any staff who had taught at the school in the last one hundred years and were still around to attend. It was a huge event and Mia had been honoured and so excited to get the booking.

Jasmine searched frantically through the folders lined up in a mesh desk organiser at the far end of the shelf on which she'd found the Filofax. This was where everything non-food related was kept, out of the way and clean. She took out the red folder she'd seen Mia leafing through when it was time to organise another picnic. 'Here…' She moved the folder across so her dad could see what was written there. 'This is her plan for the picnic and looking at this schedule…' She ran a finger down the list on the first page of details. 'Today, she should be buying up some of the ingredients and doing an inventory of everything she needs.'

'She won't miss this, surely.' Their dad clearly saw the importance of the event.

'She can't,' said Jasmine. 'She really can't.' She fired off another text to her sister's phone, the fifth in the last few hours. She glanced uneasily at the Filofax sitting innocently at the edge of the bench. Her sister never left it lying around, particularly if she had an important booking. Mia clearly didn't want to be reached and time out meant just that.

'It's okay, Jasmine.' Tim pulled his daughter to him and held her tight.

'It's partly my fault. If I hadn't been with Lexi and taken away Mia's job as the mother to go with her daughter then—'

‘Now listen to me.’ Her dad held on to each of her elbows and drew back to look at her. ‘Firstly, your mum and I are to blame if anybody is. And it sounds as though we’ve all got ourselves into a right old mess really, doesn’t it?’ He tilted her chin upwards as she smiled. ‘That’s better. Now, we can keep calling and leaving messages but I think we could be a lot more useful by making sure your sister doesn’t lose this job and her reputation in one fell swoop.’

Jasmine wiped her eyes. ‘We should go and tell the others. It’s too late to do anything tonight, but tomorrow we need to salvage what could end up being a disaster.’

‘Come on then, we’ve no time to waste.’ And her dad led them both next door, Jasmine armed with the Filofax.

Chapter Twenty-Five

Will

He still found it hard to believe his sister was going to let The Primrose Bay Picnic Company fail at this astronomical task of supplying an upmarket picnic to sixty staff at St Bartholomew's, but Mia's absence left him in no doubt that, as Jasmine had told them all last night, they had to step in and pull together as a family.

Now, as they worked in Mia's kitchen and Monica ran The Sun Coral Café single-handedly, intermittently texting for an extra pair of hands when she really needed them, it was all systems go. Tim and Rachel, Will and Jasmine were squeezed into the tiny confines that usually had no more than two people in. Lexi had gone off to school but promised she'd be on hand at four o'clock at the latest. She'd already hung her own apron on the back of the door ready to grab the second she came in.

When there was a knock at the front door to the picnic company, Will flung it open as he was the closest. He said a brief hello to Daniel and took one of the shopping bags, filled to the brim. Daniel brought the other to the back of the kitchen where there was a bit of space. At the front, Jasmine was busy with her parents doing an inventory of everything required. Rachel was finding the said items – handcrafted napkins, cutlery, serving spoons – and Tim was taking them upstairs to the apartment to line up on the dining table. Nothing would be packed today but they had to know everything was in place before they even started cooking.

When Daniel had brought round the box of wineglasses yesterday the tension between the two of them was still high as they'd sat and talked about Mia. It was diluted with his mum's presence, but it was nevertheless there. However, during the time it'd taken Jasmine and their dad to let themselves into Mia's business premises and have a talk, the atmosphere had softened and the crease across Daniel's brow, which was still there now, told Will what he most needed to know. This guy may have moved position in his life from best friend to sister's lover and father of her child, but deep down he was still the same Daniel, the guy with a heart of gold who was worried about Mia.

Now, Daniel opened up the bag he had. 'Is this the right chocolate?'

'I've got no idea, mate.' Will laughed and for the first time in years he patted Daniel on the shoulder. The man who'd had no qualms about taking the day off work, the guy who'd cancelled important meetings so that he could be here to help the family. All for Mia. He called out to his sister. 'Jasmine, is this the right chocolate?'

Jasmine looked calmer than she'd been in those first days in the café. She flipped through a lilac ring binder that held recipes, tomorrow's picnic clearly defined by a divider, and all the details she needed. 'It's perfect. How much did you get?'

Daniel counted up the bars once again and Jasmine held up both thumbs. 'Pop it upstairs in the apartment on the chest of drawers in the box room,' she said. 'The heat in here might kill it and to make good food you need good ingredients,' she instructed.

'I'll show you the way,' Will said to Daniel. 'Here, let me take those.' He grabbed an old plastic container that his dad had filled with the posh silver knives. 'I'll come back for the forks,' he added as Jasmine began to count those out too from the boxes she'd pulled from the storage cupboard. She was polishing each of them before they were counted off and placed in the containers.

Will led the way up to the apartment with the chocolate and cutlery and went straight into the tiny box room. He'd given up the bed for his parents and bunked down in here, so he moved the sleeping bag and pillow out of the way with his foot to clear a route to the chest of drawers. Making brownies for sixty people took a lot of bars of chocolate and he patted the top of the furniture to show Daniel where to leave them.

'Jasmine's a shocker for using the air conditioning,' he told Daniel, 'so it'll never get hot up here if she has her way.'

'Just as long as you don't get peckish in the middle of the night.' Daniel grinned but his joviality gave way to concern. 'How's it going, living with your little sister again?'

'Actually, not too bad. We've done a lot of talking.'

Daniel looked as though he was desperate to make an escape. The rift between them had only widened over the years.

'Do you think Mia will be back for this tomorrow?' Daniel asked.

Will shrugged as they made their way through to the lounge. 'I bloody well hope so. I mean, we can all cook, we have all the details – Mia was meticulous that way – but it's her baby. I don't think we'll put all the frills and personal touches on like she would.' He sat down on one sofa and Daniel sat on the other.

'Some of her photographs on her Facebook page are awesome,' Daniel told Will. 'This business isn't a slapdash effort, it's the real thing. She knows how to match fabrics of tablecloths and napkins, uses fresh flowers – even the blankets and the hampers look like something out of Fortnum & Mason.'

'I don't think any of us lot could recreate it quite the way Mia does.' Will looked at Daniel. 'Have you tried calling again?' His look told him what a ridiculous question that was.

'Jasmine tells me Mia left her Filofax behind.'

Will shook his head and laughed. 'She's the only person I know who has one nowadays.'

'She never goes anywhere without it.' The look Daniel gave Will told him this was another thing that was out of character for his sister.

'Come on, we'd better get back. We're not going to do much good here.' Will stood to go but Daniel's voice stopped him.

'I'm sorry, you know.'

'For Mia disappearing?'

Daniel shook his head. 'For what happened all those years ago.'

'It's water under the bridge, mate.' Will knew they had more important things on their minds now.

'It's not though, is it?' Daniel waited for Will to look at him. 'Your sister tore herself apart over the effect our actions and decisions would have on you. She beat herself up when we were seeing each other and when she fell pregnant with Lexi the most worrying thing for her was losing you because of what we'd done. And she's worried about losing you every day since.'

'She never lost me.'

'She did, Will. She lost the brother-and-sister bond you two had for so many years and she knew she'd never get it back.'

'I was angry.' Will slumped down on the sofa again and Daniel sat on the arm of the sofa opposite. 'I was angry at my family and Mia took the full force of it. I didn't really understand that at the time. In fact, it's taken years and this family disaster to really see it.'

Daniel had no idea what his friend was talking about and so Will started from the beginning. He talked about how he was the older sibling and put in charge of Jasmine in particular, how he missed out on some of his teen years, how he felt as though he was constantly relied on and was always picking up the pieces for other people.

'I suppose when Mia got pregnant part of me thought, *Here we go again, I'll have to somehow step in and help a sibling*. I wanted my own life.'

'But you're stepping in now.'

'That's different.'

'Is it?' And with that Daniel went through the front door and back down to help out.

The worst thing was, Will knew he was right. This was the same: they were pulling together as a family. He only wished he'd been able to realise what he'd done to Mia over the years before she upped and left.

*

By mid-afternoon Lexi and Jasmine were in the café helping with the post-school rush, Tim had gone off to pick up the fresh ingredients they needed from the South Melbourne market, Mia's preferred place for produce. The picnic hampers were all lined up in his parents' apartment and Will tilted the blinds to block out the sunshine and keep it cool inside. Jasmine had already bumped up the air conditioning and now, with his mum, they divided the hand-sewn linens between the hampers.

'Are you sure Mia didn't write down which linens to use?' Rachel asked now.

They were using the red gingham set for no other reason than it had been one of the patterns scribbled beside the amount needed. Other suggestions were lilac flowers, tartan, or plain green, so it had been a judgement call.

Will smiled. 'You're a woman. You've probably got a better eye for this than I have.'

Rachel playfully slapped her son on the arm. 'That's a bit sexist isn't it? I'm afraid I've got no clue. The colour scheme for the café is so basic. No, it was always Mia who was the arty one – she pays such attention to detail. I wonder if she got that from Grandma Annetta. She was a homemaker extraordinaire. I never matched up to her standards.'

Will folded another napkin from the collection he'd ironed that morning. They'd been creased from the wash and, rather than ignore it, he'd realised these were the small details that made his sister's business the success it was. As with everything, sometimes it was the little things that mattered. 'You never really got on with her, did you?'

Rachel sighed and sat down after she'd slotted another four napkins into one of the hampers. The plan was to do as Mia did and take all the food via esky, then set up when they got to the school's grounds. The manicured fields would be the perfect setting and now they were in the first throes of March there was a hint of autumn in the air that promised sunshine and a lack of rain, yet a cool breeze that would lift the city out of its summer haze.

'Your grandma,' Rachel began, 'was a traditional woman. And when your grandpa died she relied on Tim.' She looked at her son. 'A bit like we relied on you, I suppose – and, yes, it was wrong, but at the time you barely know you're doing it.' She waved her hands in front of her. 'I'm not excusing it, not at all. But I'm trying to explain that it wasn't as clear-cut as all that. Grandma Annetta also had a longing to return to Italy and I think your dad would've gone, but then he met me.'

'And the rest is history.' Will sat down beside his mum.

'She fought it as much as she could. She kept Tim close to her side by renting us the café premises, ensuring we didn't leave for Tasmania or anywhere else.'

'She could've tried to persuade you to make a move to Italy, open a café there.'

Rachel smiled contentedly. 'Australia is my home and I didn't want to go too far afield. I think deep down she knew that, the same as deep down I knew how strong her yearning was to return home. We were similar in that regard, both of us obstinate enough to want to hold on to our roots. And ultimately it came between us. Annetta was way too stubborn, or perhaps afraid, of making the move on her own. I think she thought we might forget about her if she left. And she wouldn't have seen much of her grandchildren either, and she loves you all so much.'

'I wish she was still in the bay.'

Rachel put a hand over her son's. 'We all do, even me. We may not have seen eye to eye but there was an acceptance between us at least.'

When there was a knock at the door Will went to answer it and found Tess standing on the other side.

'Any news?' she asked before he had a chance to ask the same.

‘None.’ He smiled at her anyway. ‘The job for the school function is tomorrow so it’s all systems go in here.’

Tess noticed Rachel sitting on the sofa. ‘Mrs Marcello. Hi!’

Rachel waved her hands in front of her. ‘Please, you and I have known one another years, it’s Rachel.’

Will poured three glasses of fresh orange juice and dropped a couple of ice cubes into each as the women chatted. He discreetly watched Tess talking to his mum with such ease. He tried to imagine how he’d feel if he and Tess became serious about each other and his mum did as Grandma Annetta had done and tried to push them apart. It must have put an incredible strain on his parents’ marriage.

‘Here you go.’ He handed out the drinks and sat down. ‘Are you on your lunch break?’ he asked Tess.

‘I took the rest of the day off,’ she said. ‘I’m too worried about Mia to be anything other than useless right now. I don’t want to be booking people on flights to the wrong destination or making deals with hotels that in my right mind I wouldn’t usually consider.’

Will watched as a ringlet of hair she’d pushed behind her shoulder refused to stay there and fell down again in front of her chest. He looked away when his mum noticed his attention was no longer on anything other than Tess.

‘I even went to Yoga on the Bay this morning,’ Tess continued. ‘Mia and I used to go there all the time and for some reason I thought maybe she’d go there now. Stupid, huh?’

‘Not at all,’ said Rachel with a smile. ‘You two were forever doing…what was it? Hot Yoga?’

'Bikram. We were devoted yogis back then,' Tess replied.

Will couldn't help but conjure up an image of Tess in her yoga gear – tight leggings and fitted top, perspiration running in a line from her collarbone, down further.

He crunched on an ice cube to bring his mind back to the present.

'I've phoned old friends of ours,' Tess went on, 'most of whom we've lost contact with but it was worth a try.'

Rachel nodded in appreciation. 'Of course it was, and thank you.'

'I can't imagine she won't come back for this big job she has on tomorrow,' said Tess.

'We all thought that.' Will looked around at the linens and the cutlery, all waiting for the grand event tomorrow. 'But it looks like she isn't going to be here at all. We could use a woman's touch though.' He ducked when Rachel swiped the top of his head with her hand. 'I don't mean it in a sexist way, but come on – you both have to admit you'd have more of an eye for what looks good than I would.'

'True,' Tess agreed. 'So what can I do to help?'

'We're about organised with everything we can do today,' said Rachel. 'Mia would never dream of using day-old food so everything will need to be made fresh tomorrow. And there's quite a list.'

'I'm not bad in the kitchen; what time do you want me tomorrow?'

'Don't you have to work Saturdays?' Will wanted nothing more than to have Tess by his side in whatever he was doing, but she had her own life.

'Not this weekend.' She held his gaze a little longer than he'd expected. 'What time do you want me here?'

All night, he wanted to say. Although if she stayed with him tonight and he woke up with her next to him in his bed, he was pretty sure he wouldn't be helping with any picnic.

'We're all starting at 4 a.m.,' said Rachel.

'You don't need to be here that early,' Will added.

'I'll be here by then.' She stood to leave.

'Why don't you two take a break?' Rachel suggested. 'Go for a walk along the beach for half an hour. We can manage the café and we're all set for the early start tomorrow. Get some fresh air and recharge your batteries for the morning.'

Will knew his mum was on to him when both he and Tess agreed to take a walk and as he was leaving the apartment Rachel smiled at him and winked.

They crossed over the road outside the café so they could walk along the sand. The beach was quieter than usual, with sensible people staying out of the sun in the more dangerous times. Tess had pulled on a straw hat and Will had a cap covering his dark hair, which he swore he'd spotted a fleck of grey in this morning. He'd laughed though. If this family stress was anything to go by, it was only a matter of time before his whole head turned that colour.

'What are you thinking?' Tess asked as they walked along the shoreline and let the waves creep up to touch their feet.

He hadn't realised he'd been so quiet. He was worrying about his sister, but he also knew she was sensible. His main concern was that she'd let her business go, and if she was prepared to do that then it meant she was even more upset than he'd first realised.

'I think Mia will be fine.' He stopped Tess now and holding her hands he turned to face her. He put his hand to her cheek and ran the back of his fingers down and beneath her chin as she looked up to him. He bent his head until their lips touched lightly.

'I feel like we're betraying her.' Tess looked down at the sand and her toes, which she was squidging in and out of the wet sand. 'Mia wasn't happy and she took off before I'd even had a chance to talk to her about us. She's my best friend, Will. It would break my heart if that were to change.'

Will pulled Tess to him and they stood there, the breeze warm and mixed with salty air. 'It won't change, I know it won't. I gave her a hard time over Daniel and never really moved on, but my reasons were more than about him, they always were. If anything, I think she'll understand about us – once she calms down.' When he pulled a face that spoke of the trepidation he felt at facing his sister eventually, Tess couldn't help but smile. 'That's better. Now how about an ice-cream?'

'As long as it's rum and raisin, you've got a deal.' This time Tess wrapped an arm around him and when he put his arm around her shoulders, she wrapped her other around his waist as though she never wanted to let go.

They stopped at the ice-cream shop on a side street in Primrose Bay and strolled along, chatting and making the most of the double scoops they'd bought in the waffle cones.

'I'd better get going.' Tess smiled up at Will as they reached the café. 'It's an early start tomorrow. Let me know if you hear anything.'

'Of course.' He kissed her on the lips unabashed that anyone might see him. 'I wish you could stay.'

She grinned and kissed him a second time. 'I'll see you in the morning.'

‘See you tomorrow.’ He leant against the glass window of the café and watched her go, grinning like a teenager when she turned back to wave.

He pulled himself together and ventured inside. The Sun Coral Café was a hive of activity and he felt obliged to lend a hand, but when he offered Monica swatted him away with a motherly gesture and so he grabbed a can of Coke and sat at the smallest and only available table out the front of the café. There were only three tables here and usually they were occupied so he made the most of the great outdoors, soaking up the sun. The winters in New York could be brutal and he hadn’t realised just how much he missed the Australian summer until he’d come back this time.

He’d almost got to the end of his Coke when a familiar black Hilux pulled up outside. ‘Leo, good to see you.’ He stood and spoke through the open window to his mate.

‘I know where she is,’ said Leo without preamble. ‘Get in.’

Chapter Twenty-Six
Mia

When she was eighteen Mia had been introduced to stress in a big way: she'd crammed for exams, she'd faced the wrath of her brother when she fell pregnant with Lexi, she'd come up against disapproval from her parents and Grandma Annetta. But Mia had never felt so strung out from it all as she had when she'd left to come up to the beautiful Golden Wattle Homestead.

After Leo had told her he'd secured a job for her to supply picnics for a new TV show to be set here, and she'd spoken with the TV company on the phone, she'd allowed herself to get excited. It had taken away all the family hassle and made her feel as though, despite everything, she still knew which direction she was going in. She'd searched the homestead on the internet and after she'd had the showdown with Jasmine and found out about her best friend and her brother, her first thoughts had been the photographs she'd seen of this place. And it had given her the perfect escape.

The Golden Wattle Homestead was set in a peaceful thirty-two acres of land in Victoria's Yarra Valley. Once a dairy farm, new owners had taken over and converted disused barns and the old milking shed into accommodation. They'd added other cottages too, with further bed-and-breakfast rooms up at the main house. Mia was staying in Cowslip Cottage, a cream-and-fawn-painted one-bedroom self-catering accommodation with a small veranda out front upon which sat a white wrought-iron table with two chairs.

For the last four days Mia had woken up to sunshine streaming in through the windows she left locked ajar each night, and to the unfamiliar noises of Australian wildlife. It was a different sound to the waves crashing on the shore of Primrose Bay or the noise of chatter drifting into her apartment from groups of cyclists out on an early-morning ride. And different was exactly what Mia had needed. Over the years, Mia had rarely done *different*. She'd grown up in the bay and raised her daughter there, never wanting to leave its tranquillity and ambience. But here in the Yarra Valley, her body and mind told her that this had been the perfect choice.

As she made her way back to the cottage after her early-afternoon walk Mia waved to the couple staying in Kookaburra Cottage, high up on the hill that looked out over undulating pasture-land dotted with horses belonging to the owners of the homestead. The Golden Wattle Homestead was escapism at its best. It offered horse-riding lessons for those who were willing, long guided rambles through the countryside, spa treatments in your accommodation and seasonal produce cooked by a professional chef to be eaten in the restaurant or delivered to your door.

Mia kicked off her shoes and immediately went inside Cowslip Cottage for a glass of water. The heat was beating down on the valley and she was parched. She popped three ice cubes out of the tray and into a glass, topped it with water, downed the lot and refilled it. She grabbed her Kindle, on which she'd downloaded four rom-coms and had already read two in her time here – reading was something she'd been too busy to do lately – and took it along with her drink out to the veranda to sit at the iron table. By her reckoning she had another hour until she had to check out and hotfoot it back to the bay, back to reality. She was already packed but hadn't been able to resist a last-minute walk and a final soaking up of the Yarra Valley, because when she got to Primrose Bay – after a detour to the markets – she'd be on all systems go, ready for tomorrow's picnic.

Already Mia knew she'd left it very late. But she'd confirmed everything with the member of staff at St Bartholomew's and she wouldn't let them down. She was a business woman and she'd worked too hard for this to let it all fall apart because of family strife. When she'd left the bay she hadn't thought about it at all but on the second day in to her escape she'd had a lightbulb moment when she realised this wasn't her. She didn't run, she didn't avoid. She faced things head-on. But she hadn't been able to go back to the bay then; it was too soon. And so she'd planned her stay. She'd stay until Friday, just after lunch, then drive home to the bay via the markets. She'd already made a shopping list from the folder of details so she knew exactly what produce to buy and what she already had back at the picnic company. It'd be full on and she'd probably be up all night, but this time away had done one thing for sure: it had reminded her of the business she'd built and how she always saw things through right to the end.

She pushed thoughts of tomorrow's busy day out of her mind and sat outside, but instead of opening her Kindle she watched a tall figure walking down the sweeping lawn towards the cottages that sat in line with hers. She was glad of her sunglasses so she could watch the man, who was gorgeous even from a distance. Tall and, as he got closer she could see, blond, he was muscular and he had tanned legs in khaki shorts. But as he got further down she realised he was heading in the direction of her cottage and it was then she saw who it was.

‘Leo?’ She pushed her sunglasses onto the top of her head.

He removed his too. ‘We’ve been worried about you.’

‘We?’

‘Me, and your entire family.’

She sat down and gestured to the other seat so he could do the same. ‘They’re too busy worrying about themselves I’m sure.’

‘Even Lexi?’ Leo asked. The hairs on his legs shone golden against his tan, even here in the shade.

Mia looked into her lap. ‘I left her a note.’

‘Do you think that stopped her worrying?’

‘Why do I feel as though I’m being told off?’ Mia had been churned up about Lexi but she also knew that if she’d called, Lexi would’ve been in tears begging her to come home. And she couldn’t have done that. She’d needed space – more space than another room could’ve given her, the space she could only find out here in the country, somewhere entirely unfamiliar. Maybe she wasn’t so different from Jasmine and Will after all.

Leo was watching her and she felt uncomfortable beneath his gaze until he lifted up a small cool bag she hadn’t even noticed him carrying and pulled out two cans of soft drink: one Sprite and the other a Coke. ‘Can I tempt you with either of these?’

She grinned. It reminded her of the first day they’d met, down by the river after the rowing regatta. ‘Always.’ She took the Sprite and he cracked open the Coke.

Leo sipped his drink and looked around him at the vast expanse of green, the trees lining the land, the enormous single-level homestead that looked so far away when you were in one of these cottages. ‘This place is pretty spectacular. A great location for filming.’

Mia flicked the top of the open ring-pull absent-mindedly. 'How did you know where to find me?'

'Lucky guess,' he said. 'I've thought about you a lot since Will called to say you'd gone walkabout. And then this morning my manager was talking about the homestead. He's hoping the new TV show will lead to more – there's already talk of a second series following the first. And that was when it clicked. I remembered when I'd told you about this place, when you knew you had the job. Your face lit up and you told me it sounded like the ultimate escape. Do you remember?'

Mia nodded. 'I was right. I mean look at it…it's gorgeous.' She waxed lyrical with Leo about the place – the stream trickling down close to the edge of the gardens, the stunning sunsets, the gourmet food, and the kangaroos she'd seen as well as more birds than she even knew existed.

'I was always coming back before tomorrow,' she told him. He'd moved his chair around next to hers as the sun did its best to creep onto the veranda after him. 'I've got a huge job with St Bartholomew's and I was never going to let them down. Never in a million years.'

'I didn't think you would. But you had us scared.'

'I'm sorry, it's not what I intended.'

'What happened? Why did you run?'

'Lots of reasons.' She looked away but turned back when she felt a hand on her shoulder.

'I'm here to listen,' he said. 'Not to reprimand you.'

'I think it's been building up over the years, ever since I had Lexi, and finally I just snapped.'

'You mean the tension between you and Will?'

'Will, Jasmine, my parents, my grandma. It's one thing after another in our family. God…' She pulled a hand through her dark hair all the way to the ends and looked up at the pitched roof above. There were cobwebs galore but not a spider to be seen. Maybe they were lurking somewhere nearby waiting for an unsuspecting insect to become tangled in their web. '…Are all families like this?'

Leo shrugged. 'I've had some ups and downs with mine. But yours does seem to take things to a new level.' He'd coaxed a smile from her at least.

'Mum and Dad have always been fiery with one another but I admired it in a way. I certainly didn't see it as anything bad and I figured it was better than being one of those couples who never spoke. But look at them now. They've split, gone their separate ways, left their kids to cope with the mess.'

'But they're your family – I bet you wouldn't have them any other way. And everyone has faults.'

She looked doubtfully at him and then sighed. 'I love them all, to bits.'

'But it's time you thought of yourself for a change?' he guessed.

'Does that make me a horrid person?' She sipped her Sprite, unsure if she wanted the answer.

'Mia, everyone needs to think about others, but they also need to think of themselves sometimes too. Will did when he went off to New York. That was his way of escaping. Jasmine went to London to gain perspective and sort out her own life. You stayed in the bay with Lexi and managed single motherhood with a new business. By coming out here, all you're doing is showing how normal you are. You're one of the thousands of people who sometimes need to find a different way to cope.'

They were so thirsty their drinks had gone in no time. Mia picked up the empty cans and took them inside to the bin. Back on the veranda she took a deep breath and looked at Leo. 'I'd better get going. I've got a really important assignment to organise for tomorrow.'

'I know. The school's centenary.' He held out a hand and when she took it he pulled her to sit on his lap.

'I don't remember telling you about that,' she said, her face so close to his she wasn't sure where to look. She'd wanted to be close to him for a long time, to kiss him and have him hold her, but this was almost overwhelming.

'You didn't.' He hooked her hair behind her ears as she looked into his deep-set hazel eyes.

'Then who…?'

'Will,' With his hands on either side of her face as she sat on his lap, he moved his thumbs closer to her mouth. 'Lexi, Jasmine…' Her lips tingled and her body responded as it hadn't done in years when he closed the gap and kissed her.

The warmth from his lips tasted of sunshine, heaven, dreams. And what started as a tentative meeting of their mouths turned into a deeper kiss Mia knew she'd wanted ever since she'd seen Leo outside the rowing sheds that day.

When they pulled apart she asked, 'Is that what you came up here for?'

'Let's call it an added perk.'

She grinned. 'I should go back to the bay.'

'You should.' But he didn't move to let her go. Instead they fell into a second kiss that she'd have been willing to let go further, but he pulled away.

'I'd like nothing more than to scoop you up and take you inside right now,' he said.

She ran her fingers along his jaw towards his lips. 'But…'

'Well it wouldn't feel right, because of Will.'

She pulled back. He was right. Yet again family ties were going to get in the way and she'd be a fool to wreak even more havoc. 'You're right. He's your friend and I guess I've been down this road before. And with Tess and Will…' She laughed. '…It's almost incestuous!'

'I wouldn't be quite so dramatic.' Leo's fingers toyed with the strap of her cotton sundress and her skin quivered beneath. 'It's just that he's in the truck out front.'

Mia pulled back. 'He's here?'

'He's been worried too. And there's something else,' said Leo when Mia giggled and stopped his hands moving anywhere else as they glided across the warm skin of her collarbone. 'Your parents are back.'

That had her attention. 'When?'

'They came back yesterday. Something about a missing daughter, I'm not sure.'

'Oh god I can't believe I've put everyone through this.' Mia shook her head but Leo was quick to reprimand her.

'You needed the headspace, you don't need to apologise.'

Mia wasted no time checking around the cottage one last time and wheeling her suitcase out onto the veranda. 'I'll stop off at the markets on my way home – I have the shopping list of everything I need for tomorrow – and then I'd better get organised.' They reached the top of the hill and the back of the homestead. Leo waited while Mia turned around one last time and soaked up the view of tranquillity that had been her safe haven for the last few days.

He didn't look back when he said, 'No need. Your family has rallied together and hampers are organised, ready to be packed, and they've shopped for everything. Everyone's congregating at 4 a.m. tomorrow ready for the off.'

She looked at him in disbelief and with the arm that wasn't wheeling the suitcase he cradled her to him and planted a kiss on top of her head.

It was time to go home and face the family, all together in the bay. It was time to sort out the mess once and for all.

Chapter Twenty-Seven

Mia

Mia was welcomed home with open arms from every single member of her family. She'd almost been bowled over by Lexi, coming out of the café first at top speed, and her daughter had clung on to her as though she never wanted to let her mum go again. Will had held her like his kid sister and she'd remembered how protective he'd been over the years. He'd said he was sorry for how he'd treated her and she'd apologised in return for letting this thing between her and Daniel ever interfere with his life. Jasmine had tentatively held out her hands for Mia to take but Mia had hugged her instead, both whispering how sorry they were.

Tim and Rachel Marcello hadn't wasted any time being at their daughter's side either. It had been like days of old with both of them in aprons manning the café but this time they hadn't batted an eyelid at the queue of customers waiting. Their daughter came first, the way it should've always been.

Mia knew they all needed to talk a great deal more, but it was a start. She was back now and needed to hold it together for the big job tomorrow: the big job that would possibly not have been executed quite so well had it not been for her family. She'd have been up all night preparing the crockery and linens for hampers, shopping for ingredients, weighing out and sorting foods ready to be prepared, not to mention the transportation to the venue. And she'd have been hard pushed to get it all done on time and to a standard she was happy with.

Just before four o'clock the next morning Mia jumped in the shower to wake herself up and by the time she got downstairs to the picnic company her best friend Tess was already baking brownies. She'd texted her last night but they both held back tears this morning. Their friendship was strong, unbreakable, and when Will had put an arm around Tess as she fretted the brownies were going to burn he'd seen Mia watching, and Mia had smiled at him: a simple gesture of approval. They were in their thirties now – no time for childish games. This was real life, not make-believe sibling contests in the back garden of Wattle Lane. Sibling rivalry had challenged them as youngsters and evolved into sibling envy as each of them grew older, but this summer Mia knew they'd finally got to the bottom of their problems and felt sure this would enable them to recover at long last. Something not all families could claim to do.

The tiny kitchen of The Primrose Bay Picnic Company was crowded but everyone was in good spirits and the whole place was a hive of activity. Leo had gone to fetch ice from the garage as soon as it opened and he'd stashed it in the freezer here, the one in the café, plus both freezers in the two upstairs apartments; Rachel was making ciabatta bread; Tim had roasted beef so tender it fell off the bone when he carved it thinly for the rolls; Jasmine had worked in the café's kitchen and made a potato salad tossed with Dijon mustard, white-wine vinegar, shallots and parsley; Lexi had already sorted cold meats, crackers and chutneys; and Tess had made ten frittatas upstairs in her apartment, transferring five to the other apartment to nab space in the oven.

'I've got the flowers!' Lexi raced into the kitchen gasping for breath.

'Flowers?' Mia questioned. Her daughter had a hand clasped to her chest – she must've sprinted given how out of puff she was.

'You always have flowers at your picnics.'

'I do.' Mia locked eyes with her daughter and with a tear in her eye pulled her into an embrace. 'Thank you, Lexi.'

'I couldn't let you go to set up the picnic without the *pièce de résistance*!'

Mia looked at the beautiful cream roses. 'How did you know what to get?'

'Because I know you so well.' A smile passed between them. 'And I had a bit of help,' she admitted. 'When I went in to the florist in the centre of Primrose Bay and explained they were for you, the girl behind the counter asked what colour the tablecloths were, where the picnic would be held, what sort of picnic it was going to be.'

Mia laughed. 'They're used to me in there.' She breathed in the glorious scent of the flowers before she gave them to Lexi to put somewhere cool until they were ready to go.

A few hours later the cars were lined up outside the café: Mia's Toyota, Leo's Hilux, Tess's sporty Volkswagen and Tim's sports car for himself and Rachel – who, Mia had to admit, looked as though they were on their second honeymoon. Running away had seemed ludicrous a few weeks ago but it felt like a part of their family history now; and since her stint in the Yarra Valley, Mia kind of got it. She understood the need to break away and she hoped they'd all learn from this. Instead of driving each other to breaking point, from now on perhaps they could talk before things got as bad.

She smiled to herself. Maybe that would be too much to expect.

‘Let’s go!’ Will yelled as he jumped into Tess’s car alongside her. He’d winked at his sister as she bundled into her car with Lexi and Jasmine.

‘Are you ready for this?’ Jasmine asked as they made their way along Beach Road and turned off towards the school, nestled in the quieter roads of the suburb. ‘This is your biggest job yet.’

Mia exhaled long and hard as she indicated and turned right. ‘I can’t believe I thought I could do it all if I came home yesterday afternoon.’

‘No offence, Mum,’ Lexi piped up from the back seat, ‘but you’d have been stuffed without us.’

Jasmine and Mia burst into laughter.

‘Nothing like a kid to tell you how it really is.’ Jasmine smiled at her sister.

‘She’s right though.’ Mia turned into the school car park behind Leo’s Hilux. ‘Without you lot I don’t know what I would’ve done.’ And when she waved over to her parents she knew that one of the most unquestionable displays of dedication had come from them. Not by their reappearance in the bay. But because for the first time in decades they’d shut the café for the day. They’d put a sign on the door that said it was a family event but they would be open again as usual tomorrow, and they’d given Monica the day off, paid in full.

To Mia it was the biggest gesture she could’ve ever hoped for, but there was no time for tears now as they began to unload hampers and eskies, ice buckets and bags of ice, and made their way inside St Bartholomew’s.

*

‘Move your big fat foot, Mia.’ They’d returned home from the school and Will had his legs up on one of the chairs in the café, with Tess sitting next to him and resting her head against his shoulder.

Mia tried to push Will's feet off the chair with her own. 'Hey, I was here first.'

'Not in this world you weren't. I was here three years before you so there.'

Mia poked her tongue out. Sibling envy was one thing and sibling rivalry in childhood another, but there was always room for teasing.

The family, plus Leo and Tess, had worked twelve hours straight – cooking, transporting, perfecting the picnic event and hanging around to ensure everything went perfectly – and now they were sitting in the quiet of The Sun Coral Café with the blinds still shut and the Closed sign firmly in place. When someone had knocked at the door an hour ago Mia had moved to answer it but Will had grabbed her wrist and pulled her back again. 'It'll wait,' he said. 'There's always tomorrow.'

Mia had been the last to come back to the café – along with her parents, who had hovered in the car park as Mia hung around waiting to know the event had gone off without a hitch. Tim and Rachel had leaned against the car with her until it had become so hot they'd gone and found the shade of a plane tree in St Bartholomew's away from the partying teachers.

'We're sorry we upped and left,' her mum had said when they sat down.

'Don't be.' Mia shook her head as her hands toyed with the grass beneath them. 'You needed to get away to see things clearly. I'm not so naïve I can't see that, especially after getting away myself.' She raised her eyebrows. 'I hear you're back together.'

Coyly her dad explained how they'd met up and realised that a little bit of space was the magic remedy.

'It seems you needed a bit of that too,' he told his daughter.

'I did. I needed distance from Jasmine and Will, and from everything really. All my life I've been so organised and methodical – and a worrier.' She smiled at the shared look between her parents. 'But the only person I didn't worry about was me. I worried about Lexi and her future, I worried about Jasmine when she went off to London, I even worried about Will and Daniel. I took on responsibility of the café when really I should've left it up to you both. I didn't want it – I have my own business to deal with – but I suppose deep down I thought if we could keep it going it would gel you two back together. I also think that subconsciously I wanted a reason to get Will and Jasmine back to the bay. The longer we'd left it to see each other the more we'd drifted apart and I didn't want to end up middle-aged with no brothers and sisters to speak off. That was the way it felt it was heading.'

'You know we blame ourselves,' Rachel began, and when Mia pulled a face her mum told her the same as she'd told Will and Jasmine over the last few days. How they desperately regretted the time they'd taken away from their family in favour of business. 'It was wrong of us,' she said.

'Wrong to make a go of the café?' Mia asked doubtfully.

'It was wrong to do it at the expense of family, yes.' Her mum swatted a fly that was buzzing around her face. 'You know, I admired you. Right from an early age you were so capable.'

'Capable, yet not extraordinary,' said Mia.

'Is that what you think? That's the biggest load of rubbish I've ever heard.'

'It is.' Her dad passed them each a bottle of water he had in the small esky he'd kept back for them. 'We didn't say it enough but all you kids made us so very proud. We realise now we should've taken more time to stand back and appreciate that. If I could turn back the clock, I would.'

Mia gulped.

'Mia,' began Rachel. 'You were the girl I always wanted to be. I'm in awe of you, I still am. You were hardworking when you were little, got good grades, helped out at home without question, and when you had a baby you didn't let it change who you were. You raised a daughter without a long-term partner by your side, and you started and managed a very successful business. You only have to look at the picnic you set up today for these people and think about the contract with the television company to see how amazing you really are. No matter how tough things got for you, you always stood your ground. You never cease to amaze me – not for one second, Mia Marcello.'

Tears sprung to Mia's eyes and she had difficulty holding them back.

Tim smiled. 'Do you remember Jasmine's thirteenth birthday party?'

'Should I?' Mia pulled a face, wondering what this had to do with anything.

'You should,' he told her. 'Rachel was in a flap and had no idea what to do. There were ten friends due to show up at the house and all of a sudden the party games your mum had planned looked ridiculous and babyish. You confirmed it. They were, and you had no qualms about telling us. At twenty-one and a parent of a toddler you still had more idea than us, parents of a teen and two grown adults. You took over. You went to the supermarket and bought nail polishes of all colours, hair ties, sets of makeup brushes and makeup palettes. You supplied us with music that wouldn't make Jasmine run a mile when we put it on, and the party was a raging success.'

Mia giggled. 'I remember now. Didn't I ban you from the party too?'

'Yep.' Rachel covered her mouth when a laugh escaped. 'You told us we were a bit uncool for a thirteen year old so we should make ourselves scarce. Apparently it would be the best present we could give her.'

'Even then,' said Tim, 'you were organised and always had a way forward.'

'I always felt as though Will was the one who had the authority – whatever he did was fine, he never had to prove himself to anyone. He was the natural patriarch. And then Jasmine had all the fun and none of the responsibility. I longed for someone to notice me and for me not to blend into the background. But I didn't go off to New York or to London, I stayed put in the bay.'

Rachel put an arm around her daughter. 'That's what makes you the Mia we love, the girl we know so well. We always noticed all of our children, don't you worry. But we messed up by not telling them enough. And for that we are both truly sorry.'

They talked some more about Jasmine, Daniel, Will, Tess and Leo and the complexities that were sibling rivalry. Her parents blamed themselves; Mia placed part of the blame on all three of them – but by the time they'd finished talking and brushed the grass from their shorts and made their way back to the car, satisfied there was nothing more to be done here, Mia realised this was family life. With all its ups and downs, with its good and bad, its complications, it was all a peculiar type of normal.

In the café now, exhausted after the early start and delivering the ultimate picnic event to the school, Will and Mia still battled for their footrest with that chair until Leo brought over an extra one and Mia swapped her feet to that.

'Fighting is healthy,' Leo concluded. 'But I for one am too tired to watch anymore.'

Jasmine looked at her watch. 'What time is Lexi back?'

'Any time now,' said Mia.

Daniel had picked Lexi up from the café this afternoon and he was taking her and Harry out for pizza at an Italian restaurant in Albert Park. He'd decided it was about time he met his daughter's boyfriend given they were getting serious. Mia was so glad this man was still in both of their lives. He may not be perfect for her but he was a good person. They'd talked a lot about Lexi before she went away to the Yarra Valley too. Daniel had more trouble thinking of the sex part of their daughter's life but he accepted she was growing up and Mia knew they calmed each other down by talking. They were both still worried about their daughter but knew she must make her own way in life. London was still on the cards for her one day too and Mia and Daniel had agreed to give Lexi some money towards her travel, but on the understanding she did it after uni. Lexi had agreed – she'd go ahead and get her education first and then she'd have some fun. Mia wasn't sure how she felt about the 'fun' but she'd accepted it as a compromise. Jasmine was right – it was better than alienating her daughter. She wanted the channels of communication to remain open for always and as long as Lexi needed a role model other than her own mum, Mia was now more than happy to let Jasmine step in. Her sister had surprised her in the past few weeks and, since yesterday, she'd begun to see her for the individual she'd grown into.

Mia groaned. Everyone cooking today had made extras in case they'd underestimated the amount they'd needed. They'd been ravenous when they returned from St Bartholomew's and tucked in to a meal of breads, cheeses, cold meats and brownies. Now, she couldn't fit another thing in.

Mia had shut her eyes for a second but when she opened them her mum and dad were looking at each other. 'What is it?' she asked, suspicious there was something going on they didn't yet know.

Her dad ushered the three siblings around one table and sat in front of them with his wife by his side. 'It's about Grandma Annetta.'

Mia clasped a hand to her chest. 'Oh god…is she…?'

'No, no.' Her mum shook her head. 'She's still alive and kicking and she had a good day yesterday. You tell them, Tim.'

'She asked to see me late yesterday evening and I drove up there. I went on my own and we talked for a long time.'

'So she was lucid enough to make sense?' Will asked.

'She wrote a letter a few months ago, a kind of explanation I suppose,' said Tim. 'She gave me the letter and we had a good half an hour together where she was like my mother – like she was before this disease got a hold of her.' Mia didn't miss the tears pooling in his eyes. 'We didn't talk in any depth. She told me she'd written the letter for that. We talked about Rachel and me, and how we'd repaired our relationship with time away, and we talked about Manarola. Oh she loves to talk about that place.'

When he faltered Rachel put a hand on his shoulder.

'Have you read the letter?' Jasmine wanted to know.

'We both have,' her dad confirmed.

'So what did it say?' Will asked.

Mia didn't miss the trepidation in Will's voice or the anxious look on Jasmine's face. She wondered if they were both speculating about what the words contained – were they laced with accusations about the family's imperfections? Were they going to upset their memories and leave them without the grandma who had once been the focal point of the Marcellos?

'It was an apology more than anything else.'

'An apology?' Mia asked.

'She asked for our forgiveness. She asked that we all try to accept what has passed and can't be changed, and instead, look to the future.'

'That's a bit cryptic isn't it, Dad?' Jasmine fiddled with the napkins in the dispenser on the table.

'She apologised for the hold she claimed over us with the business premises. She said she was old-fashioned and stuck in her ways and that she hadn't been prepared for me ever to follow a path she hadn't predicted. She apologised to Rachel…' He looked at his wife and she winked back at him to let him know it was okay. '…She's written up a new will and enclosed a copy.'

'Go on, Dad.' Will urged.

'She's left your mother and me her house in Manarola on the understanding it'll never be sold, but kept in the family always. She wants Rachel and I to take time to work at our marriage and take the holidays we never took over the years, spend time together and appreciate one another. We've already booked a holiday to

Manarola in August, and Mum is more than happy with that.

'She also told me how she and my dad were in love until the very end. She says it's all she could want for her boy.' His voice broke and he cleared his throat. 'She also apologised to you.' He was looking at Mia and Jasmine now.

'Me?' Jasmine asked.

'Or me?' said Mia.

'Both of you,' Rachel answered for her husband, and then he took it from there.

'She favoured Will when he was growing up,' said Tim.

Jasmine harrumphed. 'We weren't blind.'

'And she is truly sorry for that. She blames her traditional, staid, old-fashioned values…' He laughed a little now. '…This disease doesn't appear to have interfered with her ability to use very descriptive words.

'Your Grandma Annetta wanted me to apologise to the both of you and to tell you that she loves you very much. I'll let you read the letter later; it's almost poetic in its content. She's remembered the days in the back garden with you, Jasmine, after Will built you the cubby house and, Mia, she remembers you and her making perfumes out of petals and the stand you made out front of the house to sell perfume to the neighbours. She called you "the little entrepreneur".'

Mia blinked. She'd loved those days and had fond memories, but hearing that Grandma Annetta actually shared the same recollections made up for being turned away at Appleby Lodge or for being looked over sometimes in favour of her brother.

'And Will,' their dad continued. 'She says she loved you a great deal but never more than the girls.'

‘Ouch, that hurt.’ He grinned though.

‘She said she felt sorry for you. She hated the way your mum and I put upon you with looking after the girls when she couldn’t; she was angry at the way you missed out on some of your teen years because of it.’ Tim’s voice shuddered. This was hard for him to hear – his mistakes out loud and committed to paper. ‘That’s why she favoured you.’

‘Wow, it sounds like quite a letter,’ said Jasmine.

Tim and Rachel both nodded before Tim continued. ‘It was. And the will had more too.’ He waited until all eyes were upon him. ‘Mia, there’s a lump sum of money to come your way for your picnic business, which your Grandma Annetta says is the result of a hardworking girl who never let anything get in her way. She told me you were a beautiful child from the inside out and equally beautiful is the daughter you’ve raised. And she says you should use the money to upgrade your premises before too long because no woman can be expected to cook in a kitchen as small as the one in The Primrose Bay Picnic Company.’

Mia laughed then, they all did. ‘Don’t mind me,’ she said when she blew her nose. The words were lovely to hear but the emotion behind them took Mia by surprise.

‘To Will she’s leaving the same sum of money and she tells me that it’s for you to spread your wings and fly away. She says she always saw travel in your blood and you are free to go away, live in another country, do what you need to do. But she asks that you always come back, and that one day you do your best to meet someone and settle down and produce cousins for Lexi – perhaps a son to carry on the Marcello name.’

Mia didn’t miss Will smile across at Tess. Tess and Leo were doing their best not to overhear by sitting well away from them all, but Mia didn't care if they did. It felt good to be talking finally. She didn't care if the whole bay bore witness.

'And Jasmine...' Tim began, looking at his youngest daughter. 'Grandma Annetta wanted me to tell you that she may not have approved of your wild ways but that you often reminded her of herself before she met my dad.' He laughed. 'I'm not sure I want the details of those days and thankfully she didn't elaborate.'

Mia knew Jasmine was waiting to see if she'd treated them all equally in this will.

'She isn't going to leave you a sum of money,' their dad began.

Mia's heart sank. Sibling rivalry was about to go full on into sibling envy and even a level of despising they hadn't ever reached if this was Grandma Annetta's final word.

'To you, Jasmine...' (their dad made sure his gaze went to each of them as though to gauge their reactions) '...she's leaving the business premises.'

'What? I don't understand.' Jasmine, wide-eyed, was as shocked as the rest of them.

'She said she saw a passion in you, a tenacity that would take you far. She knew that when you left the bay it wasn't because you didn't want to be here, it was that you couldn't be. She blamed a lot of that on us and said all she'd hoped was that one day you'd come back. She hoped that this would be the incentive for you and with our blessing she wants you to take over the café.'

Mia watched her younger sister take it all in.

'But that's not fair,' said Jasmine. She looked at Mia and then at Will. 'We should inherit the café as a trio, three siblings running the family business.'

The room was silent until Will, smiling, said, 'You're welcome to it. Even on day one I knew I wasn't cut out for the café life.'

Mia looked at her sister. 'I've got my own business and I'm quite happy. You're the only one who can make the perfect coffee. It's yours, with my blessing.'

Jasmine put a hand across her mouth. 'What about you?' She looked to her parents.

Rachel smiled, her eyes glistening in the same way as her daughter's. 'It's time for us to take a step back. It's been a long time coming and I've no desire to return to the demands of a full-time business.'

'Do you really think I can do it?' Jasmine almost pleaded. 'What if I fail?'

Tim covered his daughter's hands with his own. 'You won't, Jasmine. And I think I can speak for everyone when I tell you you've got the full support of the family.'

Mia nodded, as did Will.

'But you guys have never trusted me with anything,' Jasmine said almost to herself. 'Never. I've always been the youngest, the one with least responsibility.'

'Jasmine, you bought a ticket to London not knowing anyone,' Mia began, 'and you went over there, found a job and a place to live. And you're still in one piece. I think that tells us all we need to know about responsibility.'

'She's right,' Will joined in. 'If anyone can do it you can – and you're a natural. You're great with customers, even difficult ones, you're a whizz in the kitchen, you don't get stressed at busy times. I think it's in your blood.'

The look Jasmine gave the rest of her family was one of understanding and acceptance. And Mia knew this was a huge thing for her sister. The level of responsibility could end up being overwhelming but Jasmine had the full support team behind her and this was really the best decision all round. Neither Mia nor Will had ever wanted the café that badly – they'd just wanted their parents together and a family business that didn't fail.

'All this time,' said Will, 'we thought we knew exactly what Grandma Annetta thought of every member of this family.'

'She knew us better than we realised,' said Jasmine.

'She did,' Mia agreed.

When the events of the afternoon had settled and the plates and glasses cleared from their table, Will cuddled Tess against him. 'Thank god I'll never have to work a shift in this place again now that it belongs to Jasmine.'

'Now hang on,' Jasmine panicked. 'You might need to give me some time to sort through who I need and when, and perhaps hire another member of staff.'

Will pulled a face. 'I guess I could help out for a bit longer, but Tess and I have been making some plans of our own.' He looked at Mia for approval, which was something he'd never done. It had always been the other way round. 'We're going to Manarola to see where Grandma Annetta grew up. And then we'll spend a month touring round Italy.'

Mia nodded. 'You look after her.'

'I promise,' he said. 'And Leo…' He looked over to his mate. '…Don't hold back with Mia on my account. She's a grown woman and it's about time I let the past go.'

Mia sat next to Leo, a little uneasy under her brother's watchful eye but with a feeling that everything was going to be fine.

Will told everyone about the trip he and Tess had discussed. They wanted to see the colourful houses of Manarola, the canals in Venice, the architecture in Rome and the Duomo in Florence.

'We'll do a lot of cheese and wine tasting,' said Tess. 'I'd like to visit some smaller towns if we can, really find out how the natives live.'

'What about your job in New York, Will?' Leo wondered.

'It's a contract position and they're keen to have me back so I'll see how I feel. Maybe I could persuade this one to come with me, only for a while.' He looked to Tess.

Mia smiled at them both. 'I'd be gutted if my best friend left the bay.' She reached for Tess's hand. 'But I'd be more gutted if my friend wasn't happy. If this relationship is what makes you smile like that every day, then I say go for it. But I warn you, if you go to New York I'll be saving up to come visit and shop my way around the city.'

Tess and Mia talked about the next big job she had for The Primrose Bay Picnic Company out at the Golden Wattle Homestead and Mia felt her excitement rising. She couldn't wait to get started – and to do it with Leo close by would be a bonus.

'Right, I need a walk,' Jasmine announced. 'I'm full of food and I need to work it off.'

'I've got a better idea.' Will went out the back entrance and after some rummaging and clattering around, he returned with a baseball bat, a ball and a set of plastic cones.

Tim threw his head back, laughing. 'We haven't played a family game of baseball in years.'

'Well then,' said Will. 'It's about time.'

‘It sure is.’ Rachel stood up as they all filed excitedly out of the café.

‘Are you sure this is a good idea?’ Leo whispered to Mia as they crossed the road over to the beach that had quietened enough for them to find a huge space to play. ‘Don’t board games and sports games bring the worst out in a family?’

‘Oh I think we’ve brought out all the skeletons we possibly can,’ said Mia, standing on tiptoes to kiss Leo.

‘Hey, Mia!’ Will yelled across at her. ‘Enough of that, unless you want to lose.’

Lexi came running along the sand with Daniel and Harry tagging behind. She kicked off her shoes and took first base. Mia watched Daniel shake hands with Will and her brother patted him on the back at the same time, a gesture that told her everything was going to work out just fine. She even thought she might have overheard them talking about surfing and a trip down to Bells Beach one weekend.

‘Boots!’ Will hollered across the beach at his youngest sister. ‘You’re up to bat next.’

‘I’m useless at batting!’ She yelled back.

‘Rubbish…have a little faith in yourself!’

Mia grinned at the family banter playing out across the sand and she was still smiling when they finished the game amidst a family stand-off at whether Jasmine had run inside one of the bases or not, and Will filled a cone with seawater and chased both his sisters with them laughing the whole time.

This was family, a peculiar-shaped arrangement of people with different traits, different ambitions. And members of a family made mistakes time and time again, but the best families pulled through those hard times. They may not always like one another but they all needed to make an effort to embrace their differences rather than fighting them. Grandma Annetta, despite her faults, had been at the helm of the Marcellos for a long time. She hadn't always steered them on the right course in the early days, but with her letter and her wishes to follow now, they were finally being navigated in the right direction.

THE END

Acknowledgements

Thank you to Katharine Walkden for editing my manuscript and helping me get to grips with those wretched commas! I'd also like to thank my proofreader, Edward, who helped me polish my manuscript to a high standard, ready for my readers.

Thank you, Berni Stevens, for a beautiful summery book cover. It's perfect! I'm already looking forward to working with you again.

My biggest thanks goes to my husband and two children, for supporting me every step of the way with my writing. I'd also like to thank The Write Romantics, as always, for their unwavering support and advice along the way.

Helen J Rolfe.

What Rosie Found Next

One house, two strangers, one very big secret...

A shaky upbringing has left Rosie Stevens craving safety and security. She thinks she knows exactly what she needs to make her life complete – the stable job and perfect house-sit she's just found in Magnolia Creek. The only thing she wants now is for her long-term boyfriend, Adam, to leave his overseas job and come home for good.

Owen Harrison is notoriously nomadic, and he roars into town on his Ducati for one reason and one reason only – to search his parents' house while they're away to find out what they've been hiding from him his entire life. When he meets Rosie, who refuses to quit the house-sit in his parents' home, sparks fly.

Secrets are unearthed, promises are broken, friendships are put to the test and the real risk of bushfires under the hot Australian sun threatens to undo Rosie once and for all.

Will Rosie and Owen be able to find what they want or what they really need?

The Chocolatier's Secret

Will one mistake ruin everything?

Andrew Bennett has an idyllic life in Magnolia Creek, Australia. He runs a chocolate business he adores, is married to Gemma, the love of his life, and has a close relationship with his father, Louis. But when Andrew receives a message from his high school sweetheart, it sends his world into a spiral, and the relationships he holds dear will never be the same again.

Molly Ramsey is looking for answers. After her last attempt, she believes the only way to get them this time is to face her past head-on. But to do this, she has to fly to the other side of the world – and she's afraid of flying. Her search for answers lands her in an emotional tangle, not only with her past but also with a man very much in her present.

Family is everything to Gemma Bennett and she longs to have a house full of kids, but it just isn't happening. And when Andrew's past makes an explosive impact on the family, Gemma must decide whether she can accept the truth and open her heart in a way she never thought possible.

In this story of love, family ties and forgiveness, will past mistakes be the obstacle to a Happy Ever After?

In a Manhattan Minute

It's the most wonderful time of the year… but when the temperature dips, can Manhattan work its magic?

Jack exists in a world that has seen its fair share of tragedy, but also success and the wealth that comes with it. One snowy night, he crosses paths with Evie, a homeless girl, and it changes everything.

Three years on, Evie's life is very different. She's the assistant to a prestigious wedding gown designer, she's settled in Manhattan, has her own apartment and friendships she holds dear. But the past is lurking in the background, threatening to spoil everything, and it's catching up with her.

Kent has kept a family secret for two decades, a secret he never wanted to share with his son, Jack. And even though she doesn't realise it yet, his life is inextricably tangled with Nicole's, the woman who was his housekeeper for thirteen years and the woman who helped Evie turn her life around.

It's Christmas and a time for forgiveness, love and Happy Ever Afters. And when the snow starts to fall, the truth could finally bring everyone the gift of happiness they're looking for.

Grab a hot chocolate, turn on the twinkly lights and snuggle up with this unputdownable heart-warming novel.

The Friendship Tree

Why do good girls fall for bad boys?

Tamara leaves London and puts ten thousand miles between her and her ex. But as she vows to start over, she meets Jake – and life gets more complicated than she could ever have imagined.

Jake is the direct competitor for the family business, and a man with a dark secret, and Tamara struggles to fight her attraction to him as she deals with secrets of her own and an ex who refuses to give up.

Tamara is soon drawn in to the small community of Brewer Creek where she becomes the coordinator for an old fashioned Friendship Tree – a chart telling people who they can call on in times of trouble. And before long, she realises the Friendship Tree does a lot more than organise fundraising events and working bees; it has the power to unite an entire town.

Should you ever try to run from your past?

Printed in Great Britain
by Amazon